Callous

Callous

A novel of subversive wit and irony about murder, faith and the end of days.

T K KENYON

AUTHOR OF *RABID*

LARGO, USA

CALLOUS

For information, contact Kunati Inc., Book Publishers in both USA and Canada.
In USA: 6901 Bryan Dairy Road, Suite 150, Largo, FL 33777 USA
In Canada: 75 First Street, Suite 128, Orangeville, ON L9W 5B6 CANADA,
or e-mail to info@kunati.com.

FIRST EDITION

Designed by Kam Wai Yu
Persona Corp. | www.personaco.com

ISBN-13: 978-1-60164-022-2 | EAN 9781601640222 | FIC000000 FICTION/General

Published by Kunati Inc. (USA) and Kunati Inc. (Canada).
Provocative. Bold. Controversial.™

http://www.kunati.com

Library of Congress Cataloging-in-Publication Data

Kenyon, T. K.
Callous / T.K. Kenyon. -- 1st ed.
p. cm.
Summary: "A fictional exploration of small town paranoia inspired by fear, false memory and confession and mob psychology juxtapositioned against religious fervor"--Provided by publisher.
ISBN 978-1-60164-022-2 (alk. paper)
1. Fathers and daughters--Fiction. 2. City and town life--Fiction. 3. Psychological fiction. 4. Religious fiction. I. Title.
PS3611.E685C35 2008
813'.6--dc22

2008011758

Dedication

To Krish and Dylan

Acknowledgements

Writing a book is probably the best illustration that nothing in one's life is a solitary endeavor. Even though sitting at the keyboard, typing out the lies in one's head, would seem to be the most insular of pursuits, a writer is bandied about by the influences of other minds. It feels more like channeling than solitude.

I'd like to thank my parents, Tom and Juleen Kenyon, and my extended family for a lovely childhood and a great life. It's made being a writer more difficult than if I was screwed up, but it's made living much more pleasant.

I'd like to thank Charles Grose, my Ph.D. mentor, for his friendship and tolerance during my Ph.D. program. Other professors would not have been so tolerant of my wild hypotheses.

My husband, Krish, and my parents-in-law, Krishnan and Janaki, encouraged me and helped care for Dylan, our son, so I had time to write *Callous*. Time is a gift beyond measure.

Many, many sources of information were instrumental in writing *Callous*. As always, these sources helped me on the things that I got right. Mistakes are my own.

Among the many books I perused, *Hyperspace* by Michio Kaku and *The Road to Reality* by Roger Penrose in particular brushed up and expanded my physics. Every book that Carl Sagan ever wrote was crucial in forming my view of the universe. Dr. Paul R. Auvil, Jr. of Northwestern University kindly discussed physics with me and corrected important points.

The series of articles "Fundies Say the Darnedest Things" by "True American" at Gather.com (trueamerican.gather.com) was a source of both ROTFL humor and traumatic flashbacks during the composition of *Callous*.

All the folks and other authors at Kunati Book Publishers, especially editor James McKinnon, have been inspiring and instrumental in writing both *Rabid* and *Callous* and surviving the aftermath.

The Iowa Writers' Workshop at the University of Iowa gave me an MFA, so much instruction in the craft of writing that I am still sorting it out, and the thick skin necessary to survive in this business. Thom Jones, Bharati Mukherjee, and Frank Conroy were my most influential professors there.

Mr. Nemo Turner won a charity auction benefiting Polaris Project (polarisproject.org) and his name appears in this novel as a tribute to his generosity. While a character is named for Mr. Turner, the character is, of course, a figment of my imagination and was written before Mr. Turner made his generous contribution. Mr. Turner's website is www.protocolpower.com.

I thank you, dear reader, for picking up this little book and reading what I have to say. Please visit my Myspace page (www.myspace.com/tkkenyon) or website (www.tkkenyon.com) for more fun stuff, including more on these characters and those in *Rabid*, and to email me. I hope you enjoy *Callous*.

Thursday

When a phone rings in the dark, the shrill is an unknown, and the fearful bloody alternatives of car crash, bar fight, suicide bombing, knife attack, heart attack and murder exist as smeary possibilities out in the dark, empty night until they resolve into one voice speaking on one phone.

Zeke scrambled through the darkness for the phone on the rough-hewn nightstand and dragged the receiver to his scrofulous mouth. The phone's number pad glared. "Hello?" he asked. "Essie? What's the matter?"

The young woman's voice was familiar, but it wasn't his daughter Ester. Her friend Nessie said, "Mr. James? Essie's not here."

Zeke switched on the light, cocked the phone receiver in his neck, and reached for his pants on the floor, nearly upsetting himself. "What do you mean Essie's not here?"

"She wasn't waiting outside the Lone Star Grocery, like she said."

"Essie got off work at eleven," three hours earlier. Zeke's baby could be halfway to Mexico, destined for a *maquiladora* slave brothel. She could be lying under a log, smothering. She could be tied up with fishing line with a cigarette nearing her leg. "Why didn't you pick her up?"

A pause, and the girl's voice was quieter. "She wasn't outside at eleven, and people were still inside, so I thought she must be working late, so I left and came back. Now the store manager came out and said Essie left right at eleven."

Zeke pulled his pants up to his thick middle and hopped, zipping them. "Where are you?"

"In my car, outside the Lone Star Grocery."

He reached for his leather jacket and cowboy hat hanging on the tall post of the empty bed. "Lock your doors. Don't you get out of your car." He patted his coat pocket for the hard lump of his cell phone, yanked boots over his bare feet. "Takes about twenty minutes for me to get to town. I'll be there as soon as I can."

He hung up and started toward the bathroom to brush his teeth.

Outside his bedroom window, the night leaned against the glass. That dark had rolled over Ester three long hours ago.

Zeke ran three steps to the bathroom, grabbed his toothbrush, smeared paste, and shoved it between his clenched teeth as he ran out of the house and through the chilly Texan night to his truck. He clambered into the high cab using the steering wheel and seatback as handholds and inserted the ignition key.

Bing—the big diesel engine chimed while it primed itself—*bing*—the truck's headlights burrowed a tunnel through the dark, and a chill wind worried the bare trees—*bing*—the night, held at bay by the cab's light, crept around the black truck tires—*bing*—Zeke's intermittent breath flurried around the toothbrush while he held the keys, poised to crank them—*bing*—and the truck's engine thundered.

He brushed his teeth with one hand and drove like the very Devil himself, hopping over crumbling country roads that rushed out of the night through the truck's headlights.

When he turned left, he opened his door and spit foam into the gravel, drooling toothpaste scum onto his orange beard.

"Please," he said aloud as he drove, and he was so sorry that he had allowed her to work so late at night even though he didn't have a choice in the matter because she was grown.

He hit redial on his cell phone, and her phone rang but cut to her voicemail. Her phone was off or dead. Her calm voice running through the earpiece was sweet, but it meant nothing.

"Please pick up, Ester. Please call your dad. Please. Please. Please."

Vanessa sat in her dark car and ran the wan heater. Warm air streams wound through her sweater, driving away the prickling chill. She twisted her long, blond hanks around her shaking fingers into ever-wilder curls. Ester, this was Ester who was missing, her teen-years friend, her "twinnie."

This wasn't some random New Orleanean zombie dragged out of the filthy waters flanking the city that she could be professionally blasé about. Essie was missing, and that made her throat clench.

That's the way this wicked old world works. It could have been anyone. She couldn't let maudlin sentiment sway her. Finding any forensic evidence tonight would be difficult. The stars were unnaturally bright, probably due to the lack of light pollution way out here in the sticks. She had forgotten how dark the wilds of Texas were.

Essie's father's red-whiskered face emerged out of the darkness into the green glow of her dashboard lights, like a drowned suicide, surfacing. His blue eyes jittered, and crazy foam flecked his auburn moustache. She rolled down the window.

"Have you heard from her?" he asked and tipped his cowboy hat with two fingers. Trust Essie's dad to wear a straw hat like a farmer instead of a manly black felt hat. His breath smelled like mint and green cow cud.

"No." She smiled at him to cover her nerves.

Essie's father sniffed and asked, "You been drinking? Never mind. Doesn't matter. I called that boy she broke up with, Bobert. Sounded like he was in a bar and didn't care none." The parking lot lights shone down, but the brim of his hat blacked out his face. "Where else would she go?"

Vanessa chuckled. "You'd think she'd call me if she hooked up with somebody."

He took off his cowboy hat and wiped his face with his sleeve. "She's not that kind of girl, so we can stop joking around."

Vanessa dialed down the jokes. "Most missing people aren't really missing. They're just misplaced, and they show up. The police only call us, the forensic science folks, in one out of ten cases, when they have an actual crime scene. Let's look around town and call people."

Zeke adjusted his hat. "That's sensible."

For an hour and ten minutes, they dialed their cell phones, listened to sleep-befuddled people deny hearing from Ester, and drove in caravan to the couple of all-night restaurants. At each, Zeke flipped open his wallet and offered them a look at his pretty, blond daughter, but none of the truckers or sobering drunks had seen her that night.

Vanessa finally said, "We should call the police. I see this at the lab all the time. You have to call first thing, right when someone is missing. Most crimes are solved in the first forty-eight hours."

He glared at her like she had said something stupid. "She probably just got sidetracked."

"Right." Hours had passed. Ester could be in a hundred places or in a hundred pieces by now.

Vanessa pulled her phone from her hip pocket and flipped it open.

Max had been asleep for an hour and a half when the phone trilled. The sheriff's office called him often at night, so his heart accelerated to bleary consciousness. Such was the price of being a known teetotaler.

Down the hallway, Max's two children slept the deep sleep of children even though they were teenagers. All the doors between them stood wide open.

"Chief Deputy Konstantin," Max said into the phone as if he were at his desk. He yanked the chain on the bedside lamp. Beside him, Diane flapped the blanket over her brown hair, cocooning herself in a quilted lump.

The dispatcher told him a girl was missing. New Canaan's police department—Larry Wunderlich, the traffic cop—had formally asked the sheriff's department to handle the case as was their long-standing arrangement. The girl's father was on the phone.

"How young?" he asked. Missing kids were the worst, the very worst. Max readied himself to call the Texas Rangers and initiate an Amber alert.

"Early twenties," the dispatcher said.

"Oh." His shoulders slid in relief. She was probably out drinking somewhere. "Okay. Put the father on."

In some ways, missing adults are more problematic than children. Most adults either came home the next morning with their underwear inside out, or they were runaways, or if you found them after significant investigative effort, they preferred to stay lost. You check things out, but it's usually a waste of everyone's time.

Max pulled his pants over his grimy body. Besides a long day's worth of waxy secretions and shed skin flakes, his skin had misted sweat during bench presses in the Sheriff's office gym. Mud clung to his rattlesnake hide boots, though he had brushed them off.

"I'm sorry to bother you so late," the man on the phone said right off. "I'm probably worrying over nothing."

Max launched into his usual lecture for worried parents. "Sir, it's always better to call the police earlier rather than later, and we're all relieved when it turns out to be a false alarm." He buttoned his shirt. "This isn't New York City. The Sin Nombre County Sheriff's Department isn't too busy to look into something to ease a citizen's mind."

The father went through the details while Max dressed. Sounded like Ester James was going to get a razzing from her friends when he hauled her out of a bar and told her that her daddy had the police looking for her, and she was going to harangue her worried father for it in turn.

Just the same, when the time came, neither of his kids was ever going to work late at night. It wasn't worth the heartache.

Max was a twenty-year man in an office with an average turnover of eight years. In that span, either a deputy got a higher-paying job in one of the cities or else a new sheriff was elected, who cleaned house and hired political cronies. There were few big busts or debacles in Sin Nombre County. Most crime was transitory—the coyotes running illegals from Mexico to Dallas and into the Midwest to work at the slaughterhouses, drug runners freighting everything the DEA tried to intercept, and the occasional secluded cult that found itself on the wrong side of the federal government.

Every new sheriff kept Max. He knew everybody, and it was likely that if they set him loose, they would lose the next election to him. A few years ago, he had investigated some funny rugs found out in the woods, recognized them as Islamic prayer rugs, and infiltrated a coyote pack that specialized in smuggling OTMs (Other Than Mexicans) across the border. A language school right across the Mexican border taught Spanish to Arabic speakers. He shut down that route.

Locally, he got good press, the Texas kind of good press, where the citizenry muttered, "No better than the varmint deserved," or "Saved us taxpayers the cost of a trial, didn't he?"

Max was as tough as a roping Quarter Horse that could outrace a wily old steer to the end of an arena and turn him back for the heeler to come in, and he could win the sheriff's office in a landslide, but he would never run.

Diane listened to Max's deep voice while he talked on the phone. He was going out again in the middle of the cold night, the poor guy. From the dim light under the warm quilt, she muttered, "You need coffee?"

"I'll be okay," he said.

She tossed back the covers and grabbed her robe. "Coffee machine is set up anyhow. You can take those folks some." She smoothed her woolly hair. Max was still hunched over on his side of the bed, exhausted. "Don't forget your gun."

"You, too." Max stood, buckling his belt. "And I'd rather see you in a nice forty-four. More stopping power. The nine you've been carrying is a little girlie."

She tried to flirt, "I'm a little girlie," but the dark hours of the morning caught up to her and she yawned through it.

She stumbled down the hall. So many times she had done this, made coffee when Max got an overnight call, or if she did. Her office rarely called her in the middle of the night, but sometimes they did when something particularly brutal happened and they needed someone from the county attorney's office on the scene.

Brutal things seldom happened in the small town of New Canaan, Sin Nombre County, Texas, but the cities of Dallas-Fort Worth, Houston, and New Orleans were close enough that their demon-haunted chaos rafted the highways, restrained only by the tenuous law and prayer and God's grace.

In the hallway, Diane paused at each of their two kids' bedrooms, checked on them in their beds to make sure each was safe, and closed their doors so they wouldn't wake because someone else's child was missing and alone somewhere in the woods between the sparse towns.

Zeke watched the alien stars traverse the cold firmament and asked, "Nessie, you give me your word that you didn't see Ester tonight?"

"Nope, I didn't." Vanessa shrugged. "Wish I had."

Zeke sighed with the regret of waning hope and wanted a cigarette even though he had given them up twenty-odd years ago, before Ester was born. Zeke's wife, Christy, had stipulated his cessation before she would marry him, and he loved her enough that he gave up tobacco, alcohol, and swearing, and he even came to Jesus for her. Christy, up in Heaven with Jesus, must be glad that he had the love of Jesus to sustain him through the last two decades without her, because without a personal relationship with Jesus Christ, he would have been terribly bereft without wife or family, trying to raise their baby girl alone. Christy was his own personal saint, like those idolatrous Catholics have, and she interceded with Jesus for him.

Their daughter, after a few rough patches in high school, had turned out to be a high-spirited but gentle woman, much like Christy, and he found no fault with that. Zeke found little fault with most people. He was as generous and gentle as Christy could have made him, had she lived. He was a huge, roan gelding of a man, a draft horse made human, but not dumb. He had funneled his other drives, now useless to a man who believed in the sanctity of marriage, into various works, some religious, some secular, all of them meant to be good.

He held two fingers over his mouth, a habit that hadn't fallen away, along with patting his breast pocket for his pack. He rubbed his chapped lips instead.

He didn't want to say anything more to Vanessa. He might be accusatory, and he himself had been five minutes late picking up Essie more than once.

A car turned into the parking lot. The parking lot's lights glinted navy and maroon on the roller bar on the car's roof. Brass lettering read Sin Nombre County Sheriff's Department on the dark paint.

Zeke waved. The car pulled up. Its motor growled hard beside him, and heat drifted out of the hood.

The driver's side window scrolled down. The deputy inside looked in his mid-thirties, maybe a decade younger than Zeke, though Zeke looked older because ranching in the Texan sun and rain weathered his skin and bleached his red hair and whiskers.

The man wore a straw cowboy hat, well shaped, its recent steaming and shaping a mark of good grooming. Zeke trusted him immediately. Straw cowboy hats are for everyday wear among gentlemen who are of the class to own their own horses, whether they own horses or not. Bull riders and bronc busters wear felt hats, and generally choose those events because they don't own a horse. Contrarily, luxurious fur felt hats are worn at formal occasions such as weddings. You can always spot a dude or an Easterner because he's the one wearing a tuxedo hat with skinny designer jeans.

The deputy tipped his hat and asked, "You Zeke James?"

"I am." He smoothed his jagged beard. "Deputy Konstantin?"

The man's sharp chin dipped as he nodded.

Vanessa said from her open car window, "I'm Vanessa Allen."

Zeke added, "Essie and Nessie. The two pretty blond girls in high school."

They had dressed alike in high school. Now, however, Vanessa wore a shirt with a gang-related calligraphic design that read Love Kills. When she left New Canaan seven years ago to go to college in New Orleans, he had been surprised. Nessie was bright enough but had not excelled at school, a classic layabout underachiever. Her emails to Ester, detailing her accomplishments and employment by the New Orleans Police Department, had surprised him too. Perhaps he was not imaginative enough. "Yep, they were like twins, freshman year anyway. They don't look so much alike anymore, Essie and Nessie."

Nessie said, "People call me Vanessa now. I was going to pick Ester up but," the police car's engine grated, "I got delayed."

The police detective got out of his car and handed them each a travel mug. Coffee aroma drifted into the cold air. "Hope you like it sweet and light, sir, ma'am."

Zeke sipped. His grandfather, who had had a hard time during the Depression, had admonished Zeke when he was nine that if you're going to drink coffee, you take it black. Milk and sugar tasted cloying to him, but the sentiments mattered more than the condiments. "Thank you kindly."

They went over details again, and Zeke tried to look calm, but his chest clenched like he had stomach flu. He sipped the thick coffee to cover.

"Okay." The deputy stroked his chin, "I'll take a look around for a few minutes."

The deputy got back in his car. Zeke redialed his cell phone. *Please God, please God,* he prayed and then stopped. Prayers are answered by God, but if you selfishly make wishes, Satan will intercept the prayer and take it as an infernal contract, and your soul will be forfeit.

Zeke prayed for strength. *Please God, please God.*

Ester's voicemail cut in. The strength left his legs.

The police car cruised the parking lot. A strong flashlight beam probed the grousey bushes and lingered on the trash bins. The detective stepped out of the car and peered over the edge of the trash receptacles, and Zeke's throat closed. The cop was looking for his baby's dead body among broken-down boxes and rancid food.

He had held Ester's slippery baby body for the first time just a few minutes after she was born. He was not, as the lady doctor admonished him, squeamish about birthing. Being raised on a farm teaches you to overlook blood and mucus. Ester was a few weeks early, a skinny puppy of a baby with a pink puff of hair. He fell in love with her tissue-paper skin and wrinkly face. Later, when she plumped out to be a beautiful baby, almost as beautiful as her mother, he almost missed her old-man face that he alone thought was magnificent.

The sheriff's deputy pulled out a long stick and tooled around in the garbage bin for a moment, then looked around the edges of the trash area with his flashlight. Thank God and all His angels. She must be somewhere else and all right, drinking a beer that she knew Zeke should disapprove of, but he promised God that he would never ever bring it up if God would just let Essie come home safe.

Or, if God preferred, he would give her holy Hell and drag her to church three times a week on Sundays and Wednesday and Thursday nights, if God only would let her come home safe.

If God would give him a sign of what He wanted, Zeke would do it.

Zeke was ready to deal with the Devil to get his baby back. He wished for a puff of brimstone and an infernal contract with a pen that siphoned his own blood, but the night was quiet except for the rattling of the sheriff's car.

Beside him, Vanessa clicked on the radio. Music moaned, the sonic equivalent of a horror movie, about gruesome things. She sang along.

By the bins, the deputy got back in his car and completed his drive, then coasted to a stop next to Zeke. The deputy buzzed down the window. "Don't see anything suspicious. Not much we can do here tonight. You two come into the office tomorrow morning to give a formal statement, all right?"

"A girl is missing," Vanessa said. "The first few hours are critical."

"Now, Miss Allen," the deputy said. "Most adults find their way home. The Sin Nombre Sheriff's department will do its job."

She buzzed up her window and turned away, dismissing them. Vanessa's engine cranked, and her silhouette leaned inside the car as she engaged the gears. Her car sped away, flashing a vanity license that Zeke couldn't quite see.

The deputy asked, "Mr. James, you married?"

Zeke couldn't take his eyes off that fermenting trash bin squatted in the dim light like its hundred cousins in Sin Nombre County. "I'm a widower." He still hated saying that.

Deputy Konstantin asked, "Is there someone I can call for you?"

Zeke nodded and gave the deputy his pastor's phone number. Sometimes Zeke felt defensive that he belonged to a church with an African-American preacher because some folks might not cotton to it, like the good ol' boys who were neither old nor good. Brother Daniel was a fine man, an excellent Christian who had deep ambitions for his church and was an inspiration to Zeke. Zeke respected him, and he would take it outside with anyone who thought wrongly about Pastor Daniel.

Deputy Konstantin saw Zeke to his truck and told him to drive home safely, slapping the truck bed as he moved back, a courtesy telling Zeke that the deputy's toes were clear of the dually tires.

Zeke drove the twenty minutes out of town to his ranch. His headlights sniffed the road ahead, and he dodged stones on the dirt road and the odd tumbleweed, trying to feel the steering wheel with his numb hands. His nerves had shut down. Worry saturated his brain.

The James spread was a thousand acres of good grazing land for several hundred head of Red Angus cattle. In the perimeter of his headlights, the land turned green. Shadows of his herd huddled in the dark.

When Pastor Daniel arrived, Zeke would ask him to look, too. He couldn't think of doing anything else. He must look for her, to find her shivering, cold form lit in his headlights so he could have her back, safe.

That morning, P.J. Lessing hitched up her black backpack stuffed with three physics books and one World History text while she jimmied the rusted knob on her front door, trying to lock it. She shoved her black bangs out of her eyes and her draping, black sleeve up her thin arm so she could see the key in the lock.

The school bus passed her house and rumbled up the block. If she ran, and if the driver saw her, it might wait.

On the door, she found a teardrop with horns in the unvarnished wood grain and pressed her palm on it. She curved her maple-syrup fingers with black-painted fingernails into the sun-rotten wood, willed herself less anxious, and turned the key.

The lock clicked.

She looked up. The school bus rounded the far corner and was gone.

Damn. Now she was going to be late for school, which meant she had to spend first period in the Hole. Crap. She had not been absent or tardy since she figured out they were serious about it.

A sheriff's car coasted to a stop in front of the house. The man getting out of the car was tall and built like a Greco-Roman wrestler. He could squash scrawny foundling P.J. like a skinny grass snake under his boot.

P.J. was not a typical high school student. Her teachers had already tagged her, in her permanent record files, as the one who was going to receive scholarships to a far-away elite school. She was a *rara avis*, an intellectual peacock who would fly the Texan coop.

The physics teacher, Keith Mitchell, had arranged to accidentally stumble over her between classes and invited her to the geek-laden physics club, visions of prestigious Science Talent Search prizes dancing in his head. When she had modestly corrected an exponent in a grandiose equation he was copying from a Physical Letters Review paper, he remembered that Isaac Newton had invented the calculus when he was all of twenty-four years old, and Albert Einstein was twenty-six during his "miracle year," when he published four astonishing papers that changed the universe, based on his patent office doodlings of the previous three years.

In physics, if you aren't somebody by the time you're thirty, you never will be. P.J. Lessing, at fourteen years old physically pre-pubescent, was accelerating toward the sound barrier of her genius. Home schooling and the Internet had allowed her to find physics early in a country of die-cast curricula where slow children were flogged to catch up and bright children were leashed to ensure equitable standardized testing scores. In India, elite students as young as twelve years old are introduced to calculus to prepare them to sit for the grueling Indian Institute of Technology exams. P.J. had cheetahed ahead of them by two years.

Her knowledge was expanding, filling in the wastelands, and connecting fields of study.

Genetically, P.J. was a great grand niece of Subrahmanyan Chandrasekhar, the Nobel Prize–winning physicist who, to pass the time on an ocean voyage when he was twenty, calculated the critical mass needed for a star to collapse into a black hole. She was thus four generations removed from Chandrasekhar's uncle, Sir Chandrasekhara Venkata Raman, who won the Physics Nobel Prize for his work on the Raman scattering of light the same year as P.J.'s uncle's ship sailed for Cambridge.

P.J.'s biological mother, who dropped her off at an Indian orphanage at six months old, did not divulge this. She stayed with an aunt in a grass-hut village for over a year to have the baby and nurse it and then ran back to her Triplicane family lest it be known that she was ruined and no respectable Brahmin family would allow their son to be arranged in marriage to her.

P.J. knew only the deprivation of the orphanage and her rescue by a blond woman who talked funny and let her eat all she wanted.

P.J. looked up the row of modest homes. The working-class neighborhood was emptied of two-income wage earners, school kids and daycare babies. The appearance of the authority vehicle just when the last witnesses had departed echoed with the ominous vibes of the

Gestapo rounding up the stragglers from the Prague ghetto, which she had a test on this morning in third period.

P.J. rattled the key in the lock, trying to get back inside the house.

"Young lady," the man called and removed his hat.

The metal key bent in her hand against the recalcitrant lock.

"Young lady!" he said again.

"I'm going to school!" she said. "I'm not ditching! I'm just late!"

"I'm not the truancy officer." He walked across the dead lawn. "I'm Deputy Max Konstantin, Sheriff's department. Wanted to ask you some questions."

"I'm going to be late for school," P.J. said. "I missed the bus, and I'm going to have to go to the Hole."

He smiled. "The Hole? Sounds dire."

"It is. You can't talk. You can't read. You can't even do homework. You just have to sit there and wait until second period." At least P.J. could retreat into physics equations in her head. If she missed first period, she wouldn't see Janelle, and Janelle had said that the "in" clique was throwing a party and she could get P.J. in, even though P.J. was a Goth geek.

"Tell you what." He nudged his hat brim up. "I'll give you a ride to school and ask you a few questions on the way, so you won't be late, and you won't have to go to the Hole."

Her parents would kill her for accepting a ride from the Fuzz. She dilly-dallied. "Can I see some identification, sir?"

"Sure." In his wallet, he had a sheriff's department identification card with his picture and a chrome badge. "You're a smart lady. Glad you asked that."

"Yeah, well, I guess it's okay then." She trudged over the frost-dead grass and got in the passenger seat of his car. The stale air inside smelled like skunky coffee breath. He got in the driver's seat and set his cowboy hat on the seat between them, brim up, like he was collecting for the

Sheriff's Ball.

Other kids her age would know not to get in a car with a stranger, even one with official-looking identification and a nifty shiny badge, all of which are available to the highest bidder on the Internet, but P.J. had been home-schooled. The non-didactic, dialectic pedagogy had been lean on the dystopian aspects of society, like the common tactic among sex offenders and serial killers of impersonating law enforcement officials.

As the car drove away from the curb, the door locks thumped in unison.

The Deputy asked, "Shadow Mountain High School?"

"Yeah," she said.

He turned left at the end of the block. "What's your name?"

"P.J. Lessing." She stared out the windshield at the cold-grayed world.

"What's the P.J. stand for?"

"Peace in Jerusalem."

His black eyebrows rose. "Quite a name."

"You don't know the half of it. My sibs are named Equality for Women, Justice for Africa, Humanity Will Save Us, Conscience in the Rain Forest, Community is our Strength, Freedom for Tibet, and, um, Harmony for All Nations. We all have nicknames, to survive public school after Saffron stopped home-schooling us."

"Who's Saffron?"

"My mom."

"Call your mother Saffron?" he asked.

"That's her name." She should shut up. Saffron and The Tower had enough trouble with law enforcement without P.J. mouthing off.

"Right." The deputy nodded. "Your phone number?" She recited it, but he didn't write it down. He asked, "What time were you up till last night?"

"I don't know. One, maybe."

He looked away from the road and glanced at her. His dark brown eyes were set in a singing-idol face, and not one of the heroin-wrinkled seventies singers, either. More like a matured boy-band hottie. He looked like he might be part-something, like her friend Guadalupe O'Shaunessey, half-Mexican and half-Irish. P.J.'s Indian soul sized up other brown people, looking for an ethnic connection.

He asked, "What were you doing up that late?"

"Computer. Studying." God, she was so going to get her parents in trouble. Authority figures didn't grok her parents.

"You hear anything last night?" he asked. "Any screams, gunshots or anything around the Lone Star Grocery?"

"No." The Lone Star Grocery's prices were high, but people generally kept their composure about it. P.J.'s family grew most of their own food.

"You hear anything from those woods out there?" The deputy gestured at the copse of trees out beyond the last houses of her block.

"Naw. Not much out there besides rattlesnakes and armadillos."

The deputy turned the car onto the highway leading out of town. "You have the radio or television on loud?"

"No. I just surfed around. Some chatting. Some IM."

"You instant message friends or strangers?"

"Just friends. Look, did I do something wrong?"

"No. There's a girl missing, and I wondered if anyone had heard anything. You should be careful about weirdoes on the Internet."

"I don't do anything stupid. Hey, you missed the exit." She pointed as the highway exit for her school slid behind them.

"Oops," he said. "How old are you?"

"Fourteen." P.J.'s finger crept up, pointing at the hard plastic ceiling of the police car. Her matte black fingernail polish was chipped. Unbidden, her finger started to draw equations in the air. The swooping Greek letters, sigma and theta and chi, calmed her.

"So you didn't hear anything last night. You see anything this morning that looked out of place? Trash cans knocked over? Stains on the ground?"

"No." She drew an equation that measured the force with which she would hit that tall evergreen tree if she jumped out of the squad car moving at sixty-seven miles per hour. Her other hand tested the door handle, but it wouldn't budge.

"You see any unusual signs of animals? Coyotes? Buzzards?"

"No. You should take this exit." She pointed at the upcoming asphalt ramp, glittering black in the sun.

"You sure you didn't hear somebody? Maybe a struggle?"

He was going to pass this exit, too. He wasn't a real cop. He was taking her out into the piney woods, where the scum-topped swamps and jagged trees hid everything. Her thoughts jumbled in her head like a wind-swirled pile of dry leaves, mixing what she remembered into what he had told her. "I heard animals. Or people. In the woods. Around midnight."

The nose of the car swung right. They coasted down the exit ramp. P.J. breathed and her finger furiously wrote equations describing the contraction of time at various fractions of the speed of light.

He said, "So you did hear something."

"Yeah. I didn't hear it very well, 'cause I was online."

The car accelerated up the access road toward her school. If the car was one-half a metric ton and accelerating from 80 kph to 100 kph, how much power was required to achieve that acceleration in five seconds? She drew the equation in the sun-slick air.

He said, "You said 'animals' or 'people.' You sure that it was more than one animal or person?"

"Yeah." The car coasted up the round driveway of the school and into the traffic jam of parents trying to rescue their teens from an idle hour in the Hole. "I'll jump out."

He stopped the car. The doors unlocked. She opened the door and swung her backpack out.

He leaned halfway through the car and looked up at her through the open door. "Did it sound like just a few people, or a lot of people?"

"I don't know. A dozen, maybe. I don't know." She slammed the door. A pristine Ford Mustang convertible barely missed sideswiping her. The license plate, which read XIAN was framed by a holder than read, *My God Is An Awesome God,* like half the other license plate holders in the parking lot. The band had sold them as a fundraiser last year.

She had escaped. Barely. In another three miles and three more minutes on the highway, they would have been out of town and into the dripping woods. She could barely remember hearing some mumbling or rattling in the woods last night as she typed long equations into the computer that spun into the ether, through the black of space to satellites and back, to India. Her hands shook so hard that she couldn't even inscribe equations in the air to calm herself.

Janelle shimmied through the scrum of underclassmen scrambling for classes. "Hey, the people giving the party wanted me to ask whether you're really into the Satanism and vampire stuff or if you just, like, dress Goth."

P.J.'s breathing was still ragged as she tried to figure out what the hell Janelle was talking about. "What?"

Janelle's head bobble was mean-girl cruel. "'Cause you hang around with the Trenchcoat Mafia and those Billy Bob–era Angelinas. So are you a Christian?"

The throng of teens jostled them, over eighty percent of whom, plus or minus three percent, wore vestigial crosses around their necks. "Not really."

"Okay," Janelle said. "Then you can come to the party."

Vanessa lay on her old twin bed in her mother's house. Tufts of yellow insulation grew through ceiling cracks like inverted, dead weeds.

Vanessa forced herself to roll off the bed. Depression felt like muddy water splashing against her legs as she scrubbed her teeth in the olive sink and swirling around her ankles while she dressed. She rested a few minutes after each task to rake together energy.

She was destroyed. Maybe if she hadn't stopped for a drink, things might have been different. Things always went wrong when she drank, like there was some sort of a God, punishing her for taking even a nip, but that was the way the nasty old world worked. Randomness sneaked up on you and smashed you over the head.

Still, she should lay off the sauce until she got back to New Orleans.

Vanessa's mother maintained that all she needed was a nice, fresh cup of tea, so Vanessa drank the pucker-inducing green tea and ignored her mother's incoherent conversation, leveraged herself into her red-laced, black corset and clothes, and drove to the sheriff's office. Keeping the car on the road required attention. Sometimes her depression mimicked fatigue or drunkenness. Maybe she wanted the car to ram into the ditch and burst into flames.

Max Konstantin's desk was near the back of the sheriff's office. As she strode through, a wave of hat-tipping rode over the sea of deputies.

She whirled and sat in the chair beside Max's desk, perching on the edge and arching her back to deemphasize her stomach region. The corset from a fetish shop in New Orleans cinched her waist to about twenty inches. The pose accentuated her bulging bustline. "Hi."

The deputy's head ticked sideways before he half-stood and shook her hand. He was a handsome man, almost pretty, with a V-physique that was usually achieved via liposuction. She hadn't noticed his looks last night in the dark, probably because she was so tired. And drunk. But no one could tell when she drank. Or when she was angry.

"Nice setup you have here," she said. "Nicer than we have in New Orleans."

"We?" Max asked. "You law enforcement?"

"I'm a forensic technician," Vanessa said.

Max's eyebrows rose and his lips curved up, barely. "You starting a department here?"

"No." Vanessa smiled big. Vanessa was just what men want: blond and pretty and flirty and funny, and even if she was a little hefty around the hips, men liked her big boobs. Her mother hadn't given her any svelte Fräulein genes, just fat German ones that strained lederhosen. She rubbed the back of her neck, dragging her fingers through her blond, blond hair. The pale curls around her fingers were translucent. "I'm just visiting my mom. She's sick. I hadn't even seen Ester for years. I feel just awful. When are you going to officially call her a missing person?"

The detective shrugged. "General rule is three days."

"And when she doesn't show up?"

"Then we'll put out a missing person's sheet. She's probably somewhere with a guy, still asleep, drunk. There's no evidence that a crime has been committed."

She had to bring this cutie cop around. Vanessa rested her elbow on his desk and leaned her head on her hand, exposing her neck and dropping her eyes below his so she looked up at him. "Ester isn't that type. She's been attending the Country Congregational Bible Church. You know about it?"

The detective shrugged but raised his chin, a body language feint: I'll play.

Vanessa nodded and widened her eyes. "Her emails have gotten really orthodox. She worried about wearing pants to work because pants aren't 'women's clothes,' like the Old Testament says. On the Christian spectrum, that church is somewhere between Hasidic Jews for Jesus and the Amish."

Max the deputy smiled at her and nodded.

Vanessa dangled her hand over his pencil cup and toyed with the phallic eraser tips. "She wouldn't have a one night stand. I'll bet she's a born-again virgin, which is kind of like being a bottle blond."

"Okay." The deputy was patronizing her. He should ask her more questions. Because she was the first person to miss Ester, the chances were fifty-fifty that she was the culprit. She was, however, female, which meant that there was less than a five-percent chance that she was the murderer. Female murderers poison their spouses or smother their children for personal or financial gain.

Vanessa leaned on her crossed arms and squished her boobs together, creating truly impressive cleavage. Some chub concentrated in convenient places. "You don't think that church would stone her to death, do you? A scapegoat? Or an honor killing?"

He smiled in a flirty, arrogant way. He knew he was pretty. "Imagine we'd have heard about that."

"Churches get weird when they're left to themselves. They spiral crazier and crazier, everyone trying to outdo each other with ostentatious piety, like they're keeping score. They convince themselves that the end is near, and then they brew the cyanide fruit punch, or else the federal government flies in with their black helicopters and sets fire to the compound. We're pretty near Waco, here."

Max crossed his arms and stared at his pen, no longer flirting. "New Canaan is not Waco. Most of them Branch Davidians were from California." He said California with an emphasis on *forn,* as in *fornicate,* and so it rhymed with Gomorrah.

"I know that," Vanessa said. She let her accent broaden from its acquired Cajun patois drawl into Longhorn Texan twang. "I was born and raised here."

"We don't have suicide cults here. This Bible Church just has some pious folks. Nothing wrong with pious folks. And Ester is not a missing person yet," he said. "She's overdue."

Vanessa didn't like his stalling. During the random carnage of September 11 that played out like a real-time disaster movie, those four planes were listed as overdue for hours before they were upgraded to missing, even though there was enough burning wreckage around to suggest something might have happened to them. It was like she could smell volatilizing kerosene and smoldering metal while some officious person spouted *overdue* like Essie was a stupid library book.

Vanessa settled farther down her arm. If she slid any farther, she would be lying spread-eagled on his desk. Maybe if her ankles were actually hooked behind her ears, he might pay her closer attention. "In New Orleans, if we had a missing pretty blond girl, we'd have a crime. I don't think I'm psychic or anything, but I have a knack for this. When I wonder if a serial killer is out there, a serial killer is out there. It feels like that now. More girls are going to end up dead."

"We don't know that. There's no use riling everybody up. And I've found that hunches are generally useless. Solid investigation works."

"So you're going to wait for him to kill again? A lot of police departments wait for more crime scenes to gather more evidence. The evidence being, of course, dead women. Usually in pieces." She leaned in to whisper. This should be conspiratorial, not threatening. She widened her blue eyes, and her big boobs pooled on his desk. "If something is wrong, people will say the sheriff's department 'made mistakes early in the investigation.'"

Max the deputy continued clicking his ballpoint. The peeking pen point was phallic, though repressed. He was still playing. She wished he would listen.

"The feds always blame local law enforcement," she said, "and call them country rubes or say they 'bungled' the investigation, or like when the federal government said the New Orleans mayor wasn't specific enough during Hurricane Katrina. Then the liberal media show the pattern of abductions like only an idiot could miss it. That's the way this nasty old world works. First on the scene is first to get screwed."

He nodded. Ah, he was listening.

"Ester wasn't the type to blow me off to go fuck some guy."

Max rolled his pencil between his teeth like a cigar. "You used the past tense," he said. "'Ester wasn't the type.' Why?"

"I'm in forensics. Most of the people we deal with are in the past tense. The job fosters the past tense." Vanessa shrugged. "And a really dark sense of humor."

Max nodded and smiled wryly.

Vanessa pressed. "So, should we start with victimology? What elevated Ester's risk for becoming a victim?"

Max smiled out of one side of his mouth, either rue or condescension. "Around here we ask, why her and why now?"

"Right," she said. Max was one of those folksy neo-Luddites who didn't go for scientific lingo. "I like that. More down to earth."

Max nodded again. "When was the last time you saw Ester?"

"Three years ago. Give or take."

"And what do you know about her lately?"

Vanessa shrugged. "Our lives went different directions. She stayed on the ranch. I went to undergrad and then work. I live in New Orleans, Mardi Gras central. We kept in touch through MyOwnRoom-dot-com. It's a social website. Her NamePlate is EssieTex."

Max nodded but didn't write anything down. "You see anybody around the Lone Star Grocery last night? Hanging out near the trash bins or around back?"

"No."

"Did you see any groups of people walking, or a pack of animals?"

That was an odd question. "No. Look, if there's anything I can do to help, you'll let me know? I don't have a lab, but I'll bet I could cook up some kitchen chemistry or commandeer the high school chemistry lab, if there's something quick and dirty you want."

Max shook his head and his dark brown eyes darted up and right, a near roll. His manner said, Here's the little science detective who thinks she can solve crimes because she's seen it on television.

Vanessa didn't cotton to condescension. This backwater policeman didn't know who he was dealing with. She smiled, squished her boobs so they bulged above her low vee neckline as if they were eyes goggling him, and spoke simpering Southern. "I realize that you're the lead detective, but if you need any little thing done that might confirm what you already suspect," Max puffed as she stroked his machismo, "I can help."

"That's fine, now," Max said. "Might do that."

That was the most commitment that she was going to get about keeping her in the evidentiary loop, so she wrote her cell phone number on a slip of paper.

Sometimes it took months for the authorities to listen to Vanessa. She felt like Cassandra, prophetic, raising the alarm, but unbelieved. If she had ever proverbially cried wolf, their skepticism might be warranted, but she was a veritable dead body dowser.

Mists of depression thickened the air around her again.

As she left the sheriff's office, she passed Zeke James, Ester's dad, coming in. His windblown hair and beard bushed out like a red chow dog.

She wanted to duck her head and go home and sleep until the fog cleared, but she raised her hand. "Mr. James," she said. "Did Essie come home?"

Zeke shook his head and sighed. "No. There's a meeting at the church at six tonight to look for her in an organized fashion."

Vanessa could sleep off the watery depression later. "I'll be there."

Diane read a motion to suppress in which slimy defense lawyers wanted to exclude DNA evidence because the defendant had not signed a waiver before the police obtained the sample, nor had the police obtained a court order to collect a DNA sample. Said "sample" had been recovered from the defendant's holding cell, which apparently contained chunks of ear, after he had bragged to another inmate about molesting a little girl.

She smiled. Easy motions made her morning. Any decent attorney could quash it. Precedent: blood and DNA, like handwriting, voice, and fingerprints, *quae est eadem*, are considered physical traits and thus collecting them is not a violation of the Fifth Amendment guarantee against self-incrimination. Plus, there is no expectation of privacy in a county holding cell, so the defendant shouldn't have left chunks of himself lying around *in pleno lumine*, literally, in broad daylight.

That should screw 'em. As a prosecutor, she had a proctologist's view of the dark cabal of the legal profession.

How do you know that God, who created the world out of chaos and darkness, was an attorney?

Because He created chaos and darkness first.

She adjusted the waistband on her black skirt, which dug under her ribs through her control-top panty hose. The microfont on the page blurred, and she rubbed her eyes. Eyestrain already, at only ten in the morning. Granted, she had been reading since four when her husband Max got that phone call about the missing girl. She rubbed her aching temples and jaw joint. Eyestrain and hairstrain. Her scalp felt like thirty thousand splinters tweezed all at once. Diane strictly knotted her hair. Hanks of hair are a handy rope around your neck.

Her cell phone rang, saving her from the indignity of bifocals. She answered, "Assistant Criminal County Attorney Marshall."

"Sister Diane? This is Pastor Daniel Stout." The pastor's voice thrummed through the phone to her ear.

"Reverend?" The Christian vernacular, *Brother, Sister, witness, the Good News,* still came awkwardly to her, and she hoped in time it would become more comfortable. With rigor, anything is achievable. "What can I do for you?"

"We have a problem," he said. "Zeke James's daughter Ester—Essie—went missing last night. She isn't the type to run off, no matter what happened in church last weekend. I'm worried that her disappearance might have something to do with the Temple Project. Is there anything you can do?"

Diane plucked a pen from the cup on her desk and snagged a fresh legal pad, jotting the time, date, phone call, at the office, and Pastor Daniel Stout. Her memory was good, but living with Max's photographic memory reinforced how faulty everyone else's memory is, so she wrote notes about everything and filed them. "Tell me what you know."

She funneled into outline form the names and details that the Reverend told her, that Zeke James had told him: Vanessa Allen, 11:00pm; jewelry: gold cross necklace, no earrings; Lone Star Grocery.

"Any indication of CSA in her past?" Diane asked.

"Those medieval people?"

"Sorry. CSA means child sexual abuse. Was she ever attacked by a stranger or abused as a kid?"

"Not that I know of."

"A history of CSA can make people do strange things. With every kid in the system, you find some sort of abuse, usually CSA."

"My Lord, Diane," Pastor Daniel said with a lilt of pity. "What must this job do to your soul?"

"Gives my soul something to fight for." Diane stretched her achy body in her chair. That was a very different answer than she would have uttered even six months ago, when the answer would have been, Oh,

I don't have one. In the second year of law school, they roll out a big machine, stick a hose in your right ear, and suck it out.

"What should we do, Sister Diane? Call the FBI?"

Calling the feds would cast aspersions—personal aspersions—on the sheriff's department, and Diane didn't have any aspersions to cast. Part of the lawman's code was professional envy for a really nice bust, and Max had much to strut about.

"It looks best if local law enforcement calls. The FBI doesn't pay much attention to individuals. They'd shuffle it into the low-priority pile."

"But a County Attorney could call them."

"It's awfully early to call in the Feds. My husband is the deputy who went over to the grocery store last night. I'll talk to him." An anxious tremor wavered. "Since Essie is over eighteen, the sheriff's department would customarily wait three days before officially declaring her a missing person, but I can ask Max to look into it right away."

Pastor Daniel said, "He called me about four this morning about Brother Zeke. I didn't make the connection at first."

She cradled the phone in the crook of her shoulder. "You didn't, um, mention me, did you?"

Pastor Daniel's throat clearing sounded like staccato static. "I wouldn't interfere in things between a husband and wife, Diane."

Diane exhaled. "I appreciate that. I'll call him now."

"Just to let you know, Sister Diane, there's a meeting at six tonight at the church to pick up flyers and divide up to search."

Diane glanced at the solid, squared stacks of caseload on her desk. Every binder held details about the ways a child was abused, physically, sexually. Each case was clipped into a binder, color-coded by the month of the trial date. February was red. March was green. The tall April binder stack was purple. April was going to be murder. Later months and years carefully stacked on the floor around her desk. It looked like she was imprisoned in a child's fort, built with vivid plastic blocks. "I'll see if I can get there."

"We appreciate anything you can do, Sister Diane."

"Thanks, um, Brother Daniel. I'll look into holding a press conference." News reporters only responded to the lurid. With no blurred pictures of a body to bleed for the cameras, she would be lucky to get ten people there. Oral advocacy in the courtroom was difficult, and Diane had become very good at it through diligent work and micro-preparation, but dealing with the media was worse, with their reliance on titillating sound bites instead of elegant, loophole-free legalese.

Max jotted a few notes on his meeting with the neighbor girl to document when he knew what, while Zeke James meandered toward his desk.

The deputy at the desk in front of his, George, the whitest man in the sheriff's office and all of East Texas, said into his phone, "Yeah, missing. Like a UFO snatched her. Let's pick the kids up from school today, huh?"

George must be talking to his wife. He talked dirty to his girlfriend, lacing his vocabulary with references to her black pubic hair and sucking hole. Max disapproved in a tired way by rolling his eyes when George swiveled to ensure Max was listening, though he wondered if "Jojo-Baby" was actually a big, strapping dude who shaved his balls, considering George's overcompensation. Max just hoped he didn't catch George and Jojo-Baby sucking dick out at Loser's Lake during one of the annual panty raids to clean up the county's parks. Dallas homosexuals drove down to Sin Nombre County for summer gay-ins. Their reasoning was a mystery—nicer parks, maybe, or taller hedges—but it scared the swingset kids and the horses so the sheriff's office enforced the blue laws.

George said into the phone, "UFOs do too exist. A college buddy of mine saw the lights over Phoenix a few years ago. He swears that they were alien spaceships."

Max had been busy that morning: walking the Lone Star's parking lot again in the daylight, interviewing the neighbor girl, back to the office for a gym session, and meeting Vanessa Allen and Zeke James. He stretched his arms to wring out the sore lactic acid from a set of high-weight pyramid reps in the office gym, and his uniform shirt strained across his back.

He had walked the parking lot with little hope. The dusty gravel, undisturbed garbage bin, and complete lack of anything suspicious failed to meet even his mildest expectations.

Television forensics shows often quote the widely held belief of evidence dynamics called Locard's exchange principle, which says that any two items that come in contact will exchange matter, meaning that a perpetrator leaves something of himself at the scene and takes away something with him.

Bullshit.

Well, not precisely bullshit, but very often fragmentary evidence left behind is microscopic and impossible to find, and the evidence that was taken away is never found because you don't know who the guy is or where to look for it.

Conviction rates had dropped since those forensics crime television shows started because juries expected a perfect Locard exchange, and often, even at murder and rape trials, all the evidence was circumstantial.

Before those shows, lots of murderers were convicted if the prosecuting attorney had means, motive, opportunity, and even a shred of physical evidence, even if it was circumstantial—lots of guilty people were convicted on circumstantial evidence. Murderers, even sadistic sex serial killers, were caught by old-fashioned investigation or dumb luck, not mad forensic scientists, not near-psychic profilers, and certainly never by actual psychics.

Max's cell phone blared the boo-boo-baby rap crap his daughter had downloaded into it this week. Standing joke. The other deputies' head-swiveling and elbow-nudging was also a standing joke. George sneered. Max mimed shooting him, and George slumped across his desk. Max snatched up the phone. "Hello?"

"Hi, Honey," his wife Diane said, breezily, without that overly careful, professional tone that usually overlaid her voice. Her office must be empty except for those compulsively color-coded case folders.

Max was not being properly chivalrous. Diane was meticulous, organized, and had an eerily high conviction rate. Even the best defense attorneys from Dallas and Houston plea-bargained when they saw her at the prosecution table. Her fanatical intensity made her a one-woman defense team–wrecking machine. She made him proud.

She also made his job easier. When he arrested an abusive parent or uncle, she made sure they stayed arrested and stayed in prison for a good long time.

Besides, a little OCD is beneficial in a spouse. She always knew where the kids and the good scissors were.

Diane said, "I was wondering about that case you went out on last night. A missing woman, Ester James."

They didn't discuss their work at home when the kids were around, like this morning at breakfast, because their work vacillated between tedium and tragedy. Their pillow talk often started with her asking, "So who did you arrest today that I'm going to have to arraign tomorrow?" Oh, they were a cheerful couple. Law and order. "Meeting with her dad right now."

"I just had a call from a *friend*," Diane said.

That peculiar emphasis was code for someone important for Diane's career, and annoyance tightened in Max's lips. County Attorneys had friends. Deputies had snitches.

Diane continued, "A *friend* who is interested in the case. He'd appreciate it if you didn't wait the usual three days to declare her a missing person. This might be a problem case, and jumping on it hard might prevent worse problems later."

"Right," Max said. "Look, Zeke James is standing in front of my desk right here." Zeke stopped by the donut table on the other side of the room, raising his orange eyebrows askance and pointing to the pink box. Max nodded and waved him over. To Diane on his cell phone, he said, "I'll call you after I talk to him."

"Who have you talked to so far?"

Max made a pretense of consulting his notes. "Vanessa Allen, Essie's friend who was supposed to pick her up from work but was late and didn't see her. Stayed in the bar until the second commercial break after eleven o'clock during that college basketball game last night, so around eleven-twenty, and then she was back five minutes later. Regular credit card charges. She didn't wait long outside the grocery store. Bobert the ex-boyfriend. Pretty much airtight alibi. In a bar with four friends up near Dallas-Fort Worth, regular charges from that bar on his credit card, bartender remembers the lot of them, and security camera footage shows that Bobert did a drunk striptease standing on the bar around midnight. He has a Navy tattoo on his butt. And P.J. Lessing."

"Who is this Lessing person?" Her tone cooled to semi-professional.

"A high school kid whose house backs up to the grocery store. She was the only person around that neighborhood this morning. She looks Mexican or Apache or something, but skinny. And Zeke James, her father, who is here right now."

Across the office, Zeke selected a donut and dropped a bill from his wallet into the honor jar beside the box.

"What did P.J. Lessing say?" Diane asked in a creamy alto.

"Not much. She thinks she might have heard something, some animals or people, about one in the morning, but says she can't be sure."

"Animals? People? Plural?" Diane asked.

His little wife was indeed perceptive. She deserved *friends*. "Seemed unusual that she consistently used the plural."

"Interesting. Who do you like?"

"Wouldn't lay a Jackson with an English bookie on any of 'em, except the 'unknown persons or animals.' Don't even like them. We need more information about Ester, her contacts, her acquaintances, the people at the store that night. Good old-fashioned investigation. Say, do you know anything about her church, this Country Congregational Bible Church?"

"Nope," Diane said, and her voice perked up to its wifely pitch. "By the way, I'm working late tonight, again. I probably won't be home until nine-thirty or so. Bye, Honey." The phone beeped.

Zeke James sat down in the vinyl-covered chair beside Max's desk, chewing the side off a jelly donut. "Thank ya. Ran out of granola bars."

"You sleep at all last night?" Max asked, a question that would tell him a lot about Zeke James's relationship with his daughter.

"Before Vanessa called, I got a few hours," Zeke said. Strawberry jelly leaked from the donut onto his auburn beard and hung, bright as a ruby, on one straw-stiff whisker. "I drove around, first in town, then in the woods. With that full moon, I shut off my headlights, and I could see pretty well. Didn't find anything."

Lunacy is an urban legend, but one that holds sway among law enforcement, ER doctors, and elementary school teachers.

Max went over the timeline again, and Zeke wrote down Essie's friends' names and a few phone numbers. Finally Max said, "We're starting the investigation now, not waiting the customary three days."

"I mightily appreciate that, Deputy. Essie wouldn't run off. I always told her that if she eloped, I'd elope with her, 'cause I wouldn't want to miss her wedding. When she was dating that Bobert fellow, I didn't like him much. He treated her all right, but he just isn't going places. But I shut my mouth."

That didn't seem like too much protesting to Max. "Is there anything missing from her room?"

"I haven't checked. Been driving around all night."

"She do anything unusual in the last couple days?"

Zeke looked down at the half-eaten donut in his hands. Max watched sadness and worry creep around his eyes. "No," Zeke said. "Nothing."

Zeke James was lying. Max was sure of it. He could come back to it. "I want to ask this delicately, you understand. Is there any history of mental illness?"

Zeke quirked an orange eyebrow. "No."

The majority of adults who are reported missing are psychiatric patients who go off their medication. "She on any medication? Anti-depressants? Bipolar? Anti-psychotics?"

His expression deepened to profound embarrassment. "She took a little aspirin once a month or so."

The lack of mental illness dramatically increased the chances that Ester James was just fine and was taking a vacation or had found somewhere innocuous to spend the night. In cases of a missing, competent adult, no crime scene, no threats, no suicide note, law enforcement usually does nothing at all. "How's the ranch doing? Cattle doing well?"

"Been a mild winter. They're fat and sassy." A little tender pride crept into his voice. "My Red Angus aren't as big as Black Angus cattle, but they're better marbled."

"No money problems, then?" Max noted that with a black marker.

"Selling all of them that I want as fast as I can breed them. They're a genetically superior herd. I've identified one PCR-restriction fragment length polymorphism that co-segregates with better mothering ability and thus higher weight gain and better survival in calves. That's an interesting bit of behavioral genetics, a neurotransmitter with an estrogen-sensitive promoter region."

"That's just great, Mr. James. Did Essie have life insurance?" Max doodled a cow with googley eyes on his notes because, while he could recite what Zeke James had just said, he could not make head nor tail of it.

"None that I know of. Maybe something through her work. I don't have any. Don't need life insurance when you've got land, horses, and cattle."

Max nodded. Due to his own life insurance, Max was worth a great deal more dead than alive, but that's the way it is in law enforcement. Being a hero doesn't pay well. Being a soulless attorney, however, pays quite well, as he noted twice a month.

"You sure nothing unusual happened in the last week or two? Anybody threaten her? She act funny?"

Zeke shook his head. "She's been fine. She has been reading the Bible a lot. I approve of that. She knows a lot about the Word, especially the Old Testament, and that makes me proud. She was growing out her hair, stopped bleaching it and was reviling worldly things, like hard music and immodest adornment. You know, bling."

That was a lot of protesting about Essie's faith and churchly rigor. Max needed a handle. Any lead was better than nothing. "Right. She goes to your church? The Country Congregational Bible Church?"

Zeke nodded.

Max should call Zeke James's pastor, Daniel Stout, and have a word with him about Essie.

When P.J. got home from school, she flopped on the couch and turned on the television. Her thin body bounced on the dilapidated cushions, and her long black skirt flowed over the couch and onto the floor like the gown of a medieval princess in a Dante Gabriel Rossetti painting, "Gothic Maiden in Repose" or "The Witch Queen." When P.J. had gushed about Dante Rossetti's poems, her friends rolled their eyes opulently and one-upped her with Dante's sister, Christina Rossetti, who wrote *Goblin Market* with its orgasmic lists of fruit and *After Death*, which was so *As I Lay Dying*. P.J. wasn't even the Gothiest of her friends. Asphodel had a headband with real bone devil horns, so he looked like he had implants. Gaystat was gay vampyre Goth. Lucyfer wore black lace underwear every day, just in case she was raped and murdered. That was so, like, fatalistic. P.J. really should choose a Goth name soon.

Even they didn't really understand P.J., though. Whenever she tried to explain physics to them, even antique Newtonian physics, they were, like, "Blah, blah, blah, geekspeak, nerdtalk." Those angsty people wept over nineteenth-century, psychosexual romances, and they called her a nerd.

None of her dweebie Goth friends were invited to the party at Hi-Falutin' Row. Going without them wasn't exactly betraying them. It was exposing the scrubbed-pink kids to alternative culture. It was practically Goth charity work.

On the phosphorescent television screen, a microphone-studded podium eclipsed a woman up to her chest. She looked stern, like her jaw was always clenched. Her dark brown hair was scraped back into a tight bun on the back of her head, and she wore a skirt suit and matched pearls. She was the uptightest tight-ass P.J. had ever observed in its natural habitat.

Saffron shouted from behind the kitchen's beaded curtain, "Are you watching that tool again?"

P.J. shouted back, "How do you know what to protest if you never watch the news?"

"Read a book!"

"The publishing industry is enervated by cronyism and nepotism, and bestsellers are pre-ordained by advertising budgets and self-fulfilling bookstore polls. And thanks again for the HDTV, The Tower!"

Saffron and The Tower squabbled like angry ducks in the kitchen.

He said, "But I really like basketball."

On the television, behind the tight-assed woman, a man had orange hair all over his head and face that looked like he hacked it with a Bowie knife.

Triangulated with the orange man and the woman stood a man wearing the most somber black suit she had ever seen. She squinted. The suit didn't have buttons. His shirt didn't even have buttons. Her melanin radar activated. He was light-skinned African-American, she thought. Or Puerto Rican. Maybe he just sprayed the self-tanner on too thick.

The woman consulted her notes and read into the microphone, "Ester Christina James has been missing for sixteen hours, since she was abducted from the Lone Star Grocery last night. We're asking anyone with any information or who has seen her to please call our tipline." She said a toll-free number, and the digits appeared across the bottom of the screen. The woman pressed a bulge of brown hair, and it succumbed. "To help search for her or pick up some flyers, come to the Country Congregational Bible Church," she gave the address, "tonight at six o'clock. If you think you might have seen anything, or heard anything, please contact the Sin Nombre County Sheriff's office."

A reporter yelled, "Ma'am! Is a serial killer involved?"

The uptight woman looked down into the throng and said, "At this time, we have no evidence of a serial killer."

The crowd rumbled, and P.J. felt their contagious nerves. Even the denial of a serial killer was frightening. If she encountered him, maybe she could talk him out of his life of crime, or perhaps he would seduce her to Bonnie-and-Clyde thrilling darkness.

An anchorwoman's pretty face filled the television screen. "In other news, in Arizona, a white buffalo calf has been born on a ranch. This white calf has blue eyes, not the pink eyes of an albino genetic mutation. To the Oglala Lakota Native Americans, the birth of the white buffalo means that White Buffalo Calf Woman has returned because the world has become filled with sin and suffering, and the universe is about to end. For more on the end of the world, we go to Joseph Blythe in Arizona."

P.J. clicked off the television. Ester James was the missing woman the deputy had asked her about. It was like she had jumped off the Earth. No, P.J. thought. It was like Schrödinger's physics-cat experiment. No one knew if Ester James was alive or dead, so in physics, she was both, a dual wave of probability traveling through reality.

P.J. really should tell her parents about the deputy accosting her that morning, but they were still arguing. If she waited a few hours until they were mellowly stoned, they wouldn't bawl her out for accepting a ride from a stranger and, even worse, from the pigs.

She had, however, avoided tardiness and the Hole.

"Sister Diane!"

Diane walked two more steps away from the sun-blasted podium before she remembered she was Sister Diane.

Zeke James swam over the bubbling crowd to reach her. His shaggy hair and beard looked strawberry blond in the strong sunlight. "Sister Diane," he said. "Do you have a minute to talk about Ester?"

She had to get back to the office to depose a witness in the Jorge Martinez case, in which a coyote, slang for a facilitator of illegal immigration and human trafficker, strangled a six-year-old boy because he cried that his feet hurt because he had no shoes.

The video camera nozzles tracked her and Zeke James. She took Zeke's arm and turned him away from the reporters. "Walk and talk?"

Zeke climbed the courthouse steps with her. "I'm worried. I'm sure your husband is doing a fine job, but maybe the sheriff's department is understaffed."

Polarized sunlight flashed off the camera lenses. She ducked her head to hide her face behind Zeke's bulk. "Is there something specific you're concerned about?"

"Well, the deputy said that he would come over and look at Ester's room, but he didn't seem real interested."

"Really?" Diane had worried that Max might be blasé. Sin Nombre County was a quiet place except for drug dealers and coyotes and domestic things. The budget shortfall last year had cut three deputy jobs out of thirty.

Zeke said, "I know her email passwords."

"Really." Ester James's computer should have been carted away first thing that morning and checked by at least her department's tech guys. The sheriff's department should have looked over her room, at least to see if she took anything with her. "Let me ask some questions. Maybe there's a reason."

"Thanks mightily, Sister Diane."

She smiled and patted Zeke's arm, carpeted with stiff, orange hairs. Zeke's wife must have been a pretty woman, and Ester must have taken after her.

After the Jorge Martinez disposition, she had a child prostitute trafficking case to deal with. The coyotes dragged them in then turned them over to the pimps. Most of the traumatized kids spoke Spanish, but this time, she needed a Russian translator for the thirteen-year-old girl, and she had no idea where to find someone who spoke Russian.

Max denied knowing Russian and said no one in his dad's family spoke it even though they all had cheek-mangling accents, but Max was weird about his family.

The Country Congregational Bible Church boasted fewer than two hundred families, a micro-church by today's standard of commercial feel-good giga-churches and brittle crystal cathedrals. Pastor Daniel's wife sent an email to the mailing list, and the church grapevine showed its true face: a kudzu weed that shot tendrils into many homes in Sin Nombre County and even neighboring counties. The emails will virally proliferate across Texas, then the country, then the world.

At five minutes to six o'clock, over a hundred people crowded into the fellowship hall. Texans are punctual. Soon a hundred hungry, worried people will go forth into the cold woods and dark streets. By nine o'clock that night, everyone for three counties around will have seen a flyer and been asked about Ester.

In the church, theories of the crime rolled through the air like night-calling bullfrogs.

"It was a white SUV with a license plate starting DMN."

"The sheriff's department has a sketch of the man who grabbed her, one of them neo-Nazi, white-supremacist, skinhead, prison-gang types. Looks like Hitler scribbled on him."

"Them Utah Mormon polygamists took her. They like them blond."

"Which one was Ester James again, the blond or the redhead?"

There was also less focused gossip: "At a snake goddess temple in India with hot springs under it, every year the sand turns black for six months, and then it turns white again for six months. It's a miracle."

"Have you read that book, *Miracles for Non-Majors?*"

"Then the white mist moved through the hotel bathroom, and I said, Begone, ghost! I have to wash the conditioner out of my hair!"

"Boy, you have got to stop being so believin' all the time. White snipe, jackalopes, and global warming are all hoaxes."

Vanessa Allen stood in the crowd and listened to the Bibles thumping. The churchies spouted self-aggrandizing crap, like their lives amounted to so little that they had to invent sanctimonious, compensatory shit so others wouldn't see what worthless worms they were. Why they bothered to continue living was a mystery.

At noon, the head of the church, Pastor Daniel, a light-skinned black man, stood on the three-man dais on one end and raised his hands. Conversations among the crowd dwindled.

"Thank you for coming," he said. "One of our own Christian ladies, Ester James, has gone missing. Now, no matter what you think about what happened last Sunday, she's one of our own, and we need to find her for her sake and for the sake of her father, Zeke James."

Zeke James, Ester's father, joined him on the dais and stood silent, his eyes on the foam coffee cup in his hands. Zeke touched Daniel's arm, pointed into the crowd right at Vanessa like a bullet could cruise down his long, fat arm and chubby finger, and he whispered to the pastor.

Vanessa thought about running for the doors. The last thing she wanted was some kind of a confrontation amongst the right-thinking churchies, but she didn't. Seriously, it didn't matter if these people thought anything weird. Everything they thought was weird.

Pastor Daniel leaned down and separated her from the crowd with a green-eyed direct stare. His eyes were not contact-lens emerald, but sallow khaki. "Are you Vanessa Allen?"

The churchies stared at her. Sense prevailed over annoyance. "Yeah."

"Come with me." He unfurled his long-fingered hand to beckon her forward.

She stepped onto the dais. Vanessa was a big girl, and she wore stiletto-heeled black pumps that matched her corset, so the reverend Daniel was only a few inches taller than she, which made her feel almost normal in the valley of the shrimps.

"Friends," Pastor Daniel said. "This is Vanessa Allen, the lady who was to pick up Ester James." He turned to her. "Did you see Ester that night?"

He stared at her with those dull cat eyes. Vanessa did not like cats, the sly, slithery creatures. She was a dog person. His cat eyes made her distrust him even more than she would an ordinary churchie person. "Not unless I was too drunk to remember."

The pastor frowned, wrinkling the skin over his faint eyebrows. He inhaled to say something, then gulped those words and asked, "Did you talk to her that night?"

Coming to the church was a waste of her time. These idiots weren't going to be able to find their own pew-flattened butts using both hands. "No. Not really."

The minister's displeased glance was uninteresting to Vanessa. He asked, "She disappeared some time between eleven o'clock and eleven-ten, say?"

Vanessa nodded and scanned the religious propaganda on the walls, assuring her that "God is Love," and "Jesus Loves You!"

God is Love. What an idiotic sentiment. Only a complete imbecile would believe that a loving omnipotent Being presided over this bitter, nasty old world. *God is War* would be more accurate, or *God is Death.*

Daniel the minister said, "Let's all pick up some flyers by the door and paper this town. We're looking to get the word out that this young woman has been taken under duress, and if anyone has seen her, get a description of the car, the license plate, anyone she's with, or which way they were headed, and notify the police. We are looking to bring her home, friends."

After she escaped the dais, Vanessa sat in the corner of the Fellowship Hall on a metal folding chair with her arms crossed. She prided herself on being able to control or at least conceal her depression, but this was all too much. Two hundred people patted her shoulders until handprints were permanently eroded into her flesh. Each one had told her that it wasn't her fault or that the Devil had delayed her. A few people remembered to comment that it could all be a mistake.

One older woman with a face like a sagging hound whispered she thought that Essie had run away in shame after what happened last weekend. The search was not for naught, she hastily added and scratched inside a fold of skin near her mouth. "It's a chance for us to do the Lord's work," she said. "It's a mitzvah."

"A what?" Vanessa asked, because she was so tired from not sleeping.

"A small blessing. An opportunity to clothe ourselves in good works before we stand before the Lord in judgment. We need all we can get of those."

"Certainly." Vanessa leaned to walk away but was not quick enough.

"Have you been saved, dear girl?" the woman asked. "The Good Book says, 'he that believeth and is baptized shall be saved.'"

"Yeah." Vanessa inched along a long table with her hands like a tightrope walker. "Sure."

At the end of the table, a teenage Goth girl stood alone, holding a flyer in her black-gloved hands and staring at the orange paper like she was trying to set it on fire with eye lasers. She looked high school age and the India kind of Indian, but the girl wore very American Goth makeup, swaths of chalk and coal dust.

"Hi," Vanessa said, then whispered, "Help me."

The girl looked around Vanessa to the earnest woman standing there. Her eyeliner smeared from dark circles around her eyes to her temples like a robber's mask. "I didn't know you'd be here! Come on." She walked into the crowd.

Vanessa followed, ecstatic that the girl had the presence of mind to help her escape the woman who wanted to dunk Vanessa in a vat. Baptismal immersion rippled with similarities to dissolving a corpse in caustic lye or other strong base. She had burned the shit out of her hands on a vat corpse once.

They passed the faithful.

A blond man chugging an energy drink said rapidly, "I heard it was a prison gang of those neo-Nazis. It's an initiation: blood in, blood out. I heard they had a lot of tattoos, and they all rode in a white SUV."

An old man with crippled hands talked to a teenager with shiny clothes and hair. "Have you read that new book, *The Prayer*? It says that if you pray hard enough, God will give you anything you want: money, cars, jewelry."

Vanessa and P.J. slithered through the crowd. Vanessa's shoulder bumped a woman in the back of her braided head. The woman turned around. She wore an angel pin as big as Vanessa's hand, gaudy with electroplated gold and cut glass. It looked like spinner bait to fly-fish for angels.

When they were across the room, Vanessa muttered, "Thanks."

"No problem," the girl said. Sunlight glinted on green streaks in her night-black hair. "You go to this church?"

"No," Vanessa said. "I'm just here for flyers. You?"

"I thought I'd get some for my high school. I don't go to church."

"Sensible of you. Christianity is just an unsubstantiated promise of a consolation prize for people who fail at life." Vanessa stuck out her hand. "I'm Vanessa Allen."

"I'm P.J." The girl shook her hand. Her brown fingers stuck out of studded leather half-gloves, and her black nail polish was chipped.

Vanessa gestured to a silver skull dangling from a chain looped around P.J.'s slim neck. "Quite a *memento mori* you have."

The Goth girl brightened and then glanced around nervously. "You have one?"

"I work with dead people. I don't need to be reminded of my own mortality."

"Wow," P.J. said. "That's dark. You're a mortician?"

"Forensic tech, in New Orleans." Vanessa dredged up data. "The net number of murders is down, but half as many people live in New Orleans as before Hurricane Katrina. The murder rate is way up. In most cities, the murder conviction rate is over eighty percent, but ours is only twelve percent. You have to be stupid and unlucky to get convicted. The police and the District Attorney's office point fingers at each other, but the problem is that a jury won't convict if a witness is a police officer."

"Wow." P.J.'s black-rimmed, black-irised eyes were wide. "Lawless."

"Yeah, well, that's the way the world is. Bad stuff happens. You gotta be tough." Vanessa felt a hand clamp on her shoulder.

Essie's dad, Zeke James, an orange haystack of a man, said, "Nessie, I'd like you to meet a friend of mine, Diane Marshall."

"So you're Vanessa Allen." A very thin line of partially gray roots lined the widow's peak in Diane Marshall's dark brown hair, swept and sprayed into a stiff bun on the back of her head. "You were the last one to see Ester."

"No," Vanessa corrected. "I was supposed to, but she didn't show."

"Oh, that's right." Diane twisted her pearl necklace as if it was a jeweled garrote and she wanted to strangle herself, which was a funny image. Vanessa wondered how to make someone autostrangle. Threat? Torture? Sounded like a good horror movie.

Diane turned to the Goth girl. "And you are?"

The girl presented her hand at heart-height. "P.J. Lessing. Tragic to meet you."

Diane's head cocked sideways, like her head was partially severed by an inexpert executioner, and shook the girl's hand. "P.J. Lessing? Did you speak to a Chief Deputy Max Konstantin this morning?"

The girl's eyes widened. She nodded.

Diane said, "Max is my husband. Can we talk?" She took P.J.'s arm and gently led her away.

This left Vanessa alone with Zeke James, Ester's father.

Vanessa did not like hanging around with victims' families. Their questions and surmises introduced amateur theories into her head when she tried to remember only facts, and impaired her judgment. Even though she had known Zeke as Essie's dad for twelve years, he was becoming "a family member" in her head, probably because Essie had become something of a stranger over the years, and now she was gone. Vanessa looked for a way to escape but the only person whose eye she could catch was the hound-dog woman who wanted to dunk her.

Zeke stared over the crowd wistfully. "I appreciate all these folks being here today. You don't realize how many friends you have until you need them."

What sappiness. Vanessa had never been that sappy. Even as a child, she was tough. Essie had been a wuss, too.

In high school, Essie and Nessie had been lab partners in sophomore biology. The football coach slapped a cow eyeball in their black wax-filled dissection tray. "Here you go," he said. "Don't eat the whole thing at once, Nessie."

Ester refused to dissect it. She stared at the corners of the room the whole time, squalling, "It's, like, gross! It's grosser than gross. Gross-erino!"

The leathery eyeball looked like a goo-filled kiwifruit with a limp, beef cometary tail. Grosser things than that excised eyeball moldered in pots on the stove in Vanessa's house.

Vanessa dissected. First, she cleaned meat off the orb and teased out the ligaments and ocular nerve.

"This is cool," she said to Essie and probed where the ocular nerve infiltrated the back of the eye. "Look."

"No!"

Vanessa stabbed the eye with her scalpel. Clear vitreous humor squirted Essie's notes, smearing the curly blue ink, which was funny as all hell.

"Ewww!" Essie ran out and squealed down the hall.

"Come back and take notes, you wuss!" Vanessa yelled. "I've seen you eat steak rarer than this!"

In retaliation for Ester's wussing out, Vanessa carefully excavated a lab pig's gummy heart and left it in Ester's locker atop her clarinet case.

Ester didn't get the joke.

That macabre sense of humor helped Vanessa a lot, over the years. In lawless and homicidal New Orleans, cartilaginous toughness was essential.

Diane held P.J.'s elbow gently. The studied gesture inculcated familiarity and suggested light restraint. P.J.'s stark kohl makeup was contrived to look ghastly but turned concubine-exotic on her.

It was interesting that the girl had shown up. First, P.J. admitted hearing something. Then, at Ester's church, she was watching the search parties convene.

Congruencies broke cases open. In one case last year, a little girl had too many appointments with too many doctors, and a nurse suspected Munchausen's by Proxy, the deadliest form of child abuse, usually by a serial killer mother. Within five minutes of entering the house to question the parents, Diane called a judge for a search warrant and found, in the basement, an autistic and battered child who needed the medicine. Not Munchausen's, just abuse of the disabled.

Diane's suspicious gaze roamed over the thirty children in the room, eighteen girls and twelve boys. Statistically, nine of the girls and four of the boys would be sexually attacked or were being routinely abused. None bore visible bruises.

Diane said to P.J., "Could you tell me what you told Deputy Konstantin about what you heard last night?"

"I didn't tell him, like, anything." The girl looked away, evidence of nerves or falsehood.

"He said you heard 'people' or 'animals' before one o'clock."

"I don't know what I told him."

P.J. pulled away and crossed her arms. Her black lace top showed off her sternum, brachiating ribs, and black bra, precociously sexual. That wasn't disapproving prudishness festering in Diane's heart. It was the evaluation of the Assistant Criminal County Attorney who prosecuted cases involving sex crimes against children. Early sexualization correlated with child sexual abuse. They learned to be sexual somewhere. Often, classical conditioning was at work: abused kids displayed sexuality for rewards or to escape punishment.

Diane said, "He seemed sure that you said that, and that you'd used the plural: people, animals."

P.J. scowled. "O.M.G." Oh-em-gee. "I didn't say anything like that. You're so wrong. Just leave me alone."

Her denial was out of proportion with Diane's mild questioning. The girl might have been threatened, perhaps by her parents if they were involved, perhaps by someone in the hall with them right now.

Diane surveyed the room, looking for someone who might have threatened to punch or knife the frail girl. P.J. had been talking to Vanessa Allen. Hmmm. She should talk to Max about Vanessa Allen's alibi.

The noisy church fellowship hall was not conducive to interviewing a potential witness. Diane would visit the Lessing family and have a proper, legally binding conversation.

"Sister Diane!" Diane recognized Pastor Daniel's mellifluous voice before she turned. P.J. slipped into the crowd behind her like a fish submerging in murk.

From the crowd, a woman's voice said, "Now, you don't really believe that evolution they're teaching you. You gullible enough to believe people evolved from monkeys? Do I look like a monkey? Where's my tail?"

"Hello, Reverend," Diane said. She patted her hair. The left side felt loose.

"Now, now, 'Brother Daniel.' The press conference was a fine idea. People are picking up flyers." His smile was gently sad. "While the cause is terrible, the community is coming together with Christian spirit."

Pastor Daniel's kind smile heartened her resolve to be a better Christian. "Have you heard anything about Ester?"

Pastor Daniel shook his tidy, groomed head. If he were any more delicately groomed, and if she hadn't met Daniel's wife and three kids, Diane would have assumed he was gay. He said, "No. No word. No leads. It's as if she vanished." Pastor Daniel looked sharply at her. "You?"

Diane shook her head, and a wisp of hair slipped out of her up-do and fell across her vision, obscuring Daniel and half the fellowship hall with a brown smear. She smoothed the stray hank into her chignon, repositioning a hairpin to nail it down. "I'm going to check a few things. If I find something helpful, I'll tell you."

"All right," he said. "Who was that young girl you were talking to? It worries me when young folks dress like that and have truck with infernal things. The fear of and the hunger for death gets in them."

"Right." Sometimes, the zealotry that infected Pastor Daniel was baffling, even to Diane.

P.J. took her flyers and left. The lady lawyer should not be suspicious of P.J. Since when did helping out mean that she was the prime suspect, or maybe it was just because she was a non-Christian that the law was so suspicious. Dubya Bush had insinuated that non-Christians should be relegated to second-class status, like they shouldn't be able to hold public office, in some weird evangelical permutation of the restrictive Islamic Dhimma laws that non-Muslims suffer under in the Middle East.

She had to redo her makeup before the party on Hi-Falutin' Row that night. Such a serious party required more black, more Goth, more tragedy.

Max sat in his easy chair with his feet on the coffee table in the family room, typing on his laptop, sending ultrasonic bat chirps to the wireless router, while his two teenagers worked on their respective desktop computers. He desultorily stumbled around the Internet, gazing into one portal, then another, haphazardly poking his investigational stick into information murk.

A web search found plenty on Pastor Daniel Stout, now the leader of the Country Congregational Bible Church.

Stout's picture had been published in *The New York Times* when he was indicted. His eyes shifted left, and his mouth revealed many pointed teeth.

The article said that Mr. Daniel Stout was a broker in New York City, touted as a golden boy at Silverman Bachs, a market maker in power as well as commodities and precious metals futures, until his too-fair trading became foul play and he fell from grace.

Pastor Daniel Stout had come to Jesus with the Commodity Futures Trading Commission hellhound-snapping at his heels. Max covered his mild amusement by secreting his lips between his teeth. There are no atheists in prisons, not when a suitably profound expression of faith will spring you. Perhaps Max was too cynical from years of watching his arrestees profess deep spiritual enlightenment.

Stout had been on Wall Street on September 11 when the planes hit, the indictment article mentioned. He was briefly listed among the missing by one "Venice Dorchester of the Boston Dorchesters," a New York socialite "of some reputation." Evidently the snarky reporter thought Max would be privy to the rumors about Venice Dorchester's reputation if Max was important enough to be rumor-privy.

Max declined to care about Venice Dorchester of the Boston Dorchesters, other than to note that the right reverend Stout used to socialize with besmirched socialites.

Sympathy welled in him, however, that Daniel Stout had been caught in that inferno, running through the chaos and dust.

The kitchen door slammed. Diane yelled, "Hey! I'm a burglar! Come to rob you!"

Max yelled through a yawn, "Bang-bang, bang! Stop or I'll shoot!"

The teenagers, Tatiana and Nicholas, their glossy black-haired heads leaning toward the computer screens, rigorously ignored them. Parents can be so embarrassing, especially when one was a cop and the other a prosecutor, and both of them liked to sit in the same room with you whenever you were on the computer, the most horrifying manifestation ever of POS.

Max had worked on Internet predator stings, and he reduced his kids' chances of being victimized with the industrial-grade spyware that emailed random screencaps to him, tracked their every click, blocked chats and IMs, and monitored website keywords. The spyware came in handy last year when his perfectionist daughter had a disastrous physics semester, and he found tutoring help for her before she ruined her GPA or, more likely, imploded from the stress of hiding her struggle.

Max met Diane in the kitchen. She dumped scarlet and green binders on the counter, emptied the dregs from her travel coffee mug into the sink, and plucked hairpins from her hair. "You've really got to start locking that front door. And disparity of force. A big, strapping hunk such as yourself would not get a legal shoot against a slip of a girl such as myself."

"King in his castle, shots fired during the commission of the crime of breaking and entering, eminent domain, blah, blah, blah." He took her pistol out of her purse and secured it in the kitchen's locked hidey hole. "Lots of work still tonight?"

"Yeah. Sorry. And that is not what 'eminent domain' means." She shook out her dark brown hair, which curled with the memory of its tight windings past her shoulders. Diane touched the refrigerator. "Did you save me some supper?"

He chin-pointed at the fridge. "Man Pie."

After he had been teased at the office for lunching on cold quiche, Max had remonikered the dish. "Kids are doing homework."

Diane found the Man Pie in the fridge, cut herself a slice, and microwaved it.

"Take a bigger piece than that. You didn't get any bacon." Max gestured toward her briefcase carelessly. "What case of yours is producing all this work?"

"Oh, the usual," she said.

Max's proverbial K9-unit ears perked. Diane was a lawyer and the perfectionist role model around the house. She didn't answer questions imprecisely. Max felt like rubbing his chin in ponderation but halted the movement. If she picked up he had noticed her evasion, she would be more wary. He wanted to know what she was hiding.

As a sworn officer, he had seen the wreckage of confrontations, and many confrontations were better avoided. Some storms blow over.

He said, "Oh. Okay."

She removed her sputtering plate from the microwave. She had overnuked it, as usual. Never merely enough, always too much: that's how Diane did things. She didn't attend college; she matriculated to an Ivy League law school. She didn't diet; she low-carbed. "About the James girl, anything new?"

"Nope," Max said.

"I met that P.J. Lessing you mentioned."

He tried to sound casual. "Oh?"

"Ester James's church organized search parties."

"Her church? The Country Music Church?"

Diane's brows twitched down, almost a scowl. "The Country Congregational Bible Church."

"Oh, right."

"P.J. Lessing wouldn't admit she'd heard anything. In fact, she was adamant that she hadn't."

"How adamant?" Max asked.

"Really adamant. All-out-of-proportion adamant."

Max nodded. "Lying adamant."

Diane picked up her plate of melted quiche. "Do you think she's protecting herself or someone else?"

"I'd say someone else. She's not a good enough liar."

"Yep," Diane said. "Did you check Ester James's computer?"

"Her father said she didn't email much." Max had thirty open cases he was working on, everything from bar fights to domestic abuse to human trafficking to people cultivating pot in the piney woods. Ester James, a grown woman, not a mental case, had been missing less than one day. She was probably going to call home any time now or else she didn't want to be found. All this commotion over her was unwarranted. Max stretched and rubbed his flat belly, rippling his fingers over the lumped muscle.

"Did you have a chance to go over there, check her room, see if she took anything with her?" she asked.

"Her dad said she didn't. I'll get to it tomorrow or so, if she doesn't come home."

They fell into the usual conversations about television as they walked back to the office, and Max noticed that the kids were absorbed in school work and did not hurriedly close any chat windows. They settled in the easy chairs, resuming their POS presence, now doubled in appalling embarrassment potential. Diane ate her Man Pie while Max filled in a Sudoku.

Again, no work conversation in front of the kids. The two people they loved most in the world, their little babies, knew nearly nothing about most of their waking hours, about how Diane was a paladin jousting with a ballpoint pen, writing flawless legal briefs, saving their friends and other children from the worst kind of human pedo scum, and how Max relished the thrill of battling the bad guys.

It's night now, when the sun pours light and warmth on the other side of the planet, on the Muslim and Hindu and Chinese commie atheist Antipodes, while our hemisphere stumbles in the dark.

The withering things come out at night. Sunflowers droop. Birds hide their heads, except owls, but owls are ill omens. The black dogs of depression snuffle and savage anyone they find alone.

Ester James is out there in the dark somewhere, while Diane and Max tuck their teenagers into bed, while Pastor Daniel and his wife sleep, while P.J. drinks a spiked cocktail at an upperclassmen party that she isn't cool enough to attend and tries to cover this by expressing sophisticated and tragic ennui, and while Zeke clutches a pillow on the couch where he has collapsed, exhausted, because he cannot bring himself to lie down in his own bed, because normalcy is acquiescence.

On the ten o'clock news, more people were murdered by strangers and those who were supposed to love them. More businessmen cheated the people who trusted them. More politicians lied about campaign-donated money or campaign-damaging sex.

New Canaan feels the change. The foggy unknown has reached into their quiet town and taken one of them. It slides under doors and steals the light from the eyes of their friends. Everyone seems dull with anger, ready to snap.

There must be a reason for the change. A physical reason. A biological one.

Maybe a virulent germ like Legionnaire's Disease that colonizes air conditioners and drifts on cool currents, contaminated the dark, underground water rushing through subterranean pipes, unnoticed until someone dies.

Maybe a cardiotoxic poison, callusing the heart with scar tissue, seeped into the soil, leached from an underground vein of adulterated ore or dumped by a corporation that chose to risk punitive damages rather than pay for remediation.

Maybe a parasite is possessing people. The toxoplasmosis parasite infects mice, making them recklessly dart about in broad daylight. The parasite jumps to the cat that eats the suicidal mouse. In the cat, the parasite breeds and changes the cat's behavior, too, makes it irritable and aggressive, and then the parasite rides saliva into new cats during cat fights. When the cat defecates, the parasite travels the fecal-oral route to new mice or to humans, and causes birth defects.

Such germs are insidious and omnipresent.

Friday

At dawn, Zeke levered his creaking bones into the upright position from the couch and tottered over to the rumbling back door. Someone knocked on it, hard.

He should have fed the cattle an hour ago, but the alarm clock was dead. He was so tired after driving around the night-deserted town, fighting weeds to peer into abandoned cars and derelict houses, and he was nodding off behind the wheel and a danger to others, so he came home even though Essie was out there somewhere.

Maybe he should have slept in his truck so he could resume searching.

Yet he wanted to check at home, hoping for a phone message or a ransom note.

The answering machine was filled with his own messages, begging Essie if she could hear the machine to please pick up and tell him she was all right.

Zeke opened the door to Pastor Stout. He covered his mouth to deflect his night breath and said, "Good morning, Brother Daniel. Come on in."

"Good morning, Brother Zeke. Melinda thought you should eat." He held out a foil-covered plate and shuffled past him inside.

"Your wife's a right Christian woman." Zeke took the plate. Under the foil, toast and scrambled eggs with cheese and green chile smelled really good. "And a good cook."

"She's all that," Daniel agreed. "Any word?"

"No, no word at all." Zeke led the way to the kitchen, eating the toast because he had not realized until he smelled the eggs that he was ravenously hungry. He ate a few granola bars and donuts yesterday. Since the food came from the Pastor's own kitchen, it was kosher.

His refrigerator held five casseroles and a raisin pie that neighbors baked and slid into his fridge, using their keys to Zeke's house. While they might not be technically kosher, such as the chorizo-and-cheese tamale pie, any food baked with such kindness must be kosher in the eyes of the Lord, but he could not eat last night.

It was seven o'clock in the morning. Essie had been out in the dark and missing for thirty-two hours. Zeke set the breakfast plate on the Formica kitchen table and clutched his stomach, suddenly sick. Had she eaten? Was she hungry, out there?

It seemed impossible that he had raised her, that they spent every day of her life and more than half of his in each other's company, that he had kissed all her scraped knees, that his DNA twined in every cell of her body, and yet he couldn't feel whether she was alive or hungry or hurting or dead. All he felt was an ache to find her and then follow her around and stand guard over her bed with a shotgun loaded with deer slugs and blow a ten-inch hole clear through anyone who tried to hurt her.

Zeke inhaled clear air, held it, and tried to push down the panic and the toast.

Brother Daniel patted his back. "We'll find her."

Zeke nodded and felt eye water wet his eyelashes.

"Brother Zeke," Pastor Daniel said, "you haven't mentioned our friends the Israelis to anyone, have you?"

"No." Zeke wiped his eyes and glanced at Daniel. "Why?"

"Well, we don't want outsiders interfering."

Cold horror flushed through Zeke. "You think someone took her to get to me, to stop the shipment?"

"I'm sure that's not it, but non-Christians might not understand."

"I didn't think about it." But he had to get to the Sheriff's office and tell them. If it would help find his Essie, he would buy a full page ad in

The New York Times and storm the studios of CNN.

"I'm sure it's not related," Daniel said. "And if it was, we'd want them to contact us to arrange for getting Essie back. Telling the police or the media might jeopardize her, if they want to stop us."

"But we should tell the sheriff's department. They'll keep it quiet."

"Diane Marshall understands the situation. You don't have to tell anyone else."

"Right." Zeke groped his pocket for his truck keys.

Max laid two jelly donuts on the far side of his desk and waited for Zeke James. Zeke had called from his cell phone, sounded frantic, but he had no word of Essie nor a ransom note. Maybe the strain was wearing on him.

At the desk in front of his, George manned the phone. "No, ma'am. There was no break-in at the Cart-Mart or a hundred guns stolen. It's just a rumor."

Max's phone rang. Sheriff Carlos Garcia was on the line. "Hello, Carlos," he said. "What can I do you for?"

"Anything on this James woman?" Garcia's abruptness would have insulted anyone else, but Carlos and Max went way back. Max, as Carlos's Chief Deputy, took care of actual law enforcement while Carlos worked the elections.

"No, and I doubt there will be. She's an adult and not a mental patient, so she's not at risk. I'm asking around, but there's no sign of anything wrong. No one saw a struggle. No crime scene."

"Should we call out the mounted posse?"

While Max appreciated the volunteers, and their knowledge of the land and environs was indispensable when they had a problem, activating the posse would cause a furor. "We don't have anywhere to look. Her church is putting up flyers. I'm looking into her contacts. If we knew her body was in the woods somewhere, I'd say yes, but at this point, she could be on her honeymoon in Aruba."

Carlos reluctantly agreed and hung up. Max hoped he had done the right thing. If this case caused an embarrassment for Carlos, he might lose an election. Texas is an "at-will" state with cowardly unions and no civil service tenure. The job of sheriff was usually bequeathed to an anointed successor when a sheriff retired, but job insecurity, even a little, even imagined, can rile a man's nerves.

Max stared at the donuts and waited for Zeke James.

Minutes were precious commodities in Max's life. Cases could be broken in minutes. Triggers could be pulled in seconds.

On the computer, he pulled up the social networking site Vanessa had talked about. The MyOwnRoom site was a conglomeration of jiggling boxes and flashing frames. Kids these days could sort through the hullabaloo, but establishing a hierarchy took Max a minute. Finally, he found a search box, typed in essie tex, and began clicking through 65,719 results.

Ester James's homepage was unremarkable. She was interested in meeting people as friends but not, as the site suggested, "friends with privileges."

Max shuddered at the thought that Tatiana might advertise for "friends with privileges" on social networking sites at college next year.

The picture showed pretty, blond Ester James next to a well-formed Red Angus cow. The caption under the picture read 4-H Champion Heifer SweetieBoo. An insignia at the top was a red silhouette of a heifer in a yellow triangle. It looked vaguely Masonic, in a down-home way.

Ester had eighty-three RoomMates on her MyOwnRoom page, quite short for a social networking site where some people had hundreds of thousands of friends. Among them was CapnVanessa-Of-The-

Starship-Forrestal and a picture of Vanessa Allen.

Odd. Was the Allen girl a science fiction geek? Max clicked.

Vanessa's MyOwnRoom page was a mishmash of science fiction alternate universes. Her picture gallery included her wearing pseudo-militaristic uniforms, all of them with plummeting necklines, and she obligingly leaned forward for the camera. She looked like an ad for a porn flick called *SpaceBoobs*.

Vanessa's motto, "Never tickle a sleeping Nessie," was translated into Latin and several languages that Max was pretty sure were not human. One of the alphabets looked like Elvish, and a few of Max's neurons that he had not used since high school reconnected. Yep, Elvish. Vanessa also listed her height as five feet, three inches and her build as "slender," which was damn amusing.

Most of Vanessa's RoomMates were disaffected young people (a stupid term because their affect is prodigious), many of whom were into science fiction, Goth music, booze, "nothin'," violent computer games, the New Orleans party scene, meth, horror movies and novels, nouveau pharmaceuticals, "the tragic darkness of my own soul," prescription painkillers, archaic British comedies, pot, "the great god Cthulhu and Him-Who-Is-Not-To-Be-Named" (surely they hadn't started a religion around that snake-eyed movie wizard, Max thought), heroin, Poe, and methamphetamines.

Black *in memoriam* ribbons adorned several roommates' pictures.

Yeah, well, when you list your hobbies as "DWI" and "selling crank," that kind of thing can sneak up on you.

Funny, though. Vanessa did not seem like a science fiction geek. Most sci-fi geeks Max had known—and he had known some serious geeks in high school—popped off knowing, insider comments that labeled them faster than an AV Club tee shirt.

That was funny. Vanessa had not spouted obscure quotes. Her street clothes seemed mainstream, even mall-gangsta. She was out of kilter.

Funny, out of kilter, those types of incongruities made him suspicious.

Vanessa's timeline and alibi pretty much cleared her. The bartender remembered her boobs. Her credit card receipts documented that she had left late, well after Ester James's manager had seen Ester raise her hand in greeting and trot with purpose off the end of the sidewalk. Vanessa was a dead alley.

That church of Ester's was odd, though. Max did not like what Vanessa had said about them being Branch Davidians or a suicide cult.

Max clicked back to Ester's homepage. She had an HTML link for the Country Congregational Bible Church at the top. The description was, *The Lord is coming. Click here to learn more.*

As his mouse pointer hovered over the link, Max glanced up at the ruffle disturbing the bullpen.

At the office door, Zeke James removed his hat and charged into the deputies' room. His head swung from side to side like a Red Angus fighting bull as he strode over to Max's desk. "We need to talk."

"You get here all right?" Max closed the computer windows and handed Zeke a donut. Considering the situation, he could fix a speeding ticket.

"Fine." Zeke took the donut. "Thank you kindly. Is there somewhere we can talk out of earshot of these nice folks?"

"Sure." Max led him down the hall to the conference room where they held staff meetings and interviewed suspects, such suspects as they had in law-abiding, God-fearing Sin Nombre County. He didn't switch on the video equipment. Zeke James seemed het up but not overwhelmed with guilt.

The maple-veneered table could seat twelve. Max sat at the head and kicked out a chair beside him for James. "This all right?"

"There's something you ought to know." Zeke James sat and set his donut and napkin on the table. He smoothed his red beard down to a point with both his hands. "There're these folks I'm doing a spot of business with."

"What, Cali Cartel?" Max plucked his notepad from his shirt pocket. He should have flipped the recording switch. "Drug runners? Coyotes?"

"No," Zeke said. "Jews."

"Jews?" Max laid his pen on the table. No need to take notes, not that he ever needed to take notes, but it showed people he took them seriously.

"Israelis. Now, I'm not worried about the actual folks I'm doing business with. They're right fine folks. I heard tell about Jews when I was a kid growing up, but these folks are fine and upstanding. I'm worried about people who might not like that I'm doing business with Israelis."

"Like, Nazis?" Max asked. "No problems with that sort around here."

"I don't know who," Zeke James said earnestly, "but I'm doing business with Israelis, and I thought you should know."

"Received threats about it? Phone calls? Letters or emails?"

"No. We're not advertising."

"Well, then," Max said. "I'll take their names in case I need to call them, but it's unlikely that's the problem, Mr. James."

"Zeke," he said. "Call me Zeke. You're looking for my daughter. We should call each other by our Christian names."

"Right. Call me Max, then. Don't you worry about it, Zeke. You would have heard by now if there was a ransom, or if they were threatening you, and you haven't, right?"

"Right. Nothing." He seemed certain but not protesting. Was this what Max had sensed Zeke was hiding? Maybe. Zeke fidgeted with his cowboy hat. "She's been missing a day and a half. What're the odds at this point she'll come home safe?"

Max hated that question. You can spout statistics about children and young women who go missing, but the fact is that most are dead well short of four hours. The other fact is that for the few who live past four hours, many of them will be rescued days or years later, abused and shell-shocked, but alive.

The question is whether or not they have survived those first four hours. Like Scheherazade, if they can beguile their captor, they can survive.

He tapped his empty holster, musing.

Zeke might not be able to handle statistics right now. His bloodshot eyes were as red as his pelt, but his skin seemed chalky under that bright hair. Max thought about a hole in his life where Tatiana had occupied space and quailed. A daughter vanishing could crack a man.

Max said, "This isn't a horse race, Zeke. Each case is different from every other. There's no way to make odds on it. We are doing everything we can. Every law enforcement officer within two hundred miles has seen her picture and knows her name. If she can be found, we will find her."

Zeke nodded, chastened, and ate a bite of the jelly donut. "Did you talk to the FBI or the Texas Rangers yet?"

"I don't think we need the FBI on this, Zeke. We don't know if there's been a federal crime committed. Don't know if any crime has been committed."

"Oh?" Zeke asked. "That lady lawyer, Diane Marshall, said she was going to call them."

That dinged Max's professional pride a little, but Diane might have told Ester James's daddy just about anything, depending on whether he was painfully grieving or being a pain in the neck. "I'll check into that."

From: AgentJohnJohnson@nvavc.fbi.gov
To: ACCA.Diane.Marshall@texas.gov

Hello Diane,

Agent Hal Blackstone forwarded your email to the Behavioral Analysis Unit 2, crimes against adults, a division of the National Center for the Analysis of Violent Crimes. In response to your email, yes, we are those brilliant profiler guys.

The best analyses ("profiles") are based on multiple crime scenes and victims who are known to be related by specific evidence, such as DNA. Without a crime scene or a body, there is little to base a profile on. Nevertheless, we have drawn up an informal assessment of your likely perpetrator.

Organized Type: Because you have not found the victim's body, we can assume that the serial killer is organized. Organized serial killers attack strangers, often miles from home. They destroy evidence and hide or destroy the body. To contrast, disorganized serial killers kill friends and acquaintances, often in their or the victim's home. Some serial killers may, however, be considered "mixed," meaning that they fit neither the "organized" nor "disorganized" types.

Gender and Ethnicity: Every single sexual deviation is overwhelmingly dominated by white males. As your assumed victim is also Caucasian, this lends credence to the white male theory as serial killers generally kill within their own ethnic group for psychological ("signature") reasons.

Age: As you have not found the body, we assume this serial killer has killed before and thus is probably at least 30 years old. However, as many serial killers begin killing at a young age, your serial killer may be as young as 15. As most serial killers stop murdering around 40 years old, we can assume that he is probably younger than that. This is, however, his psychological age. As many serial killers are psychologically immature, your serial killer's chronological age may be up to 50.

Prior Abuse: Many serial killers who kill women were abused as children by the mother. As you have a missing mature female, this is probably accurate. Perpetrator will probably bear scars or brain trauma to the frontal lobe from prior abuse.

Signature and MO (Modus operandi): Though there is no evidence, no victim, no body, and no crime scene, we may make some predictions about your serial killer's signature and MO.

Signature: (Ritualized evidence left at the crime scene that relates to the serial killer's unconscious, psychological state.) As your serial killer is organized and accomplished, signature evidence will probably be present.

MO: Serial killers develop techniques that are effective and provide the perpetrator sexual pleasure. Often, killings are "hands-on," such as strangling by hands or ligature. However, some serial killers use weapons as a projection of power, especially phallic-type weapons, such as blunt, bludgeoning objects (baseball bats, etc.) or stabbing weapons (knives, daggers, etc.). Guns are rarely used; however, because your crime took place in a state with fewer restrictions to gun access (Texas), your serial killer may utilize a gun.

Alcohol or illegal drugs: Many serial killers use alcohol or, frequently, illegal drugs to lower their inhibitions and heighten the thrill of the kill. Your perpetrator will likely have used alcohol or illegal drugs, or even legal drugs, within the last two weeks.

Other traits: Most serial killers work alone, capture their victims alone, and kill them alone. As there was very little or no struggle at the scene of the kidnapping, it is possible but not likely that there may be a team of killers. If there is more than one killer in this case, then it is likely that your perpetrators are two males (Garcia/Doody in the Buddhist Temple murders in Maricopa County, AZ, or Hickock/Smith in the Clutter family murders in Holcomb, KS). It is less likely but possible for the killers to be a male and a female (Bonnie/Clyde or Homolka/Bernardo).

Childhood/Background: Most serial killers committed crimes as juveniles. When you have suspects, you should look for juvenile convictions such as arson, animal cruelty, or assaults against other children.

Education: Very few serial killers graduate from high school. The exceptions to this are Ted Bundy and Ted Kaczynski. And Paul Bernardo. Or Jack Unterweger. Or Richard Cottingham, Gary Ridgway, or John Wayne Gacy. Unless your serial killer is one of these very rare exceptions, he will be a high school drop-out.

Most serial killers could not hold their urine through the night until well after their peers. This may have exacerbated the abuse at the hands of their mothers, or it may stem from frontal lobe neurological damage. It may have created a sense of shame in the perpetrator.

Over 90% of serial killers were breast-fed as infants.

Final Notes: Delete this email after reading it. We tried to contact you by phone, but Agent Blackstone's contact information must be out of date. No profile is perfect, as profiling is an art based on experience in law enforcement and gut inclination rather than a hard science. Perpetrators have used artifacts in FBI profiles to base defenses in court. Also, because no profile is perfect, we prefer not to have written documentation.

When you have a suspect in custody, please advise BAU so that we may revise this profile to more accurately correspond with your suspect.

Zeke braced his arms against the fence of his ranch and squinted against the strong sun at a car trailing a gravel tail, slowly driving up his road. He should be out in the woods, looking for his daughter. He hated coming back to the ranch, but this meeting had been scheduled for months. A man had flown eighteen hours.

The car, a cherry red rental from the Dallas/Fort Worth Airport, held a small, round man who Zeke had met on three previous occasions, once here in Texas, and twice in Jerusalem. Zeke raised his hand. "Howdy, Rabbi."

"Shalom!" Rabbi Saloman raised a hand and waddled like a bipedal rabbit over to Zeke. The Texas breeze fluttered the Rabbi's beard and blue zizith fringes peeking from under his coat. His accent was Boston Brahmin, for he had grown up in Massachusetts, tinged with yeshiva Yiddish. "How are you, my friend!"

"Not so well, Rabbi. My daughter Ester went missing, night before last. Can't say that I've slept."

Rabbi Saloman covered his mouth in horror. "Ezekiel, why did you not call? We could have postponed."

"You were already on the plane. Didn't seem fair, dragging you halfway around the world. Pastor Daniel at our church is organizing the search for Ester mighty fine."

"This will take only a few minutes. I am so sorry." Rabbi Saloman clasped Zeke's hand in both of his. "My parents' families were all murdered in the Holocaust. They lived in terror of people disappearing. They paced the house at night, standing guard. I find myself doing this.

This breaks my heart, I tell you. I am so, so sorry, Ezekiel. If there is anything that I can do, anything at all, please tell me."

"I appreciate it, Rabbi." Maybe he should have walked around the house at night and stood guard. If Ester came home, he would.

"Is there a reward for information about her whereabouts? The Institute is not wealthy, but we can contribute some money."

"Not yet." Water rose in his eyes again. "Just pray for her."

"I can do that." Rabbi Saloman released his hand. "And let us do this quickly. You are a strong man, Ezekiel. I do not wish to tax you further."

"The heifers are back here." Zeke led the Rabbi into the barn. Their eyes adjusted to the relative shadow. Five young Red Angus cows levered their heads over stall doors, bobbing. Their eyes and noses were dark against auburn hides. "Under normal circumstances, I would have groomed them."

"Under the circumstances, I think you are exceptionally kind. But Ezekiel, what will we do about the plane on Wednesday night?"

Exhaustion smote Zeke. "Wednesday is a long way away, Rabbi."

"Surely by then Ester will be home."

"From your lips to God's ears."

"So these are the five heifers?"

"Four, Rabbi. These four cattle here are the stock you'll want to inspect. That last cow down there, Lilypie, is a project for LeBonGene Pharmaceutical Company."

Lilypie lowed at Zeke.

"Yes, darlin'." To the Rabbi, he said, "She's attached to me. You just take a look at them and I'll be scratching Lilypie. Here's a footstool."

Zeke ambled down. Lilypie butted his chest, sliming him with grassy spit. Zeke scratched her ears. He loved this cow, not in any sick, twisted way forbidden by the Bible, but with the affection one reserves for one's favorite dog.

Lilypie loved him back with an intensity that wildtype cows cannot.

The Rabbi carried his footstool to each of the stalls and stood upon it to look over the cow within. At each, he nodded approvingly.

The Rabbi reached Zeke, standing at the last stall cradling Lilypie's head in his arm. "They are all fine examples of cattle, Ezekiel."

"Yep," Zeke said. "They're all homozygous, twenty-first century, high-tech cattle. They'll start you an excellent herd."

"And who is this cow?" Rabbi Saloman patted her neck, and Lilypie swung her head over to look at him with her large, dark eye. Saloman looked bedazzled. "Oh, my."

"Yes, Lilypie is a looker."

"She is perfect. May I?" Rabbi Saloman ducked through the door of her stall to take a closer look. He ran his hands over her legs and checked around her udder. "She is the most beautiful cow I have ever seen."

"Yup," Zeke said. "But she's not part of your project."

"Oh, Ezekiel. She would be perfect."

"She's not an ordinary cow. She's genetically modified."

Rabbi Saloman looked over Lilypie's haunches. "Are there embryos?"

"I admit, there are two wildtype embryos, without the pharmaceutical gene, of her line in the freezer."

"We will pay double for them."

Zeke waved him off. The Rabbi's intense look worried him. "I only have two left, and those embryos are very robust at taking up DNA. Lilypie here is a double knock-in. Very rare."

Saloman's eyes bugged. "Triple."

"Rabbi, those wildtype embryos are important for controls."

"Ten times!"

"If I can divide the two embryos into four, I'll give you two at the negotiated price. I don't want more money. I'm not seeking to take advantage of you as you turn back to God."

Rabbi Saloman's hand covered his heart. "Ezekiel, I did not understand you. I apologize. It makes me tremble, though, that yours are the very same words that Dama ben Natina, a Gentile jeweler, said to one of our high priests. The jewel had fallen out of the high priest's breastplate and had to be replaced to perform our sacrifices. Dama ben Natina said that he had a jewel, but it was under his father's bed, and his father was sleeping. The priests thought it was a bargaining tactic and, like I did, bid up the price. Finally, the father awakened, and Dama ben Natina retrieved the jewel, but he would take only the previously agreed-upon price because, in exactly your words, 'I am not seeking to take advantage of you as you turn back to God.' Oh, Ezekiel, surely this is most auspicious."

Zeke was flattered. He hugged Lilypie's head, and she nudged him. Her warm head was a comfort in these days when he ached for Ester's return. "Well, surely, Rabbi. I'll see if I can split those embryos for you."

Rabbi Saloman stood back and surveyed Lilypie, who chewed her cud contentedly. "Oh, Ezekiel. This heifer will change the world."

Later, Saloman's memory of the event, the one that he recounted to the other rabbis in Jerusalem, was that he had not looked at any of the other cows but homed in on the transgene bovine at the end, as if that particular, beautiful cow was preordained for them, and surely this meant that God smiled on their plans.

Deep down in his cells, he wanted that story to be true, and soon, his cells exchanged a few packets of neurochemicals, and he could not remember it any other way.

With a perfunctory knock on the church office's door, Diane Marshall shimmied around the grinding copier and sat in the chair before Pastor

Daniel's schoolmarm desk. On the drive over to the church, she had debated sharing the profile with Pastor Daniel, her husband, or both, or neither. Pastor Daniel might use it to good effect, telling parishioners where to look for Ester. Showing Max the profile would just rile him, maybe prejudice him the other way.

She held the sheaf of paper out to Pastor Daniel. "FBI emailed about who might have taken Ester."

He took the pages, scanned, and stroked his sharp chin, which he did when she had inadvertently stumped him on a Biblical question. He said, "It's not very specific."

"No, but they seem pretty certain we have a serial killer problem. It's warm in here today." She stood and fanned the door, beating out the heat. Her pearl necklace swung on her blouse in counterpoint.

Daniel nodded and rubbed his wiry hair. "The copy machine has been running red-hot, making flyers for Ester. Ecclesiastes?"

Though she had brought the FBI profile, Diane had come to Pastor Daniel's office for their weekly Bible study. The Old Testament with its emphasis on laws was enjoyable, which she imagined was because of her lawyering and others would find it stultifying. Daniel did give her a lot of homework, though, and some of her law school professors had been less mocking if she didn't make a good showing.

"Ecclesiastes is depressing." She pointed to the onion skin paper. " 'One generation passeth away, and another generation cometh: but the earth abides forever.' Sounds like my job. We have families who are 'system families.' A girl gets taken away from her parents for abuse, then she gets pregnant at fifteen, then her kid gets taken away for abuse, then ten years later, the next-generation kid becomes a ward of the state. Bad parenting and child abuse must be genetic." She stretched her mouth in a smile puckered with rue. "Sorry. Bad day at the office."

Daniel nodded sagely. "I worry about what it must be like to make these snap, life-or-death decisions."

Diane had nightmares about decisions she had made, wondering if she had left kids in too much danger or destroyed their spirit by ripping them out of their parents' arms, several times quite literally. She shrugged, a gesture used at the Criminal County Attorney's office to express the thankless helplessness of their jobs. "The problem is that there are no good choices. Little kids' natural instinct is to stay with the people they've imprinted on, to love their parents, even though the parents beat the tar out of them. It's probably self-defense that most little kids who stay near their parents survive better. All choices are 'vanity and vexation of the spirit.'"

Daniel's wise nod was reassuring. "Yes, perhaps the son of King David was experiencing a dark night of the soul. You know, last week after we discussed how few women played prominent roles in the Bible," he sat straighter and leaned forward, "I realized I had forgotten that one philosophical interpretation of the Bible is that Biblical women represent the soul seeking God, and that's why they're always suffering. Like when Rachel wanted a child to love and she said to Jacob, 'Give me children, if not, I die.' That's the dire longing for God. Mary Magdalene went out during the night to seek Jesus' dead body, because she knew that her Beloved was shut up in a sepulcher sealed with a great stone. That represents the intoxication and daring of the soul in love, that she is in darkness and feels herself without him, so the wounded and bereft soul goes bravely to seek God."

Diane's smile parted and became wry and wary. "So feeling the absence of God is feeling the presence of God?"

Daniel let his head bob side to side. "Oh, those Catholics. Parsing everything."

They laughed together, and again Diane wasn't sure what to make of these meetings. Most new church members attended Bible studies with Daniel, but sometimes he seemed intent on converting her, even though she was pretty sure she was a Christian.

Ecclesiastes was a short book, and next was Song of Solomon.

The Devil could quote Scripture for his own purpose, and in this case, Diane felt that the Devil had planted that erotic poetry square in their path.

Perhaps they should skip straight to Isaiah, the first of the major prophets, who foretold the Messiah and enumerated the sins of the nations that would evoke the wrath of God and end the world.

Skipping to Isaiah would avoid temptation.

P.J. slunk around the edges of the crowd, wanting more flyers to post at her school but hung over from the party last night. She held the edge of the table and swayed. Her eyes hurt. Her skull hurt. Her sinuses hurt.

Everything, *everywhere*, hurt.

People's murmuring splashed around her like she was treading water in rough seas. She tried not to listen, but you can't shut your ears.

A shrill female said, "I prayed, and I believed, and I found these blue shoes on sale for half off."

A child exclaimed, "And then he gave me candy!"

A woman said, "I was in New York City, and a homeless man asked me for money. I gave him five dollars and told him, you go and buy food with that, because that's from Our Lord."

A woman's voice stated, "Vedic astrology is much better than Western. If you know the exact minute that you were born, the exact minute, then everything they say is one hundred percent accurate."

A man's sad voice said, "I don't know where else to look for her. Seems like we've looked all around the piney woods and the vacant lots, and put up these flyers. I fear for her."

P.J. turned. The Mexican man wore a baseball hat with NYFD and an American flag.

The pastor and the lady prosecuting attorney came out of an office. She held a stack of paper under one arm, probably flyers.

Dry, green bile gurgled in P.J.'s stomach. She was so tired. P.J. would just grab a handful of flyers and go home. Janelle had told her to sleep off the hangover. Everyone had one, she said.

The lady lawyer caught P.J.'s eye and cocked her head suspiciously. She pinched her pearl necklace and twisted it. She walked over to P.J., and P.J. tried to not look like she was going to puke. The floor tilted and she grabbed the table.

The woman leaned toward her. Her brown hair did not move. "Hi, I'm Diane Marshall."

"Yeah, I, like, remember." The woman's pale, warm palm clasped hers. P.J.'s hand was clammy and limp and must feel like a brown, dead fish. Diane-the-lawyer didn't flinch. Either she was used to dead-fish handshakes or was too polite to recoil.

Mrs. Marshall said, "We should talk. I could give you a ride home."

P.J. didn't want to talk to The Law about anything, but it was already dark outside. Ester James had gone missing in the dark. Walking to the church at dusk was foolhardy when she would have to walk home later, especially since she had dry-heaved twice walking here. The room swirled.

Her house was only a mile and a half away, but she had to pass the now-notorious Lone Star Grocery. Elementary school kids dared each other to sprint across the parking lot. On her way to the church, P.J. kept noticing black pick-up trucks, as if the same one was circling the sidewalked main drag.

But lots of people owned black pick-ups. P.J.'s neighbor had one.

Ester James had gone missing in P.J.'s neighborhood.

At her high school that morning, P.J. stapled up the flyers, between puking in the bathrooms. Other kids said the kidnapper might kill her for interfering.

"I'm not afraid of that poser." She stapled harder, choking down vomit. On Ester's MyOwnRoom page, some dude called "The Satan Incarnation" left a message saying he had killed her because his demons hounded him. "You're just afraid that 'The Satan Incarnation' will break into your big houses and steal your fancy shit and ruin your stupid parties."

"Yeah," the football team's running back had said. His simple gold cross caught on the top button of his shirt. "Tough words from the main event at our stupid party last night."

Last night's party was a miasma of menacing shadows in her memory, swirling around the fractured rainbow of a hazy chandelier.

Those 'fraidy-cat *booboisie* teens had no frame of reference for how good they had it, living with a family their whole lives, never having childhood terrors that there were worse fates than a third-world orphanage, eating soup and rice. Skinny, dirty children cried outside the gates of the orphanage, wanting in. But for the luck of an open bed when P.J.'s mother left her, P.J. could have been left outside. Most boys outside ended up as hoodlums, drug runners, or petty thieves and were murdered before they were fifteen. Girls ended up as prostitutes and also died before they turned fifteen, usually in birthing the next generation of children who lived on scraps outside the orphanage.

Saffron had picked P.J. because a lady at the orphanage said she had good stars. P.J. did not believe she had been saved because she was special. Luck was a fallacy. Random chance, local statistical anomalies, and outliers governed the universe. Anything else would be frightening.

Survivor guilt dogged her. She fantasized about going back and scooping up the outside kids and saving them, living with a passel of them in a small but clean apartment, feeding them apples and peas and dahl and fresh milk. America's most abject poverty is orders of magnitude better than their wildest dreams.

"I was just going to, like, pick up a few flyers and leave," P.J. said to Mrs. Marshall. She kept her eyes on the floor in case she barfed.

"I'm leaving, too," Diane Marshall said. She grabbed a handful of flyers off the top, far more than P.J. had planned on picking up, and set the rest of the stack on the table. "I don't mind dropping you off. We've got one girl missing. We don't need more young women missing and presumed in the bottom of a bayou somewhere."

P.J. didn't want to walk home. Let her parents freak. It was weird out there. And she was sick. "Yeah. I'd appreciate it, Mrs. Marshall."

"Call me Diane."

P.J. was in that age range where it was pretty impressive for adults to grant her the privilege of using their Christian names, and she was barely savvy enough to realize that Diane probably wanted something in exchange for this familiarity.

They walked to Diane's car, a sleek, steel-blue Jaguar. P.J. tried not to be impressed by material goods, like the big house where the drunken party was last night. She was cognizant of her parents' desire for her to not be impressed by materialism, so she was all impressed by the very cool car to spite them. She hoped she wouldn't ralph in it. "Wow."

"My husband gave it to me for Christmas." Diane peered at her. "You feeling okay?"

"Yeah. Fine." She was so lying. Alcoholics were stupid to poison themselves thusly. She would never drink booze again.

Diane beeped the car and the doors unlocked. Naive little P.J. again slid into the passenger seat of a car with an official-sounding stranger, her waif body barely denting the soft upholstery. She rested her feverish face against the cool window.

Diane drove slowly out of the church's gravel parking lot and, before P.J. could point, swung the car right.

P.J. asked, "Do you know where I live?"

"I talked to some people. This is your first year in public school, you're far above grade level in all your courses, and you're a math prodigy."

The sudden exposure of her private life felt like the top had ripped off the car and the cold February air slapped her face. She felt friendless. "I'm not a geeky prodigy. I just like physics." They drove past the First Christian Church of Christ. The sign planted in the dead grass read: If you take Satan for a ride, pretty soon he'll want to drive. "Who did you ask?" P.J. wrapped her arms around her chest.

"Your teachers, your principal," she said.

"Not my parents?"

"No," Diane said.

"My parents don't need to know about me talking to you." They didn't know about the party last night, either. Her legs hurt. Her lower back hurt. She closed her eyes and didn't quite vomit, but the car undulated.

"We need to talk about what you heard that night. Animals, you said, or people."

"I don't know," P.J. said.

"Yes, you retracted what you said, but it's normal for a young woman your age to worry about getting adults in trouble. I assure you, the adults who took Ester need to be stopped. It looks like we might have a serial killer on our hands. Maybe more than one. Maybe a team of serial killers. Now, you heard something, didn't you?"

"I don't know," P.J. said. Man, the kids at school would tweak when they found out that there was not just one serial killer but a team. She swallowed hard.

"Take your time." Diane drove through a green light and swerved, avoiding a roadkill armadillo. P.J.'s stomach lurched.

Diane glanced at P.J. and must have mistaken P.J.'s grievous illness for trepidation, because she joked, "Hey, how do you know when a lawyer is lying?"

P.J. shrugged and swallowed hard. Her head whirled circles within circles within nauseating circles. "How?"

"His lips move."

P.J. grunted a laugh but did not open her lips for fear of barfing. Those jokes Janelle had made this morning about P.J. barfing last night—meeting Ralph, praying at the porcelain altar, shouting at one's shoes, shooting the bazooka—were not damn funny.

The Lone Star Grocery's long parking lot blighted the land on their left. Diane turned the car into the parking lot and drove up to the front doors. The front doors slid open, as if Diane was going to smash-and-grab the grocery store. Diane asked, "Where's your house?"

"Round back." P.J. pointed with a motion like leaping over the store.

"Do you think you could have heard something if it happened in front?"

"I don't think so," P.J. said.

"They must have been closer." Diane drove around to the back service entrance. Two forklifts offloaded pallets of laundry detergent from a tractor-trailer with the abrupt maneuvers of wind-up toys. "Can you see your house from here?"

A low brick wall ringed the property's perimeter and separated the asphalt from the weedy lot and her back yard. P.J. pointed over the wall at her back porch and kitchen garden.

Tumbleweeds and scrub brush thicketed the lot. In the distance, barricading trees wove winter-bare branches.

Behind the windows of her house, shadows moved. Her parents must be home. If they saw P.J. in the car with Diane the Man, they'd freak, and they'd freak all over her Internet privileges. P.J. ducked, slumping under the dash.

"Are you all right?" Diane asked.

"My parents are, like, non-traditional but, you know, they're great and everything. They just aren't into law enforcement types. We tried living off the grid for a while, but my dad likes TV too much and he whined until my mom hooked us back up, and solar cooking takes forever."

"Do they have any reason to worry?"

Other than a little drug dealing and the occasional Ponzi scheme, "No." P.J. felt her face betray her equivocation.

Diane nodded, braced herself on the passenger seat so she could look out the rear window, and backed the car around the store. The engine wound up convincingly, and P.J. bet that the Jaguar could outrace both her parents' cars, even in reverse. P.J. swallowed some sick from the sudden acceleration. Her face went hot.

When they were safely around the front of the store, Diane said, "You're a smart young woman."

"Saffron just taught us more than kids get in public schools." She climbed back into the seat and unlocked the door in case she hurled.

Diane's eyebrows flickered at the name Saffron. "I've seen your testing. Some of your teachers think you're a prodigy. Have you thought about where you're going for college?"

"I'm, like, a sophomore." P.J. hadn't thought about where she was going that weekend. Most of her Goth friends thought college was a waste of time, except for the parties and the Pre-Raphaelite Literature classes, because the world was going to zap out of existence on December 23, 2012 because that's when the five millennia Mayan calendar runs out.

Diane said, "Never too early to be thinking about entrance requirements. If you want to go somewhere with a particle accelerator or a cosmology program—MIT, Caltech—you'll need friends."

"I have friends," P.J. said. Was that what the teachers told this old lady? That P.J. had no friends?

"Not the social kind of friends," Diane said. "I mean friends who can help get you into good schools."

"My parents can't afford to send me out of state. That's why I'm going to public school, so I can get a scholarship to a Texas university."

"If you had friends, you could get scholarships to Caltech or MIT."

P.J. had a bad feeling that Diane wanted to be her friend, in addition to the bad feeling that wound around her arms and legs and squeezed her gut. According to kids at school, adult friends usually wanted sexual favors in exchange for goods and services. Cynda got her Kurt Slate purse from a guy she met in the MyOwnRoom chat rooms in exchange for a blow job.

P.J. touched the door handle. "Um, I'm not into that."

Diane's eyebrows lowered and her lips opened. "What?"

"Never mind. Go on."

"Okay. For example, when I was your age, one of my friends' dads helped me get into UT and then Cornell Law School, and then I helped him run for Congress." Diane stared at her hands resting at the nadir of the steering wheel, as if gravity had drawn them downward to rest at the point of maximum entropy. "My parents didn't want me to go to college, you see. They thought that, because I was a woman, I should stay home and have babies, so I didn't need a high-power education."

"So you defied your parents?"

Diane shrugged. "Many times. But it helped to have friends who told me what tests to take, how to prepare, give recommendations."

"Yeah?" P.J. scraped black nail polish off one thumbnail. Black flakes fell into the black carpeting on the floor of the car. Even sick as she was, P.J. could see the benefit of this conversation if she could abstain from vomiting long enough to finish it.

"Yeah. P.J., if you remember anything, anything at all," Diane handed P.J. a blank business card with only a phone number in black ink across the middle of it, "call me. Friends help each other, right?"

"Sure." P.J. tried to remember that night, listening to a Goth Internet radio station and chatting with a physics grad student in India. She turned up the music around midnight, because shushing and clattering outside bothered her. "There wasn't a storm that night, was there?"

"No. No storm." Diane peered at her in the dimly lit car, illuminated only by the store's neon sign. In the dim light, her dark hair and black suit disappeared into shadow, and she looked like a vampiric, floating face.

Maybe P.J. had heard something. "I turned up the music at one point because there was noise outside, like tumbleweeds smashing into things. And sounds, like talking, or chattering, like cats going after birds." The whole car and her body shimmered sideways and she grabbed the door handle. "Chat logs have time stamps. I can tell you exactly what time I turned up the music."

"That would help a lot, P.J." Diane smiled at her and drove out of the parking lot toward P.J.'s house. "You and I should talk more often. Getting into college is hard enough, and it's really hard if your parents don't support your goals."

P.J. smiled back shyly. Oh, God, she was, like, getting a girl-crush. Not in a lesbo way, but Diane had defied her parents and gone to Cornell. That was so, like, cool.

P.J. jumped out of the car and made it to the bushes of her house before she heaved the handful of sharp popcorn she had eaten at the church.

Diane drove her Jaguar equidistant between the dashed lines on the road and at a precise and legal speed back toward the church. The discussion with P.J. weighed on her mind. That poor child seemed so lost, like Diane had been at that age, trying to figure out whether to adhere to her parents' suffocating religion or break away. When she had announced her full-ride scholarship and her intention to leave the house in two weeks, her father had berated her for taking someone's place, and he meant a man's place, who would use the degree.

After taking P.J. home, Diane returned to the church for group Bible study. The class, led with a light hand by Pastor Daniel, was a lively discussion about a chapter in Luke. When Diane had started attending Bible Study, the discussions had seemed sophistic, each argument phrased to sound better and thus prevail regardless of its logic. Now, she saw the cohesion of the Bible, and the arguments seemed more elegant, like legal briefs.

A woman in the group, When-Dee, had a master's in history and provided context for the Gospels' writing. "The anti-Semitism in the Gospels," she said, glancing at her notes, "is merely to divert the Romans' attention. Rome crushed a Jewish uprising with the Sack of Jerusalem, when the Romans burned the Temple, in 70 A.D."

Everyone in the little circle nodded. Some jotted notes.

When-Dee continued, "The early Christians did not want to offend Rome, because Rome did not tolerate insurgencies."

Driving home from Bible study, residual peace suffused her. Peace was a fleeting emotion for Diane, and she savored it.

Before they had Tatiana, Diane had put in hundred-billable-hour weeks at the esteemed Dallas firm of Gibbs, Wilder, and Stimson, drawing up contracts between their giant corporate clients and the other giant corporations and litigating cases based on those contracts when things went wrong. After a while she didn't care if her robber barons won, or the other guy's. Dread permeated her whole life, and she scurried between her house and the office, locking her doors and clutching her concealed gun.

Some people meticulously clean their houses before they go out, lest they die and strangers find dust on their end tables or crumbs on the rug. Some real freaks use rulers and compasses to perfectly orient the dustables. Cleanliness and order become charms. If the house is immaculate, they will not die before they return.

In defiance of her own reaction to her parents' religion, churches became a charm for Diane. Being in a house of worship, even for a few minutes, even alone, placated the dread. At first, it was a couple times a month. Merely sitting for a few minutes in a hard pew that mortified her butt made her feel better.

The last couple years, she had been trespassing several times a day: before work, before and after lunch, heading home, and sometimes sneaking out at night. She crept into any church, from garish Catholic cathedrals to self-conscious Episcopal churches to austere Quaker meeting houses, but she had not belonged to any of them.

When she met Pastor Daniel, he told her that God was just as important as her other commitments. Joining his church was a relief. The lurking things were bound for whole days at a time.

The only problem was that if she told him, Max wouldn't understand. She had tried to explain her wisps of panic once, years ago, and he had suggested a hunting trip for boar or bear to relieve stress.

She knew that she must broach the subject eventually. Keeping the secret from him felt wrong. Considering the church's plans, she should introduce him to her church soon. Maybe tonight.

Diane got home around nine. Max had cooked a big pot of beef stew. He was handsome and a good cook, and she was a lucky girl.

Yes, maybe she could tell him tonight.

The dark brown lumps and gravy bubbled in the pot and looked like enough for two meals, hallelujah. Her parents still occasionally rumbled that Diane was going to lose her husband if she didn't mind the home and have supper on the table for him by six o'clock, but they didn't understand their arrangement. They didn't know about the housekeeper who came on Wednesdays, either.

"Kids home tonight?" Diane asked.

"Yep." Max smiled.

"I have some reading to catch up on." She pulled hairpins out of the heavy bun on the back of her head. Her hair unfurled, and the tension at her temples eased.

"What, bringing work home again?" He rubbed his knuckles under his sharp chin.

"Oh, there's always more to do." She tasted the stew from a wooden spoon. It scalded like a pin scraping her tongue, but the gravy was smooth and flavored with cumin and green chile, like a big pot of *carne asada. Fantastico.*

"You're doing a lot of reading lately," Max said.

That's because she read her Bible at work so she had to bring work home. She felt like she was having an affair with the Messiah. "Caseload is horrendous. April is staggering. These idiots commit crimes and then I have to stay late to put them in jail. Speaking of people I need to put in jail, anything more on Ester James today?"

Max grumbled, "Her dad came to see me, something about Israelis."

The second sip of broth congealed in Diane's mouth and filmed her throat, nearly choking her. Zeke James shouldn't be talking to anybody about Israelis. "What did he say?"

"If he had a ransom note or threatening phone calls, then I'd worry." Max rubbed his hand through his curly black hair. "He retracted it almost as soon as he said it. Sounds like he's mixed up in that weird church, too. Those Jesus freaks creep me out, always proselytizing and witnessing, trying to convert you. Reminds me of my creepy cousin Cassie."

Cassie, who died with David Koresh and the Branch Davidians.

"Right," Diane said. She stirred the stew. Maybe today was not the day to tell him. She had procrastinated telling him one more day, every day, for months.

"I called your office this afternoon about four." Max tapped his thigh where his holster usually hung. Fondling his gun was a nervous habit that she had never teased him about. "They said you'd left early."

A carrot chunk surfaced hesitantly in the stew, capsized, and submerged. "I had a few errands to run. Did you call my cell?"

"Left a message."

She retrieved her cell phone from her purse. Four new voice messages. She had silenced it during Bible Study. "The dead zones must have gotten me."

"What errands?" Max asked. His black eyes sharpened, and he stared at her, watching and calculating, and then he looked away. In Hispanic culture, it's not polite to stare too long, so Max had a thing about that, but he was such a good investigator that his need to watch warred with his upbringing.

She didn't want to lie, but he obviously wasn't receptive right now. Soon. She would tell him soon. Maybe tomorrow. "Had to interview some witnesses for an upcoming trial."

"Oh? Which witnesses?" He reached for her jingling purse, extracted her pistol from the inner holster, and locked it in the kitchen gun safe.

"Jorge Martinez. Thirty witnesses, and none of them speak English."

She handed him her cell phone, and he plugged it into the charger.

He asked, "Did you call in the feds on the Ester James case?"

As a Christian, she should not equivocate like a lawyer. Since her commitment to Christ, her soul, which during law school had been sucked out her ear into the big machine with the flashing red lights, felt redeemed. Diane held tight to her in-probate soul and said, "Nope."

That wasn't lying, exactly. No FBI agents were going to arrive. It was an email consult. Precedent: in several divorce cases, cybersex had not counted as adultery. Surely cyber-consulting did not count as consorting with the enemy.

"Okay," Max said. "I've got a truckload of paperwork to do at the office, and then I want to get a good look at the Lone Star at night."

Odd. He usually looked at things once and then reviewed them in his bizarre, perfect memory.

However, Diane could finish a whole week's homework while he was gone. She wouldn't have to skulk around at work, hiding her workbook and journal and Bible in her office. Bringing so much work home might make Max suspicious, like she was hiding something. Max alternated between being jealous and cavalier about Diane's male work friends.

Indeed, when she did tell him about the church, she would introduce him to When-Dee first, then a bunch of other women, then Pastor Daniel. She didn't want Max to get the wrong idea.

She smiled. "Okay, honey. Good hunting."

Some thoughts are poisonous.

Like mad cow disease prions, they wrap normal thoughts and catalyze a deviant reaction, twisting them into malignancies.

Some people with a predisposition, a weakness, an aberrant genetic makeup, cannot detoxify what is mostly harmless. Like a phenylketoneuric who cannot metabolize the amino acid phenylalanine, what is nutritious to most is slowly fatal to them.

Some improperly digested philosophies become neurotoxic. Religion has taught this for millennia, to be circumspect in your thoughts lest they betray you.

If thine eye offend thee, pluck it out.

If thine brain offend thee, bash it out.

Saturday

Just before midnight in the dark, Vanessa walked the chilly parking lot of the Lone Star Grocery, watching her sneakers traverse frosty gravel, looking for anything to indicate a scuffle, maybe some threads from Essie's white shirt or long strands of blond hair. She found only rocks.

Outside on the road, a car turned and drove into the parking lot. Its headlights flashed as one tire hopped the curb. Yellow sodium lights slid over the car. It cruised slowly, like the driver was returning to the scene of the crime, like murderers are supposed to do.

Even if the driver had been the killer, it didn't worry Vanessa. Ester and Vanessa had been twins during their freshman year of high school, before Vanessa had undergone a growth spurt of eight inches. After that, they called each other "Twinnie" only out of mutual memory. Essie had been an itty-bitty woman, five feet three inches, one hundred and twenty pounds. Vanessa could have bench-pressed Essie.

The car circled each stalk of lights, winding through the parking lot like a child swinging around poles. Vanessa sat on the trunk of her car and waited. She lifted her face to the light.

The sheriff's sedan stopped beside her. The glass reflected the parking lot floodlights like four circling UFOs. The window motor whined in the still, cold night, and the descending window gradually revealed the deputy's handsome face from hairline to neck, as if his pretty-boy head were emerging from of a jar of formaldehyde.

She unzipped her jacket and hopped off her car. "Hi, Deputy."

The sallow lights jaundiced his face, and he tipped his hat to her. "Hello, Ms. Allen."

"Call me Vanessa. What are you doing out here?"

He leaned one elbow on the door. "Just seeing what there is to see."

Vanessa nodded. "Nothing to see. I've looked."

"You sure you'd turn over any evidence you found? You wouldn't try to analyze it in a kitchen chemistry lab?"

She smiled. Little jokes were meant to be cute, even though they were more often irritating. "Ethidium bromide might be hard to find at the Lone Star."

Ethidium bromide is the highly carcinogenic agent that makes DNA bands in gels glow under ultraviolet lights.

"Right." He looked out into the parking lot.

His distant demeanor meant that he hadn't expected company out here, she surmised, amused. He was in the dark parking lot of the closed grocery store to be alone. Finding evidence was incidental. "Are you okay, Deputy?"

"Call me Max. Yeah, fine."

She pulled her jacket away from her front and bent over his window so that her heavy breasts fell deeply into her bra.

He looked at her breasts then looked away. Yep, some interest.

She smiled. "Okay, Max."

He frowned a little. "You been drinking?"

"A little. Two."

"'Two.' That's what all the drunks say." He glanced at her car behind her. "Get in. I'll drive you home."

"Don't you have somewhere you should be, Max?"

"If I don't drive you home, I'll have to arrest you for DUI, and I just caught up on all my dad-blamed paperwork. Faster to drive you."

He shouldn't see the hovel that her mother lived in. Vanessa hated pity with its accompanying haughtiness. Still, a ride with him was better than spending the night in a Texan jail.

"All right." She sauntered around the car and opened the passenger door.

Max started to point his thumb toward the back seat but acquiesced as she slammed the door. "Where d'you live?"

"New Orleans." She grinned.

He smirked. "And where's your mother live?"

"Turn left out of the parking lot."

"How's she feeling?"

"Who?"

"Your mother. You said you were in town because she was sick."

Good memory, there. "She's better."

"What's she got?"

Needed to be serious enough for her to come home but not serious enough that she should not leave the house. "Autoimmune thing."

She directed him several miles into the nicer suburbs. "You usually pick up drunk women in grocery store parking lots at night?"

"No." He glanced away from the dark road and caught her smile. "My wife works a lot. Usually I'm at home, making sure my kids do their homework."

"How many kids?" Men love questions.

"Two. Nicholas, twelve, and Tatiana, seventeen." He emphasized Tatiana, probably with pride.

"I'll bet she's pretty," Vanessa said.

"She's not bad. Not that I, her father, notice such things."

Yeah, she was pretty. And he was a proud daddy. "Oh?"

"Yep, took her on her first hunt when she was thirteen. Bagged a whitetail."

A little thrill of revulsion or something shuddered through her. "Hunting? Jesus, Max. That's barbaric. It's like murder."

"Hunting is not murder. Hunting is a natural part of the cycle of life. You aren't one of those vegetarians, are you?"

She shook her head.

Max continued, "Have you ever seen a three-year-old playing hide-and-go-seek, stalking? It's like watching a lion cub practicing on a wounded rodent. We're predators. We kill things and eat them. Our eyes are on the front of our faces like lions, not on the sides like prey. Yeah, I hunt."

This was evidently a touchy subject. His wife must feel differently. "Well, I suppose it's morally no different than dissecting a frog."

"Right." His curt nod was angry.

She changed the subject before he offered to teach her to hunt. Deliberately setting out to kill something was bizarre. Accidents happen, sure. Planning and executing were different. Maybe if she started on cats. Vanessa hated cats. "Tatiana, that's Russian, right? One of the four grand duchesses?"

He rubbed his sharp chin and grimaced at oncoming headlights. Glare played over his smooth skin and sleek, black hair. "My wife didn't want to name her after someone who was murdered, but it was my grandmother's name. My dad is Russian."

"Oh." She sang it down through half an octave.

"Yeah," Max said. "My mom is Mexican."

That was where the machismo and closely held gestures came from. Vanessa let a note of admiration ring in her voice. "That's where you get your dark eyes."

"Yeah, and the brown skin," he said. "I'm a half-breed."

Vanessa shrugged. "Everyone's a half-breed. I'm a quarter Apache."

Max laughed. "Yeah. You look it."

She twirled her blond hair and batted her very blue eyes. Deputy Max was a hottie, for a guy on the far age ranges of her attraction. The depression was lifting, and her blooming nervous energy usually precipitated a sexual triathlon. Such things were easier to arrange in New Orleans. She would keep Max in mind for when the impulse turned to an urge, which would dry into ravenous thirst.

She said, "My dad was half-Apache, half-Norwegian, and my mom is blond. Her name is Inga Allen, but she changed her last name from Von Something when she emigrated from Argentina. Those dominant Apache genes can be drowned out by recessives, if enough recessives gang up on them." She didn't say anything for a few minutes, trying to think of something to talk about besides her warped family. "So," she finally ventured. "You much closer to finding Ester?"

"Nope."

"First forty-eight hours, you know." She referred to the fact that the vast majority of crimes were solved in the first forty-eight hours. After that, the arrest rate drops by orders of magnitude.

"Forty-eight hour rule is a self-fulfilling prophecy," Max said. "There's nothing magical about it. If the perpetrator is so stupid and obvious that it takes you less than forty-eight hours to decide who it is, then it's an easy case. If it takes you longer, then it's a hard case, which means it's less likely to be solved."

"Still, forensic evidence degrades in forty-eight hours."

"There is that," Max conceded.

"And if there is a serial killer around here, more girls are going to end up dead."

"Yeah, you've mentioned that." His annoyed timbre spurred her on.

"Shouldn't you be checking the alibi of every white male in town? It's a small town."

Max chuffed a sarcastic chuckle, his annoyance reaching high irritation, which pissed her off that this idiot wasn't listening to her. He said, "White males. You should know better. Half of all serial killers aren't Caucasian. Twenty percent are female. Like female pedophiles, female serial killers are unrecognized and underreported."

His twenty percent statistic and bland grimace were both absurd. Like other feminine demons such as succubi, female serial killers did not exist. Men liked to tie people up, rape them, and kill them. That wasn't a woman's territory. The knife was a sharp-edged dick, fucking victims in piqueristic permutations of rape. Jeffrey Dahmer admitted that he incised vaginal orifices in his victims, and he was a homosexual. It must be a Y-chromosome thing. What would a sexually sadistic woman serial killer do, whittle a new dick on a victim? It wouldn't stay stiff.

"Gotta play the odds. Eighty percent is a pretty good start. Stop here." She pointed to a nice house.

He pulled the car over. Lights glimmered gold through the sheer drapes of the picture window.

"Thanks for the ride." Vanessa opened the door and hopped out. She bent over and gave him another good look at her boobs. He looked. That should keep him busy. "I appreciate the ride, Max. See you around."

She slammed the door and sashayed up the sidewalk, watching the house's windows. No one peeked out.

The drone of Max's car motor fell in the distance.

Vanessa turned off the sidewalk and trudged over the frost-killed lawn to the street. Her mother's house was a mile and a half away.

She had analyzed the writings of serial killers and psychologists' reports about serial killers. Their delusions of grandeur, of being Nietzschean *übermenschen* or vampiric top predators, disgusted her. Those arrogant bastards deserved to get caught. The way out wasn't to win, to become a superman above the law, but to surrender and crawl under it. If you're not trying to win the race, you walk away. Without hope, nothing matters.

That's the way this bastard world works.

She shuffled through the cold gravel of the street, wishing she had brought a proper coat. She kept her head up; it took a hell of a lot more than that family dog barking to unnerve big ol' Nessie. Walking under the stars warmed her. Her long legs stretched. In fifteen minutes, she had walked a mile.

The last half-mile was a different neighborhood.

Past the bus depot, past the pawn shops, the houses squatted lower, meaner. These circa-sixties houses with seven-foot ceilings were built for stooped folks whose growth had been stunted by bone-leaching phosphate soda pop, greasy fast food made of ground up stray dogs, and tinned ravioli bought at convenience stores when the kids' whining got on the parents' nerves. Crabbed people cycled through generations in these houses, each generation falling lower, and the houses degenerating more.

Vanessa turned down her childhood street and hesitated because the shadows were crawling. She took a good look down the block.

The streetlight was long gone, torn down by the residents and sold for scrap metal when aluminum prices made it worth the trouble. The moon cast dirty chalk light where overgrown yards spilled into the broken asphalt. In the last six years, some yards had sprung high, chain-link fences with padlocked gates.

Some people tried to keep the criminals out and preserve their few belongings.

Some fences, however, kept crime in. The second house smelled like sun-rotted dog shit. Pit bulls barked their hoarse *raff raff*, from cages in the back. Pit bulls are natural psychopaths. Those trained to fight look like normal dogs, slobbery and wiggly most of the time. When you rile them up with a rabbit or a cat or a baseball bat, the demon emerges.

Vanessa was still tipsy from five vodka shots at the Foxhead and she stumbled, drawing the attention of any nefarious persons crouching in the shadows. She felt around in her purse, discarding perfume and a switchblade, and found pepper spray.

Adrenaline snaked through her happy alcohol buzz. Her stride lengthened. She walked proudly because she wasn't ashamed. This neighborhood toughened her. Tough people survive. Wussies never know the thrill of making it home without a gunshot wound. She smiled when she walked through this neighborhood, like she smiled when she worked with a dead body, because she was that tough.

A dead, half-eaten orange cat lay on the street. Cats were stupid creatures that convince yet stupider people to feed them and sift their shit out of sand. She kicked it into the gutter for sanitation's sake.

Behind the dogfighting house, celebratory automatic gunfire jackhammered the dark sky. Muzzle flashes lit intermittent shadows through the fences. Gunpowder smoke mingled with the dog shit stink.

Someone's dog must have won.

That meant that someone else's wounded dog, the one that curred out, was being electrocuted with a car battery and jumper cables clamped to its tongue and crammed up its ass. The execution of the loser is part of the show.

That's how this fucked-up world works.

Deputy Max Konstantin left Vanessa walking up to her house and drove back toward the center of town. He had two errands now.

The first was to examine Vanessa's car in the Lone Star parking lot. She was the first person to miss Ester, a suspicious position, and Max had seen something on her car. Threatening her with DUI to persuade her to abandon her car in a public place was a nice touch.

The other errand, he had not fully decided to pursue.

Scrutinizing Vanessa's car would buy him some time while he decided whether or not to indulge in a little felonious trespassing.

Streetlights rose out of the dark road, slipped over the roof of the car, and trailed away in the rear-view mirror. Most businesses were dark. Muted lights shone through the stained glass windows of Martini's bar. Four cars hunkered in its cold parking lot. New Canaan is a small town, even though it is the Sin Nombre County seat.

Max drove, his thoughts tussling. He discounted Vanessa's serial killer hypothesis even though local law enforcement always denies the possibility of a serial killer until it is painfully obvious that there is one. Local law enforcement denies the existence of a serial killer in cases where there isn't one, too. A thousand true negatives exist for every false negative, and there are no false positives.

He drove into the Lone Star Grocery's parking lot. Vanessa's sedan reflected the emergency lights glowing in the store's entrance. The car was last year's model of a domestic brand. The parking lot's yellow lights muddied its color to swamp gray. Max got out of his car. His growing beard itched in the cold air, and he scratched his cheek absently.

Max leaned over the driver's side and noted the VIN number, then crouched and aimed his flashlight at the license plate. The Louisiana vanity plate read CALLUS.

Yes, law enforcement work did rub against you until you built up a callus, until you became calloused to the terrible things that people did to one another. He felt a sad kinship for her, that she wore her damage, wounded in the name of others, so proudly.

As he had noticed, a brown wipe smudged the passenger door handle. Probably good Texas mud or spontaneous Louisiana rust. If he luminoled it to test for blood, the iron in dirt or rust would catalyze the chemical reaction, producing a false positive.

He walked back to his patrol car. In the trunk, he found a white box, a forensic sample collection kit.

Back at Vanessa's car, he donned blue nitrile gloves, moistened cotton-tipped swabs with distilled water, and swabbed four brown smears: two for the state crime lab, one for a spare, and one for Vanessa Allen to test to shut her up.

Probably shouldn't tell her where he had collected it. He chuckled.

He inserted the swabs in the white sample boxes barely bigger than the swabs themselves and labeled everything with careful block letters, then double-entered the sample codes on index sheets on his clipboard. He dropped the tiny box containing two swabs in the sample envelope, put the envelope into a mailer, and addressed it to the state crime lab. He tossed the kits into his duffel bag in the trunk, found the digital camera, and took pictures of the smear on the car.

On those television shows, they drop swabs in plastic baggies so the camera can focus on the ominous smudge, but plastic retains moisture, and moisture degrades DNA. Just another example of how they screw it up.

Max stripped off the sweat-stuck gloves. The acrid scent annoyed him. Evidence collection was important for Diane's end of things, but the lab results took months to come back, far too long for most investigations. They confirmed what the investigator had already found out through police work: suspects, interrogations, alibis, means, motive, and opportunity.

Now it was time for his other errand, if he chose to do it.

It was close to one in the morning, not that he could sleep if he went home. Insomnia had snuck up on him a couple days ago, carrying questions about what the hell his wife was doing, staying out in the evenings, not answering her cell phone, taking off from her office, and not able to do her casework at the office such that she had to bring it home every darn night. Her tardiness and missing chunks of time had been going on for months. That was too long for a simple affair. Since he had gone out tonight, he had trapped her at home with the kids. To make sure, he swiped her keys from her purse when he stowed her gun.

Max slid into his idling car and drove through the night.

He had never thought of himself as a trusting soul, but he had never spied on his wife. His kids, sure. Minors are not legally responsible, so they are not afforded constitutional protections. With responsibility comes privacy.

Max considered driving home with his questions unanswered. That would be the ethical choice. He should either trust his wife or prepare for the worst, but trespassing at her office and rifling her belongings was unethical.

Yes, it was unethical. There was no escaping that. And criminal.

The traffic light at the intersection of Sagebrush Road and Sixteenth Street was red. Left would take him home. Straight ahead, the road led to the county office building. The signal poured red light over the hood of his car. Max slowly scratched the handle of his gun with a couple fingers, as if he was scratching a cat's ears.

To Hell with it.

Max turned on the red and blue flashing lights atop the car and blew through the deserted intersection. Max couldn't pretend that he wasn't an investigator any more than he could forget he was a man. When things went wrong, he asked the questions and looked for evidence. That's how he made his money and spent his waking hours.

On the other side of the intersection, he clicked off the flashing lights.

Most men would blast into orbital trajectory if their woman screwed around on them, but Max worried that it was not a tawdry affair. He hoped for evidence of tawdriness as he pulled up to the county office building.

As he twisted the clanging keys in the lock on the lobby's glass doors, he clicked into investigator mode. He needed evidence or lack thereof. He hoped for nothing, assumed nothing. He only looked. He could surmise later.

In Dallas or Houston, a County Attorney's office building would have round-the-clock guards, security cameras, and an alarm system. In New Canaan, however, in rural Sin Nombre County, such frivolities were not tolerated by down-to-earth taxpayers. Locks were good enough. Most of the doors could also be opened with a swipe card in the card reader, but Max brought Diane's key because he didn't want her card recorded. Max rode the smooth elevator up two floors, scratching his gun the whole time. The doors opened.

Rudimentary lights glowed in the ceiling and illuminated the entry part of the office with a vague, yellow light. The furniture looked like sketches of desks with one side blocked in black.

At the secretary's cubicle in the front, a cheap vase of dying flowers parked next to the computer. He leaned over the ledge and plucked the note. *To Josie,* it read, *Thanks for having the abortion.* He put the note back.

He walked around the secretary's desk to the individual offices. The third one down had a brass nameplate: Diane Marshall, ACCA.

Some of Max's friends had razzed him about Diane not taking his name when they married, but they were clods who would do something stupid like let a beautiful, smart, funny woman get away due to nomenclature. Most of them had divorced at least once. Besides, Marshall was a good law enforcement name. He had been tempted to change his name to hers, just so people would refer to him as Deputy Marshall, or Sheriff Marshall, and maybe someday, Marshal Marshall. It wasn't too late to do so, assuming that Diane wasn't on the verge of running away to Mexico.

He unlocked Diane's office door and paused with his hand on the knob. This was a big step backward in their marriage. He didn't like it, but he twisted the doorknob.

No vases of flowers perched on the file cabinets.

He could stop now, with that good omen.

Squared, color-coded stacks of three-ring binders and manila folders made a fortress of her wide desk. She may not be neat in the classical sense of the word, but she was organized. Max had seen her find a particular document deep in those piles by sliding her hand into the middle and whipping it out like a card trick.

The computer screen glowed with lifelike phosphorescent fish, so he logged on with her usual password and perused her case files. No suspicious-looking folders or files within any of the case-named files.

In her web browser, he found her recently visited sites by pressing Control and H. Mostly religious stuff, for the Ester James case, he assumed. That church Ester James had belonged to was weird, all right. Maybe there was more to that creepy little church.

In the browser, Max tapped in the website that supplied the professional-grade spyware he used for the home computers and downloaded the worm.

There. Now, her computer would email screencaps to him. He flagged the keywords hotel, motel, sex, affair, oral, anal, and, after a moment's hesitation, love. If Diane typed in those words, a screencap of whatever she was typing would be sent to Max, besides random screencaps and a list of visited websites. He dumped the browser's memory of webpages and passwords.

His fingertips roved her desk, touching her pens and her drawer pulls, and he found her date book in her shallow desk drawer amid the clutter of sticky note pads and packets of hot sauce.

Among the usual clutter of court dates and meetings that he knew her codes for, her date book held cryptic entries: 3:30–BS Dan.

Dan. Who was Dan?

And the initials BS? They might stand for what he would catch for snooping on her like this, but maybe they stood for something sinister.

Bull Shit? Bill Short? Brake Service? Butt Sex?

Her printer was on. Max spread her date book on the glass top and pushed the copy button. The machine grated, and paper extruded. He folded the copy and tucked it in his shirt pocket.

Well, she had some kind of code, but he still had no direct evidence.

Could have been worse. He could have found dying red roses, jewelry boxes, love notes, and tickets to Mexico. The escape route for love affairs always ran through Mexico. He wondered idly if the Federales or drug cartels had rat lines for illicit lovers buying a cheap Mexican divorce.

He felt a little wrong for spying on his wife, but it was like that old story about the scorpion and the frog.

He was an investigator. It was his nature.

Diane slept badly that night, thinking about P.J. Even when Max finally finished his paperwork and dragged himself into bed after two, Diane was still awake, gleaning yet more disturbing items from the conversation.

"Did P.J. Lessing look sick to you?" she asked.

"What? No." Max rolled over in the dark to look at her. "Why?"

"She looked sick to me."

"Probably the flu. It's going around." He closed his eyes.

The girl looked sick. Diane stared at the pebbled, dark ceiling.

Diane asked, "Did she say anything weird to you about her parents?"

"No." His voice was hoarse from his long day.

"There's something weird going on."

"Yes, dear."

"Don't yes-dear me."

He squinted in the dark at her. "You don't have one of your panicky feelings, do you?"

"No," she lied. He denigrated her panicky feelings as intuition or hunches that were supported by an unusual statistical anomaly of random chance.

Maybe P.J. had been sick with nerves. Maybe she was hiding something so terrible that it made her sick.

Panic.

Saturday morning was bright and cloudless. Diane puttered around the house for two hours before the panicky feelings, driven by snippets like "My parents wouldn't like me talking to you," and the nervous waver in her eyes when Diane asked if they had any reason to worry about law enforcement, made her jittery enough to go meet the non-traditional parents for herself, just to make sure that nothing terrible was going on. Diane had seen a lot of terrible situations in her job.

When she had finally decided to go, just to check, just to make sure, her darned keys were missing. She was sure she had hung them on the chunky blue moon-adorned ceramic key rack Tatiana had made when she was nine, but the freaking keys turned up in the silverware drawer.

Diane had nearly dropped her purse when she came in last night, carrying folders. Maybe they had dislodged. Max had stowed her gun for her. Maybe the keys had latched onto the trigger guard and fallen.

Now that she thought about it, she had heard a clang as she closed the silverware drawer. That must have been her keys. She must have imagined hanging the keys on the rack or thought that she had because it was habitual.

Diane turned down the tidy residential street and counted houses. The neighborhood was middle-class, where people believed that the condition of one's lawn equated with the cleanliness of one's soul. In the affluent sections of town, people hired illegal Mexicans for fifty bucks a day plus lunch. Their immaculate lawns belied the states of their malingering souls.

The Lessing house was a curious commingling of poverty and diligent manual labor. The lawn was a brown square of crew-cut, frost-killed grass. No dead leaves, no weeds. Diane parked her ostentatious Jag behind the tree. A thin gap ringed the yard's perimeter and vacant flowerbeds, evidence of edging. Fresh paint glistened on the wooden post-and-rail fence. Both cars were twenty years old but clean.

In contrast, Diane's Jaguar was dusty and needed vacuuming. Tatiana had spilled diet soda in the back seat. Diane rubbed the leather headrest to wipe away some of the deposited hairspray. The grime stuck.

Diane dragged her heavy purse out and slammed the door. Her purse clunked against the door and she winced, hoping she hadn't dented it. Though Max had given her the car, its pristine condition figured in his machismo, somehow.

At the front door, Diane pressed the chime and waited. Inside, stillness gave way to scuffling and muffled shouts. They must sleep late. Oops.

A woman answered the door. Her mussed hair and rough complexion was indicative of a woman around fifty, though her slender body under her cotton nightgown suggested younger. The woman cleared her throat and asked, "Hello?"

Diane held out her hand for a shake. Her gaze flicked down to her own navy blue pumps and back up to the woman's blue eyes in a ceaseless struggle between shyness and her chosen advocacy. "I'm Diane Marshall. I'm with the County Attorney's office." She didn't add that it was the Criminal County Attorney's office. Better to sound like she was a toothless contract lawyer. "I'm sorry I didn't call ahead."

The woman crossed her arms over her white nightdress. Her unfriendly posture blamed Diane for waking her. "Saffron."

Diane retracted her unshaken hand. "Nice to meet you, Saffron." On Saffron's driver's license record, her name was Jenny Barkowski. She must have renamed herself, a hippie affectation. "I'm looking into a crime committed over by the Lone Star Grocery. I'd like to ask you some questions."

She finger-combed straggly blond hair. "We don't know anything."

P.J. must take after her father. She had much more melanin in her brown skin and glassy black hair than her mother. Diane said, "If you didn't hear anything, that might be important. Or maybe you did, and if

I asked the right questions, you might remember. May I come in?"

"All right." Saffron slouched aside to let Diane pass.

Diane walked inside. Her nose twitched and investigated molecules floating in the air. Neurons fired, and she recalled a trip to India with a friend during law school, vetting the rural Indian justice system. They visited a temple town in Southern India, and the whole town had smelled like pungent Hindu temple incense and fried onions. Well, this older house probably didn't have adequate ventilation.

Not that poverty is a sign of anything. Diane had worked in the Criminal County Attorney's office for ten years, and crime victims, valuable witnesses, innocent bystanders, and perpetrators came from every demographic.

Her olfactory neurons discarded the onions and incense, felt around underneath, and hoovered up a few stray molecules that activated decades-old memories.

Dorms?

For a minute, Diane remembered the sunlight streaming through the industrial curtains that draped the dorm rooms' windows at the University of Texas, followed by random memories of frat parties.

Oh. The house smelled like pot.

Diane wasn't here to investigate drug possession charges. The marijuana residue, however, clicked the house into a column in her head titled: illegal activities.

Saffron said, "Have a seat. I'm going to start the coffee."

Diane sat on the sagging sofa, wondering whether she should drink the coffee. The couch's upholstery was brown paisley tapestry, decades out of date but not worn. The fabric gathered clumsily over the arm of the couch. Saffron had probably reupholstered it herself. The end table beside the couch held a collection of china figurines, all white and blue and clean.

You had to give Saffron credit for trying. For work, Diane had visited the seedier parts of town, and for an under-populated county, they had some scary districts. Pawn shops, drug dealers, and prostitutes parasitized each other in vicious social feedback loops.

A kitten scampered up the hallway. Saffron returned. "Coffee will be ready in a few."

Diane started, "A couple days ago, Wednesday night, we think a young woman was abducted near here."

Saffron didn't grimace or look askance. Nothing. Her expression looked like a studied, determined non-reaction.

Diane asked, "Did you see it on the news?"

"No," Saffron said. "I don't watch television. Rots the brain."

"Yes, indeed." Diane inhaled the secondhand pot smoke. "Ester James was the girl's name. She worked at the Lone Star Grocery behind your house."

"What's that got to do with us?" Saffron asked.

"Did you hear anything that night? See anything?"

"No." That quick answer's rehearsed cadence was evident. Diane did not like people who concealed evidence, even in adherence to a misguided, anti-establishment philosophy.

"You sure?"

"We didn't hear anything," a girl's voice said. P.J. Lessing stood in the hallway. Her long black hair snagged on her rumpled concert tee shirt and flannel shorts, swaying on sleepy, stick-like legs. She was pretty without that horrid black makeup.

Saffron glared at P.J. The malicious stare continued long after interruption irritation should have ended and became a silently replayed fight.

Tampering with a witness is a crime. Knowing which witness to tamper with suggested a worse crime. Diane wondered why P.J. had been so nervous in the car in response to a few questions. She smiled at P.J. "Hello."

P.J. looked down to the carpet. "I don't, like, know you."

Of course she didn't. "I'm Diane Marshall. I'm looking into the kidnapping of a young woman near here on Wednesday night. Who are you?"

P.J. didn't look up. Her shyness seemed cruelly forced. "Nobody."

Diane asked, "Did you hear anything that night?"

Saffron said, "I said no one heard anything."

P.J. nodded and rubbed her cheek. Diane squinted. Was her cheek slapped-red? Sometimes it was hard to tell with dusky skin. She had some scabbed-over abrasions on her right forearm. Yesterday, she walked like her legs or back hurt her.

Beside P.J., a chubby black toddler wearing a cloth diaper and a tee shirt that read, *That's it! I'm goin' to Grandma's!* tottered out. He asked P.J., "Coffee?"

Diane glanced at Saffron, who studied the crushed carpet. Diane asked with a big smile, "How many children do you have?"

"Eight."

"Bless your heart." Diane meant it. "All yours?"

"Yes, all mine," Saffron said, "and all adopted internationally. Our family is like a rainbow. P.J. is from India. She had some problems with her legs, but we got those straightened out."

Eight adopted kids seemed more like a residential orphanage than a nuclear family to Diane, but she wasn't the one saving kids from foreign institutions, so it was none of her business.

Without Gothic make-up, P.J. looked like one of those lovely, sari-draped child brides married off to an older man for her dowry and virginity. Sunlight picked emerald streaks from her black hair.

The toddler demanded, "Coffee!"

P.J. wiped her cheek again as if she was silently crying and walked after the toddler into the gloomy hallway. Livid scars traced the backs of both her legs. She turned and stood like a shadow at the mouth of

Hell, silently entreating.

"Wow," Diane said. "It takes a special person to adopt that many kids."

"Not really. I love kids." Saffron didn't look up. Her flat intonation concerned Diane.

Diane wanted to call to P.J. to come over, but she did not want to draw attention to her. "Your husband must be a special guy."

Saffron said, "We don't use limiting role words like 'husband,' 'wife,' or 'mother' that are based in Christianity and repress natural relationships. We prefer 'partner,' not that he's much of a partner sometimes."

"Oh?" Diane leaned forward with her forearms resting on her knees and hands clasped, the classic *I'm listening* posture. Under her feet, crosshatched backing showed through the threadbare carpet.

Saffron lit a cigarette. "No matter what I do, he insists on participating in degenerate American culture. He doesn't get it."

"That must be tough." Diane risked a glance at P.J. The girl bit her lower lip. P.J. leaned against the wall and stared at the floor, unwilling to leave them alone but not wanting to be there. Something was wrong, something bad.

"Yeah," Saffron complained. "See, I knew a woman would understand. Men just don't get it. I thought he was different, that he got it, even though the women in my women's group tried to warn me that men never get it. He watches television like it's got some kind of hold over him, like he's addicted. Especially college basketball. What kind of man watches every Iowa Hawkeye game and every damned NC-double-A playoff game? I mean, every one of them!"

Diane's lawyerly interrogative habit resumed. "Did you go to the University of Iowa?"

Saffron sucked on her cigarette as if she might get high from it. "We went to Maharishi University and studied ayurvedic medicine with the Maharishi Mahesh Yogi. It's in Iowa, near Iowa City. I would never have gone to a traditional university." She said *traditional* with the same distaste as if she had dipped her cigarette in toilet bowl cleaner and then chewed it up. "Those traditional universities are all the same. They indoctrinate people and train you to be a cog in the establishment machine, so you can further the aims of the IMF and the trilateral commission run by Yale Skull and Bonesmen. That's why I home-schooled the kids, but P.J. here wanted to go to public school so she could get into a traditional university. She convinced a majority of the kids, and they voted it through."

"Wow. That's interesting," Diane said, encouraging Saffron's diatribe. Saffron's iron insistence was worrisome. What had Saffron been home-teaching her kids: anarchy, free love, and obsessive yardwork? Diane clasped her hands hard, and her cheeks ached from smiling. How far did this woman's free love theories extend?

Diane glanced at P.J. The girl's eyes were huge, frightened.

A large tapestry hung on the wall beside the hallway entrance. A flaming sun surrounded a pregnant African woman, like a gravid Icarus. Children of various ethnicities cavorted near the fringe. The disturbing impression was less one of fertility than of burning hellfire and scrawny, hungry demons.

"They come home with the weirdest ideas. You home-school your kids, don't you?"

Diane nodded.

Saffron continued, "Most people don't realize that they're tools, used by the government to repress the people's creativity. If the damn government would get off our backs, we could live in harmony with nature and stop destroying the planet with our cars and our televisions and airplanes. All religions are used to control the people's minds. Can you imagine anyone who thinks that God is good, if the Christian God is responsible for Hurricane Katrina, and September eleventh, and racism, and the income tax?"

"Far out," Diane said. Her molars clenched. She wanted to tell Saffron that God didn't create wickedness but gave us the strength to fight it.

Saffron said, "And Christianity represses women. They suppressed the Gospel of Mary Magdalene, turned a beautiful fertile woman into a mockery of a virgin, and destroyed the pagan Goddess religions."

"Yeah," Diane said. "The patriarchy." Goddesses? *Yikes.*

"But pagans really get it. I'm a Wiccan High Priestess. You seem like an enlightened woman, ready to be freed of the shackles of oppression. You should join our coven."

"What?" Witches and Satanists met in covens. Diane must have heard her wrong. Maybe she said convent or covenant.

A curio cabinet stood in one corner of the room, entirely dust-free in a way that nothing in Diane's gritty house was, even with the Wednesday housekeepers. A morbidly obese Buddha squatted on the top shelf, panting to force blood through his congestively diseased heart. Below that, a naked onyx figurine with six arms danced in a circle of fire, suggestively thrusting its pelvis. On the lowest shelf, a Mayan feathered serpent-god slithered.

"And," Saffron continued, "the Catholic Church dictates that women have to be virgins or married, and if they are married, they have to be constantly pregnant. They're repressing women's natural sexuality." She inhaled. "And male circumcision, the removal of the foreskin, is just another attempt by the all-male Judeo-Christian patriarchy to reduce women's pleasure during sex. That's what the ribs on the expensive condoms are, you know, to replace the foreskin."

Diane didn't want to discuss sex or penises with this insane woman.

Movement in the hallway startled Diane. A man, butt-naked, stood scratching his beard. His barrel chest had a light sheen of hair, but his pelt really started at his cauldron-sized belly and flourished over his thighs nearly to his knees, satyr-like. As Saffron had evinced a preference for, he was indeed uncircumcised.

"Oh!" Diane said.

Saffron gestured at the naked man. "This is The Tower."

Diane stared at the carpet. "Hi, Tower."

"*The* Tower," he said. His voice was smudged with cigarette soot. "Like the Tarot card. What, does me being sky-clad bother you? Are you so repressed that a man can't be unclothed in his own house?"

"I don't know anything about Tarot cards," Diane said. Her smile condensed as if a drawstring knotted her lips with worry about genetically unrelated men wandering naked around young teenage girls in a house in which parental roles were undefined. The panic found its answer. Should she go back to the office and call a judge for a warrant or arrest them on the spot?

"You know the Tarot," Saffron said. "The Tower is the card of destruction and change, like the Hindu God Shiva, the Black God who dances at the destruction of the world." She gestured toward the black idol dancing in the curio cabinet.

"The Black God?" Diane asked. "Isn't that a name for Satan?"

The naked The Tower raised one hand toward P.J. The toddler at her feet shrank and hid behind P.J.'s bare thighs.

"Most people think The Devil is the worst Tarot card," Saffron continued. "But The Devil means freedom."

"The Devil!" Diane wanted to jump up and push the raw-naked man out of the room. Everything that Pastor Daniel had preached about the Devil rang through her head: that the Devil himself tempted people to sin, to the *worst* sins, that he was present on Earth in the hearts of People of the Lie and in a corporal form when called by Satanists, and that The Great Serpent would give rise to the Anti-Christ who would reign over all the nations on Earth during the Tribulation.

Saffron, still smoking her cigarette, said, "The Devil card in the Major

Arcana means your Antagonist, not Evil. It's more like self-bondage, because what is really holding you back are your own inhibitions and delusions. I can read your cards for you."

The naked man's hand descended toward P.J.'s head and caressed her hair.

P.J. flattened herself against the wall to escape his touch. Her wild-eyed fear was horrible.

That man was sexually abusing P.J.

Panic slammed Diane, sucking her legs and arms limp, but she stood. Lord in Heaven, Saffron had adopted eight children to feed the carnal, pedophilic lusts of The Tower, a man who named himself after his own erection. This house was an orphanage turned child-prostitution ring.

Diane said, "Get away from her."

"What?" The Tower asked.

"Get away from her!" Diane whipped her cell phone off her purse strap where she clipped it and speed-dialed Max's phone. It beeped and clicked as he picked up. "Max! I need you in your official capacity over here right now with three vehicles. And Child Protective Services. You!" She pointed at The Tower, who raised his hands in front of his chest as if that was the naked part of him he should cover. "Stay away from her!"

The Tower said, "What!"

Diane jammed the phone between her shoulder and ear and drew the cumbersome handgun out of her purse. The sights snagged on a thread and she jerked it with trembling arms. "Stay away from her! Put your hands in the air! Get down on the floor!"

"Lady," he said, "where would I hide a weapon?"

"Get your hands out in front of you and get down on the floor!"

Saffron stood. "What the hell's going on?"

The Tower half-lowered himself to the floor like he had a hip problem and leaned against the wall with one hand. "She said something about

Child Protective Services."

Saffron asked, "What're you calling them for?"

In her ear, through the phone, Max's tiny voice asked furiously, "Are you all right? Are you all right? Where the hell are you?"

Diane couldn't stop yelling. "Get away from her! Max, I'm at P.J. Lessing's house behind the Lone Star Grocery, on Happy Trail Road."

"I'm coming!" he yelled. "I'm calling it in. What the hell happened?"

"Just hurry." She held the gun on The Tower, who crouched in a football-ready stance. "Get down on the floor. Now! Down on the floor!"

Saffron's hands shook and her cigarette fell to the floor. "You can't do this to me, to us, in our own home."

"I'm sorry," Diane said, "but I have to make sure that this isn't what it looks like, and it looks like that hairy pedophile is sexually abusing that minor. Lie down on the floor, please, Saffron. You probably didn't even know what's been going on."

"That's not true. That can't be." She kneeled and then lay on the floor. "What the hell is going on? The Tower?"

The Tower braced himself on the wall and leaned on one knee. "I don't know."

Saffron turned to the teen girl. "Peacey?"

P.J. cringed with her back against the dark wall. Her black eyes were huge. The toddler cowered between her legs and the wall.

Saffron picked her cigarette out of the carpeting and carefully placed it in an ashtray on the side table above her. "Peacey, did you say something that could have been taken wrong?"

"Just stay down," Diane said, "Max, are you on your way?"

"I'm in the car. Called it in. Cars inbound. ETA, three minutes."

"Do you know the address?" Diane asked.

"I was there a couple days ago."

"Okay." Max had been there, so he knew the address perfectly. In the distance, Diane heard sirens.

Saffron said, "You can't do this. You can't just walk in here and see something that doesn't jibe with your bourgeois morality and break up my family!"

"Saffron, ma'am," Diane fell back on officious politeness, an authoritarian pretense that government agents and citizens have equal rights, which Diane utilized every day from the superior position, "ma'am, I'm sure this will all be rectified soon. Your children will be well-cared for. P.J., take the child and go to the bedroom. Keep the other kids back there. Don't come out until the sheriff's deputies arrive."

P.J. froze.

Saffron said, "Peacey, do what she says." She gasped a sob. "Everything will be all right. Go to the girls' room, take the rest of the kids in there, and come out for the officers." She gasped again. "I love you. Don't forget that I love you."

P.J. whirled the toddler onto her hip and bolted down the dark hall.

Saffron laid her head on the carpet. "Where will they go? You won't make them eat meat, will you?"

Diane said, "I'm sure it won't come to that."

Saffron buried her face in the carpet and wept. "Why are you doing this? Because The Tower is sky-clad? Because seeing a naked man makes you think that there must be intercourse going on? Because your narrow mentality won't let you see the human form as beautiful but only as a sex object?"

Diane, the prosecuting criminal attorney, knew that she should shut up and maintain the situation until the far-off sirens arrived. "Because casual nudity is a common grooming tactic for pedophiles."

P.J.'s recoil was a common reaction to sexual abuse. Saffron's blindness to P.J's clinging to the wall to escape his groping hand was a common symptom of an enabling, negligent, stupid parent.

"He's not a pedophile," Saffron said.

Diane said, "No one can judge his own case." *In propia causa nemo judex.*

From her cell phone, Max said, "Diane! Are you all right!"

"Yes," she said to the phone. "The situation is under control. Tell the deputies to come in with minimal interruption. We don't need to traumatize the children with helicopters and SWAT teams."

Saffron sobbed, "You're really going to take them away?"

"I'm sorry." Diane wasn't sorry that P.J. would be safe tonight, but she had to figure out who could take them all. Breaking the eight of them up and sending them to different families would make things worse.

Max asked, "I'm almost there. Is the front door unlocked?"

Diane edged over to the door, still pointing her gun at The Tower, and pinning the miniscule phone to her shoulder with her cheek by cranking her neck at a right angle. Taking her support hand off the gun, she reached behind her back and unlocked the deadbolt and doorknob. "It's unlocked."

"Good." Garbled mumbling. He must be radioing the others.

She moved away from the door. "When you come in, I'm on the right."

"Just stay there. How many people are in the room?"

"Two adults plus me. Children in one of the back bedrooms."

"Okay. We're coming. Just stay all right. When I come in, lower your weapon and get the hell out of there. Run out the fucking door. All right? Are you all right, Diane?"

"I'm all right," she said.

The wails converged on the street outside, and brakes screeched. Footfalls pounded over the lawn and clattered up the wooden porch.

The front door slammed open and her husband Max jumped in, arms braced around his gun. His head swiveled wildly to apprise who might shoot at him, and his arms and the gun's muzzle swung toward Diane and then back at the two prone people on the floor. Max yelled at her, "Are you all right?"

"Yeah," she said.

"Then get out. Go!"

"But someone should be here, for backup."

Max stared straight ahead at Saffron and The Tower. Anger twisted his face and poured off him like heat off an engine. "Get out of here! The kids, think of our kids! What will they do if both of us are in here when the shooting starts? Go!"

Diane said, "Arrest the two adults. Suspicion of child sexual abuse and child rape."

Max sidestepped toward her, grabbed her arm and pulled her backward toward the door. All the time, he watched Saffron and The Tower and threatened one, then the other, with his gun.

Diane said, "Take the children in the bedroom into protective custody. Bedroom walls are there." She pointed to the interior walls with the demon tapestry so he would not shoot through them if it came to that. Against a decent caliber bullet, drywall is as much protection as rice paper. "There should be eight kids."

"Eight kids? He's been abusing eight kids?" The anger lines on his face morphed into insane rage. Max jerked her behind him and pushed her out the door. "Go!"

She turned and fled the house, gun held low, her finger along the barrel.

She ran around Max's sheriff's car and crouched. Red lights from the blazing rollers on top of the car swirled on the trees and houses. In the house across the street, a wide-eyed woman and two curious kids looked out a plate-glass window. When they saw her looking at them, the woman pushed the kids down and ducked.

Into her cell phone, Diane yelled, "Max, can you hear me?"

Her voice recycled from the car, where his cell phone lay on the front seat.

She stretched over the hood of the car trying to see inside, but sheer curtains blocked her view.

Inside the house, Max shouted harsh commands. A tornado of rage roared. Diane crouched beside the car and gripped her gun to run back inside.

A siren-blaring car screeched onto the curb in front of her. A tubby, sweaty sergeant deputy she recognized struggled with his seatbelt before he swung out of the car and dashed over to her. "What's going on in there?"

"I don't know," she said. "Max is in there with two suspects. Max Konstantin."

The deputy looked at the open door, where Max's shouting escalated. "He's in there alone?"

"He had the situation under control," she said, "and he told me to leave."

A gunshot blasted. The sound wave crashed over them. Jackrabbits bolted. An armadillo, uprooting a neighbor's lawn, scuttled under a bush.

Diane stood and stepped toward the house.

Another shot cracked and echoed down the cold street.

"Oh my God!" Diane tried to run into the house but the deputy pulled her down behind the car. His wet grip pinched.

Another shot splintered the chilly air and pounded Diane's chest. "Max!" she yelled. "Max!"

The sergeant deputy shouted, "Stay here! Stay right here!" and ran in a long arc toward the open door, yelling, "Officer requires backup!" into his shoulder radio. His shouts echoed through the car's receiver.

"Max!" She fumbled her pistol and looked over the car hood. The other deputy was already inside.

Over the car's radio, men shouted, "Get down! Get down!"

A woman screamed, "Stop! Stop! Please stop!"

Three more sheriff's cars screeched to a stop. Brown-uniformed men holding rifles or pistols scrambled from the cars and ran to the windows and door. Two went in the front door. An ambulance turned up the block.

Diane scrambled from her safe spot behind the car and ran in a wide arc toward the door like the deputy had. She could see only a sliver of the brown couch inside the living room. She edged through the door.

Max stood, pointing his gun at Saffron, who cowered and sobbed on the floor. Max's raging face was still, but his lips were drawn back like the rictus of a psychopathic eagle. His focused fury was frightening, like he was trying to kill Saffron by projecting his hatred at her skull to shatter it. Diane gasped and backed up a step.

He was alien, demon-possessed.

The first deputy pointed his gun at The Tower, who lay crumpled on the carpet. Diane could see his naked, hairy back, but his right leg spasmed like in a grand mal seizure. Other deputies stood over Saffron, pointing guns.

More deputies pushed past Diane into the house. One wrenched Saffron's arms and handcuffed her, then half-marched, half-dragged her out the front door. One deputy aimed his gun down the hall.

Diane yelled, "Kids are back there. They're unarmed. They're all kids!"

Three different octaves of crying vibrated the windows of the house, from teen hysterics and children's sobbing to toddlers' wails.

The other deputy said into his shoulder radio, "Send in the EMTs. We've got one wounded."

Saffron screamed back into the house, "I love you! Don't forget that I love you! Stay together! You're a family! Stay together!"

Max jerked his gun up to point at the ceiling and stalked out the front door. He pulled Diane across the lawn and around to the other side of the car and grabbed her. His roughness scared her. He said,

"Don't ever do that again. Don't ever do that again."

"What happened?" she asked and was afraid to shake off his hands.

"The man wouldn't get down." Max's brown shirt and curly, black hair smelled like acrid gunpowder. His anger solidified to cold remoteness. "He rushed me."

"Oh, God. Oh, God!" She held Max and shook. The heavy muscles under his clothes were solid and reassuring, but the shaking felt like an earthquake rattling her. "Is he dead?"

"I don't know."

They were safe. She was safe. She and Max were safe and this was over.

She thanked God for defending her and Max against those people who were—something, and she couldn't put a name on the idols and infernal tapestry and conspiracy theories and covens. She gasped and sobbed on Max's shirt. Gunpowder stung her nose. Grit and something wet rubbed from Max's shirt onto her cheek. Max's strong arms held her tight. Diane wiped tears off her face, and her palm came away pink with blood.

This was why people said the glory should go to God, because Diane could not have stood up alone to save eight children from that hairy pedophile and his enabling procurer.

That afternoon, shell-shocked P.J. stared through the dust-filmed windows of the Child Protective Services mini-bus.

This couldn't be happening. They couldn't just arrest her parents for no reason. Her parents had saved her from the Indian orphanage and fixed her legs. She had just begun to depend on them. Lobbying the other kids to go to public school had been the first thing that P.J. had ever stood up for, because she assumed that if she talked back or got out of line, Saffron and The Tower would ship her back to the orphanage in India.

Would the government ship her back because she had no parents? She didn't remember how to speak Tamil.

Her gritty eyes burned. She had cried out all her tears under the bunk bed when the cops had kicked in the unlocked door and swarmed into the bedroom. She had railed at them to tell her what had happened to her parents, but they shouted incomprehensible orders and pushed her down on the floor.

Her tear ducts scraped together some moisture, and another mucus-slimy tear oozed out of her eye.

In the front of the bus, Diane Marshall gestured for them to exit through the front door.

Hate boiled through the turgid fear. Marshall had interrogated her without her knowing it and then used what she said—innocently said!—to rip her family apart. Saffron and The Tower were the only family she had ever had.

She cradled Dom, holding him for her own comfort as much as his, and stepped down from the mini-bus with him on her hip. The dazed black toddler clutched a stuffed orca and a sippy cup with one handle. P.J. almost fell and skinned her knees because her legs shook with shock. She was amputated from her parents.

At the sheriff's office, they had told her that a local pastor could take them all in so they wouldn't be broken up.

P.J. hadn't known that they could have dealt the kids out like poker cards to any foster family that might ante up. That's when she started crying again, along with the rest of the kids. Even a stoic Goth can't cope with someone cleaving your parents and your babies away.

Diane Marshall rode over on the bus with them, holding Moonie, the youngest. P.J. hadn't looked at her the whole trip because she was afraid that she might lose it and scream at Diane and slap her, and then they might haul her away to juvey, and she couldn't leave the babies alone.

Outside the bus, a man handed her down. He was light-skinned African-American, so light that his eyes were hazel green. "You're all one family?"

"We were all adopted internationally," P.J. said. "Our family is like a rainbow." The toddler on her hip wailed and hiccupped.

"I'm Daniel Stout," the man said. He was tall, and his arms swayed like weeping willow fronds. "You can call me Pastor Daniel."

P.J. didn't like any of this. She was a stoic Goth, but her parents had raised her to resist authority. She needed to be strong for the babies, but she wasn't going to help this foster-father-crap-monster one bit. "We won't be here long. This is a mistake."

"Of course," he said, but he didn't sound like he believed her, and he waved her into the house.

Max pulled his official car up on the sidewalk, where a man hugged Max's wife.

No man should hug Max's wife.

Max stepped out of the car, setting one calm snakeskin boot on the blacktop at a time, and strolled around the nose of the car. His gaze panned down them, noting pelvis proximity, and his hand rested on the handle of his gun. The man was of some ethnicity, only a shade darker than Max himself, but not Hispanic or Indian. His pelvis was tipped back, less sexual, which was probably why Max's gun was still in its holster, though he already longed to tag this interloper with a Mozambique drill, a firing pattern of two shots to the center mass and one to the head, a guaranteed take-down drill that the British had developed during the Boer War.

Max recognized Pastor Daniel Stout from his picture in *The New York Times,* when he had been indicted for lying and cheating.

The man retracted his arms and asked Diane, "Are you all right?"

She nodded and slapped both hands over her scrunched face.

Max tucked Diane under his arm and didn't bother to make his face look neighborly. "Howdy."

"Hello." The rangy man held out his spidery hand. He was taller than Max by several inches, another strike against him. "I'm Pastor Daniel Stout of the Country Congregational Bible Church."

Dan. This was the Dan in Diane's date book, the Dan who wanted her to BS with him. He was the Dan of the Country Congregational Bible Church, which might be a creepy suicide cult.

Max's arm tensed to punch this guy in the head. Against his inclinations, he kept his voice civil. "I'm Deputy Max Konstantin, Diane's husband."

Dan the Dead Man addressed Max's wife. "What happened that the whole family is in foster care?"

"It's a long story." Her voice was muffled by her hands. "The adoptive father walked around naked."

"Around the girls? That's pedophile grooming behavior." Dan rubbed his mouth in about the place where Max was imagining his knuckles splitting it open.

Diane sighed and dropped her hands from her forlorn face. "Yes. They're going to be shell-shocked, especially P.J., and some of them may be from war regions. This may have reactivated PTSD or just scared the living daylights out of them. If they need clothes or anything," Diane dug a county debit card out of her purse, "here's five hundred in emergency cash. Please keep receipts. If they need to talk, listen, but don't push."

She sighed again, like she always did when her work forced her to make harsh decisions. "They've been through a lot. From what I saw in their records, some of them were old enough when they were adopted to remember the orphanages, and now the adoptive parents have been taken away, and the father is in the hospital. It's just a mess." Diane covered her face again. "But they might have been in an even worse situation. If that disgusting man was raping them, and if that woman adopted them so he could," her voice was hollowed by her hands, "at least they're safe now."

Max tightened his grip around her shoulders and rubbed her arm. She let her hands drop away from her face, and her arms hung at her sides, limp and exhausted. She was traumatized, too.

Dan said, "They may be People of the Lie, Diane, and you rescued the children from them. God was with you today."

Diane nodded, but her face was still scrunched with distress.

Dan glanced at Max. Max's other arm twitched. The preacher was taller than Max and wiry, but Max could beat the holy crap out of him. Max ran his palm over his holstered gun, which still smelled like burnt gunpowder. "We should talk, Pastor Daniel, about your church."

Dan smiled way too big. "Anytime you want to talk about our little Church and what we believe, you just stop by my office and I'll be glad to share with you. Or call me on the phone. Here's my card."

Saturday afternoon, Zeke walked to his barn. Three glass tubes of blood samples from his cattle clanked in his jacket pocket. His only child had vanished sixty-three hours before, and he had slept eight of those sixty-three hours. He tugged his leather jacket closer and clutched the broken zipper against the chill.

When he went out to check on his cattle a few hours ago, he found them hayed and watered, and one of his fences was newly mended. His neighbors had been tending his cattle for two days, and you never know what right fine people you have for neighbors until you can't take care of your livestock for a few days. He hadn't even rung them up. The care of his cattle had just happened, like the benighted secular humanists promulgated that humanity had evolved out of the sludge and just happened, as if there was no beneficent Hand that guided its progress as a single phagocytic cell begat primitive chordates begat ape begat man.

Zeke pushed his barn door open. The door dragged on straw, and a dry puff of air rushed past him. He tugged the recalcitrant door closed behind him, and dark enclosed the barn. Spectral gray scurried along the tops of the stalls and hay bales, sketching horizontal lines in the charcoal gloom. In another minute, gray twilight crept down the stalls and spilled onto the floor and hay bales.

Zeke sidestepped three paces and felt the splintery wall for the switch. Beneath his fingertips, the wall had the texture of tightly woven, thorned rose vines. His index finger grazed the switch, and he flicked his hand upward.

White light blinded him where dark had closed his eyes a moment before. He rubbed his eyes. Blue dots marched across the whited-out barn, and the barn resolved as his eyes acclimated to the glare. Light poured in like a flash flood, revealing color. Gold swarmed into the hay, and raw red filled the boards of the wooden stalls. The horses nickered at the light. One sneezed.

Blazing white showered a blond woman who sat on a hay bale.

Ester! His heart leapt up and his body twitched backward.

The blond girl sat with her long legs crossed, but she was too chubby around the bosom and hips to be Ester. Blond hair, black clothes, and segmented wasp-waist made her a black and gold hornet. Discordance buzzed in his head.

Vanessa Allen.

Thankfulness and hope knotted and popped, leaving him empty and yearning for Ester again. Zeke panted with the torrent of hope and loss and removed his hat to fan away the scalding shock. "What are you doing in here?"

Vanessa said, "I was just looking for something that might mean something."

"What's that supposed to mean?" His hope had burned out, and anger swelled in its place.

Vanessa twiddled her foot impatiently. "I'm a forensic tech."

"You aren't with this here sheriff's department. You're not investigating. You're trespassing." Zeke had pined for Ester these last few days, and oscillating between work and despair left him unable to stop his words. "Get off my property."

He regretted saying it as he walked away, but grief drove him away from the barn. He tugged his hat firmly onto his head.

He blamed whoever had taken Ester, for he couldn't believe that she had gone of her own free will or, worse, done herself harm. Vanessa was probably negligent, careless, but the Devil was in the person who had taken Ester. He knew that Vanessa was not the one to blame, but he couldn't turn back.

Footsteps pittered behind him on the good Texas loam. "Mr. James!"

Zeke should thank God for a chance to apologize, dang it. He pawed the ground with his boots and removed his hat. A lady is a lady until proven otherwise. "Vanessa, I do not blame you for Ester disappearing. I apologize."

"That's all right, Mr. James. Tempers are running high for everybody." She smiled and blinked, batting her eyelashes.

Her flirting got on Zeke's nerves. "My temper is not 'running high.' I do not care to speak with you right now."

Surely that was not a sin, to choose not to speak with someone. Zeke strode for the house, hoping that he would not hear her running after him.

"Mr. James!" Running footsteps, again.

Mwah Dang. His spirit cringed.

She said, "I just want to see her room, her computer. I'm a forensic tech. I might find something to help find her."

"Dusting for fingerprints would do no good," Zeke said. "She hasn't had anyone over in months."

"Maybe I can get on her computer and see if one of those Internet predators has been emailing her. In the Slavemaster case, a man cajoled, manipulated, blackmailed, even threatened women into meeting him, and then he killed them."

"She wouldn't have truck with people like that," Zeke said. "She was coming to the Lord, forsaking worldly things like rock music."

"There are lots of bad people around, Mr. James." Her bright blue eyes were wide and honest, dismaying him because he did not want to talk to her. "At Ted Bundy's trial, everyone said how nice he was. Pedophiles and serial killers are psychopaths, and they know how to play us psychotypicals. Please let me see her computer."

Well, it couldn't hurt. Maybe Vanessa would come up with something, a threat that Essie had discounted, or a man she stopped corresponding with because Jesus had come into her life. "All right. I have some work in the house."

Zeke showed Vanessa to Ester's bedroom, still a little girl's bedroom in many respects. He had bought her furniture from a yard sale when she was six months old and painted it fresh. Christy had stenciled the roses.

He missed Ester so much. If her clomping footsteps, loud for a delicate young woman, were to fall on the linoleum floors, he would fall on his knees and thank God, but the wooden house was silent. He told Nessie, "Her password is John-three-one-six."

Glass tubes filled with blood clinked in his chest pocket. He needed to process the samples. He walked through the kitchen and opened the closet door. Raw wooden steps led into the basement's gloom.

Zeke's biological lab was purely utilitarian. His only concession to decor was that when he attached fresh white bench paper to the black lab countertops, he used colored masking tape correlating with an upcoming holiday, like red and green for Christmas or pastels for Easter. It rivaled a university lab though it was paltry compared to a pharmaceutical start-up. Two lab benches were composed of kitchen cupboards that he reinforced to hold the heavy equipment, topped with impermeable lab resin countertop that resisted stains, acids, caustics, organic solvents, cuts, scratches, and dings. He would have installed them in the kitchen, but they were danged expensive.

Zeke had registered a chemistry consulting business with the county so he could buy the reagents he needed. Chemicals like radioactive tags for Southern blots were regulated, so he filled out the business license form at the county and printed stationery on the computer to buy them from the manufacturers.

Zeke patted his breast pocket as if checking for cigarettes, found the tubes, and held them up to the light. Fluorescent lines striped the ruby red. He inserted the blood sample tubes into the round voids in the centrifuge, slid the lid closed, and set it spinning to separate the blood cells from the flaxen plasma. The centrifuge revved like a whining model airplane engine.

Zeke waited. He hated that he was sitting in his lab feeling the closed centrifuge vibrate as if everything was fine. At that thought, Zeke whipped his newly charged cell phone out of his pocket, thumbed the Send button twice, and listened. It rang one and a half times and Ester's *dulce de leche* voice said, "You've reached the cell phone of Ester James. I can't come to the phone right now," and he flipped the phone closed. When she did turn her phone on next, she would have hundreds of missed calls from him. His earlier reticence at calling her and infringing on her independence seemed stupid.

Above him, louder than the soprano drone of the centrifuge, Vanessa yelled, "Mr. James! Where are you?"

"Down here!" he yelled back. "In the basement!"

Her shiny black shoes and chubby ankles appeared on the wooden stairs. Vanessa ducked to see the basement from the middle of the stairs. "What on earth have you got down here?"

"My lab," Zeke said. "Essie didn't tell you about my lab?"

Vanessa's lips pouched in amused condescension, as if she was kissing a baby. "No. And what do you do in your lab?"

"Genetics," Zeke said. "My herd is the best-studied cattle in the country, genetically speaking."

"So you're cloning milk cows?" She advanced another step.

"Cloning is a circus trick. I'm working on genetic markers, single-nucleotide and restriction-fragment-length polymorphisms that co-segregate with desired behavioral traits, and knocking in pharmaceutically relevant genes." He smoothed his beard and tried not to feel prideful. Repressing pride was easier than normal. The malaise of missing Ester overwhelmed him. "And Red Angus are beef cattle, not milk cows. Dairy cattle have been artificially selected to produce enough milk to feed five calves at once."

Vanessa sashayed down the stairs. "So you're trying to build a beefier cow?"

Zeke felt like his life's work was being reduced to trivia. He squelched the urge to rise in anger. "No. Behavioral genetics."

"All that behavioral genetics stuff is crap."

Zeke shook his head. "Some studies have been flawed, like that Maori 'warrior gene' study. The researchers didn't control for variation in the normal Maori population. Cattle have less intra-breed variation than humans."

"You're making warrior cows?"

"I found a variant of a gene, the monoamine oxidase A gene, which I call 'Mao A' because folks shorten all that to MAOA. I kind of picture it like some little bald Chinese guys sitting on your mitochondria. Anyway, Mao A breaks down all those proteins that anti-depressants keep from breaking down, and it's X-linked. A mutant of Mao A that makes less of it makes cows bad mothers."

She stepped into the basement lab and looked around. "People are bad mothers because they don't give a damn about their kids."

"No, Mao A causes behaviors. Low Mao A correlates with violent behavior in humans."

Vanessa stared at him. Her stare wasn't the guileless glance that Christy slid over his face across a pre-calculus classroom, but a burrowing glare. "It's all upbringing. I'm a quarter Comanche and half German. The Comanche were a gang of serial killers who egged each other on to greater brutality, and the Nazis created a culture of death. If it was genetic, Apaches and Germans would all be murderers."

"It's not a high penetrance gene. My great-grandpappy was Frank James, Jesse's older brother, but that doesn't make me a Rebel insurgent murdering Union soldiers in the Civil War." This argument was unproductive. "Did you find anything on Ester's computer?"

"No," Vanessa said. "Looks like she wiped her hard drive. Did she have a virus recently?"

"I scan them and haven't found any malware. Good thing I back up all our files on a safety site."

Vanessa nodded. "You should have the police look at those, or I can."

Zeke shook his head. Deleting files was an odd thing for Ester to do. Maybe she had met some fellow online and run off with him. His heart swelled a little with hope. Any day, he might get a message from her from Las Vegas or Bermuda, saying that she was a married woman. Elopement must run in families, like violence, or else his sentimental stories about him and Christy had swayed her. But dang, he had wanted to be there. "Essie broke up with her boyfriend, Bobert, a week or so ago. I thought it was strange at the time. Maybe something was going on with her."

"She mentioned that. Have you checked your email lately?"

"Before I went out to see to my cows." He edged toward his computer.

"Okay." Vanessa wandered around his lab, examining bottles. She glanced at everything dismissively, as if even his buffer solutions, organized first by major ion and then by concentration, were as irrelevant as his genetics.

"You must be used to a far grander lab in New Orleans," he said.

"Naturally," she said.

Zeke allowed that a government lab, even a city one, would have more gadgets and gewgaws.

She trailed her fingers across his whining centrifuge. A Mettler balance, a scale for weighing micrograms of powders and worth several thousand dollars to a drug dealer to accurately price his inventory, was next on the bench. She brushed it, and the digital numbers flashed up to 2.470g, then returned to zeroes.

Beside that was an apparatus to run agarose gels.

Vanessa's bare fingers dipped toward the watery buffer reservoir.

"Hey!" Zeke shouted. "That's for Southern blots."

"Oops," she said blandly and retracted her fingers.

That buffer was contaminated with ethidium bromide. He shook his head at her stupidity or recklessness. "Doesn't your fancy lab do Southerns?"

Vanessa shrugged, more the expression of an annoyed teenager than a negative.

"Let's go upstairs." If she was going to be so danged cavalier around chemicals, he didn't want her in his lab. If she didn't kill herself, she would screw up his experiments, and he was in the final stages of submitting a paper for PNAS. One of Zeke's collaborators at UT had been inducted into the Academy and so could submit papers to the *Proceedings*. "We can talk in the kitchen."

"Let's stay here." Vanessa sat down on a lab stool and smiled at him. He wasn't so prideful that her condescension affronted him, but arrogance was unpleasant. He did not turn his back on her in his own house and walk away, however, because that would be rude.

Vanessa ran her fingers through her hair, and long blond strands fell to the side. "I wish the sheriff's office here would listen to me, that they need to look at things like her computer, and do some forensic testing."

Maybe he had been too hard on her. She did seem to want to help. Zeke shrugged. "Deputy Konstantin came by. Inspected her room." Cursorily.

She pulled her jacket back and set her hands on her hips. Her white blouse gaped, and Zeke saw that she did not resemble Ester in breast development. Ester was like her mother had been, small and neat, which is not something that he had made it a point to notice about his daughter, but he lived with her and she walked around in a tee shirt in the mornings without the benefit of a bra. She was his baby. Her body was just a grown-up version of the chubby little legs that had stomped on him all her life.

Vanessa, however, was well endowed. Her shirt was one of those kimono-wrap things that gaped if you turn a little, and she had turned a lot.

Zeke closed his eyes, moved his head and opened his eyes to stare at a drawer on his lab bench. That drawer held boxes of fresh pipette tips, cotton-plugged and unplugged, clean and sterile, blue and yellow.

Vanessa stood up and removed her jacket. Her white shirt looked like netting in the harsh fluorescent light. Her pink bra showed though it.

She said, "It's warm down here."

"Sure is." Motors on the refrigerators and incubators exhausted heat.

"It seems like they could test something, look for fingerprints in her car, or something."

"That's true."

She fanned herself and plucked her shirt, exposing yet more bosom.

Zeke turned away and walked to his lab computer. "I'll just check her email."

Vanessa asked, "You know her email password?"

He shrugged and sat on the chair. "Naturally."

"Did she know that you know it?"

"I checked her email for her when she worked a double shift."

"How cozy." Vanessa swished over to where he sat.

She planted one hand on his chair and leaned over, eye level with the screen.

He turned to say something, but her shirt was hanging open beside him, and the round meat of her breast swelled out of her bra. Her breast trembled with her heartbeat, and a sheen of sweat bubbled from her skin. Pink nipple peeped.

It was, indeed, warm in his basement.

Zeke pushed the lab chair away from the desk and scooted two feet away. "Vanessa, your clothes are in disarray."

"Pardon me?" She stood up and her shirt straightened itself. Her eyes were innocent and sweet, and her blond hair clung to her shoulders in curls.

"Your shirt gapes open immodestly. You should be careful."

"Oh." She tucked the shirt tighter around her. "I didn't know."

"All right, then." Zeke scooted toward her but stayed at a diagonal from the keyboard to leave space between them.

"So you know all her passwords?" Vanessa asked.

"All her passwords are the same thing." He opened up the email site.

Vanessa's voice choked. "I just feel so awful. I feel like it's my fault."

Zeke sucked his lips inside his mouth for a second. "It's no one's fault but the one who took her. There's where the sin lies."

"Right." She laid her hand on his shoulder.

"Maybe you'd like to talk to Pastor Daniel. He's a man of God and can minister to you far better than I could."

She nudged the back of his chair, and it swiveled toward her. Her head dipped, and her lips swooped at him.

Zeke's chair fell over backward and he scrambled over it. His ankle wrenched. "Miss Allen, I don't know what kind of man you think I am, but I am not interested in your worldly ways. You need to leave."

"But, I," her big blue eyes were moist, "I just need some comfort."

The banked anger at her flashed. "I work hard to be a moral man. I am not the kind of man who has sexual relations outside of wedlock with girls the age of my daughter while my own daughter is out there, somewhere, lost. I don't want comfort. I want my daughter back."

Vanessa Allen leaned on the computer desk and stared at him. She drew in a deep breath and, as she sighed, her irritated gaze wandered to the unfinished ceiling beams.

He pointed to the stairs. "Get out."

P.J. sniffed crying-snot back into her sinuses and tried to corral her sibs. The kids were freaking out, and she didn't know what to do. Dom and Moonie had not been separated from Saffron or The Tower since they were adopted. No pre-school. No babysitters. P.J.'s frantic attempts to comfort them did not quiet their operatic crying. The six younger kids howled, child sopranos wailing in six-part cacophony. Every time she caught a couple of kids and tried to get them to meditate, one jumped and ran away, crying that they wanted Saffron and The Tower and to go home.

Connie's traumatized silence screamed louder than the six crying babies. Connie sat under a desk at the back of the garish yellow and blue room. Her shallow breaths fluttered silently. Years ago, after Connie's adoption from Rwanda when she was four, to teach her English, P.J. and Saffron had studiously selected a word for the day and repeated it at every opportunity, fork, fork, fork-fork-fork, until the word lost all meaning for them and jumbled itself into letters, and by supper they giggled every time they said it.

And now, Connie was back in that catatonic funk.

P.J. wiped away her own tears with the backs of her hands because crying was useless, but she couldn't seem to stop.

The three Stout kids watched her while they played video games. Their African-American thumbs, which were lighter than her brown sub-continent thumbs, clicked the plastic controls. Horned monsters lurched across the video screen. When they exploded, green ichor clots dripped down pixilated bricks.

Community, six years old, walked up to the youngest Stout child and slapped her. The girl howled.

"Hey!" P.J. yelled. "We do not engage in violence against our fellow human beings! Why would you do such a thing?"

Community shrugged, saying, "Funny."

"It is not funny, and don't do that again."

Behind her, a demon exploded on the screen.

Mr. Stout, or Pastor Daniel as he introduced himself, stared at P.J. from across the room, and then he smiled when she caught him at it.

A thick, mahogany cross splayed across the white plaster above the fireplace. A graphic crucifix complete with a mortally wounded Jew would have grossed her out, and even the empty torture device was creepy.

She wanted to go home.

The older Stout boy nudged the younger one when Moonie, the eighteen-month-old Russian girl, tugged on P.J.'s pants and asked in a whisper hoarse from crying, "Diaper change?"

Luckily, the police had allowed P.J. to take the diaper bag with them. She found a clean hemp diaper in it and laid Moonie on a towel to change her.

The mother, Mrs. Stout, came over and knelt beside her. She was a thin white woman, and considering that she had a black husband and her kids were *hapa-haole,* she probably wasn't weird about race. P.J.'s coffee-brown skin seemed suddenly rococo.

Mrs. Stout asked, "Can I help?"

"It's okay. I've got it, Mrs. Stout." P.J. wasn't sure if she felt threatened but changing Moonie busied her hands. She wiped her dripping eyes on her sleeve.

Mrs. Stout scooted her legs out from under her. "Call me Melinda."

"All right." It wasn't as impressive as when Diane had given her leave to use her first name. Maybe P.J. was becoming inured to adults.

P.J. flipped the cloth diaper around the toddler and pinned it. "We're getting low on these. Is it okay to use your washing machine?"

"I'll have Daniel get some disposable ones." She motioned Pastor Daniel over. "Pumpkin-pie, we need a couple boxes of diapers," she eyed Moonie and Dom, "sizes four and six, and some pop."

"But the environment," P.J. said. "You can't use disposable diapers."

Mrs. Stout fanned P.J.'s comment out of the air. "You'll only be with us a few days, so the impact on the environment will be minimal."

"I don't know." P.J. didn't like it. She didn't like any of it.

Pastor Daniel squatted and smiled at her. His teeth had a yellow cast, as if he used to smoke. "The environment isn't a case of always and never. Did you have electricity at your house?"

"Well, yeah."

"That has an impact on the environment, because most of our

electricity comes from coal-burning power plants. You just conserve as much as you can and reduce, reuse, and recycle."

Such waffling worried her. "Okay."

"It's like sin," Daniel continued and glanced at the big, ugly cross nailed to the wall. His eyes went soft. "We're all sinners, but you try to reduce how much and how often, because Jesus died for our sins, but He didn't die so we *can* sin."

Shiva, Parvati, and Buddha, he was talking about sin. P.J. tried hard not to let her mouth hang open in disbelief, but her molars were not in contact. Her tongue lay in an unfamiliar cavern. "Okay."

Pastor Daniel smiled at her and revealed too many teeth, like an orca grinning at a seal sunning itself on the beach. "Are you a Christian, P.J.?"

"I don't think so." P.J.'s anxious fingers twitched, wanting to inscribe equations in the air, but she clasped her hands in her lap. They might think demons had infiltrated her and decide an exorcism was in order.

He said, "I'll pray for your soul, P.J."

Under the desk, Connie moaned without lifting her head off her knees.

"Okay. Um, thanks." Her whole world was ass-end up, and her two-day hangover headache pounded her skull.

Vanessa pinched the sun-hot steering wheel with two angry fingers of each hand as she drove her car down Sixteenth Street of stinkass New Canaan, Texas.

That asshole Zeke James thought he was so fucking morally superior because he didn't get his fuck on. What an ass. He thought he was the fuck-all just because she didn't freakishly repress the natural instinct to fuck by submitting to the injunctions of some Imaginary Friend in the

Sky. She slapped the hot steering wheel.

And now she had a case of blue bean. Fuck him. Fuck them all.

She stormed around town in her car, raced by the Foxhead bar where she had been drinking before she was supposed to have picked up Ester, and slid the car around a corner by Shadow Mountain High School, from whence she had graduated with no particular distinction.

Skidding around one neighborhood corner, she hit a cat. Stupid thing didn't deserve to live if that's how stupid it was that it didn't run when a thousand pound car barreled at it. Evolution in action. Law of Natural Selection. She hated cats anyway.

She rubbed her face where the tears she had sprouted for Zeke's benefit had streaked mascara under her eyes. She must look like a tattooed Maori hunter with a stupidass warrior gene. Looking in the rearview mirror, she stuck out her tongue, which is fearsome in Maori warrior culture, but nothing looks dumber than a mascara-streaked blond with a protruding tongue.

She looked back to the road's cracked asphalt and rubbed the hollows under her eyes.

The Country Congregational Bible Church, a beige building with prim, plain glass windows, occupied a corner. If the building had been a woman, she would have worn a long skirt, pinned her long hair back from her face, and sat up straight in her high-backed, hard chair with her wrists and ankles crossed. An older blue sedan with vanity license plates BR DAN was parked beside the front door.

Ah, Pastor Daniel. Maybe he could help her. Coolness reinstated itself. Vanessa whipped her car into the parking lot. In the mirror, she rubbed most of the mascara off her eyes, leaving enough to look smoky and sexy but not enough to look like a skull.

Inside, the church looked like an architectural interpretation of Noah's ark. Wood paneled the walls and formed the long, parallel pews like skinny stalls. Foot traffic had delaminated the long hardwood floor planks.

At the front, a door closed behind the empty pulpit. Vanessa trotted up the center aisle, past the pews and up the steps.

Below a huge mahogany cross nailed to the wall with galvanized spikes, water filled a glass-fronted tank for full-immersion baptisms. It looked like a Jacuzzi some porn director had thought up to film underwater piston shots.

Churches felt alien to her, like a mystery denied. Her mother hadn't bothered to baptize her, so Vanessa had nothing specific to rebel against. She flailed against the nebulous, overwhelming, irrational fog of it all.

She pushed open the door to his office.

Daniel Stout leaned over the desk with his back to her, one hip cocked like a resting horse. She had not noticed how round his butt was—not fat, but muscled, and images of wild nights in New Orleans trickled through her pelvis. She could just walk up behind him and grab him. Maybe she could have him on the desk.

Vanessa was a little chubby, but she had a pretty face and was young and buxom, and men like big tits. Plus, her fetish-wear steel-and-silk corsets cinched her waist. She tamped the anger that Zeke James had provoked into the stillness below and composed her face into an expression of pretty sadness. "Pastor Daniel?"

"Yes?" He turned around, holding a sheaf of papers in his hands.

"I'm really upset about Ester. I feel like it's my fault, and I don't know what to do." The muscles in her face twisted, and she sniffed.

He blinked the round blink of cluelessness. "I apologize, Miss, um, Vanessa, wasn't it?"

She nodded. Her eyes burned as she tried to conjure more tears, but she had exhausted her meager supply.

"I'm very sorry," he said. "I just stopped off to pick up tomorrow's sermon. I must get back home. There's been a problem."

She stepped forward and wrapped her arms around his waist,

huffing dry sobs on his shoulder. "I lost her, and it's my fault."

Pastor Daniel's hands patted her back, but between each pat was a beat to allow her to pull away. His pelvis tipped back. He was taller than she was, maybe half a foot, which felt odd. She was accustomed to being eye-level with most men. Made it easier to plant one on them.

His hands settled on her hips. His long fingers almost touched around the steel bones that encircled her waist. "What is that?"

Maybe he liked fetish wear. She inhaled and plumped her breasts against him.

"I can't counsel you right now." His hands pattered at her shoulders, pushing her away. "If you need to speak to someone now, Brother Vincent, First Baptist, is a deeply religious man, very conservative. I can call him for you."

Shit! "I'll be okay." She sniffed and tried to make it pretty and pitiful.

"If you'll excuse me, I have to lock up the church and go." He hustled her out, locked the church's doors behind them, and trotted to his car, leaving her standing in the gravel parking lot.

Well, fucking-dammit. Stupid, idiot Christian, turning down a chance for a quick screw. Fuck him. Fuck him and everyone like him in this fucking hick town. Vanessa kicked the shit out of her car, and the back quarter panel dented.

What the fuck kind of cheap-ass fibershit was this fucking car made of that a limp girl like Vanessa could put her fucking foot through it? Fuck whatever piss-ant country made this ass-sucking car. Fucking stupid car in this piss-ant town where there wasn't a man hard enough to fuck a big-tit blond.

She kicked the fucking car again, this time in the tire.

Surely some dick in this hick-stick town was up for a quick fuck.

Max sat at his desk near the bullpen, reading his wife's email, looking for anything from Pastor Daniel Stout or the Country Congregational Bible Church that may or may not conflagrate into an Armageddonish funeral pyre.

The extra uniform shirt that he had found in the lost box was too tight through the chest and arms. Blood had sprayed on him, so he had bagged and logged his uniform shirt as evidence. He had washed the blood off his face with paper towels and coconut and rose foaming soap in the bathroom. Between the soap, the residual gunpowder, and the tinge of fear-sweat, he smelled like a gunfight in a Thai whorehouse. If he luminoled himself, he would glow like a turquoise banshee.

At the desk in front of Max's, George played computer solitaire. An ace was flipped up, but George didn't move it.

Other officers go on leave after they kill someone, but Max, *Feo, Fuerte y Formal,* "he was ugly, strong, and serious," the Hispanic macho ideal. After he shot someone, he typed up the paperwork. The typing took a little longer because his hands shook, but no one could see that.

Max scanned Diane's email. She logged on several times every hour. Once, he had been called away from his desk while hacking her account, and she had been locked out and had gone freaking nuts, nearly launched a hacker investigation. That would have been embarrassing, and it very well might have gotten him arrested by the ate-up anti-terrorist people.

In Diane's email, nothing seemed to be from Dan. Stout was grooming her to be seduced, if he hadn't slept with her already. If someone looks like they are doing something suspicious, they are doing something suspicious. The two of them looked suspicious.

First, Stout was encouraging her to lie to her husband. Max knew that guy was behind all those missing hours. "Dan" was all over her date book.

Second, they were too damn physically familiar with each other. When Max had driven up after Diane dropped off the Lessing kids, Stout's hands had been all over her, casually, as if it happened all the time. Typical grooming behavior.

The worst part was that a fucking hypocrite like Pastor Daniel Stout, so holy as the head of a church, might convince himself that he was in love, and that if he and Diane had sex, it was sanctioned and fated. Stout could not simply fuck. Sanctimonious types like Stout broke up homes.

Max's teeth grated. His jaw clicked.

An image of the two of them bumping uglies in the missionary position ran across his imagination. Diane's face was hidden in the flowered sheets of their own bed. Pastor Dan's shadow, cast from the lamp on Diane's nightstand, sprawled over the white walls and blue drapes.

Max grabbed his empty holster.

If they only fucked, Max didn't care. He had had more lovers than he cared to count before he married Diane. She had been active, too, she admitted. Max did not know why it was an admission but went along.

So what if she scrogged someone after their wedding ceremony instead of before? It was just genital stimulation. Did not mean shit.

Two pale hands thumped Max's desk, and Max looked up at Vanessa Allen.

"Good Lord," Vanessa said. "What are you so mad at?"

"Nothing." Max minimized the computer window with Diane's email.

Her breasts were practically hanging out of her white shirt, and he tapped his pencil on the desk to focus his eyes away from them. The shirt had no buttons and was wrapped around her like the top half of a bathrobe. She said, "I'm worried about Ester James."

"We all are." Max looked at her eyes to get his retinas off her boobs. Her jewel-blue eyes were moist with tears.

Vanessa drew in a shuddering breath, and her breasts bobbled in her shirt, threatening to pop out. "No, I'm really worried about her. I'm worried that we don't have any leads, and what that means."

"We have a lead. Here." He handed her one of the boxes of samples he had collected from her car last night. "Brown smear on a surface. Might be blood. Go do some forensic voodoo."

"You didn't tell me you had a lead! That's marvelous!" Vanessa opened the cardboard box and shook out the swabs. "Looks like mud."

"Thought you were going to go to the health food store for agar or commandeer the high school chemistry lab. Do what you can. The state lab always takes months or years. I already sent this over. Really, blood or not-blood would tell me a lot."

"Why didn't you just Luminol it?"

That was a dumb question. Even dumb cops knew that Luminol is your last resort, let alone smarty-pants forensic techs. "Might be rust, might be dirt, both of which have enough iron to activate Luminol. And that Luminol crap destroys the evidence."

She stroked her blond hair. "Where did you get the sample?"

Max grinned at her. "From a truck."

"Oh! A trucker. Those truckers are all screwed up." She frowned at the sample. "I'll see what I can do. She's officially a missing person today."

"Actually, she's an official missing person tomorrow."

"But you said you'd start investigating on Thursday morning." Her expression went surprised and confused. "Please tell me you did."

"Between you, the sheriff, my wife, and that preacher, this thing was in full swing by nine o'clock Thursday morning. Couple hundred volunteers ran all over the woods, poking the bushes with sticks. They're still out there, as far as I know. Other people went door to door, showing folks her picture. An APB went out that morning, and every police and sheriff's department in Texas and Louisiana has a flyer with her picture. I've hunted down tangential people, tertiary contacts, and badgered them. Her ex-boyfriend Bobert? Clean. Her dad? His call data records check out as per your call to him, and he even talked to his preacher's house earlier that night on the phone from his home. No weird cell phone tower pings from his phone. And he doesn't smell guilty to me."

"You've already gotten a warrant to tap his phone?"

"You don't need a warrant. Smith v. Maryland, 1979. Expectation of privacy of the phone number called is neither reasonable nor legitimate, so a pen register is not a search covered by the Fourth." He sucked his teeth to keep from looking immodest. "I sleep with a lawyer."

"So Zeke James talked to the preacher that night," she said. "Maybe he told them that Ester would be alone. There's something weird about that creepy little church."

Max pondered. He could check out that creepy little church in connection with the Ester James case. That kind of leverage would be interesting.

Vanessa pressed her hands to her chest, presumably to keep her hands from shaking but drawing his attention back to her voluminous breasts again. Her breasts were substantially more entertaining than the lunge-gunshots-splatter scenario that nagged his head. "She might have met someone online. She broke up with Bobert suddenly. You could check to see if some psycho was emailing her. Her dad knows her email passwords. You remember the Slavemaster case?"

Max nodded and ran his hand through his hair. A fingernail snagged on a knot. Black, curly hairs fell in his lap. He should be careful about that.

Vanessa said, "Ester was so sweet that she could have been bamboozled by a creep. There. I've given you two things to look into, and I can't do a damn thing myself." A tear rolled down her cheek. She covered her face with her hands.

George turned away from his computer solitaire game and stared at her.

Max swung around his desk, took her arm and led her to their conference and interrogation room. She covered her face with her hands the whole way. He did not flip on the videocam. No need to record the histrionics of a young woman whose friend was missing and presumed dead, and he could replay every word in his head.

At the door, he set Vanessa on course into the room and twisted closed the horizontal blinds in front of the observation booth's mirrored glass.

In the conference room, she sat heavily in one of the chairs and half-lay on the table with her head resting on her crossed arms. Her breasts squished on the table edge. That looked uncomfortable. He should stop worrying about the comfort of her breasts, and he should stop thinking about her breasts entirely.

Wow, but they were big. Not deformed-big, like those exotic dancers who have four or five implants stuffed into each boob, but pillowy.

Thinking about Pastor Daniel Stout fucking Diane had him all riled up. He needed to back off. He sat beside Vanessa.

She said, "Everything I do seems wrong and I'm sorry that I was late picking her up and I can't help. I hate it that I can't help."

He patted her shoulder. "We all wish we could do more."

"It just seems like I'm missing something."

"Yes. We're all frustrated." He fell into the habits that he thought of as daddy-mode, which meant echoing his kids' emotions back at them and waiting out the storm. He had perfected the method when his daughter hit menarche. Grown women are as logical as round robot vacuum cleaners compared to a thirteen-year-old girl in the throes of brand-spanking-new hormones. More than once, he had patted Tatiana's shoulder and asked what she was crying about, and she'd wailed, "I don't know!"

Vanessa crawled with her arms to turn toward him. She said into the table, "I deal with murders every day in New Orleans. I dust for fingerprints and I swab for DNA and I analyze gunk under fingernails, and I learn something to help the person who was killed. I can't do any of that here. I don't even know what to do with this sample that you gave me because I don't have a PCR machine or a gel apparatus or anything!"

"We don't have a crime scene or a body. She may not be dead." Max patted her shoulder again. Even her shoulder was featherbed soft.

"You and I know that three days gone means three days dead. That's the way this bitter old world works. The civilians may not want to believe it, but we know it."

"Yeah, usually the case."

Vanessa wiped her face with her hands. Her cheeks were wet.

Max handed her a tissue. "We could still find her."

She wiped under her eyes with the tissue. "Do you think a serial killer is involved?"

"Way too early to talk about serial killers." Getting the public all riled up with talk of psycho killers on the loose was irresponsible and ludicrous. They had organized search parties for Ester. They might organize lynch mobs for a hypothetical serial killer, and they might catch someone not so hypothetical. "We don't know whether we have even one murder. We have a missing woman."

"We have a missing woman *here*," Vanessa corrected. "Are there any missing women or girls nearby? There's a major interstate. There was that trucker serial killer."

"This is all premature." And wrong-headed.

"That's what the police always say," Vanessa said, and she peered at him. "The police always say that there isn't a serial killer around until they have ten victims or twenty or more lying dead in the morgue and it's so obvious that there is a serial killer that even the public has figured it out and screams for the police to do something."

"You know a lot about serial killers," Max said. She was probably one of those Ted Bundy groupie sickos who read true-crime slasher porn. She was also right. Law enforcement isn't set up to find serial killers. The term "linkage blindness" refers to how jurisdictions can't share information.

Vanessa said, "We have at least three active serial killers in New Orleans right now. I keep finding the same DNA and the same fibers on dead women, but the last thing that the police want to hear is that they have three maniacs slitting drunk women's throats, strangling them, and kicking them to death. It puts a damper on Mardi Gras. The tourism board gets upset. The prosecuting attorney couldn't convict even if a guy killed a nun in the courtroom in full view of the jury on national TV."

"Same DNA?" That might actually be something.

Vanessa nodded. "You'd think that particular idiot would wear a condom, considering he tends to kill prostitutes, but I guess he figures that, considering how much blood he wallows in, a little vaginal fluid isn't real dangerous." She sat up straighter. "It's like they're all over the place, an infestation of serial killers."

"There aren't that many serial killers around. We obsess about serial killers and such bogeymen because we have an innate, copious capacity for fear. Back when we were cavemen, we had lots of things to fear, like saber-toothed tigers and flash floods and dropping dead of an infected spider bite." Max shook his head. This was what talking to a pretty blond did to him: he became pompous, but every lawman has pet theories. "Serial killers aren't as common as people think because TV and the movies glorify the few prolific ones, like Ted Bundy and the Green River Killer, and they make up all those stupid movie villains. A real serial killer is a murderer who kills three people with a cooling off period between, not a psycho genius who leaves enigmatic clues like the

Zodiac killer or BTK."

"No," she said. "Serial killers believe they're vampires, or killer clowns of God, or top predators like sharks. They're not human. The FBI guys create those profiles of them. They always do weird things the same way, like a ritual. They betray themselves with their MO and signature."

Max nodded sideways, a gesture of equivocation rather than agreement. "Most serial killers just kill in different ways or they learn to take a baseball bat or a tarp with them the next time, or they learn a new sexual trick, or they have something different in their pockets, and then they don't have a 'signature' or 'MO' and thus the smarty-pants Behavioral Analysis Unit guys at the FBI never catch on that it's the same person."

"No. I've studied them. The FBI guys are dead accurate on those profiles." Her intent expression was amusing in its innocence.

Max explained, "Those 'profiles' are cookie-cutter jobs, 'white male, between fifteen and fifty, sexual perversions, high school dropout, thinks he's killing his mother due to prior child abuse, uses alcohol or drugs,' every damn time. That ViCAP links MOs, not suspects, so it's useless. MOs are too similar between killers and too variable over time and with opportunity. They do over a thousand profiles a year. Even a blind squirrel occasionally finds a nut."

"No," Vanessa said. "No. It can't be. I've read all this stuff for work. I've based conclusions on all this stuff." She stared at her hands, horrified, like the test tubes of wrongly concluded evidence were still clasped in her hands.

Max bounced the pen on the conference room table, and his fingers slid down the barrel. "Every serial killer who has ever been caught was apprehended by good ol' fashioned police work: means, motive, opportunity, connections, witnesses, suspects. Ted Bundy was nailed on a traffic stop for driving a car with stolen plates. Not the FBI. Not smartie county attorneys. Just little guys doing their job. Those profilers wouldn't know if their wives were screwing around on them until they got the postcard from Mexico."

Vanessa raised one blond eyebrow over her bloodshot blue eyes. She leaned over, and her breasts bulged out of her shirt at him. The touch of her hand on his surprised the hell out of him because he had not seen her hand move, but he had not been watching anything in the room other than those whipped cream breasts. She asked, "Do you need to talk?"

"Nah," he said.

Her hand flipped. He probably should retract his own hand, but didn't. In other men, every nerve in their bodies would have strained to migrate to that hand, but a cold line pressed Max's spine, chilling him.

She asked, "Did you get divorced recently?"

"No. Not getting divorced, either."

Her thumb rubbed his first finger. "Do you think your wife is cheating?"

"Nope."

"I'm sure she's not. Not on a guy like you."

"She's just working late a lot, lately."

Vanessa nodded at him. "That must be tough. Did all of your previous lady friends work a lot?"

In college it seemed like his girlfriends were all over him, doing everything from pressing his shirts to waking him up at four in the morning for spontaneous sex. "You get a house and a lawn and two careers and kids, and time gets tighter."

"She must be working really hard. I mean, it's after six o'clock. Is she home yet?"

"She's at the office."

Vanessa nodded again. "Is that why you were so mad when I got here?"

Max frowned and looked away.

"Right," she said. "I'm sure she has a very good reason. Not all women are complete whores. We have a whole different standard of conduct in New Orleans. Women do whatever because they're wasted off their asses, as you can see on the *Wild Girls* videotapes. But in Texas, things are different, right?"

"Right." Had he smelled liquor on Diane when she got home? He could not remember.

From behind the mirrored window, Max heard the sharp trill of metal blinds snapping together. Someone was watching them. He expected nothing less from his smarmy deputies.

He disengaged her hand. "Are you all right now?"

She nodded, but she looked sad again.

He said, "Go on home. I'll call you if I find anything."

"My car is broken down. I bummed a ride off a friend."

"Really? It's only two years old. Well, I'll give you a ride home. Interesting license plate you have there."

"Yeah, well, it's a brutal world, isn't it? You've got to be hard as a callus to survive."

From the observation booth, there was a rustling like someone getting the hell out of the way, and a door slammed.

She followed him out of the conference room and through the bullpen. As he passed his desk, he stopped to shut off his computer because his co-workers would plant porn on it if he left it on. He jiggled the mouse.

A square at the bottom of the screen, labeled ACCA.Dia..., blinked.

Ah, shit. Diane's email account had been open for half an hour. She had probably called the damn Homeland Security. He clicked it closed and retrieved his gun from his locked desk drawer.

At Max's car, Vanessa got in the passenger door. Policy was that ride-alongs take the back seat, but what the hell. The car had been in the sun. Greenhouse effect had heated the air inside to coffee temperatures. He started the engine and pulled out of the parking lot toward her house. The first street light was red.

Vanessa gestured leftward with one lazy finger. "Turn here."

"You can't get to your mother's house that way." The light turned green and he went straight.

"There's something I want to show you," she said.

After ruminating on the hand-holding incident in the conference room, Max had a pretty good idea what she wanted to show him, but congratulating himself on his studliness might be premature. He was on the far side of forty, past the danger zone where young women might sport. Yet he had heard that subtle zing in her voice when she talked about loose New Orleanean women, like herself.

The air conditioner chilled the police car. The cold clung to his skin.

He glanced at her and did not smile. "Is it connected to Ester James?"

"Sure."

He drove through the small business district, past the Lone Star Grocery, into the thin ring of suburbs. "You can just tell me about it."

"If that's what you'd like."

That was sexual innuendo. "Tell me."

She turned sideways in the seat belt to face him. "The kidnapping or initial assault had to have been done quietly. You talked to Ester's manager and other people working at the Lone Star that night?"

"Every last one of them," Max said. Maybe it was not all sexual innuendo. His shoulders unkinked. "She clocked out at eleven-oh-three. The Lone Star folks all said that Ester walked out swinging her purse, and she walked all the way in front of that long row of windows where they could all see her, and then she fell into a black hole. No one saw the car."

"Might not have been a car," Vanessa said. "Might have been a truck.

No one saw anything, so there couldn't have been a long or intense struggle. She probably got into the vehicle willingly or was quietly coerced. Who could have done that?"

"You, for one," Max said, "But the Foxhead's bartender remembered you in there." She had limited opportunity, unknown means, and no known motive. The Foxhead bar was across the street from the Lone Star Grocery. The bartender and his free-loading brother remembered her in the bar, and her credit card had run at ten fifty-five, eleven-twelve and eleven-thirty, not leaving time for a kidnapping and murder, and it did appear that Ester must have been transported to a second crime scene, and thus the receipts shored up Vanessa's approximate if belated timeline. Vanessa had been later than five minutes picking Ester up, but emphasizing that seemed cruel. "Ester's manager was one of our initial suspects because some of the other employees thought she might have had an affair with him, and he's married, but he stayed in the store for over an hour after she left, then he called home from his cell phone, and then a very short amount of time passed before his wife said that he arrived home."

"The wife might be covering for him. Or their clocks might be fast."

Max shook his head. "He logged into his email account from home that night, and it fits with the time frame. It's not perfect, but it's indicative."

"Any RSOs in the area?" Registered Sex Offenders.

"Most of them are registered for date rape or molestation of their own kids. We don't have any Tier Threes at all." Tier Three sex offenders are very likely to commit more crimes and are considered a danger to the community and society, yet they are tagged and released like cutthroat trout in a fish study.

Vanessa nodded. "But whoever it was, either a man she met online or someone from that church, she got in the car willingly."

"Or someone shoved a gun in her face and she went quietly."

"Yeah," Vanessa said. "Possible. Turn here." She pointed leftward.

Max turned down the street where he had met P.J. Lessing. More cars parked in the driveways on this cold, late Saturday afternoon, and a few bundled kids played outside under the careful watch of parents in lawn chairs, also wearing jackets, some reading or listening to headphones. One man read a paperback novel, which rested atop a shotgun that lay across his lap.

People were already getting paranoid, and only one pretty girl was missing.

Vanessa said, "He might have driven her right down here. The vacant lot is the nearest patch of wilderness."

"It's a pretty big lot. Walked it yesterday." Max pulled to the side of the residential street. The Lessing house's windows were dark, and the cars were in the same spots. Saffron must still be in the lockup, where she would stay until Monday morning because Sin Nombre County judges don't work Sundays. The Tower was in critical condition. He was tough to have held on this long after Max nailed him with a Mozambique drill.

Max pointed into the scrub brush zone. "The vacant lot extends over yonder behind those houses to a small bayou."

"Let's take a look." Vanessa opened the door and got out.

"Hey!" Max leaned over to call her back but the door slammed shut. *Aw, hell.* He got out and pressed his hat onto his head, careful not to crush the crease or flatten the brim. The air was still February cold, maybe in the high fifties, and he zipped his jacket.

Vanessa strode toward the brush and straggly pine trees.

"Hey!" Thorns on plants snagged his pants as he hurried.

Texas, being a large state, has different climate zones. Sin Nombre County is about eight hundred square miles in the eastern part of the state, north of Houston, a ways south of Dallas-Forth Worth, and caddywampus east of Waco. The vegetation is an intersection of tall plains grasses, scrub brush, piney woods, and Louisiana-like swamp.

"Did you see anything odd out here?" she asked.

"Looked like teenagers had a beer party out here a couple weeks ago. Those houses are close. If she had screamed, people would've heard."

"Not if she was already unconscious. Besides, people run their heaters and close their windows this time of year."

He had thought of that. Even though they had been walking only a few minutes, the thick grass, bushes, and pine trees blocked the low, ranch-style houses.

The reddening sun neared the horizon over Vanessa's right shoulder. The trees' shadows black-striped the dry grass.

He said, "Killing her out here would be risky. Someone might see."

Vanessa shook her head. "Serial killers are adrenaline junkies, considering what little adrenaline they secrete. That's one of the theories about why they kill people: because nothing riles them except the most vile acts. If you or I killed someone, even in self-defense, we'd freak. We'd be shaky and tormented. Have you ever shot someone?"

"Law enforcement doesn't talk about that," Max said. "If we have shot someone, talking about it is either psychopathic bragging or a trigger for post-traumatic flashbacks. If not, some guys think it makes them look inexperienced or wussy."

"So you have," Vanessa said.

"I didn't say that."

"You said 'we' when you talked about people who had, and you said 'some guys' and 'them' about guys that hadn't. What did it feel like?"

Astute. Diane would have caught it, too. "Ten years ago, a guy came at me after he beat the shit out of his wife and kid. The kid was only two. The bastard came at me, and I utilized the situation to put a bullet in him."

That was the first time he had killed someone. Max had indeed freaked out afterward, screaming at the man's dead body to stay down or he would shoot him again, even after it was obvious that the nearly beheaded, quivering corpse was not going to stand up. The little boy was even more traumatized by watching his father's head explode and splatter him with skull splinters and brain clots.

"You 'utilized the situation?' You wanted to?" she asked.

Her pushy needling was uncalled for. "Most of the times I've gotten into trouble in my life involved pummeling some bully who needed it."

"So you've acted the chivalrous rescuer before?" Vanessa asked.

"Yeah," he admitted. He should have handled those situations differently. Part of the reason that he had joined the sheriff's office, Diane had mused at him one night in bed, was so he could act on his protective instincts. Diane was wrong. The sheriff's office had made him more dangerous. Instead of beating the crap out of a man who had crossed the line, now he killed them, and the idiot office gave him a medal for it.

Seventeen times. The Tower would make it eighteen.

"I think you're wonderful." Vanessa stepped toward him.

He felt crowded by her even though she was two feet away. He still stank of gunpowder. "You're wrong."

"I wish someone had stood up to my dad. Maybe my mom would have turned out differently."

"How'd she turn out?" Max asked.

Vanessa looked off over the bushes, away from the setting sun. The red light turned her hair strawberry blond, and her face was shadowed. "Not so well."

"Did he hit you?" Max asked. His face warmed. His hands tensed.

"He hit everybody." She stuck her hands in her pockets.

"Would you rather that I'd been there, and that I'd shot him?" He shook one foot that seemed to be on the verge of cramping.

"When I was a kid," she said, "I thought about getting a gun to protect us. You probably saved that kid from trying to kill his dad himself."

Max's holstered gun dragged on his belt, and he grabbed the thick leather and jiggled the stupid thing. "He was only two."

"Matter of time. He would have had to either kill his father or allow himself and his mother to be beaten, maybe killed. Oedipal, in a Darwinian way."

"Your father left. Maybe that guy would have left them alone."

"Naw. He would have found another woman and had another kid, and then that kid would have to make that decision, too."

"Jesus," Max said.

"Men like that don't change," Vanessa said. "People don't change."

"That's a dark view." That was a stupid thing to say. Max thought that way, too, and it was probably accurate more often than not.

"It's the truth. When people show you their true colors, you're a fool if you don't believe them. I think you're a hero."

"I'm not." Even if he liked the sound of it, losing his temper was not heroic.

"No wonder I felt drawn to you from the very beginning. I knew that you were the one to find out what happened to Ester. You're a knight in shining armor."

"You're romanticizing, and I'm married. Step back."

She took a half-step toward him. Her breasts almost touched his chest. She was only an inch shorter than he was, if that. "I wish you'd been there for me when I was a kid," she said. "You want to go for a drink?"

"Shouldn't," he said. "Need to get home. It's getting dark."

"Your wife won't be home for hours."

The paperwork for the two Lessing perps needed to be finished for Monday. Even though The Tower was in the ICU, he was still a perp. "I have responsibilities."

She laughed. "We don't have many responsibilities in New Orleans. I keep forgetting about those things."

Coming from her, New Orleans sounded like a perennial drunken party, which was probably a half-accurate description, a drunken party with at least three serial killers. The dark side of the city-wide open bar was bar fights and lawlessness.

She said, "Come on, one drink. You've had a long week, considering that you're putting in time on a Saturday night. You deserve it." She linked her arm though his. "We're just friends, out for a drink. Colleagues. Let's swap war stories."

"Can't," he said. "Need to get home."

"Okay, let's just walk this lot, and see if there's anything to find." She set off, stepping high over the dead prairie grasses and wild maize in those thin, black pants and ballerina slippers. It was fortunate that it was February, and the rattlesnakes were hibernating.

Max had left his evidence-collecting duffel bag with a digital camera, baggies, gloves, forceps, and whatnot in his car.

"Where's that water hole?" she called.

"To your right. Maybe a hundred yards." He followed.

Long-legged Vanessa kept ahead of him. He was careful not to break one of his legs falling on the wobbly, sedimentary rocks. He had broken his ankle in his middle twenties, and the calcified break still pinged when he stepped on it wrong. A break now, in his middle age, would more than ping.

"Up here?" she asked.

"Almost there."

The soil thinned and gave way to stark limestone outcroppings. The white stone was eroded in pits and curves. Dead seedpods clung to twisted acacias' winter-bare branches. River birch, all thin lines now, grew in the moister soil near the bayou.

"This it?" she asked and swept her arm, indicating the brook trickling into the rusty swamp.

"Yep. It's small." On the other side, a thicket of black alder skeletons rooted in a patch of deeper soil. He rubbed his chin.

An evergreen magnolia tree, almost sixty feet high, shaded the stagnant pond from the red setting sun. He stopped and leaned against it. Someone had pruned the branches off the bottom ten feet, exposing its smooth trunk. In the summer, this tree would produce white magnolia blossoms a foot across, and the flat land at its base would be a fragrant, romantic spot for a picnic. Now the pond was wintry and dead-looking, like a chemical spill surrounded by dead bushes and acid-etched stone.

"How deep do you think it is?" she asked.

"Three feet. I lay on that rock on the other side there," a limestone tongue overhung the crescent pond, "and poked the bottom with a stick."

"Okay." Vanessa stuck her hands in her jacket pockets.

With her hands restrained like that, and her shoulders hunched in disappointment, she was less overtly sexual. He patted her shoulder. Even through her jacket, she was soft. He liked soft women, he had to admit. Diane was soft in the right places, though he encouraged her to eat so she would be more of a handful. Skinny women looked prepubescent. "We'll find her, but she's not here."

"If she's not here, then she might be alive," Vanessa said.

"Yeah." He did not let any hope lighten his tone.

"Yeah." She sounded just as dejected as he did.

His hand lay on her shoulder, and he stood behind her.

She stepped back with one foot.

He touched the towering magnolia tree behind him for balance. His hand was flat against her back. His biceps contracted and swelled against the constriction of his borrowed shirt. The cold night seeped under his jacket like icy water.

Her blond hair in front of him smelled like pears. Pale strands snarled on the rough fabric of her black jacket. His inner ape wanted to comb them aside, but he took half a step backward. His back bumped the tree.

She stepped backward.

If he inhaled deeply to speak, his chest would brush against her back. His palm and fingers were flat on her shoulder.

He didn't move away from her, couldn't even touch his handgun in its holster on his hip, not when she turned, not until her lips touched his.

He was numb by that point, and as after frostbite, burning set in. His hands reached into her hair for warmth and wrapped around her body to thaw him. Her mouth was warm.

The swamp grotto darkened as the sun sucked under the horizon.

He spun and pushed her up against the tree, struggling with her clothes and his. She wore a metal-laced, black bustier under her clothes, but it was crotchless.

She helped him unbutton the tight shirt, and he boned her pillowy body there against the tree in the cold February air and wind with only the tree rustling overhead.

Once, when she groaned, he hissed, "Shhhh," in her ear, but other than that, he didn't speak. He couldn't. She gasped, and he covered her mouth to keep her silent. The cold shook him, and he could barely move and couldn't breathe.

Just when Diane was ready to freak because her email account was locked, it clicked open. She checked her email with the relief she felt at seeing a level plain spread before her after driving miles on a road-hugging cliff. Sounds of typing came through her open office door. Three other ACCAs down the hall were working on Saturday night, too. For a county of eight hundred square miles, they had a large staff, but every law enforcement jurisdiction in the border states had a large caseload, between the illegal aliens, especially the OTMs, and the drugs, guns, crime, and vice that ran across the border. Even though Sin Nombre County was hundreds of miles away from the Mexican-US border, three highways ran through it.

The note from Daniel about canceling their Bible study was not unexpected, considering that he suddenly had eleven children in the house. Bible study was such a pleasure, to talk about God and morals that were not constrained by the convoluted Texas statutes and lawyer ethics, which essentially dictated rules concerning the transfer of money and little else. Bible study was a different mental task than her usual one, which was how to wrestle Texas laws to fit the crime they were confronted with. Criminal law, as it is practiced, is not an intellectual exercise. It's one-upmanship. It's scoring debating points. It's blasting a crime with bright white light to convince a jury there is no shadow of a doubt. No wonder people think lawyers are slimy.

She wondered how the eight Lessing siblings were getting along over at the Stout house and decided to drop by, just to make sure that Daniel understood what he should and should not ask P.J. without a County Attorney representative present.

Plus, now that she was calmer, she needed to talk to P.J. about The Tower's prognosis. The hospital had called. It did not look good.

Driving over to Daniel's house took a few minutes. Not much traffic congested New Canaan on a Saturday evening. Most people kept loaded shotguns on the gun racks on their pickups, even young people out on dates, which meant dinner out would be at one of the chain restaurants that served breakfast all day and sugary pie. They scurried into restaurants, greeting each other quickly in an effort to be done and go home. People peered out the dusty windows. The light was failing.

Diane called home from her cellular while driving. Tatiana assured her that she and Nicholas were fine. There were plenty of leftovers for them to eat, and neither of them had plans to go out that night. "No one's going out," Tatiana said. "It's weird out there."

"Okay, honey. Take care of your brother until we get home."

At Daniel's trim little house, she knocked.

Pastor Daniel answered the door. "Hey," he said and smiled.

Diane loved that joyful, surprised smile. "We should talk about P.J."

"Come in," he moved out of the doorway so she could enter.

Diane went into his house and waved at Melinda, who grinned at her while strapping a disposable diaper on one of the little Lessing kids.

Daniel smiled at his wife across the room and said to Diane, "She's a great mother. She would have liked to have had a bunch more kids, eight or ten, bless her heart, but it's tough on a minister's salary."

"I'll bet," Diane said. It was tough raising two kids on two county employees' salaries.

"There is one more thing," Daniel muttered to her.

She turned. "Yeah?"

"You didn't mention Ester James's outburst in church last weekend to your husband, did you?"

"No. I didn't think it was relevant."

"Good," Daniel said. "I don't think so either. Now, to what do we owe the pleasure?"

Diane dropped her voice and leaned toward him. "The hospital called about their adoptive father who was shot. He might not make it."

"No." Daniel laid his slim hand over his heart.

"We shouldn't tell the younger kids, and we should keep them home from school so that they don't hear anything."

"Yes, yes, of course."

Diane said, "And I just wanted to stress that you guys shouldn't ask P.J. anything about that night."

P.J. watched them, Diane Marshall and Pastor Daniel, sitting primly on the couch, facing her. Diane still wore the beige slacks, white shirt, and pearl necklace she had worn to P.J.'s house that morning. Her hair, which she had taken down at the sheriff's office, was twisted into its customary bun again. Her hands were folded in her lap. Pastor Daniel leaned forward, his elbows resting on his knees, his hands clasped.

P.J. pushed back farther into her chair. She was dizzy.

This morning, she had awakened in her own bed in the girls' room, covered by the quilt that Saffron had made out of their old clothes, anticipating a Saturday of lolling on the couch, reading, finishing her homework, helping Saffron with her beading and cooking, then chatting on the computer far into the night, but then that Marshall woman had arrived, and then three gunshots blasted in the living room.

At the first shot, P.J. shoved the babies under the bunk bed, then the older kids, then she crawled in front of them all as the second shot boomed.

They cowered until the deputies stormed the bedroom and dragged them out from under the bed. P.J. had bruises on her wrist where the deputy literally dragged her away from the babies and shoved her down on the floor. The long, hollow barrel was dark inside, and the deputy's face at the top was twisted with anger. She tried to crawl back to the kids to shield them from the guns, but the deputy kicked her back.

Community, the first-grader from Iraq, stared at the guns and did not say a word.

Connie, who was ten years old but had lived her first four years in Rwanda before Saffron adopted her, curled into a stiff ball.

Everything had changed so fast.

Last night, P.J. and Sanjay, a physics major at an Indian Institute of Technology, had been working on tensor math through a chat window with webcams aimed at their scratch paper. Shadow Mountain High School did not teach tensor math in freshman algebra. Sanjay would be logging on in two hours, at nine o'clock her time. He was on the other side of the world and had slept through her family's breaking apart. She wanted to talk to Sanjay.

Diane pursed her lips, as if she was going to say something distasteful. "P.J., we need to talk about what you heard the night that Ester James went missing. You told Deputy Konstantin that you heard people or animals, plural, and then you told me that you heard something like cats chattering at birds, or tumbleweeds, but then something changed. When your mother was there, you said that you didn't hear anything. We need to know why you changed what you said. Did your mother threaten you?"

"Saffron didn't threaten me. Are Saffron and The Tower okay?"

"You said your adoptive parents wouldn't like you talking to us because they were hippies. Did they tell you to change what you said?"

"They didn't do anything. Were they shot?"

Diane asked, "Did one of them hit you?"

"No. Why aren't you answering me about Saffron and The Tower?"

Pastor Daniel asked Diane, "What about saffron and towers?"

Diane raised her hands as if she was keeping them away from a hot fire. "Her parents call themselves 'Saffron' and 'The Tower.'"

Pastor Daniel sat up straighter. "The Tower? Your father is named The Tower, like the Tarot card?"

"Yeah," P.J. said. "Like the Tarot card. Where are they?"

Pastor Daniel shook his head and muttered something.

Diane said, "Saffron is in jail, but she's fine. She yelled to you guys."

P.J. nodded. She had heard Saffron screaming. Diane had not mentioned The Tower yet. Her ears felt muffled, like a thick, cotton sari had fallen over her head and she couldn't quite see Diane and Pastor Daniel sitting on the couch. Their forms were there, but the image reflected on her eye without reaching her brain.

The world-ending panic was the same as when Laxshmi, her favorite of the workers in the orphanage, had told her that her new mother was coming to take her to America, and had taught her to say Hello, Mommy, I love you, in English.

"But I don't want to go to America," she said.

"Of course you want an Amma and Appa," Laxshmi said. "All babies want an Amma and Appa. And everyone wants to go to America. I myself would like to go to America, but I did not get into university. You will have many opportunities. You must go so that one of the children who live outside the gate can have your bed."

P.J., whose name was Surya at the time, did not understand. She had hidden under the long *pallav* of Laxshmi's sari when Saffron came to take her away. She heard only, "Say hello to your Amma, Surya. Say hello to your Amma," again and again, through the muffling cotton veil.

She did not understand what Diane and Pastor Daniel were saying, and she did not want to.

Diane said, "The Tower was shot, P.J. He lunged at a deputy, and the deputy had to defend himself. He was the only officer in there at the time, which is a very dangerous situation. The hospital says he was hurt badly."

P.J.'s own voice floated in from the window, "Is he going to die?"

"The doctors are doing everything they can."

"Has Saffron been to see him?"

"She's in jail, P.J. She can't."

"When is she going to be out? When can she see him?"

"I can't answer questions about the legal status of your parents, P.J. They have a right to privacy and counsel because they're innocent until proven guilty. I can't discuss it with you. I know that sounds weird."

Saffron had been right about the government, that there was a conspiracy to control people's minds, but if Saffron was in jail, if she needed a lawyer, not doctors, then she must be okay. She must have ducked like P.J. and the other kids had.

For most of the kids, ducking bullets was habit. "Can I see him?"

Diane shook her head. "He's been arrested, even though he's in the hospital. He can only talk to a lawyer right now."

"When is Saffron getting out of jail?"

Diane's head swayed like a hypnotizing cobra. "The judges don't work on Sunday, so it'll be Monday at the earliest."

"At the earliest? It could be later?" She wanted to see The Tower and to get out of this Christian hellhole right the hell now and if she had to wait until Monday she would implode. The praying before dinner, and the crosses nailed all over the house, and the constant harping on sin and her soul all added mass, and she was wildly spinning and crushing herself. Soon, she would be homogeneously neutral, nothing but neutrons, as blank and gray as a neutron star if she didn't get the hell out of here. "Two more nights?"

Diane said, "Yes. I'm sorry. At least two more nights. We need to discuss what you heard the night that Ester James was kidnapped."

"I told you that I didn't hear anything."

Diane said, "I understand that you're mad at me." She looked up at the ceiling. "I'm so sorry about what happened, about how it turned out, but things looked wrong in your house. As a prosecutor, I've seen a lot of wrong things. I couldn't leave you there when I suspected they were hurting you. Do you understand?"

P.J. shook her head, whipping her black hair around.

"I suppose not," Diane said. "But what if someone was hurting one of your little sisters? Could you leave her where she was being hurt?"

"Of course not," P.J. said and regretted it.

"And I couldn't leave you there, you or any of your little sisters or brothers. I'm sorry about The Tower. I really am. No one should have gotten hurt. I'm so sorry, P.J., but I couldn't leave you there."

P.J. stared at the ground. Diane did seem sorry. It was not any easier.

Pastor Daniel asked, "Why did you change what you said, P.J.?"

Because Saffron and The Tower had told her to butt out when she came clean about catching rides with the Law and Diane the Man. Attention from law enforcement was not what they needed right now. "I must have been wrong the first time, when I said that I thought I heard something."

Diane shook her head and said, "Now, we don't think that's right. People's memories are sharpest close to the events, and we believe what you said the first time. Now, we think we know who was out there, who made the 'chattering' or 'tumbleweed' sounds that you heard, and we just need you to tell us the truth."

They knew that someone was out there? She should just tell them. "I don't know who it was, but I, like, checked the time stamps on the chat archives, and it was at eleven-forty."

"That's good." Diane brightened. Her eyes, less morose now, cheered P.J. a little. "That helps a lot. Now think back," Diane said. "Imagine yourself on the computer, chatting. Who were you chatting with?"

"Like, friends."

"Right. Close your eyes. What were you talking about?"

With her eyes closed, P.J. could not see the gaudy gold cross high on the wall above Pastor Daniel and Diane. "String theory."

"What?"

P.J. opened one eye, her worse eye, and Diane was a fuzzy brown and white blob on the couch. "Superstrings. Hyperspace. M-theory."

Diane's face blanked. "And what's that?"

"Physics."

"Oh, physics." The Diane blur nodded.

P.J. shut her eyes again.

Diane's voice said, "And at eleven-forty, what did you hear?"

She squeezed her eyes tight and imagined the computer room at home. It smelled musty with mold because the roof leaked. The blue and green carpeting was stained in concentric arcs in that corner. Monkey

Wrench the cat was asleep on the couch.

P.J. opened her eyes. "Who's feeding the cats?"

Diane asked, "You have cats?"

"Yeah. Eight."

"Eight?" Diane rolled her eyes. "Do you have a key? Do they eat dry food?"

"Yes to both."

"Okay," Diane said. "I'll feed the cats. Now, do you remember what you heard?"

P.J. closed her eyes again. On the computer screen, transmitted by the webcam aimed at his paper, Sanjay's words and equations scrolled up, written in English words, Greek letters, and numbers, describing ten-dimensional space.

Diane's voice said, "They were outside, maybe a hundred feet from your back window. Could you make out individual voices?"

P.J. concentrated. "I don't know. At first it just, like, sounded like a bunch of voices talking. There wasn't any one voice."

Pastor Daniel's voice interrupted, "A bunch of voices? Did it sound like a crowd of people talking randomly, or were they talking together, rhythmically?"

She had been listening to a Goth song called "My Hero, Earless Van Gogh," and the beat was thrumming double bass drums. "The talking kind of drowned out the bass line of the music. They were singing or something."

Diane said, "The voices were definitely singing or something."

P.J. nodded, and her head spun in the darkness of her own eyelids.

"Was it men's voices talking, women's voices talking, or both?"

The lead singer for the Goth group was a woman, so P.J. mentally subtracted her from the noise from outside. "Both."

Pastor Daniel's voice asked, "About how many people were out there? Ten? A hundred? Five hundred?"

She shook her head. "Nowhere near a hundred or five hundred."

Diane said, "Less than ten?"

"No." P.J. thought harder. The voices had overridden each other, they rose and fell, but several distinct voices emerged, and there were others, too. "More than ten."

Pastor Daniel asked, "Twenty?"

There were twenty-one people in P.J.'s honors algebra class, and the din every morning was insane. "Less than twenty. I don't know. I can't remember. I don't know." Her throat choked, and panic hovered on her horizon. Talking surrounded her, like everyone crowding around her. She opened her sandy eyes. "I want to stop. I don't want to talk anymore."

Diane's expression fell into compassion and sadness. "It's okay, honey. We'll stop for tonight. Give me your house key so I can feed your cats."

P.J. handed over the house key, and her ability even to get in her own house was gone, except for the emergency key in the rock. Last night, when Diane had offered to help her get admitted to MIT, P.J. had liked her. Today, Diane had taken away Saffron and The Tower and dragged her to the House of the Jesus Freaks and had maybe killed The Tower.

Good thing that P.J. was a Goth and tougher than all of them.

Max drove home directly into the huge red and gold sunset that filled the wide windshield of his official car, aghast. This morning he had shot a man, but this seemed worse.

He had blasted his life apart. If Diane found out, she would leave him. She would take their children. She was not tied to Max by financial desperation, only by love and respect and legal bonds.

She could sever those legal bonds with the stroke of a pen.

His only ambition had been a normal, safe family and a job getting rid of a few bad guys in the world. He loved Diane. Now he would end up in a crummy apartment, sitting on lawn furniture, drinking, watching college football alone. He might as well have shot himself.

The sun burned his eyes, and his eyes watered. Any other reason that tears might fill up his eyes was a waste of water. Regretting actions is stupid. The only thing you can do after shooting someone in the chest and head or figuratively shooting yourself through the mouth is to stay calm.

Bravery is not the absence of fear. Bravery is control when your body tries to panic.

When confronted with a rattlesnake, panicked thrashing will draw the snake's attack. Max had to do whatever he could to save himself, calmly.

When Max arrived home—his home with his mortgage and his line of credit and the redwood deck he had built—after sunset, Tatiana and Nicholas were eating leftover stew and cornbread and watching one of those idiot reality shows. He sat and ate with them, calmly, as if nothing exceptional had occurred. He watched the idiot reality show even though he did not care which idiot was booted out of the haunted house this week. Finally, when it seemed appropriate, he went to shower.

In the bathroom, he peeled his gunpowder-stinking clothes off his body. Spiny seedpods had infiltrated his underwear, worming their way through the denim and cotton. They scratched his muscled legs as he dragged his pants off. His hands were raw. The branch stumps on the tree had scraped his palms. Splinters poked his hands.

He scrubbed his body twice in the shower. Grit, sap, and ooze had dried into a gritty crust on his groin.

When he got out of the shower, Diane was sitting on their bed, reading a book. Her dark brown hair was down around her shoulders, gently curled from its tight coils. She wore blue pajamas. "Your jammies are here," she called.

"I'll be right out." He retreated to the bathroom to towel and dress.

In the bathroom with the door shut, he toweled his hair. He had to be careful. Diane was a smart lady. Max was not stupid enough to believe Diane would celebrate his honesty if he admitted screwing around. It wasn't that he wanted to avoid getting caught. He did not want to cause her anguish, and he wouldn't wager the kids' two-parent home that she would eventually understand, so he would live with guilt. Perfectly fine tradeoff, in his book. Ice crystals solidified around his shameful secret. He pulled on his underwear, undershirt, and long pajamas and emerged, properly clad.

Diane gestured to his overly modest pajamas. "You're so weird sometimes," because he did not walk around in the nude. She asked, "Did you arrest anyone else today that I'm going to have to arraign?"

"No one new. Met that Vanessa Allen again. She has some cockamamie idea that a serial killer got Ester James."

Diane looked up with an intellectual frown. "What did she say?"

It could go either way, here. If she already suspected something was up with him and Vanessa, she would question him with the sharp wit of a trial lawyer. She could not trap him in inconsistencies because he remembered everything verbatim, but he was not all that good at lying. "Don't have any evidence pointing toward it. We don't have even a body."

"She's a forensic technician in New Orleans, right?"

Ah, Diane was interested in the serial killer.

"Yeah," he said. "She wants to play Sherlock and hunt down Moriarty the Mastermind."

Diane nodded. "What else did Vanessa say about a serial killer?"

Her interest was piqued. Now Max just had to extricate himself. Max rolled his eyes. "It doesn't matter what else she said. We don't have one."

Diane licked her lips. "All right."

Using the non-existent serial killer to deflect her attention was despicable, but he was all right with that.

The truth never set you free.

Sunday

Zeke was in the barn the next morning, scooping oats for his horses and checking his tack. Bright pink light flooded the barn from behind him. He turned. Pink blared though the open barn door, and a person's silhouette stood amid the glare.

The barn was charcoal inside with early dawn dusk, so Zeke shaded his eyes to see better. He sure as heck hoped that it was anyone but Vanessa.

The silhouette resolved into a male figure.

When the man closed the barn door, Zeke saw it was Max Konstantin, the deputy, in his brown uniform and glinting pectoral badge. This was evidently an official visit. He hoped that they had found Ester, and she was okay. He hoped they had not found her body. He hoped they had, and this terrible, paralyzing fear that someone was hurting her was over.

From the horse stall, Zeke yelled, "Hello! Over here!"

The deputy looked over and jerked his chin up. "Hello, Zeke. Figured you would be up early."

Max walked over to the oats barrel where Zeke stood. His horses ignored Max as their attention centered on their morning oats. They both removed their hats.

Somewhere, either his baby was lying dead on a slab or was still missing. "Well, out with it. Have you found her?"

"No, I'm sorry, Zeke. We haven't found her. We have no word." The deputy cleared his throat and rested his hand on his holstered pistol, uncomfortable. "Let's talk about this church of yours, Zeke."

"My church?" Zeke blew the fear out of his chest with a horsy whoof.

"What about it?"

Max fidgeted with his belt, loaded with his gun, beeper, pepper spray, and a few items Zeke did not recognize. "Something going on there?"

Zeke settled back a bit. Worldly folk didn't need to know some things about Zeke's church. Not that they were hiding things, but outsiders might interrupt. "There are lots of things going on, Max. Bible study. Fellowshipping. Charity projects for poor folks in Dallas, Houston, and New Orleans. What do you mean?"

Max patted a horse's neck with a firm but gentle slap. Charlie whuffed and chewed his oats. It was a good pat, from one familiar with horses. Zeke noticed things like a practiced horse pat. "I get the feeling something's up. When we were talking right after Ester went missing, I asked you about them, you didn't answer much."

Oh, that. Zeke had almost forgotten about Ester's outburst, what with all the turmoil these past few days. He was sure that, if she came home, *when* she came home, all would be forgiven. "It was nothing anyway."

Max's black eyes were mild. "Tell me, Zeke."

Zeke rubbed his beard. He did not much like the beard, but the Old Testament decreed that men should not shave, so he was trying it. "I'm afraid this is going to distract you from finding my Ester."

"Tell me anyway. Since you say it's nothing, I'll give it low credence, and it won't distract me."

Zeke nodded. "And there are other things that seem more important, like that her computer has all the files wiped off it."

Max took out a little notebook. "How do you know?"

"Nessie checked it. Her personal files are gone, even programs."

The deputy's expression hardened as his jaw bulged, like Zeke had said something very wrong. "Nessie? Vanessa Allen checked it, and everything was gone?"

"Yeah."

"Were you watching her, or did she tell you that?"

"Told me."

"Need to see that." He sighed. "What else?"

"Well, Vanessa Allen thinks that Ester might have met someone online and gone off with him, and that's why Ester's computer files are wiped, and why she broke up with Bobert a few weeks ago, and why she had the outburst in church."

Max's raised eyebrow shamed Zeke. "Outburst in church? That's what the problem was?"

Zeke sighed. This was his baby they were talking about. "Pastor Daniel was preaching a good sermon last week about the literal reality of the Bible. Ester was squirming a bit, like she had something to say. Brother Daniel said that, before Noah's flood, it never rained because the Bible makes no mention of rain before that point."

Max stopped writing, and his eyebrows rose.

"That's right. Most people don't know about that," Zeke said.

"Suspect they don't," Max said.

"Ester stood up. It was unlike her, you understand. That's what makes me think that Vanessa may be right, and maybe some man filled her head with nonsense. Ester was coming to God, going to Bible study and becoming less worldly. She and I prayed more together in the last six months than in the ten years before that. It gladdened my heart, and I told her so."

Zeke took off his cowboy hat, smoothed his hair, and pressed his hat back on his head. Telling Max hurt Zeke's heart. It portrayed Ester the wrong way. "She asked Pastor Daniel, if there were no rains before Noah's flood, how the plants grew." Zeke's eyes watered. Embarrassing Ester like this seemed so wrong. If she was dead, he wanted to remember her as a good Christian and know that she died a good Christian, so he might see her in Heaven. "And Pastor Daniel shut her mouth, he did. He told her that the plants got water from the mists from the ground.

That's what's in the Bible."

Max's raised eyebrows pulled every line out of his face and redistributed them to his forehead under his curling, black hair. "Oh-kay."

"She stormed out," Zeke said. "She went home, and when I got home, she had fixed lunch, and she said that she didn't want to talk about it. Someone incited her to do such a thing. I talked to Brother Daniel, and he said that she was welcome back at the church. She didn't need to apologize to anybody, Brother Daniel said. He asked that she meet with him once for a Bible study to discuss it, and that's all. Brother Daniel said, 'No harm, no foul.' He said that she wasn't questioning her faith, just an interpretation of the Bible. So you see," Zeke sucked in a breath, "it wasn't important."

"Okay," Max said. "I see."

"Wasn't anything important at all." Zeke wiped the water out of his eyes with his shirt cuffs that smelled like healthy, green horse spit. Max was the secular type, and he would not understand. Zeke could see the challenge in his eyes. Maybe Vanessa was right, and the sheriff's office was not doing enough. They should have investigated the home and found the missing computer files, and they had not. They should have found something by now. He was losing faith in the sheriff's department.

Zeke said, "And it shan't be important when you find her. And you must find her. I'm dying. I'm dying every day she's gone. I miss her so."

P.J. crowded into the first pew with Pastor Daniel's wife Melinda, their kids, and her own sibs. She wished she could fold her arms and lay her head down to sleep, but every time she slept, she was overrun with gun-flourishing SWAT teams, rappelling Army Rangers, and suit-clad federal agents dragging her away. Exhaustion and anger vied for her attention, but shock short-circuited both. She didn't know whether to sob where she was or run down the crowded aisle and out of the church, screaming for help.

Connie hung on P.J.'s arm, pulling. Her hot cheek pressed against P.J.'s biceps, and their skin in contact was slick with sweat.

At the podium, Pastor Daniel surveyed the crowd. His chin jerked up, haughty. He swung his long arms over the congregation and said, "Brothers and sisters, we have a problem."

Behind her, cloth rustled as people fidgeted. P.J., half-hanging over the end of the pew, glanced back at the crowd.

Ester James's red-bearded father, who P.J. had seen at the press conference and in the church, sat on the right end of the fourth pew next to the eastward windows. He looked up from his Bible. His pen hovered over the book.

"We have a problem," Pastor Daniel said. Pastor Daniel's arms were spread wide like he should be hanging on the brutal crucifix behind him. "We have a problem because our sister, Ester James, has a problem. She has been taken, either by forcible kidnapping or led astray by the People of the Lie, and now we have the responsibility to find Ester and bring her home."

Head-nodding started near the back in the Turner family. Melinda had introduced P.J. to several families before church. She described the Turners as vigorous, good church-goers, stable and high-minded. Nemo Turner, the irrepressible uncle of the bunch, let his shoulders slump as he joined in the nodding.

Pastor Daniel continued, "Because we are all responsible for one another. When one of us is sick, we nurse them back to health."

The nodding spread through the church, running through the tow-headed Macintosh bunch, numbering twenty-eight strong.

Pastor Daniel said, "When one of us is despondent, we pray with them and raise them up. And when one of us is missing, we search for them."

Diane Marshall sat three pews behind Zeke James, deep in the church. Her hair was drawn back in a bun at her neck. She twisted her pearl necklace with one hand and took notes with the other. A hot flush of hate crept over P.J. that this woman who had ripped apart P.J.'s family was sitting here in church, pretending to be all innocent.

P.J. turned to face the front, her face hot.

Pastor Daniel smiled down at her from his raised podium.

P.J. felt forked, which in chess means that her every move results in her being killed.

Pastor Daniel preached, "It is a terrible thing when a young girl goes missing. Ester has her whole life ahead of her. She has not yet been married, has not yet been a mother."

P.J. glanced back, trying to find an exit that wasn't blocked. Zeke James had covered his face with his rough hands.

Pastor Daniel said, "Some of you may be thinking in terms of cause and effect. Last week, our sister Ester expressed some thoughts that did not correlate perfectly with the proper surrender to the Lord. She is a rebel who needs to lay down her arms. She is an imperfect vessel. As are we all."

The ghost of Ester James joined the fray, haunting the church from the eyes of every one of the waiting, silent congregation. They all stared at Pastor Daniel, who stared at P.J. Their combined gaze pounded her.

"As are we all," he said again. "The Book of Job tells us that the Lord allowed Satan to try Job's faith even though Job 'was perfect and upright.' No one is beyond Satan's reach." Pastor Daniel said. "Because we are all sinners. Because we are all imperfect vessels that the Lord must fire to finish. Because we all rebel against the Lord, and we must all lay down our arms and submit.

"In The Book of Job, the Sabeans stole Job's oxen and donkeys.

Lightning killed Job's sheep. The Chaldeans stole Job's camels. A great wind killed Job's children. The Sabeans and the Chaldeans were agents of Satan, People of the Lie. Of their own free will, they chose to steal, they chose to murder, they chose evil.

"And when you choose evil, you choose Hell."

P.J. glanced back into the congregation. Some people scribbled notes. Some nodded. Some scrunched up their faces and pondered the nature of free will. Others stared at P.J.

Pastor Daniel said, "Evil happens because people choose evil. Among us, somewhere near here, someone has chosen evil. They took Ester, a right servant of the Lord, with them, and they brought pain to her father Zeke James and to all of us in this congregation."

Pastor Daniel paused and looked back at P.J., catching her when she turned back from trying to find a way out of the stifling hothouse of Puritanism. His stare took in her clothes and her naked face because Melinda had asked P.J. to leave off her makeup this morning. She could see him judging her, and she shrank back into the unyielding wood of the pew.

"Someone among us must know something," Pastor Daniel continued, staring right at her. "And if they remain silent, then they choose the side of evil. And in choosing evil, they place themselves in the service of the Devil. And in doing that, they are already trapped in Hell."

Everyone else turned and stared at her. Their brown, black, green, and blue eyes reflected her own stare, but they all stared at her, and then they whispered to each other. She was trapped by their stares and their thoughts as surely as if they had grabbed her arms and legs and forced her down.

She couldn't breathe. She couldn't move. Nausea threatened and a half-remembered, incomprehensible thought beset her: her body, laid out as if for sacrifice, held down, as she stared into a circle of light and pain.

"Friends," Pastor Daniel said. "Brothers and sisters, my fellow

Christians, we are all good people here." P.J. watched him and he watched her back, and he spoke directly to her. "We all love our sister Ester. We miss her, and we yearn for her return. I ask you, I beg you, if you know something about our sister Ester, if you know anything that might help us find her, please, please, for the love of God, tell us."

Diane hurried home from church for lunch with Max and the kids.

Pastor Daniel's sermon today had disturbed her. Usually, his sermons rallied them all to do God's bidding and were hopeful, looking ahead to better times to come, but today, with all that talk about evil ones and Hell and slaughtering Job's family, his focus on the evil in men's hearts troubled her. It echoed the torture and damnation sermons that she heard twice a week during her childhood, where she learned about her own evil nature, and that her every sin and impure thought increased the loneliness of Christ on the cross at Calvary and added to the spittle on his face. She wanted to leave the guilt and fear at work and not obsess about sin and punishment in church, too.

While they ate, the local news out of Dallas was on the television. The young blond woman on the television was familiar. She was buxom, handsome, and taller than the Hispanic woman interviewing her.

Diane touched Max's hand and asked, "Isn't that Vanessa Allen?"

Max looked up from his sandwich with little interest.

Tatiana asked, "Who?" and wrenched herself around to look. Nicholas could not be bothered.

On the television, the little reporter asked, "You're a forensic scientist in New Orleans?"

The wind blew Vanessa Allen's long blond hair. "Yes, for two years now. I'm originally from New Canaan, here in Texas."

"And you believe there is a serial killer operating south of Dallas."

A black microphone pointed at Vanessa Allen's pink-lipsticked mouth. "A serial killer is operating in the rural areas south of Dallas. His latest victim is Ester James from New Canaan." The usual picture of pretty, blond, grinning Ester James filled the television screen. The Sin Nombre County Sheriff's Office tipline phone number and website were printed across the bottom of the picture.

Max tapped the kitchen table with his fist. "Ah, crap. Now every psychic nutjob is going to call us."

The reporter on the television asked Vanessa, "Have they found anything?"

"No. She's been missing for three days. Because I'm a forensic technician, I have been trying to help with the investigation. At least four other young women were reported missing in this area." An East Texas map with four bull's-eyes flashed on the screen.

The shot cut back to the earnest reporter. "Were they dead?"

"Well, yeah." Vanessa smiled. "The MO is the same in every case: murder and dumping the body in a rural, piney woods area in or near water."

Max said, "Oh, bullshit. 'In or near water.' Everywhere is 'in or near water' around these swamps." He crunched his pickle.

On the television, the wind crackled the microphone. Vanessa pulled a handful of her blond hair out of her mouth. "As several weeks had elapsed since the murder in most cases and two of the victims were submerged, no useful DNA was recovered from the victims. There were several 'signature' items, such as particular species of plants near the bodies." Vanessa nodded sagely. "The four young women even look similar. Serial killers typically have a 'type' of victim they prefer, often women who look like their mother or an ex-girlfriend."

Lord, four other girls. Diane sucked air because she had been trying to exhale smoothly to keep from choking. She grasped Max's warm hand.

"That's a myth," Max said. Diane glanced at him. His mouth was twisted like he had a fishhook on the left side, pulling. "Serial killer myths are as stupid as pedophile myths. Ted Bundy had a 'type,' but most serial killers like their victims small and weak, and most often that's kids, small women, or the elderly. It's pragmatic, not psychological. Bigger people fight the guy off, and then it's recorded as an assault, not a murder, so it doesn't fit the signature or MO, which are both just psychological bullshit."

On the television, Vanessa said, "These murders should be submitted to ViCAP for analysis."

"What's ViCAP?" The reporter's black hair blew into her mouth.

Beside Diane, Max muttered, "Vi-crap."

Vanessa said, "The FBI's Violent Criminal Apprehension Program, part of the National Center for the Analysis of Violent Crimes. It's a computer database that compares signature items and modi operandi, the 'MO,' of murders. It will at least tell us if the perpetrator has other victims."

Max chewed and swallowed hard. "Vi-crap is just another government bureaucracy created to lull the public into complacency after Ted Bundy went on that cross-country killing spree. Have you seen those questionnaires? If I filled out one on every murder that we saw, I wouldn't have time to do anything else, and it doesn't have any room for important things that they don't specifically ask. Vi-crap links MOs, not suspects, not location, not victims. Vi-crap, the FBI, and those 'scientists' at the Behavioral Analysis Unit have never caught a serial killer. They're all a waste of time." He crushed a potato chip in his fist. "All that crap does make pretty stories, though. And now Vanessa Allen has found four other dead bodies, so they must be linked somehow."

Max's dismissive mouth-set was infuriating. Diane asked, "Are you listening to this? Four other girls."

"Young adult women go missing all the time. They leave their husbands, run away with some guy, or go on a bender. And if ViCAP does link them after we catch the perp, then we law enforcement agencies get to clear our books of them, without any forensic evidence or actual police work. It clears up a lot of cases. Way too damn many cases that were committed by somebody else."

Diane shushed him and stared at the television. Pictures of four young women flashed on the flat television screen. "Those poor girls."

Max pointed. "That one, lower left, was a prostitute last seen getting into a van registered to an RSO. We couldn't nail the guy, but he did it."

Diane squinted at the text. "You knew about Soledad Watson?"

"She was a prostitute."

"And so she wasn't deserving of the protections of society because she wasn't a virgin or a wife? Because she had sex for money?"

"Not what I meant." He sounded tired. "It's a high-risk activity."

Diane glanced over at the kids, who were watching, wide-eyed. "It's okay, guys," Diane said. "Just some work stuff."

"Mom," Tatiana's eyes were huge. "Is there a serial killer?"

"I don't know, honey. We all need to be extra careful until we figure out what happened to Ester."

Tatiana looked at her half-eaten sandwich. "Have you seen her MyOwnRoom page?"

Diane and Max glanced at each other. Diane asked Max, "Have you?"

One corner of Max's mouth bent down. "Yeah, I took a look at it the next morning. We have better leads."

Diane asked, "What did her webpage say?"

Tatiana said, "There're just some comments, like some guy who says he did it. I think Admin took that comment off, though."

Max scoffed, "Idiots always come out of the woodwork after any murder. False confessions. You can't believe any of them. In the Central Park Jogger case, five teenagers admitted they did it. Signed confessions. Turns out, it was someone else. Those kids spent years in jail, and they didn't do it."

Tatiana's black eyes widened more, straining at the corners.

"Then there were the four guys over in Arizona who admitted to massacring those Buddhist monks," Max said. "After they confessed, turns out it was someone else. Over a hundred people claimed to have kidnapped the Lindbergh baby. Five hundred people claimed to have murdered Betty Short, the Black Dahlia."

Diane knew all that. "Yeah, but sometimes the bad guys really did it."

Max shrugged. "You can't trust a confession. Some of those freaks believe they did it. They can pass a polygraph. Some of them get obsessed and study the crime until they internalize it. Some of them have the memory beaten into them by negligent cops."

"As a prosecutor, I'd rather have a confession than a body."

"Juries are stupid. You've said it a thousand times. Evidence solves crimes."

Tatiana and Nicholas looked at each other, then back to their parents.

"I am so never going to be in LE." Tatiana flipped her dark brown curls behind her shoulders. "People at school are, like, carrying pepper spray to class. One girl brought a handgun."

"She brought a gun to school?" Diane asked.

"She checked it in at the office when she got there."

"Oh, okay." Carrying guns inside the fenced school campus seemed overboard, even in Texas.

Both kids wandered off and left their dirty plates on the table. Lunch together had been nice while it lasted.

"So," Diane said to Max with a smile. "Anybody confess to Ester James's murder that I don't know about?"

He shook his head. "Not even one. She hasn't gotten enough publicity yet." He gestured toward the screen. "That'll change things."

"Do you think that Vanessa Allen is right about the serial killer?"

He ran his fingers through his hair, and his black curls sprang up afresh. "There is no serial killer. Vanessa Allen is imagining things."

"What if she's not, Max? She's a forensic tech with a big-city police department. She must see that type of thing more often than we do. When was the last murder around here that wasn't domestic violence, a bar fight, or drug-related?"

"Twelve years, when you take out all the things that cause murders. Maybe Ester James was into meth."

"Oh, come on. She went to that church, Pastor Daniel Stout's church." Diane shook her head. "I don't know. Ever since you said that Vanessa thought there was a serial killer on the loose, I can't get it out of my head. And now with this interview," she flapped her hand toward the television, which droned weather, "I'm going to get all kinds of questions. Maybe we should call in those FBI profilers."

Max rubbed his sharp chin and said, "Don't need those FBI guys sticking their noses into anything. All their serial killer profiles are the same: white male, under forty years old, pervert, abused, pyro."

That email from the FBI's Behavioral Analysis Unit Two said all that: white male, thirties, sexual deviancy, child abuse, arson. Okay, but serial killers have a lot in common. For instance, they all kill people.

Diane wished that Max would read the profile, but she knew better than to push it.

Yet, the People of the Lie, the Sabeans or Chaldeans, whoever had taken Ester James, might still be out there, watching other young girls like Tatiana, preparing to take another young woman. Diane loved Max and respected his skills, but damn it, if she called in the Feds, it was going to look like she did not trust Max.

Their only real lead was P.J. Lessing.

P.J. had to stop covering for her parents or not trusting her own memory. There were techniques that Diane could use, pictures, reassurances, blandishments, that cops use all the time to elicit information or extract confessions.

Real confessions.

New Canaanites have a focus for their fear now: a serial killer. They know what to guard against. They watch through their closed and locked windows for a soulless man sharpening his knives or winding a strangling garrote.

All the other nebulous demons have evaporated. Focused fear is easier to bear than the swirling terror of everything.

Things are getting paranoid here in Sin Nombre County. A girl is missing, a pretty girl, and that sets everybody's nerves on edge. If it can happen to a pretty blond girl, a valued repository of recessive genes, it could happen to anyone.

All the chitchat about serial killers over lunch tightened Max's stomach. He did not finish eating his sandwich. Planting the serial killer hook in Diane's mind last night to distract her was loathsome, but he had done it anyway, and he had set the hook too hard. If he wasn't careful, Diane might talk to Vanessa Allen for more information. Vanessa might slip up.

Or sabotage.

Max could not fathom why he had screwed Vanessa Allen against a magnolia tree at sunset. Words like "indiscretion," "folly," or "accident" staggered past the awful truth, glancing at it like rubberneckers at the sheet-draped hominoids at a highway accident.

"Stupidity" was a pretty good word. "Callous disregard" for Diane, his kids, the sanctity of marriage in general, and Vanessa herself veered closer to the truth.

Gambling addiction was a closer analogy. He had been lured by tumbling dice and was now indebted to a blond bookie who might take his house.

His actions surprised him. He decided to do the Catholic thing and avoid further occasion of sin, but he felt dirty. No, he felt like he had made the shameful discovery that he had always been stinking filthy.

He might be able to mollify Vanessa by appearing to take her seriously, so she would not rat him out.

Vanessa thought that the creepy little church might have something to do with Ester's disappearing. He could start there.

The Country Congregational Bible Church's website was simple: yellow background, silvery white cross, black font. No pictures. No video. No sermon podcasts. Terribly Protestant.

Max clicked and found a couple of pages where someone had transcribed the entire text of the Biblical Book of Revelations. The text was annotated with hyperlinks to supposedly correlating historical events.

Somebody had too much time on their hands.

The first chapters of Revelations are the Letters to the Seven Churches, which on the website equated to seven historical Christian ages. The first letter to the church of Ephesus was about early Christians, when the church gained many converts but was beginning to lose its love of Christ, the website said.

The last church mentioned in Revelations is the one in Laodicea. This church is the "rich church," which pleads for love gifts from so-called Christians trying to buy their way into Heaven, the modern selling of indulgences. Any church that demands tithes, any church that is more concerned with its coffers than its Christians, that shorts virtue and longs vice, and all religions organized around central bank accounts, are Laodicean churches, according to the creepy little church's

Monarch butterfly-colored website.

Max was amused that Pastor Daniel Stout's definition of Laodicean churches included so many financial terms, as Pastor Daniel Stout had come to Jesus with a government hellhound snapping at his heels.

These are the End Times, sayeth the website, when God will invade this earth in force. You must choose Christ now. There is no use saying that you choose to lie down when you cannot stand up.

The penguins had beaten all this crap into Max in Catholic school. The Jesuits had Socratic-methodically deconstructed it for him in high school. Father Miguel had glared down his patrician nose at Max and allayed his fears of the imminent end of the world by saying, "That's a literalist interpretation, Maxim. And are we literalists?"

We were not literalists, Max remembered. Armageddon literalism was reserved for rice-eating Seventh Day Adventists, canned goods–hoarding Mormons, and suicide cults.

The more he learned about this creepy little church, the more he thought that someone who had gone against its brand of religion may have met an untimely end in an honor-killing equivalent.

Max jotted a list of things he was going to have to do: check into the church's finances, check alibis for major church members, subpoena computers to check for incriminating emails. It was a lot of work, considering once again that he was investigating suspicions, not a crime because there was still no evidence that a crime had been committed.

If New Canaan was harboring a suicide cult, they had best deal with it quietly before the federal government called out the Bureau of Alcohol, Tobacco and Firearms and fulfilled the paranoid prophecies of another bunch of fanatics.

Max found the church's list of sworn members on the website. He printed them for future reference and deprogramming therapy.

Mrs. Diane Virginia Marshall was the first member listed under M.

Hot shock collected under Max's skin.

Oh, Lord. Diane and Dan weren't having an affair, or they weren't only having an affair. She'd gone and joined that cult of his.

How the hell had she hidden it from Max?

She worked a lot. So did he. Both of them, at all hours and for long hours. They treated each other like adults, not like truant teenagers who needed a note from their mommies when they were tardy.

But Max did the bills. No money was missing from their accounts. To get her name in deep, bold font with a glowing outline, Diane must be an important member.

If it wasn't money, then what?

Terrible motivations for murder surfaced in Max's head: power, influence, laws, or crimes.

Diane could fix any legal problems that church had with a pen flourish.

More importantly, she could divert the sheriff's office from Daniel's church while they were investigating Ester's disappearance, which she had done that first morning when she called Max and said that a *friend* wanted it looked into, a friend who was "interested in the case. He'd appreciate it if you didn't wait the usual three days to declare her a missing person. This might be a problem case, and jumping on it hard might prevent worse problems later."

Now that he was zeroing in on the creepy little church, she was suddenly pounding away on the idea of a serial killer, those phantom murderers. At lunch today, she had been adamant. She was their front.

Max knew who the *friend* was, now. Those bastards were using her to throw suspicion off themselves.

Diane drove through the wide streets of New Canaan and called Pastor Daniel from her cell phone. Sundays were usually tranquil in

New Canaan because many restaurants and most businesses were closed. She stopped at a red light.

A wrinkle of sound, and Pastor Daniel answered, "Hello?"

"Hi, Pastor Daniel? Did you see that press conference that Vanessa Allen gave about serial killers on the noon news?"

"I'm not sure what to make of it." Pastor Daniel's voice sounded tinny through her phone. Its resonance was best experienced in person.

A car pulled alongside her. The woman driving gazed fearfully at Diane, then turned her worried face back to the road.

"You were right," Daniel said. "There must have been something going on in that house."

Diane touched her heart with her left hand in horror, then realized that she was not holding the steering wheel and dropped her cell phone grabbing the warm wheel again. She retrieved the cell phone. "What?"

"They were worshipping idols. We need to ask P.J. some very serious questions."

The traffic light turned green. Diane accelerated, and the Jaguar jumped harder than she had meant. "I've got to go to the office for a few hours first, but I want to talk to P.J. tonight."

Max had called Pastor Daniel Stout and the reverend invited him over to the church to talk.

After reloading his handgun and checking that his extra magazines were lined with fresh hollow-points, Max drove over. Ester James might have run afoul of the good reverend. The cleric might have it in him to kill a sworn officer to protect whatever they were doing in that church.

The parking lot was empty, save for an older blue sedan with the license plate BR DAN. You did not need perfect recall to remember that plate. It would make Max's job easier if everyone had an eidetic memory like he did. He found gross errors that people made all the time in concrete data like names, phone numbers, emails, amounts of money, agreements made, times that things occurred, and of course, what people actually said. The past just seemed to fade away for most people, memory myopia.

Max walked past the blue sedan. The hood ornament had been cut off with a blowtorch.

Max walked into the church, removed his hat, and looked around. Inside, the sepia-toned church looked like it had been built out of one batch of cheap lumber and varnished with clearcoat.

Typical. Protestants treat their churches like they treat their women: strip them of adornment in the name of zealous modesty. Diane might actually buy into that crap, start wearing ankle-length skirts, let her hair grow long and split-ended, and stop wearing makeup. Max would still love her, but such measures equated with deprivation in his book. He did not cotton to the repression of women, whether in Afghanistan, Nigeria, or his own backyard, and especially not his own wife. He sure as hell did not want anyone giving Tatiana such ridiculous ideas. Tatiana was damn brilliant. She could save the world.

The church echoed back his lonely footsteps.

The nave of the church was empty, if you could even call it a nave because there wasn't a proper chancel for the altar or a narthex leading in. The sneering penguins had inculcated him well.

"Father Daniel!" Max called. The glassy wood echoed his voice. He had not realized that his voice had a trace, just barely a trace, of a Mexican growl under his straight Texan twang.

No answer.

Max walked up the aisle, his hand covering the butt of his pistol. Preparing for ambush was not paranoid. Ester James, who had caused a scene in this church last week, was missing, and her father had placed a call to this church a few hours before it happened.

It was one of his better theories about the case.

Means: pretty much everyone in Texas owns a gun, and Father Daniel was a big guy, very tall, a lot of reach, while Ester was a small woman. Either way, there was a disparity of force.

Motive: the outburst in church may have been against religion. In other religions, women were murdered in "honor killings" for less. People in these wild parts of Texas died for their religion, either for traversing doctrine or for cleaving to it when the government came knocking. His cousin Cassie, for example. Churches, especially those with a charismatic leader, one who could convince a County Attorney to mislead an investigation, were susceptible to ideology amplification like a hall of crazy mirrors, each distorting and reflecting *ad infinitum*, until they thought the Day of Judgment was upon us and everybody drank the fruit punch that tasted like bitter almonds.

If a cult leader can convince people to kill themselves and their children, another one might convince his flock that only one person needs to die.

Maybe Ester James had drawn the black tile in a lottery.

Zeke had said that Pastor Daniel "shut her mouth" when Ester had mouthed off in church. He snapped at a young woman who asked a perfectly logical question in front of all those gullible people. But Zeke said that Pastor Daniel was kind about letting her back into the fold, said that "she was welcome back at the church, didn't need to apologize to anybody." He asked that she meet with him once for a Bible study to discuss it, and that's all. "No harm, no foul." He wasn't questioning her faith, "just an interpretation of the Bible."

Awfully egalitarian of him. Sometimes, too nice was a brighter red flag than threats.

Opportunity: Zeke James's phone call fit the timeline. It provided the time for Daniel to either call someone else or go himself to the Lone Star. Zeke was probably not involved or was an unknowing accomplice.

Additional factors: Ester would probably have gotten into a car with Daniel or another church member without fuss.

The theory was thin, nearly linear in its thinness, but possible. Of course, no one had found a speck of forensic evidence to support it, even circumstantial. No evidence refuted it, either. Many cases are closed without any forensic evidence.

Max called, "Father Daniel!"

The polished wood echoed his voice back again.

A door by the baptismal tank opened. Daniel Stout poked his head through, up near the top of the doorframe. "Yes? Ah, Deputy Konstantin."

The preacher threaded his limbs around the door. Max felt short and squat, watching the lanky pastor. Pastor Daniel said, "Nice to see you. What did you want to discuss?"

"Want to know more about your little church, here." He rested his hand on his holstered gun. Its weight on his belt was a spot of calm on his squirming body. "Explain to me why you are not a Laodicean church."

Daniel smiled. "Most people mangle that word."

"Twelve years of Catholic school."

Pastor Daniel tapped his fingers on the lectern. He looked like he was about to preach to an empty church. "Laodicean churches are 'rich' churches, selling options and futures on indulgences. We are a humble church. We don't ask for tithes from our members. We ask for time, and we ask for faith, but not money. Members are encouraged to contribute to our affiliated charities."

Options and futures. Yes, Stout was a fallen Wall Street player. Max asked, "How do you pay the mortgage and your salary?"

The preacher's face changed, becoming subtly professional in bearing. "We bought the property outright. We have an endowment."

Zeke had been worried about Jews and Israelis. "Where did you get that endowment?"

Pastor Daniel shrugged. "In a previous life, I made some money. I manage the church's investments. Even after maintenance of the property and my salary, we turned a substantial profit on our investments this year, enough to subsidize our charities."

Max wondered if that money had gotten Stout indicted. "Sounds like you're a 'rich church.' Sounds like you're a filthy rich church."

Daniel frowned. "No. Rich churches are concerned with the money entering and leaving the coffers. We have been liberated from that."

No wonder Max had not noticed any money missing from their common bank accounts. Diane had not had to give the church money, just time, just faith. Diane had been so damn busy lately. "How much time and faith do you demand from your members?"

Daniel leaned on his crossed arms on the lectern. "We're a community, a fellowship. We study the Bible, and we have common goals." Daniel licked his lips. "Anybody you have in mind?"

Being coy was silly. Surprise held no advantage. "Yeah, my wife."

Daniel smiled. "So Diane has witnessed to you? Marvelous!"

"Nope. Found her name on your website."

"Oh." Daniel stared at his slack hands on the podium, crestfallen.

"Yeah. So what do you believe, Father Daniel? Your website seems fixated on the Book of Revelations." Stout's equivocating pissed Max off. "Do you have a date, Father? When is Jesus coming back?"

"Ah." Daniel waved his hands. "You won't catch me with that one. Jesus said that he will come like a thief in the night. We dare not guess. We do not propose a date or a year or even a decade."

"You must have a date. All you cults have a date."

Daniel's face smoothed out. His voice was low as he said, "We are not a cult, Mr. Konstantin. We believe traditional, mainstream Christian teachings. Seventy percent of Americans believe that they will see Christ return in their lifetimes." Snake-like, or prophet-like, the preacher did not blink. "These are the End Times, Mr. Konstantin. All the Biblical signs are in place. The nation of Israel has been reestablished in Palestine. Jerusalem is in Jewish hands. The Jews are ingathering in Israel."

"So when is it? Ten years? Fifty? The whole Y2K thing must have been a big disappointment, what with the world not ending and all."

Daniel sighed. "The year 2033 may be important, plus or minus five years, two millennia after the death of Jesus Christ when he was thirty-three years old, but we dare not guess."

Max pushed the heel of his hand against the butt of his gun. "So you do have a date. You're just like Koresh and all the rest of the nut jobs. You are an end-of-the-world weirdo cult."

Pastor Stout smiled and recited, "He will come again in glory to judge the living and the dead, and His kingdom will have no end. We look for the resurrection of the dead, and the life of the world to come."

The pastor parroted selected parts of the Nicene Creed, memorized by every good little Catholic schoolchild and recited during the Mass every damn week. Max said, "The whole Mass isn't about Revelations and the Apocalypse."

"Neither is our church. Why don't you come to our meetings and see for yourself?"

Max crossed his arms over his chest. This left his gun unattended, but the chance of Pastor Daniel whipping out a gun seemed remote. The pastor's clothing had no suspicious loose jackets, square bulges, or pocketed leaden weights. "I'm not interested in churches."

"Do you believe in God?"

"That's none of your business, but I surely don't believe in churches, and I don't like my wife attending this one. Stay away from her."

"I think you should take that up with her."

"No. We need to settle this as men."

Pastor Daniel blinked, and his head turned to the side. The sunlight from the plain glass windows caught his pale, green eyes. He looked as half-breed as Max was. Pastor Daniel asked, "Settle what, as men?"

"You're gunning for Diane. You're as obvious as a creepy old guy hanging around a playground. Stay away from her."

"She's a member of my congregation. She is my sister in Christ. I am not 'gunning for her.' I have no designs on your wife."

Max was an excellent investigator, but he was not a particularly good interrogator. He could play bad cop when working the old routine, and interrogations in the department conference room are vastly different than field interrogations, especially when righteous anger was beginning to coil in his belly and his gun was heavy on his belt. He held his hat in his left hand, and his right dangled by his holster. "Have you slept with her?"

"No. I have never had sexual relations with Diane."

That answer just made him mad. "'Sexual relations.' That's the weasel words that Bill Clinton used."

"All right, then. I have never had sex with your wife. I have never kissed your wife. I have never been naked with your wife, nor she with me. I have studied the Bible with your wife. We have discussed Christ and the Living God. I have not, and will not, have sex with her. Does that suffice?"

"No. Leave her alone. Don't talk to her. Don't read the Bible with her. Don't call her on the phone."

"Diane is an adult. She chooses where she goes and who she associates with."

"And so do you. Don't 'associate' with Diane any more."

Pastor Daniel shook his head. "If Diane wants to come to Christ, I have an obligation to help her."

"Leave her alone." Max's hand rested on the grip of his holstered pistol.

Pastor Daniel's gaze followed Max's hand, but he did not react. He looked back at Max's face with no change in his cool expression. "Diane can decide for herself."

Max respected that Stout was not unnerved easily or hid it well. His own armpits grew clammy every time his palm stuck to the tacky silicone grips of his gun.

Often, amateurs facing a weapon are not as nervous as professionals, who understand the damage that even one bullet can do to a human body. Amateurs, after watching too many movies or playing too many video games, think that someone can be shot once or even a couple times and stand up and fight, if they have mental fortitude.

That's wrong. Bullets puncture skin, disintegrate into shrapnel inside muscle, and churn flesh into hamburger. Getting shot with a hollow-point bullet is like being cannon-balled with a naked blender blade set to pulverize.

Pastor Daniel should be more nervous about Max's hand on his gun.

Then again, the right reverend might have murdered a pretty young girl because they had differences of theological opinion. His calm display increased Max's suspicions.

Max turned and walked out of the church, uneasy about presenting his back as a target.

All Stout's denial was overboard, and his verbiage had been stilted and formal. The lack of contractions—have not and will not for haven't and won't—was a giveaway. In an official interrogation, Max would call a judge right now for a search warrant for the guy's property and car.

Max was right. The church had done something to Ester, and the pastor wanted to screw Max's wife.

P.J. sat under the desk with Connie, who alternately cowered silently or wept silently.

Pastor Daniel knelt beside P.J. "You're a compassionate person."

"Thanks." P.J., whose head was crammed against the underside of the wooden desk at a forty-five-degree angle, had meditated on compassion in front of the Buddharupa and Bodhisattva for ten years. Pastor Daniel, the *über*-Christian, might retract his compliment if he knew that it was the result of sacrifices to graven idols.

Maybe P.J. should give him a chance. This should be interesting.

She said. "The Dalai Lama says that you should put yourself in the mind of the other person and know that they're suffering, too. He says that true happiness only comes from compassion." Saffron's favorite Bodhisattva, the Akash Jogini Bodhisattva, wore a necklace of skulls that P.J. had always found unsettling.

Pastor Daniel smiled. His lips were pinker than his gray skin. The difference in the melanin in their skin was peculiar. P.J.'s skin was water-logged mahogany. Pastor Daniel's skin was a fainter shade of black.

"Yes," he said. "Jesus taught about compassion, too. Three parables in the Gospels relate to compassion. Even before the parables, Matthew said that Jesus looked out upon the crowds and felt compassion for them, because they were as sheep without a shepherd."

Maybe challenging Pastor Daniel was a dumb idea, especially if he was just going to spout Bible trivia. Her back hurt from crouching. She crawled out from under the desk and stretched. Her back cracked in two places. She wanted to do a backbend to pop all her vertebrae into place.

Under the desk, Connie whimpered. P.J. needed to crawl back under there. She couldn't leave Connie to the demons that tormented her.

"I don't mean to proselytize to you," Pastor Daniel said, "but your parents had some very odd ideas about religion, and perhaps your time here will be productive if you understand Christianity. You don't have to become a Christian," Pastor Daniel said, as if inspiration had struck him. "Conversion should be the result of a long road of study, not impulse. You should not convert while you stay with us. Okay?"

"Okay," she said, as if she had had any intention of converting.

"Just so you know," Daniel said, "Diane Marshall is coming over for a few minutes. She wants to know if you can remember any more about the night that Ester James disappeared."

Anxiety swarmed her like biting gnats. P.J.'s finger rose in the air and wrought equations. "We've been over that."

"Yes, but last night when we talked, you remembered more." Pastor Daniel's eyes followed her hand, tracing Greek letters and Arabic numerals in the air. "What are you doing?"

"When I get nervous, I do math." She extended out the equation. "I used to do it on paper, but one time I was in the car and we didn't have any paper, so I wrote it with my finger on the back of the seat, and then I didn't need paper anymore. It's kind of like playing chess blindfolded."

Pastor Daniel's frizzy eyebrows rose. "You can play chess blindfolded?"

P.J. bit her lip and wondered if she was showing off. "Can't you?"

"Never tried it. What math are you doing?"

P.J. hesitated.

Pastor Daniel said, "I used to be a stockbroker, commodities futures desk at Silverman Bachs. Options are priced using non-linear calculus, the Black-Shoales equation. I had a gadget, but I could solve it in my head. We used game theory to predict which commodities were going to be hot next. Kind of like John Nash applying game theory to social relationships, like whether to talk to the big, beautiful blond or the cute brunettes around her."

"Oh!" P.J. perked up. Maybe they could talk. She had not chatted online with her brainiac friends for a day and a half, and her brain felt like it had been relegated to solitary, and no one even shoved white bread and water through the slot. P.J. was a bit of an introvert but not a misanthropist.

She said, "It's quantum mechanics. Schrödinger built on Heisenberg's uncertainty principle, that you can't measure both the location and the velocity of a particle, which makes sense. If you pinpoint the location of a car, you don't know how fast it was going, and if you measure its speed, it's already moved past where you measured the speed, even though there's more to it than that when you're talking about particles. I mean, Einstein-Bose condensates, right? Wow."

Pastor Daniel's grin looked forced. "Okay."

P.J. wondered if she should stop talking. Sometimes people did not appreciate the beauty of physics and treated her like she was an autistic kid with a washing machine manual. "Anyway, I'm working on Schrödinger's equation, which describes quantum states of particles and says that, if two different paths are possible, like if a particle might jump over a wall or tunnel under it, the particle does both until you measure it. Schrödinger's equation describes the deterministic process of unitary evolution, which means that all the possible outcomes continue to exist until the quantum jump appears. Schrödinger himself didn't like quantum jumping. That's why he came up with the cat thought experiment which illustrates the illogic of probability states and quantum jumps as ways to describe reality."

Pastor Daniel scratched his neck under his collar, a good approximation of a cat in an uncomfortable situation that resorts to obsessive-compulsive grooming. "Okay."

Connie moaned again, and Melinda sat down beside her with a swirl of her denim skirt and held Connie's hand. Connie looked up nervously, her bright eyes wavering, then held Melinda's hand tighter and laid her head back on her knees.

Pastor Daniel smoothed his hair like a cat washing its ears. P.J. could not help seeing everything he did now as cat-like, Schrödinger's cat-like.

Pastor Daniel said, "I hear Diane's car outside."

P.J. drew her knees up and wrapped her arms around them. She was a solitary atom, a noble gas. She didn't want to interact. "I told her everything last night."

Pastor Daniel said, "Yes, but last night when we talked you remembered more. Maybe if you try really hard, this will be the last time you'll need to talk to her." He smiled sadly. "It must be very difficult, considering Diane had to remove you from your home, and she was there when your father was injured."

A linear core of worry spiraled tighter inside P.J., and she looked down at her hands. She could not repaint her flaking nails because her nail polish collection—black, charcoal, hematite, and steel—were in the medicine cabinet at home. Everything she needed was at home.

The front door rattled in its frame. Melinda braced Connie like an oversized backpack slung over one arm as she let Diane Marshall in.

Connie clung to Melinda just as hard as she had to P.J., maybe tighter because Melinda could use her hip as a cantilever to carry Connie. Indeed, Connie chewed sullenly on a cookie while grappling Melinda's shoulder. Luckily, Melinda was tall and strong, and Connie was undersized from starvation in Africa. Still, Saffron never carried Connie or any of the kids after they were a year and a half old. She said that they needed to learn to stand on their own two feet.

Connie looked like she needed to be held. P.J. never knew, and she was sorry that she never knew. The other little kids might need more, too. Her much-vaunted meditations on compassion had not informed her of their needs as much as she had thought. Damn. Maybe she should read Pastor Daniel's Bible.

P.J. followed Pastor Daniel and Diane Marshall into the family room in the basement. Pastor Daniel closed the door behind them. The closed door dampened the shrieks of the video games and general chatter of almost a dozen people.

Pastor Daniel and Diane sat on the beige couch again. A looming cross quartered the colorless wall above them. The family room, which Saffron would have called the communal room, was beige and ecru, like white bread toast.

P.J. sat in the wingback chair that served the computer desk, facing them. She was so tired after barely sleeping last night and cramped from crouching under the desk and beleaguered from realizing that she had not helped the little kids nearly as much as she had thought, that she could not even work up a good bout of anger for Diane Marshall.

P.J. asked, "How's The Tower?"

Diane looked at her own knees poking out from her pale skirt. "It's going to be a while before he gets out of the hospital."

P.J.'s gut clenched, and suspicions sneaked around her. "Is he dead?"

Diane looked up. Her sad eyes scared P.J. "Last time I checked, he was alive but in critical condition. One of the bullets hit his shoulder, one hit him in the gut, and one hit his head. He's in a coma. They would call me if he passed away."

"If you knew that he was going to die, would you tell me?"

"You should be prepared for it, but they said he might survive. It sounds like a fifty-fifty shot."

"Okay." P.J. felt like Diane was being honest. Even though Diane had screwed up her life, at least Diane was not lying. "Can I see him?"

Diane sucked her lips in. "He's very hurt. His injuries are extensive. He has drainage tubes sticking out of his abdomen, his head is mostly covered with gauze, and he has IVs and monitors and beeping and sucking equipment all over him. It's disturbing. I don't want you to be more upset."

P.J. had pictured him as asleep in a bed, maybe with a monitor measuring his heartbeat and a pristine saline drip. Yet, he was her father, her Appa as she called him in her head because Saffron did not like limiting role titles, and even though he smacked her around sometimes, and even though Saffron had slapped her the night before when P.J. had finally come clean about talking to law enforcement, she just wanted to touch his hand. "I want to see him."

"Okay. We'll go tomorrow during visiting hours."

"How about Saffron?"

"She's still in jail. She'll probably be bailed out tomorrow, maybe Tuesday, so you can talk to her on the phone after that. The court will probably tell her not to contact you but," Diane flipped her hand and flicked her eyes, dismissing stupidity, "I'll monitor it to make sure that she doesn't tell you not to cooperate with us, which is what the court is worried about. It seems Draconian not to allow her to talk to her kids, and not to allow you kids to talk to your mother. It's abuse of governmental powers."

Which was probably pretty close to how Saffron would have expressed it. This common sense and rebellion against authority was what P.J. had liked in Diane to begin with, so long ago. "Okay."

Diane said, "I need to ask you a few more questions about the night that Ester James disappeared, and I need you to be honest." Diane looked up at the ceiling, and her tears swelled under her brown irises on her lower eyelids. "You have every right to be mad at me. I am so sorry about what happened yesterday morning, about your dad, and about having to take you away from your family. I've seen so many terrible things happen to kids, and it looked like terrible things were happening to you and your brothers and sisters, so I had to do something. I couldn't leave you there."

P.J. felt sorry for Diane. She was all broken up about it, and she had not actually shot The Tower. The blame rested with whoever had fired the gun. Just like Pastor Daniel had said about Ester James's disappearance, the sin lay with whoever took Ester.

One more test. P.J. asked, "Did you feed my cats?"

"Yes, certainly. Last night and again just before I came over. They seem fine. I counted eight cats and cleaned the litter boxes. The tortoiseshell was limping."

"Planck always limps. He has arthritis." At least Diane had taken care of the cats. That spoke well, that she did what she said she would. P.J. found a stack of paper on the computer desk behind her. "I printed out the chat logs from that night, with time stamps."

"Thanks." Diane's forehead worry lines smoothed. "Give me a minute?" She skimmed the pages, dragging her finger down the paper.

P.J. tapped the arms of the chair with a straight sine wave rhythm, up and down and up and down.

Diane stopped with her finger on the third page and asked, "Where did you go after you said you had to turn up the music?"

"I didn't go anywhere." P.J. had worked on tensors for hours.

"You stopped typing after you said you were turning up the music. Look. You typed POS, Parents Over Shoulder, and then brb, for be right back. Did The Tower or Saffron come in?"

P.J. only remembered the math. "They must have."

"But you don't remember it?"

"No." P.J. had not meant to cross her arms over her chest, but they were clenched around her.

"Look at the time stamps." Diane held the printed pages out to her. "After you typed brb, two hours went by, then you came back and typed, SJ? SJ? and then you logged off. Where were you?"

"I don't know." She thought she had talked to Sanjay about tensor math for another hour. "Maybe I fell asleep."

"Are there any other gaps in your memory?"

"I don't have gaps in my memory."

"If you don't remember what happened those two hours, that's a gap."

The gap might have been in P.J.'s consciousness or her memory, but which one? "I must have fallen asleep or something."

"Did The Tower or Saffron call you away from the computer?"

"No. Why would I have a gap in what I can remember?" She was pretty sure that she had only worked on the math with Sanjay until about two in the morning. Right? She sucked in the left corner of her lower lip and held it between her teeth. She worked on math with Sanjay pretty much every night until two or so. Was that night different?

Diane said, "There are a lot of reasons why someone would repress a memory. Some drugs, like Rohypnol, 'Roofies,' date-rape drugs, can make you not remember things at all. Memory gaps happen all the time. Senior moments. Brain farts. Haven't you ever not been able to remember something, and then something jogs your memory, and then you can?"

"Yeah. Everybody does that."

"Right. Losing memories and finding them again can be accidental, but people hide memories they don't want to remember."

P.J. did not like the idea that she might have memories lurking around her brain waiting to pop up. Phantom memories seemed superstitious. Her right hand rose into the air and wrote a long equation. "I don't know."

"If you can do something accidentally, you can do it on purpose."

"But I want to help you guys find Ester." And she wanted this all cleared up so she and the kids could go home to Saffron. "Why would I deliberately not remember something about that?"

Diane bit her lower lip, an exaggerated gesture akin to P.J.'s equations. "Maybe something bad happened."

"Nothing bad happened." P.J.'s hand flew and traced numbers into the equation, relieving pressure. She looked at Diane's thin upper lip, her slim nose, and managed to look at Diane's eyelashes before she again stared into the equation describing states in quantum mechanics.

"You're quick to say that, considering something very bad happened to Ester James that night, and it happened in the vacant lot outside your window, and you've been very interested in the whole Ester James case, showing up at her church, putting up flyers. What is that you're doing?" Diane pointed at P.J.'s wildly flipping fingers.

Pastor Daniel waved Diane off. "It's just math. It isn't a big deal."

Diane nodded at Daniel. "Okay. P.J., The Tower was walking around naked. He reached toward you, and you practically walked through the wall trying to get away from him. Why?"

Diane was more right than she knew, P.J. surmised. Atoms are almost nothing but hollow spaces, less than one percent occupied by mass. The strong nuclear force sticks the protons and neutrons together in the nucleus, and the attraction of the nucleus holds electrons in orbit. The nucleus and electrons are infinitesimal compared to the space that the atom occupies, so atoms should slip through each other like two colliding schools of fish, but they can't. The electrons whipping around the nuclei in a cloud are all negatively charged, and thus the electrons repel each other, and thus the electrons in the atoms in the proteins in the cells in the tissues of P.J.'s cheek repelled the electrons in the calcium, oxygen, and carbon atoms in the calcium carbonate in the drywall, and thus P.J. could not walk through the wall, even though she and the wall were each ninety-nine percent empty space. P.J.'s finger moved to the right of the Schrödinger equation, and she began calculating the repulsion of the charges of electrons between her cheek and the wall.

"P.J.?" Diane asked. "Are you with us?"

"What?" P.J. looked up at Diane and Pastor Daniel, both of whom watched her like she might evaporate.

Diane said, "I asked why you tried to get away from The Tower when he reached out at you."

P.J. shrugged and thought about emptiness and repelling electrons bouncing off each other. No matter what she said here, it would be wrong. Nothing she said was right or cool. She was always the dork who got people in trouble. Getting all the kids home to Saffron seemed impossible.

"P.J.?" Diane asked. "You seem agitated when we talk about The Tower or Ester James."

"Agitated? I'm not agitated." Her left hand took over inserting Greek figures in the Schrödinger equation, while her right hand calculated the charge repulsion of electrons.

"If your parents did something wrong, P.J., if they hurt you or the other kids or even if they were involved with Ester somehow, and if you tell us about it, we can help them. We can use your testimony as a friendly witness, and we could knock the charges down to negligent homicide or even reckless endangerment. It would help them a lot. You just have to tell us about it in your own words."

"What?" P.J. dropped a negative sign in the electron force calculation. Her hand rose three inches in the air and overwrote her previous equations.

Diane said, "But if you don't tell us, if we find out that they hurt you or the other kids or if they knew something about Ester, then it's going to be a lot worse for them. There are forensic teams over at your house right now. If Ester was in there at all, or if we find her blood or clothing or microscopic skin particles that Saffron or The Tower brought back with them, the charges are going to be capital murder. They won't get bail at all, and they probably will get the death penalty."

P.J. scribed frantic equations in the air because she could not listen.

"You know, P.J., sometimes things happen that we didn't mean to happen. Like, sometimes when I'm cooking dinner, it burns. I didn't set out to burn the dinner. It just happened. P.J.?" Diane asked. "Are you listening?"

Pastor Daniel said, "It's okay, Diane. It's just math."

"But look!" She gestured at P.J., who resolutely continued working on the quantum mechanics with her left hand, calculating electron repulsion with her right, and replaying an internet chess game in which she had been walloped by a Russian Grand Master.

Pastor Daniel said, "If she says that she's just doing math, then she's just doing math. Right, P.J.?"

"Yeah. Right." Carry the *phi*, cancel the volts, and the rook moved to g6 to check her castled king.

Diane said, "I think you heard something, and I think you saw something. You must have seen something. You did see someone out there, didn't you?"

"I don't know." How would they know if she saw something?

"Did you see anything like this?" Diane balanced her briefcase on her knees and opened it. The black leather top eclipsed her face. She slammed the lid and held out to P.J. a slippery handful of eight-by-ten color photographs.

P.J. let her calculations fall and took the photos.

The overhead fluorescent lights reflected white lines across the glossy prints, but underneath the white stripes were terrible pictures, horrible pictures. At the top of the frame, a man's arm held thick bushes back for the photographer. A bloody arm with part of a woman's bare torso and breast lay on the ground.

"Oh my God," P.J. said. Horror coiled in P.J.'s legs and she wanted to jump up and run.

"Four young women have been killed south of Dallas," Diane said. "All of them went missing, and we found pieces of them."

P.J. wanted to drop the photos, to throw them away from her as if they had just turned into a writhing serpent in her hands. "Oh my God!"

The next photo was of a bashed-in skull with brown, curly hair. Some scalp still clung to the skull. The lower jaw and most of the front of the skull were gone.

"Animals, coyotes especially, eat the tongue and eyes," Diane said. "We rarely find soft cranial tissues on the skull. She was a nice girl, she went to a party, and she never came home."

The photographs rattled in P.J.'s hand. Her fingers were numb and she could not feel the slick ink and paper. The photos slipped and she tried to catch them but she did not want to touch them and they fell to the floor.

Diane said, "Ester is at least the fifth victim."

The photographs lay on the beige carpet. The only color in the room was in the photos: the green bushes, brown blood, and one blue coat wrapped around a leg. The edges of that picture were dark, like a spotlight had lit the dismembered leg for the picture at night. "Why haven't the police warned people?"

"The police don't advise the public about serial killers or any crimes during the investigation. It taints evidence. It brings out the loonies who think they're psychic and they've talked to the dead. It usurps the police and sheriff departments' authority."

Diane stared right at P.J. as if P.J. was hiding something. P.J. felt like Diane was accusing her of helping the serial killer.

Diane said, "This is what this serial killer or these serial killers do to young women. This is what they have done to Ester or will do to her. They'll rape her, chop her up, and scatter her body under bushes like she was garbage and they don't want to be fined for littering."

P.J. pressed herself back into the chair. "I can't believe this. Every time I walk home from school, I walk through the parking lot of the grocery store." Someone might have been watching her, waiting to chop her up. Or one of her little sisters.

Pastor Daniel spoke up. "Like the Sabeans and the Chaldeans, they fell on these girls and tore them to pieces. They are People of the Lie, P.J. We have to stop them."

"This is Ester James," Diane held up a glossy photograph of the young blond woman that P.J. had seen a hundred times in the last three days: on the television news and programming breaks, on the flyers that she had stapled all over her high school, and at the church. "They're going to do the same thing to her, if we don't find her, or else they already have. If they have, then we need to find her as soon as possible, to save the evidence, and to bring her home to her father, so he can bury her."

Ester James existed in a state of semi-deadness, P.J. thought, like Schrödinger's cat shimmering in Limbo. No one had seen if she was alive or dead. She was an unobserved state, both alive and dead. Only after a conscious examiner examined Ester would classicality be achieved.

Pastor Daniel said, "If Ester has been killed, she deserves a Christian burial. Her father needs to say goodbye, and she deserves her sacrament. The funeral is a holy ritual as much as marriage or baptism."

Ester's half-life and half-death were entangled with the environment, P.J. thought. The state of the observer's perception is entangled with Ester's state. It was all entanglement. P.J. was entangled.

As soon as a consciousness observes Ester, she will resolve into life or death.

The photos glared up at P.J. Black blood clotted on the chewed limbs. Those photos unnerved her, scraped raw all her nerves and excised them, leaving her weak and numb.

"Try closing your eyes again," Diane said. "Just try. Remember Wednesday night, when you were chatting on the computer."

P.J. closed her eyes and tried to remember, but jitters crept up on her. She had been sitting in the back room, the communal room with mildewed blue carpet.

Sanjay had had ten-dimensional math spread out on his metal desk, and his webcam showed his work on her computer screen. She had been following along and typed a question.

One of the photos lying at her feet was of a finger, just a finger, in straw-yellow grass. The pointed nail was painted burgundy black.

Pastor Daniel said, "Let us pray."

There must be an Observing Consciousness, P.J. thought, that separates us all from quantum probability foam. P.J. tried to reach out to that Observer, out there.

Pastor Daniel said, "Lord, we ask Thee to guide P.J. in remembering what happened that night, to reveal to her what she has repressed in her memory, so that we may bring Ester James's killer to justice. In Jesus' holy name we pray, Amen."

Diane said, "Amen."

P.J. said, "Amen," for the first time in her life.

That night, P.J. had heard something outside, over her Goth music growling through the computer's speakers. People talking. She looked up and out the window. Something reflected through the screen in the glass.

Diane asked, "What did you see?"

Lights. "There were lights," P.J. said.

"How many lights?" Diane asked.

Diane sounded so sure that she must be right. Trusting little P.J., who accepted rides from strangers in sheriff's cars and Jaguars and drinks from people who were not her friends, went along.

P.J. had gotten up and looked out the window. She tried to stop time so she could count the lights, which meant that she must be going the speed of light where length becomes zero, mass becomes infinite, and time stops. Mentally, she grouped the lights into pairs and counted the white dots outside the glass. "Seven."

"Seven?" Pastor Daniel asked.

P.J. counted the lights with her finger, even though her eyes were closed. "There were seven lights."

"Did you go back to the computer and type, 'gotta go, brb?'"

"Yeah. I must have, when I saw the lights."

"Did you go outside?"

"I don't know."

Pastor Daniel said, "Let us pray again. Lord, we ask You to help P.J. remember that night when she saw the seven lights."

P.J. felt Pastor Daniel's warm palm in her left hand. Diane's cooler hand held her right.

P.J. prayed. She wanted to remember. There were serial killers out there, murdering people, people like P.J. and her sisters and Ester. It was imperative to stop them, if she could only remember.

Pastor Daniel said, "In Jesus' holy name we pray."

All three of them said, "Amen." They let go of her hands and rustled backward.

Last week, the weather was cool, in the seventies during the day and the fifties at night. The back door in the communal room led to the screened porch. She got up from the computer, turned up the music, saw the lights, and walked outside. "I walked onto the screened porch to see what the ruckus was."

The screened porch had old rattan furniture with plastic cushions. It was too dark to see the chintz-like plastic at night. "I sat on the couch."

Her thighs felt the grit on the plastic cushions, even though she had been wearing a long, black skirt. "The moon was up," P.J. said. "It was a full moon that night."

"Yes, it was," Diane said. "How well could you see?"

"Okay. The moon was pretty high in the sky and to the east a little, over the grocery store, and the parking lot lights from the other side of the store spilled over. The top of that low wall that divides the loading docks from the empty lot was a silver line. People came through there, talking."

"Talking?" Pastor Daniel asked. P.J. opened her eyes. She had almost forgotten he was there. He was leaning forward with his long arms braced on his knees. His head was cocked to the side, and his chin was lowered, like he was thinking so hard that he had to point the top of his brain at her. "What were they saying? Would you call it chanting?" he asked.

"Yeah." People came over the wall, chanting. A crowd of people.

Diane said, "You said there were seven lights."

"The lights, like, swung in arcs." P.J.'s fingers described the lower part of a broken-up circle. "They were walking and carrying flashlights."

"Could you see their faces?" Diane asked.

"No. It was too dark. I could see their feet in the flashlight beams."

Her own right foot stepped on a glossy photograph of a naked human pelvis propped up under a magnolia tree. The magnolia flowers were out of focus but in full summer bloom.

"Were they wearing pants or skirts?" Pastor Daniel asked.

"I don't know," P.J. said.

"Do you want to close your eyes again?" Diane asked. "Maybe you can remember better. Try to picture it."

P.J. closed her eyes. Pastor Daniel and Diane were replaced by fragments of magnolia flowers, dead bodies, and swinging flashlight beams.

"Describe the people," Diane said.

"There were a lot of them. The flashlights were hidden among them and then glared around, like they were searching for something."

Pastor Daniel said, "Last time you said more than ten people but less than twenty. Can you give us a more accurate number? Were there twenty?"

"Less than twenty."

"More like thirteen?" Pastor Daniel asked. "P.J., this is very important. Were there thirteen people?"

There were seven flashlight beams, one per every two people or so. "There was one person with a flashlight out in front, and then five flashlight beams whirling around, and then there was one at the back. There might have been one flashlight for every two people for the middle five. That's about right. I think there were twelve people."

"Okay. Twelve. That's good." Pastor Daniel said, and he sighed. "P.J., were Saffron and The Tower among them?"

P.J. opened her eyes again. "What?"

Pastor Daniel held Diane's hand. Diane stared at his hand with surprise, and then she looked up at his face, alarmed. Diane removed her hand from his.

Pastor Daniel asked, "Saffron and The Tower were among the people in the wilderness with the flashlights, weren't they? That's why you didn't know where they were, because you didn't want to remember that they were among the people out there."

Panic pressed her. Thinking hurt. Those horrid pictures jumbled on the floor, like the writhing limbs of drunken people dancing. Trust mixed with residual chemicals.

Her fingers rose into the Schrödinger equations. Ester was both alive and dead in these numbers hanging in the air. Was she both alive and dead, out in the woods somewhere? Or did whoever took her see her die, and thus they were the observational consciousness? Did Ester herself count as a consciousness? Did P.J.?

Diane asked, "Did you see your parents in the house?"

Every night after P.J. had signed off with Sanjay, she climbed into her bunk bed above Connie and crashed. Had she done that? Or had she stayed outside on the porch? Her memory jerked and jarred awake. "I don't know."

"Where were they?"

P.J.'s fingers filled Greek letters into the large density matrix. Ontology stealthily shifted, and reality became the probability matrix, probably. "I don't know."

Diane gazed at the ceiling, pondering. "Okay, let's go back. You heard something, turned up the music, then went outside and saw the people in the vacant lot. Where did they come from?"

They walked from the left to the right, into the wilderness. "They climbed over the wall at the grocery store, under the moon." P.J. moved her hand to the left. Unsupported, the tensor set describing reality fell to pieces. The Greek letters fell into the photographs at P.J.'s feet, sprinkling a photo of an arm stump and an amputated foot in a bed of trampled carnivorous pitcher plants that looked like a smashed tea set.

"They walked through the dead brush, into the trees."

P.J. frowned.

Diane asked, "What?"

P.J. closed her eyes again. "They walked from the grocery store into the dead grass and weeds. The moon was above them." Her left hand moved to the middle, pointing between where Diane and Pastor Daniel were sitting if she opened her eyes. With her eyes closed, her hand extended through the screen of the porch. The tree line started a hundred yards right. What had happened between them walking over the wall and into the tall grass, but before they reached the trees? She thought hard, trying to move the people with her mind, but they would not budge from that halfway mark.

"P.J.?"

She had stood up from the computer and looked out the window and then walked onto the screened porch. It felt like she knew more. The knowledge was just beyond what she could remember, like a mental cat hair in her throat that had to be coughed up.

Out there on the screened porch, she had coughed. Maybe.

"I coughed," P.J. said. Her eyes were squeezed shut.

Once she thought about coughing, one memory sparked, the other memories surfaced, like a nuclear chain reaction. Those neuro-thingies in her head must be like the naked protons that collided with and split uranium nuclei, which released more proton debris and energy, which collided with more nuclei, and so on. Pastor Daniel and Diane had pressed inward on her soul until she reached critical mass.

"They were behind our backyard, and they stopped. The lights came together in a bunch, shining inward. Some dust got in my throat and I coughed, and they shined their lights on me."

Seven lights hit the fly screen on the porch and sparkled like a huge computer monitor. People of the Lie, Sabeans and Chaldeans.

"I just stood there, because they'd seen me." Panic had slapped her legs and chest, like the shock of getting caught with pot at school.

Diane's calm voice asked, "And then what happened?"

The panic returned in waves, like it bounced off the past and amplified. "One flashlight separated from the middle of the pack of lights and walked over to the porch. It stopped outside the screened door. It was just a yellow-white light," like the light that illuminated the arm and breast ripped from the woman in the photograph at her feet.

"And then what?" Pastor Daniel's voice asked through the dark. His voice held a tense note that Diane's had not.

"He opened the door to the porch."

"He? It was a man? Did you recognize him?" Diane asked.

Out of the dark, the flashlight had painted the screen door.

The Tower opened the screen door.

Oh, God. Oh, Jesus, Shiva and Buddha.

"It was *Appa*. The Tower opened the door. He said, 'Come on, P.J.' and I walked out into the brush with him. It was really cold out there. We walked toward the trees."

P.J. tried to calm herself by meditating on the Bodhisattva. One of them, the Akash Jogini Bodhisattva, wore a necklace of skulls.

Why would a Bodhisattva wear a necklace of skulls? Bodhisattva were nearly fully enlightened people who did not go on to nirvana but were born again to guide others to the Way. Why would Akash Jogini Bodhisattva wear a necklace of skulls?

Maybe it wasn't a Bodhisattva. Maybe they had told her it was a Bodhisattva, but it was something else, a demon, a devil.

Diane asked, "You walked out there and went with them?"

"Yes." A glimmer of light leaked through her shut eyelids.

"Oh, my Lord," Diane said. "Oh, P.J. You were there?"

P.J. said, "I was cold, and The Tower put something around me, a black blanket or something."

"A robe," Pastor Daniel's voice said. "A black robe."

P.J. opened her eyes. "Yeah."

Diane clutched Pastor Daniel's hand. She said, "I thought they might be People of the Lie, unwittingly doing the Devil's work out of narcissism, but Devil cults are just superstition. Aren't they?"

"Thus the old cliché," Daniel said to Diane, "that the Devil's greatest lie is that he convinced the world that he does not exist. In the Lessing house, did you see black candles? Knives or wands? Pentagrams?"

"I don't know!" With her other hand, Diane clutched her sweater over her heart.

"They only had twelve people, so they needed one more. With P.J., there were thirteen of them, a full coven."

"A coven?" Diane asked. "Saffron mentioned a coven. I thought that she said convent or covenant, but she didn't. She said coven."

Yes, a coven. P.J. knew about Saffron and The Tower's coven. They walked sky-clad around candles in the living room, chanting. Good thing that no one from school had discovered those naked, wrinkly, pudgy pagans.

Pastor Daniel continued to soothe Diane. "And you rescued her. You rescued P.J. before she ended up like those other girls. It's okay, Diane. Don't cry."

Like those other girls.

The people out in the woods that night were chanting. Their chanting was different, harsher. The Tower and Saffron must have gotten mixed up with these darker pagans during those long weekends when they went on pagan retreats and left P.J. in charge of the hacienda.

The Tower and Saffron were both easily swayed, and Saffron had been on some kind of megalomaniac high lately, yelling at the kids that they had better be good because worse could happen to them.

What happened in the woods was worse.

P.J. closed her eyes again.

Memories crackled in her head, blasted through thought, and

became worse, and worse, and worse. Oh, Shiva. She *remembered.*

Under the darkness of her eyelids, P.J. saw the copse of trees.

"Did you recognize anyone else?" Pastor Daniel asked.

"Saffron was there. I didn't see her face because she wore one of those black robes, but she sways when she walks. She was three people in back of me. At one point, she grabbed The Tower's arm and whispered, and their hoods came together like two shadows merging, but she didn't say anything to me. The Tower said, 'It's big magic. It'll be a long night.'"

Pastor Daniel's smooth voice asked, "What did he mean?"

"They were carrying something. That's why there was one man in front, and one woman at the back, and six people in the middle were carrying something long and heavy between them. The others were holding back the bushes and shining their lights on the ground. I saw an arm. An arm was sticking out of the bundle that they were carrying."

Pastor Daniel asked, "Of what race was the person with the arm sticking out?"

"Pale. White. A white arm. They were carrying a stretcher, and Ester was tied to it. Her blond hair fell over the edge of the stretcher. She looked asleep. I was the observing consciousness. We walked into the woods."

Diane said, "Go on."

"We walked far into that stand of trees, over to the marshy area. There's a big magnolia tree there, and it doesn't shed its leaves in the winter, but it doesn't have blooms yet. On the other side, some skinny trees looked dead." The flashlights threw spiky shadows from the trees behind them, slashes of white on black paint.

P.J. said, "There was a huge stone altar beside the bayou, a cube. There were carvings all over it."

"How tall was it?" Diane asked.

"I could see over it. It must have been four feet tall. It was a cube." The cubic altar radiated out at her like it was exploding. It was a hypercube, four-dimensional, an object that only math could describe.

"What did the carvings look like?"

"Pentagrams, pointing downward. Curly Latin, like wrought iron."

"Then what?" Pastor Daniel asked.

"They took her off the stretcher and laid her on the altar, chanting in Latin. It wasn't Sanskrit, like in Hindu temples. I picked out words. Requiem. Quantum. Equilibrium. Vacuum. Symmetry. They laid her on the altar, and they set the flashlights on the ground, facing in. When they walked around the altar, their shadows blacked it out. Ester was lying on it, but her arms and legs hung off because she was too big, too long. Her head hung off the front. It was dark, but the moon and their flashlights lit her blond hair. She was naked. She must have been cold."

P.J. covered her face with her hands, and the darkness inside her eyelids deepened. "They chanted. They walked around her. Their shadows blotted her out. The Tower was behind me, and he pushed me forward. I stumbled but he pushed me and I walked. I didn't know what they were saying. A man stepped out of the circle."

"Did you recognize him?" Diane asked.

"No. He was the man in front, leading the way. He was taller than The Tower, six feet, maybe."

"What happened next?"

P.J.'s eyes burned with salt. "He raised a silver knife with a black handle, an *athame*, over his head. He stabbed over and over while The Tower and Saffron and the others walked around, chanting. Then he cut her throat, and the blood ran down the altar and into the pond. The water turned rusty brown with it. He cut her up."

The box opened, and P.J. observed. Ester was dead. Oh, God, Ester was dead.

All this time, she had known, but she couldn't look at it. Observing made it real, and she didn't want any of it to be real. Being Gothic and tragic was a model of her life, not what she wanted her life to be.

Diane's voice was calm, but she sounded choked. "P.J., what happened then?"

Tears squeezed out of P.J.'s eyes and dripped from her palms. "And then they threw water on the altar and washed off the blood. They told me to get up on the altar."

Diane and Pastor Daniel gasped.

"And they took off the robe and my clothes, and I couldn't stop them. I couldn't move. They held me down, and the guy who killed Ester pulled my knees apart, and two others held my legs, and he opened his black robe and he was naked and he stuck his dick in me. He *raped* me. It hurt. I hadn't before, and I thought he stabbed me because it hurt so much and he was going to cut me up, and I screamed but no one heard me and I couldn't even hear myself. He grabbed me and pulled me onto him and raped me again and again, and they all chanted."

Someone touched her shoulder and P.J. jumped and she fell out of the chair but Diane wrapped her arms around her. Diane's chain of pearls ground against P.J.'s collarbone. Diane said, "Oh, Lord," over and over. "I'm sorry. I'm so sorry. I'm so sorry. I should have gotten you out sooner. Oh, God, I'm so sorry."

Pastor Daniel sat on the floor in front of her. Tears ran down his face, leaving darker tracks on his ashen skin. "Oh, P.J. You were a virgin?"

The slashing branches of the trees crossed the sky like black-handled knives ready to fall. The black robe lay under her on the stone altar, but the rough rock still hurt her back. They pulled her legs, and the man stabbed her with his dick again and again. She couldn't breathe and she couldn't talk. Every time she blinked, she saw the black trees.

Worse than the rape, worse than the murder, the ring of people watched and did nothing, like she had done nothing when they killed Ester.

"Oh, Lord," Pastor Daniel said. "A Black Mass, with a ritual murder and the rape of a virgin. Satanists." He held Diane's arm. "They've been killing these young girls. There are five dead girls now. We have to tell people. We have to warn them before they kill or rape someone else, not to mention the effects of whatever black magic they're performing. Satanists. My Lord, here in New Canaan, Texas. *Satanists*."

Yes, Satanists. Black-robed Satanists killing pretty blond women and raping virgins by the light of the full moon on a pentagram-carved altar. What could be more cliché? P.J. forgot to mention the black candles and the wild orgy afterward, but she would have been unconscious by then.

Oh, yes, I was there. Of course I was.

And you were there, too. You remember.

The moon crested to its zenith above the enclosure ringed by acacia and black alder trees, when the High Priest raped the thin girl. Terrible and wonderful moonlight poured over the ring of bystanders and P.J., splayed on the altar. Her arms and head, dangling off the cube, cast sharp shadows on the moonlit sandstone at their feet. The sun-soaked altar burned P.J.'s back, but the February air chilled her until her teeth chattered while she screamed. The black-robed figures stood silently, heads bowed.

P.J. remembers the Satanists stabbing and tearing apart the lovely, blond Ester James, just like those dismembered girls in the photos scattered at her feet. She remembers the pain of the rape. She can almost remember their faces, obscured by black hoods. If she tries hard enough, their faces will resolve.

Moonlight-capped boulders surrounded the clearing.

The dank bayou over the High Priest's right shoulder stank of rotting algae.

You remember.

Monday

At four-sixteen in the morning, Max opened his eyes and looked at the clock. When he rolled over, he was alone in the bed.

Damn it.

Three o'clock in the morning is a late night. Max sometimes worked late at the office or out and did not get home until three, but four o'clock is early in the morning. That's when your alarm clock shrills to catch an early flight or go hunting.

Max sat up and prepared to go hunting.

His cell phone lay on his nightstand, in case Diane called. He thumbed the one button and held it down to call her.

On the first ring, Max was pissed at Diane for staying out all night without calling, and for staying out all night at all.

On the second ring, Diane's destination of Pastor Stout's house had come to his sleep-fogged mind, and his fears of Stout seducing her resurfaced. Damn it, he had told Stout to stay away from Diane, *mano a mano*, and when Diane had called and told him she needed to interview P.J. Lessing one more time, he had told her to wait until Monday at the station where they could videotape it.

Stout should remember what Max had said at the church, because if Stout had so much as touched Diane, Max was going to shoot the preacher down and stuff him and mount him on the fucking wall.

By the third ring, Max recalled the photos of the four other women killed south of Dallas in the past couple years. Soledad Watson, the prostitute, worked late at night, consorting with the usual suspects. Information gleaned from P.J. might have led Diane to a dangerous part of town, to criminal types, to whoever or whatever was killing women and cutting them up.

Diane had to pick up the phone. There were dead women out there, and someone was killing them. "Damn it, answer."

That little Goth P.J. Lessing had sent Diane. She was always around when someone went missing. She was a bad omen. She was the catalyst.

Damn it, Diane, pick up. Pick up.

At four-eighteen in the dark of the morning with the phone wedged between his shoulder and his ear, Max stood to find his pants.

Diane's voice mail kicked in. Max said into the phone, "Diane, where are you? It's four in the morning. Call home when you get this message."

He hung up and redialed. Her cell phone rang and no one answered.

Max hitched up his pants and zipped them. He powered up the computer, logged into his account, and typed his username and password into an Internet site.

A map popped open. A radiating red dot showed the current location of Diane's Jaguar and displayed the nearest address by GPS.

Max had installed GPS units on all the cars when Tatiana started driving. They not only displayed location, they also measured speed. He had never thought he would need it to find Diane at four in the morning.

The car had been stationary since a few minutes after nine o'clock. Max remembered that damn address, where the mini-bus had dropped off the Lessing brood and he found Diane and the pastor clutching each other. What in the hell had she been doing at that clergyman's house for seven hours? Jealousy was not in his repertoire. It bucked him because he didn't know how to handle it.

Max knew exactly what she had been doing over there. He was right. He was fucking right. That preacher was fucking her. Righteous anger piled onto jealousy. The thought of that preacher sucking her earlobes or her elbows pissed him off to the point where he realized he was holding his gun.

Max called her cell phone again. And again. He punched the number pad so hard the light flickered.

On the second ring of the fifth call, the line clicked open. "Hello?"

Anger poured out. "What the hell are you doing over at Daniel Stout's house at four-thirty in the morning?"

Her rich voice sounded thin through the phone. "I'm sorry. I was talking to P.J. Lessing, and some terrible things came out. Just terrible, but it is a major break in the case. Probably the major break."

Max tried to lower his voice but his throat tensed and he sounded shrill. "So exciting that you stayed over there until four-thirty in the morning?"

"I fell asleep on his couch. We have to get P.J. Lessing into an interrogation room and get it on videotape, but we're going to walk the crime scene tomorrow morning. She saw them kill Ester James. We took notes. She signed them."

There were so many things wrong with that speech that Max wasn't sure where to begin. He rubbed his cheek, scraping his palm on sharp stubble. "You shouldn't be at Stout's house in the middle of the night."

"It was work. I have as much right to work late as you do. What are you doing when you're out late, like last Friday until almost two in the morning?"

Ransacking her office to find evidence of her fucking around with Stout, and now he saw he was fucking right. "Working. Looking for real evidence on the Ester James case, not," with clenched-jaw sarcasm, "'recovered memories' from a suggestible minor during an interrogation in the middle of the night without a parent or guardian present after major life trauma. Jesus Christ, Diane! That'll get knocked down by any half-competent defense attorney." He propped his elbow up on the dresser to hold the hot phone to his ear. "Even a stupid cop like me can see that."

"Her foster father and I, an officer of the court, stood *in loco parentis*. She implicated her adoptive parents in sexual abuse, at pretty much her first opportunity after ascertaining her safety. And don't take Christ's name in vain."

"That's right, because you're a Christian now, a member of Stout's church, aren't you?" And Max knew what to think about those cryptic entries in her date book: BS for Bible Study. Crap. That kind of brainwashing might as well mean butt sex.

"Pastor Daniel said that you knew. I'm sorry that I didn't tell you, but I was afraid of just this reaction."

"Anger that you didn't tell me? Or at you spending the night with him?"

"It isn't like that! His wife is here!" Her voice had lost its sleepy slur.

"Diane, you've been out all night at this guy's house. What am I supposed to think?"

"That I'm doing my job! The job that pays the bills!"

He hated that he did not provide the entire living for the family and his wife had to work, let alone this. "Son of a bitch, Diane, that's low."

"That's not what I mean, and that's not how I think of it, but I went to school my whole life to be a lawyer. We agreed that my career was important, and we would co-parent the kids. You have to let me do my job."

"Four-thirty in the morning, Diane."

"I nodded off on the couch. I'm already in my car, driving home."

He was not sure whether to wait up. If he did, they might fight more. If he did not, he was not sure whether she would come home. "Where are you?"

"Corner of Fifteenth and Rio Hacienda."

Fifteen minutes away. "Why did you do it, Diane? Why join his church?"

"Max, it's four-thirty in the morning."

His teeth ground in his mouth. "You want to remind me of that?"

Her voice was a little hysterical, but it waned softer like she was looking around while holding the phone to her ear. "I was searching for something. Meaning. A strategic theory."

"The kids and me and your job and putting perverts behind bars aren't enough for you? Do you believe that crap?"

"It's not crap. And there's precedent. I exist. Why shouldn't something of me, my soul, exist in perpetuity? Something should be eternal, and it isn't the earth or the stars. There's nothing out in the universe except chalk and fire. Surely, something endures. I wish you would come to church with me."

"No." He hung up without waiting for her to say anything else, took off his pants, and lay on the bed.

This bed was their fourth bed. Their first one was from his bachelorhood. When she had changed the sheets the first time after she moved in, her eyes had creased and then widened at the mandala of brown-rimmed stains on the ticking, not to mention the blood of three virgins and a charred blip. Two days later, she announced that she had found an excellent sale and a bed would be delivered the next day. Max, so enamored of her smooth linen skin, thin gold hoop earrings, and molasses scent of her breath that he argued with nothing, signed for it and paid the man.

The first night on that bed, the sex had been gymnastic, like she was trying to make him forget the other bed. The middle two beds had come and gone due to changing lumbar needs.

When she sneaked in the room, he played dead on their fourth bed.

She undressed, put on pajamas, lay far over on her own side near the edge, and turned off the lamp. Black air snapped closed over the bed.

She had not showered, as guilty parties are wont to do, when they come home from screwing.

Hell with it.

He rolled over in the dark, reached, and dragged her over to him.

"Max, I thought you were asleep."

He kissed her to shut her up. He investigated her, every nook and cranny, as thoroughly as an adultery-sniffing K9 unit. The sex was incidental.

She gasped into the night, but no alcohol, neither wine nor whiskey, soured her breath, merely a hint of garlic under a strong breath mint. If she had screwed around, it was a decision, not a loss of control, as far as such things are ever a decision.

When he licked her breasts, he checked for other saliva or foreign tastes, specifically, for any Eucharist or priestly residue. Her perfume left a bitter, dry residue like alum even after the scent was gone, and that aftertaste was still there.

He maneuvered his fingers into her panties under the dark blankets, which she was wearing the customary way, seams inside, and into her crotch, which was moistening but not already slimy from another man.

Fine, Diane had not been screwing around tonight. As she had said, Daniel's wife was home. Or she might have blown him. But at least she hadn't been getting screwed this particular night.

With this assurance, his opinion returned to its previous philosophical bent, that they had both had relationships before marriage, and as long as one was devoted to the home, extramarital sex was unimportant.

His own jealousy revolted him. His opinions of sex had been formed carefully, over years. They were not a knee-jerk reaction to some nirvana-esque initial sexual experience nor a rebellion against religious inculcation.

Opinions chiseled from a red-hot block of rage and pain do not erode.

Max screwed his wife in the dark, in perfect silence.

Later, her breathing in the black room was shallow and regular, not quite asleep. He asked, "How can you believe that stuff, Diane? It's lies."

Her breath inspired and exhaled in soft shushes three times before she said, "It's comforting."

"Lies aren't comforting. If I told you that you were going to win the lottery after you die, you'd think I was full of shit. Why is it different when Father Daniel tells you about golden palaces and heavenly choirs?"

Her breathing deepened, asleep.

Max asked, "Do you believe everything that faker tells you?"

In the dark, Diane's snores softly reverberated on the blue walls.

Early the next morning, from the front room window, Zeke saw Pastor Daniel stroll up the gravel walk. The preacher's tread on the gravel was heavy. Gravel scuttled out of his way.

Foreboding rose in Zeke's throat, and his legs ached.

Only a moment ago, unknowing had been a curse, and now it seemed like the deepest comfort. That shard of hope that he had regarded as a spike through his feet, tripping him, had been the only thing keeping him pinned to this earth. If only he could die now.

He rested his hands on the windowsill, short of breath.

Knocking radiated through the silent room.

All Zeke's vitality was gone. He could not move to open the door.

More knocking disturbed the quiet air.

Zeke moved his hand enough to twist the deadbolt and knob.

Pastor Daniel entered, his hat in his hand.

"You found her?" Zeke asked. He leaned on the deep windowsill. Grit ground into his palms.

"No," Pastor Daniel said. "But we have some information. It's not good. Indeed, it's nothing we have hoped for."

"But you have not found her, nor her earthly remains?"

"No."

Zeke still could not stand on his own, even though that spike of hope had returned. He again wished it gone, so he might fall to pieces and walk into the arms of the Lord. Yet if she was not dead, there was hope, and as long as she might still live, he would wait for her. "What's the news?"

"We must keep this quiet, for we don't want them to know before we have rounded them all up."

"Them? All?"

"Yes. Satanists, a coven of Satanic witches, are operating here. We have information that they murdered her in a Black Mass."

"But you have not found Ester."

"No. The informant is going to be questioned by the County Attorney today, and we and the sheriff's deputies will look for evidence and for Ester's remains. Ester was a good Christian, Zeke. If this is true, and all signs point to it, then she is in Heaven with Jesus, beyond all pain and all want. Anything they did could not change that she was Saved. Her acceptance of Jesus as her Lord and Savior cannot be abrogated."

They had not found her. Zeke cradled that knife blade of hope that sliced him, for the pain of superstitious hope kept him alive.

Vanessa watched the small television perched atop the older, larger, broken one. She was tweaking, having filched a snort off her mother's methamphetamine stash, and her own jitters irritated her. She hated crystal meth, but she usually lost a few ass pounds when she visited her mother, though she usually gained it back in booze and beignet when she went back to New Orleans, plus a few.

On the television, the prosecuting attorney Diane Marshall, standing behind a too-tall podium, looked like a decapitated head floating in a bell jar of formalin on a shelf. Her hair was drawn back so tightly that she looked like she had shaved her head and lacquered her skull brown.

Diane Marshall held a piece of paper and read directly from it: "The County Attorney's office has new information that may lead to imminent arrests in the Ester James missing person case. Much of this information must remain secret until reviewed by a grand jury to indict current persons of interest; however, some information must be disseminated for reasons of public safety."

The paper in Diane Marshall's hand trembled more than it would have in Vanessa's vibrating hands. Wouldn't prissy Diane Marshall freak if she knew Vanessa screwed her husband? That would really fuck up her day. Vanessa jumped off the couch and paced. She hated meth.

Diane Marshall said, "Some information relates to a group of people in New Canaan or surrounding communities who have been practicing Satanism. These Satanists are an immediate danger to the lives and health of our citizens, and thus we are releasing this information under the federal terrorism guidelines. These Satanists have been acting as a gang of serial murderers and rapists. They have murdered and dismembered at least five young women and raped a young teen girl. Ten Satanic cult members are still at large."

Vanessa stopped pacing and bounced in place like she was speed-skipping a jump rope. She hated meth, but she hated idiot prosecuting attorneys even more.

Satanists. Jesus H. Fucking Christ.

She hated meth.

There was no fucking Satanic cult in Sin Nombre County. There was a fucking serial killer, and once again, law enforcement couldn't investigate their way out of a paper bag with a compass and a Bowie knife.

Jesus Christ. Satanists. They should have just said space aliens.

On the television, Diane Marshall said, "These Satanists may kidnap more young women for Satanic sacrifice or rape."

Satanists. Jesus H. Fucking Christ. Vanessa hated meth. She bounced and paced on the brown shag carpeting, which was as limp and greasy as unwashed hair.

All the evidence pointed to an organized type serial killer. Not a fucking Satanic cult. Fucking idiots.

Diane Marshall said from her roost behind the podium, "We ask all Texans to be vigilant, especially during major moon phases. Parents, keep close watch over your daughters." Her voice choked.

Diane Marshall was thinking about her own virginal daughter, Tatiana, who was seventeen and smart enough to make her daddy proud.

That idiot should realize that one of the victims had been a whore, a literal whore, and the other women all utilized barter instead of currency. It was part of the serial killer's MO, his fucking signature. Jesus, Vanessa had written a whole report for the Dallas police and the Sin Nombre County Sheriff's Office, and they acted like they hadn't read it. Serial killers had an MO and a signature. That's how you knew they were serial killers.

Well, that's the way the whole stupid, fucked-up, ass-wipe world worked. The truth is too complicated so idiots make up superstitious crap to explain it.

Satanists. Jesus H. Fucking Christ. She hated meth.

Vanessa dialed Max Konstantin on her cell phone. "Did you know that your wife has some fly up her ass about Satanists? She just told the whole world that there's a bunch of Satanists running around slaughtering young virgins? Why in hell is your wife talking about Satanists?"

Max's low voice was too soft, and Vanessa beep-beep-beeped the volume rocker on the side of the phone until she could hear him. "I don't know what she's talking about. As if your serial killer press conference yesterday wasn't bad enough to rile everyone up, now we're going to have mass hysteria."

"Black Mass hysteria," Vanessa quipped.

"You know," Max's voice coming through her phone was still tinny, "any other time, that would be funny. But the house phone just rang, and my idiot boss Sheriff Garcia is going to call us all in and put us all on seven-day duty and twenty-four-hour call until we round up a bunch of Satanists. The weirdoes are going to be crawling out of the woodwork, tattling on neighbors who don't mow their lawns often enough and expounding on their psychic dreams. Hold on."

Vanessa heard him muttering in the background while she grapevined across the living room, crossing in back for ten vamps, then crossing in front. She hated meth, which compelled her to perform aerobic dance steps when she hated aerobics classes.

Max came back on her cell phone and said, "Yep. The Sheriff's office is already swamped. Jesus Christ."

"Why the hell would she do that? And why Satanists?"

"Diane said she had a major break in the case last night. That must have been it. Shit, Satanists. Does she have no sense?"

"I was going to ask you that."

"Diane said that they were going to walk the crime scene with P.J. this morning."

"P.J. Lessing, the little Goth?" The one who had been hanging around Ester James's church, which in cases like this was sometimes indicative of the perpetrator, of someone who wanted to come forward, or of someone who was generally fascinated by murder and death, like a Goth.

Or like a forensic technician, come to think of it. She giggled.

Max said, "Yeah, that P.J. Lessing, and considering that she lives right in back of that grocery store, I'll bet they're going to that vacant lot back there."

"The one with that fantastic magnolia tree? I'll meet you there."

"*Don't.* The last thing I need is you showing up, grinning."

She grinned. "Okay."

"Especially since I'll bet Diane's going to bring that preacher."

"Pastor Daniel?" She still wanted to fuck the preacher with the high, tight ass, and fucking on meth is so much fun, almost as fun as on ecstasy. It's bunny-fucking.

"Yeah. You aren't a member of that church, too, are you?"

She laughed and laughed. He was so funny. She hated meth. "Lightning would strike me dead."

He sighed. "That's my other damn phone again. I'll tell you anything I find out from Diane, okay?"

"Okay! Thanks!"

They hung up, and Vanessa filched a little more of her mother's stash, just to keep her going for another couple hours because she hadn't slept at all for two days and had slept only badly the last five days, and coaxed it into a line and snorted it.

The exhilaration hit her from her long toes to her swelling boobs to her blond roots.

She hated meth.

Diane waited in her car outside the Lessings' house, sipping bitter, black coffee out of a travel mug and hoping her breath wouldn't be too skunky. Despite sleep deprivation, Diane had awakened at seven o'clock with a jolt of frightened energy. Max rolled over and slept on. Sleeping so deeply, so long, seemed negligent. Women were dying out there. If what P.J. had remembered last night was true, and she thought it was though she prayed it wasn't, then a gang of truly evil people were murdering and raping young women.

Lord Jesus, the moon was waning. If they had some demonic ritual planned for the new moon, they had a week and half to stop them. If their ritual was for the waning quarter moon, they had only a few days.

God, Lord Jesus, please let the girl be mistaken. Or lying. Or on drugs. Or psychotic. Schizophrenia sometimes broke brilliant prodigies, like John Nash.

Diane should be able to spot if something was wrong today, when they walked the scene with her, and she retold her story.

That morning, when she had dropped Tatiana off at the high school, her teenaged daughter had sauntered, head down, inattentive and completely unaware of the other cars and even the huge van that pulled up beside her and blocked her from view for agonizing seconds, until she was inside the fenced perimeter.

An anxious armada of cars scrutinized their own disembarking teens.

Pastor Daniel's humble blue sedan stopped in front of Diane's car. Diane secured her coffee in the car's cup holder and scrubbed her oily teeth with her tongue, hoping to ameliorate the worst of the coffee breath. P.J., in the passenger seat, dozed against the window. Pastor Daniel reached over and gently nudged P.J.'s shoulder. The girl woke slowly and shook her head. Her black hair was mussed from sleeping, but she was not wearing her severe make-up. She was a pretty girl, but her jaw was thin and her owl-like eyes were large.

They met in the Lessings' front yard.

P.J. asked, "Can I check on my cats?"

Diane answered, "I fed them and cleaned the boxes before you guys got here, but you can go in if you want. You shouldn't go in the living room because the Sheriff's office hasn't finished investigating what happened Saturday morning." And no one had cleaned the walls. "I went in the back door. The cats met me there."

P.J. borrowed the key back from Diane and went in through the back.

Pastor Daniel and Diane followed P.J. in to make sure that she did not move anything or destroy evidence, but the girl concentrated on the cats. Diane had performed the chores, and P.J. seemed relieved to see all eight of them swarming around her like children to a cookie-wielding grandma.

In the computer room, Pastor Daniel pointed to a slim, black-handled knife resting on a shelf. "That's an *athame*. It's a ritual knife used in witchcraft. Have it tested for blood."

Diane noted it. She would come back later.

People can believe some crazy things. Whether or not there was a Devil, whether or not he could be called to Earth and perform Satanic magic, did not matter. If twelve people thought it could happen, then young women were dying for it.

Figurines populated a wall-sized bookcase.

Pastor Daniel said, "Lord in Heaven, Sister Diane. They have Hindu deities, Buddhist idols, Native American kachinas, everything except Our Lord and Savior. This idol here," he pointed to a cast iron, slender idol dancing within a circle of flames, "is Shiva, the destroyer god in the Hindu religion. Did you know that some Hindus think that the current cycle, the Kali cycle, and the whole universe and all of existence will end in the year 2036? The Mayans, however, who believed in this dragon-like, feathered serpent god, here, thought that the world would end in December of 2012."

A lot of information. "Wow, Daniel. Were you into this stuff?"

He scratched his smooth, shaved cheek. "Know thy enemy. I've studied many Satanic cults, from Hinduism to Wicca to Islam."

"But," Diane felt odd debating theology in front of the ebony statues of Shiva and Kali, who stared at her with white enameled eyes, "I kind of thought those religions were different paths to God."

Pastor Daniel laughed. "No. Christianity is the path to Christ. As Jesus Our Lord said, 'No man cometh unto the Father but by Me.' Jesus is the Lord's 'only begotten' Son, not *one* of the begotten sons and daughters and nieces and nephews of God. Those other religions are inspired by, and paths to, Satan, trying to confuse people and damn their souls. I'm glad we're talking about this. You have some weird ideas."

Diane inspected the dancing demons. "I suppose so."

"You saved these children from far worse than death, Diane." Pastor Daniel inspected a black, writhing, grinning goddess idol. "Their immortal souls were in more danger. You saved them from damnation. They have a chance to come to Christ before the End of Days, and the end is coming."

Diane needed to start working on Max and the kids soon.

P.J. came back into the computer room, holding some stuffed animals. "The little kids need these."

Pastor Daniel nodded. "We'll put them in the car before we go to the vacant lot, where it happened."

It, Diane thought. Where *it* happened. Where the ritual murder of a young woman and the rape of a child happened. Where a Satanic black ritual happened. Where people willfully murdered a young woman and raped a girl because they thought it would invoke black magic.

At the Criminal County Attorney's office, if they spelled everything out in vivid terms, not in legalese or bland euphemisms for all the crimes and collateral damage but real words, every day would be a devastation of raped kids and dead women and mourning families that they calmly coerced into accepting plea bargains.

After stowing the stuffed animals in the trunk of Pastor Daniel's car, they walked to the vacant lot and began by the grocery store.

Pastor Daniel held out the digital video camera that Diane had signed out of the County Attorney's office that morning. Hatless, he peered at it and gingerly pushed a button on top. Diane had never known him to wear a hat, even though he had lived in Texas for three years now. To Diane, born and raised in Texas, a man outside without a Western hat looked vulnerable to the sun.

P.J. said, "I was standing on my porch," and she pointed to her back yard, "and the Satanists came over this wall, about here."

The dust was unmarred, no footprints, but the ground was hard-baked with a light powder of dust. Tracks would be gone in minutes.

Pastor Daniel asked, "And then what did you see?"

It irritated her that Daniel asked that question because Diane was the prosecuting attorney and Pastor Daniel was the foster parent who should be safeguarding P.J., but he knew more about Satanists than she did, as evidenced by the fact that she hadn't recognized Satanic paraphernalia. Plus, if the interview went awry, she might be able to toss it without compromising other evidence. Lawyerly tactics might be disgusting, but they were useful.

P.J. said, "They walked across here." She stomped through the brush, which was trampled in places. Diane took a digital camera from her bag and shot a few frames of the trampled places and then a few with a disposable film camera. Digital photos are easy to manipulate, and defense lawyers and juries know it. A corroborating film negative can save a case, even though manipulating them is easy, too.

"Oh, hello!" A woman's voice shouted at them.

Diane looked up. A zaftig blond woman hailed them, hand up, and tramped through the winter-dead bushes toward them. Her sunglasses were so huge that they looked like black goggles. Diane squinted and recognized the woman from the church and the news conference, Vanessa Allen.

Vanessa reached them and stretched her trembling hand toward Diane. "Hi! I didn't think I'd find you guys here! I thought I'd walk this lot one more time to look for evidence. Can you believe it's already been four days? I can't. I can't believe it's been four whole days."

Diane was about eight inches shorter than Vanessa. Diane was used to tall men, but a much taller woman made her feel shrimpy. "This is an official visit, Vanessa. We're investigating a crime."

"I saw your news conference this morning. Are you investigating the Satanists in this vacant lot? Are you going to investigate the space aliens and Sasquatch while you're at it? Huh? Sasquatch?"

"This is an official investigation." Diane easily squelched the impulse to respond to the taunt. She was a litigator and measured everything she said by whether it had its intended effect. So, the Allen woman was a bitch.

"And I'm officially offering my help. I may not agree with your whack-job theory, but at least you're investigating something. You have a trained forensic tech at your disposal while you walk the, I presume, 'Satanic ritual murder scene.' Do you want me along or not?"

Pastor Daniel stepped up next to them and said, "Hello, Vanessa. I'm sorry we haven't been able to talk. Things have been hectic, and I haven't had time for parishioners, let alone petitioners."

"That's okay. I'm gonna be a Sikh."

Pastor Daniel looked confused and worried. Diane wanted to tell him not to respond because it was just a provocation, but Daniel did not say more.

Vanessa turned. With the huge, dark sunglasses, she looked like a bug-eyed robot mechanically turning its head. "Hi, P.J."

"Hi." P.J. scuffed the dirt with her black sneaker.

"You don't look so Goth today," Vanessa said.

"I was too tired to do my makeup."

"In the long black skirt and pretty white blouse, you look like a proper little Christian. Have you been hanging around the preacher too much?"

P.J. frowned. "Shut up."

"Did you see the Satanists?" Vanessa's derisive tone twisted her mouth. "What kind of Satanists were they, orthodox or reform? Southern Satanists? Missouri or Wisconsin Synod Satanists?"

"It's none of your business." Tears dropped from P.J.'s eyes.

Diane considered intervening, but P.J.'s contained reaction suggested that she was sincere in what she said. Liars expounded on their lies and hotly defended them. If nothing else, P.J. believed in the Satanists.

Vanessa said, "Right. Shall we walk this vacant lot and look for evidence of the coven of Satanists? Or see if the Loch Ness Monster dropped into the pond? Maybe a *chupacabra* has been vampire-sucking goats." Vanessa stomped on a weed and moved off a few yards, trampling brush with her big feet, on which she wore ballet flats, not good hiking shoes. Diane thought that it was too bad that the rattlesnakes were still hibernating, but at least some of these bushes had wicked thorns.

Diane put her arm around P.J.'s shoulders. "It's all right, honey. Don't listen to her."

A man's shout echoed across the dead grass. "Diane!"

Diane turned and saw a man in a proper hat, Max, stomping through the thigh-high dead grass toward her. She yelled across the waste, "Max, this is County Attorney's office business."

"And this is Sheriff's office business," Max Konstantin said. "We need this information, too, no matter how cockamamie it is." He reached them, touched his hat to Diane, a vestigial removal of his hat that always melted her heart a little, and noted Vanessa's presence five yards away with a nod and a hat touch. "Hello, Miss Allen. What are you doing here?"

"Offering my forensic services." She held her long, blond hair back with one hand, which lifted her breasts toward the two men. Diane closed her eyes to keep them from rolling up into her head at such a stupid trick.

"Peachy." Max's mouth tightened, and he turned his shoulder away from Vanessa.

"Look, Max." Diane frantically tapped her thighs for her cell phone. The rectangular lump in her pocket was tangled with a rosary. "We're just walking the scene with P.J. to see if it jogs her memory."

"Yeah." Max's jaw jutted forward, like his teeth were set together, and the muscles around his nose spasmed. Diane had seen this particular expression when he had found his then-fourteen-year-old daughter necking in a car with a nineteen-year-old college freshman, and a poetry major at that. "I want to see this interrogation technique of yours. Or maybe it was the good reverend's confessional technique that got P.J. to admit she's a Satanist."

"I'm not a Satanist!" Transparent tears brimmed over her long black eyelashes and fell down her cheeks.

Vanessa said, "Of course not. It's everyone else who's a Satanist."

Max looked back at Diane. "Do you know how many phone calls we've had down at the Sheriff's office since your little press conference? Hundreds. Probably thousands by now. Everyone is pointing fingers at their weird neighbors or asking if we're going to distribute silver bullets to the general population."

"No." Diane fidgeted with the crucifix in her pocket that she had bought at St. Mary's that morning and hoped that people were not so stupid as to load silver bullets into their guns.

"Yes. I don't know which military contractor supplies silver bullets. George is telling them a wooden stake works just fine." Max turned to Pastor Daniel. "I imagine you're doing brisk business in crucifixes and holy water."

His chin rose. "We do not use the superstitious trappings that the Roman Church has integrated into their ceremonies to appease pagans."

Diane poked her crucifix down in her pocket.

"Oh, yeah, we're the freaking crazy ones." Max half-jumped toward Daniel, who flinched and raised his hands up, warding off an attack. "You could use a vow of celibacy."

"What's that supposed to mean?"

"It means to stay away from my wife."

Diane's legs tried to step back and run away and cower behind a tree. She stepped forward, between them. "Stop it. Stop it, both of you."

She jumped. The silenced cell phone in her pocket jiggled her thigh like a rattlesnake had crawled up her pant leg and rattled a warning.

"You two stay away from each other." She opened the phone, noted Zeke James's name on the screen, and walked a few steps. She worried that he had found some other piece of evidence, something different. "Hello? Zeke? What's wrong?"

"We have a problem." Zeke's voice through the phone was hoarse and exhausted. "This morning, when I went out to the pasture, I found a couple head of my cattle dead."

Diane's chest tightened. "How many?"

"Three. They slit the cattle's throats and disemboweled them."

The thought of dead cattle made Diane woozy. She held a hand to her temple. "Oh, Lord."

"They were trusting cattle. Never been hurt. They would've watched whoever did it walk right up to them."

"That's horrible." Diane covered her mouth with her hand. "I can't believe it. I'm so sorry, Zeke."

Zeke's voice was clenched. "I can't help but think that it's a warning that they will do this to Ester. Sister Diane, what should we do?"

Diane glanced over at the others. Vanessa stood away from the group, watching the treetops, her blond hair writhing in the wind. She and Max stood near but not facing each other. Their postures were tense.

P.J. sat down on the ground.

Diane said into the phone, "I believe what P.J. told us, Zeke. She is adamant that she saw Ester. I'm so sorry."

"I'm canceling the plane Wednesday. We can ship them next month. I'm sorry about the timeline, Sister Diane, but she's my baby. If there is even a small chance that someone might do this to her, I can't."

Retching sounds trickled through the phone.

Diane said, "Zeke, Please talk to the sheriff's office before you do anything. Are you all right?"

The gagging slowed. "I'm fine."

"Has anyone threatened you? Atheists? Vegetarians? Satanists?"

"No." Zeke's breath crackled over the phone. He panted.

"All right. Call the sheriff. Even better, you've been dealing with Chief Deputy Max Konstantin, right?" Diane looked up and locked eyes with Max. His tanned face was flushed. "He's right here."

Max's hands strained into claws, like he was repressing their desire to wind into fists. Diane held her cell phone out. "Honey, Zeke James needs to speak to you. Several of his cattle were killed last night."

Max lifted the phone out of her hand. "Yes? Zeke?"

Diane stepped back. Zeke's call might divert him from throttling Daniel.

Vanessa walked over to Max. Her blond hair blew across her face, and she peeled it away. She said loudly over the wind, "Max, I can take a look at them. I've been around enough dead bodies to have an opinion."

Max nodded to her. He glanced at the phone, spoke into it for a minute, then walked over and handed it back to Diane. "You've got a call on the other line. I'll call Zeke back from my phone."

Nemo Turner, a fellow parishioner, was on the line. They had co-organized the shipping documents for Zeke's cattle. Diane often sat near his family, and they answered her whispered questions in church. She thought of them as her cheat sheet. She answered.

Nemo asked, "Sister Diane? Is it true what we've been hearing? Satanists?"

"Yeah, it seems so."

Max answered a call on his own phone and walked over by a boulder.

"I've been talking to some folks," Nemo said. "We want to have a prayer vigil tonight at the church."

"Oh, Nemo. It might be wiser to stay home."

"These Satanists could commit home invasions. We might be safer in numbers," Nemo said. "We can bring bedrolls and post guards at night."

Diane had to admit the sense in it. "That's a good idea, Nemo. Why don't you call Melinda Stout about it? She's at home."

"Right. See you tonight." Nemo's line clicked closed.

Diane hung up and heard Max say into his phone, "No, ma'am. The sheriff's office will not be issuing guns to the general population. There is no civil war against the Satanists and atheists. Thank you for inquiring." He snapped his phone closed. "Idiot."

"P.J.," Pastor Daniel said. The whole gang turned toward him. "Would you please show us all what happened?"

P.J. had played in this vacant lot since Saffron and The Tower had bought the house when P.J. was five. Before, their small apartments had been in bad neighborhoods. "There's a swampy area back there."

Vanessa said, "It's farther left."

Deputy Konstantin glanced at Vanessa and looked away, but he did not ask, so P.J. did. "Do you know this place?"

Vanessa shrugged. "In high school, all the good parties were in this vacant lot."

Deputy Konstantin nodded like he knew.

P.J. wondered if he knew about the other places that high school kids went to party around there, like Loser's Lake and Hi-Falutin' Row.

P.J. led the way into the bushes. "The Tower was standing about here when he saw me on the porch," P.J. said.

Standing in the field, looking back at her house, it hurt so much. Repressing it would have been easier. She could almost remember his face. The hood on his robe flapped around his acutely angled chin, his orthogonal jaw, his right eye, as he held her knees apart.

It was for the best that she remembered, though. Ester's family could grieve now instead of worry.

Still, she had survived and Ester hadn't, and guilt ate at her. She had stood in a black robe when they slit Ester's throat. The other Satanists were in too deep. She was more culpable because she knew better. They were brainwashed but she, the Goth perennial outsider, should have stopped them.

P.J. said, "We all walked back through these bushes, into the trees."

They stomped through the brush. Pastor Daniel watched P.J. through the video camera. Diane snapped pictures with two different cameras.

Deputy Konstantin and Vanessa Allen walked behind them. They did not talk, and he bounced away when she strayed too near to him, two like magnetic poles repelling.

Thorns snatched and tore their clothes. Diane misstepped and it looked like she twisted her ankle, but she didn't complain. The dead bushes gave way to the sandstone steps around the bayou.

The land in front of the scummy pond was barren. A limestone layer under the poor soil stymied any root deeper than a weed. Dead lichen limned the rocks. P.J. said, "The altar was right here."

The adults looked at the ground.

Deputy Konstantin paced the perimeter of the area. He shoved bushes and squinted at the dirt.

Vanessa Allen peered into the rusty pond like she was scrying. P.J. could hardly hear her mutter, "This is stupid. I hate Beth."

P.J. wondered who Beth was.

Diane took methodical pictures of the ground and climbed a rock for a better vantage, favoring the twisted ankle.

Pastor Daniel swept the video camera across the area in panoramic shots. Those shots were going to be blurry and vertigo-inducing, bad amateur videography.

P.J. pointed to the ground. "It was right here, this high," she held her arm at chest-height, "and, like, this wide." She spread her arms far apart, nearly her full wingspan. "It was hard and rough, gritty stone, like granite."

Pastor Daniel pointed the video camera right at her. "Yes?"

"And they pulled Ester off the stretcher. She flopped. They dragged her onto the altar and they all pointed their flashlights at her." That night, the white light glared on Ester's pale skin like cars about to run her down. Now the morning sun glinted gold on the smooth, beige dirt. "When they dragged her up on the altar, it didn't move. It must have been heavy, because they half-heaved her up and dragged her across."

Vanessa muttered, "This is stupid. I don't care. This is stupid," and trotted around the pond, clambering over rocks and trampling dead thicket. Again, "I hate Beth."

P.J. should have grabbed Ester, run into the brush, and hidden her in the fossil caves back behind the river, where Saffron and The Tower hid their pot stash.

Saffron and The Tower would have looked in those caves. A fourteen-year-old girl cannot outsmart and outrun twelve adults, dragging an unconscious woman who outweighed her.

Diane climbed down off her rock and stood beside P.J. "What then?"

"They walked around her, pointing their flashlights at her while they chanted in Latin. The circles of light climbed all over her. I didn't have a flashlight, and I didn't know what to chant. I just walked."

"Which direction?" Pastor Daniel asked.

"Um," P.J. said, "this way." She took a few steps to her left.

Pastor Daniel said, "Widdershins."

Diane raised her eyebrows at him.

"Counterclockwise," he said. "You walk clockwise for white magic, and widdershins for black magic." He kept the video camera pointing at P.J. even when he spoke to Diane. "And then?"

She said, "They chanted for a long time. Ester moved one foot. A few times, they stopped and pointed their flashlights up, and it got really dark." The parallel flashlight beams soared into the black sky, catching dust motes. "Then they all pointed their flashlights at the altar again." P.J. pointed at the center of the void, "and a man was standing there. He had stepped forward in the dark."

That night, beams caught the back of the man's black robe, but more shone on Ester's pale skin and blond hair. Because he was surrounded by light, the man cast no shadow on the sandstone ground or the massive altar.

P.J. said, "He drew an *athame* from his belt, and he stabbed her. She didn't move. He cut her throat, and the blood ran down the altar and through here." P.J. pointed at the shallow dirt and drew a line to the limestone rocks and to the water. "It came pouring out of her, like someone was emptying a gallon of milk on the ground."

Vanessa Allen, who had stepped toward them, inclined her head. "That's a pretty good description of someone slicing a jugular vein."

P.J. said, "They all watched the blood pouring out. Someone came forward and caught some of the blood in a cup. I don't know what they did with it."

Diane asked, "What kind of cup?"

"A goblet. It was a heavy goblet, medieval-looking, gold and rubies."

Diane nodded. "And then what happened?"

"He cut her up. He took that *athame* blade, as big as a butcher knife, and he hacked her to pieces in about fifteen minutes. No one said anything. He cracked bones and sawed her muscles. Sometimes it sounded like carving meat and sometimes like hack-sawing metal. He worked hard, like there was a time limit, and he flung the pieces away. When he was done, he swept his arm across the altar and all the pieces fell off, and he looked up. The moon wasn't quite overhead yet. The flashlight beams and the full moon hit him, and I saw him smile up at the moon."

Vanessa tossed her golden hair in the sunlight. "It takes longer than that to chop up a body."

Diane pressed her hand to her chest. "And then what happened?"

"I don't know where they got the buckets, but they sloshed water from the pond on the altar to wash Ester's blood off." The brown and red water ran down the sides and drained into the sand.

"Thank you Lord that Zeke James isn't here," Pastor Daniel said.

Diane sighed. "P.J., then what?"

Gravity yanked P.J., and she fell to her knees. She was free-falling in a vacuum, accelerating harder and harder, and the curvature of space-time stretched her. She couldn't breathe. Her heart thundered a bass line. "They grabbed me. The Tower and someone else grabbed my arms, and they pulled me over to the altar. I fought. I fought like hell but I couldn't move. I yanked and I tried to fall on the ground and I tried to kick them but they dragged me over there so fast, like I wasn't anything, like I had no mass." Like she was a massless particle, a wave in the ether, and their inertia was irresistible. P.J. rubbed the deep, scabbed-over abrasions on her right arm.

"They dragged me over the altar," she said, "and they dragged me up on it. Four men held me down. It smelled like the slimy pond water. The guy who had killed Ester opened his robe. He was naked underneath, and he pushed my legs apart."

Diane had one hand over her heart and was breathing through her mouth, horrified. "Go on."

Pastor Daniel's mouth was set in a line of rage, staring where she pointed, where the altar had been.

On the other side of the clearing, beyond the circle, Vanessa Allen watched P.J. One of her dark blond eyebrows was cocked, like P.J. was an interesting specimen under her forensic microscope. She smiled.

Deputy Konstantin squatted on the ground, leaning against a rock, eyes closed, but no one else noticed him doing that because everyone else was watching her and had their backs toward him. One of his hands covered his mouth like he was trying to not throw up, and his other hand clutched his holstered gun like it was his only handhold before he fell down a ravine.

Max rubbed his sweating palm over the cool handle of his gun and tried not to vomit. Cold sweat slapped him.

Her story stabbed him. He couldn't shut his ears, so he heard, and he wanted to scream. Later, he would recall it perfectly, word for word.

He reached up to his head, removed his hat, and covered his face with it, staring into the sun glinting through the straw-woven crown. Anyone who saw might assume he was covering emotion at hearing P.J.'s story.

In her soft, frightened voice, P.J. said that the man, "opened up his robe. He was naked underneath, and he pushed my legs apart."

Max's Aunt Anna had always been a hugger, grappling her nieces and nephews and smearing them with kisses. She was a lean, patrician woman, slimmed by dieting, who could have been the daughter of the lost Grand Duchess Anastasia Romanov, had not Max's father's family been descended from unabashedly peasant stock. Anna herself, however, was an Anglophile and called herself "Anne" to her friends. Her nieces were invited to high teas. She wore her platinum hair swept up in a French twist and wore slim-skirted suits.

When Max was nine, Anna babysat him and his younger siblings so his parents could go to dinner and a movie and she introduced him to wine coolers. When Anna tucked Max into bed, she opened her robe, and she was naked underneath. She got into bed with him and touched him. Then she showed him where to touch her.

Over by the bayou pond, in her little-girl voice, P.J. said, "It hurt when he raped me. I thought he'd stabbed me between the legs and in my back and he was cutting me up while I was still alive."

Pain sparked through Max's temples because he was squeezing his eyes closed so tight, but tears slithered through his clamped lids. He was lost in P.J.'s nightmare and his own. His back hurt from the hard rock behind him. His rattlesnake skin boot heels dug into his ass.

She said, "It went on forever. It felt like hours. I kept crying for him to stop, and he pushed in harder. It hurt."

In Max's job, rapes of an adult are more violent and bothered him less because an adult knows that a crime is being committed and fights. The few times he has chanced upon a molested kid, Max backed far down into himself and called for a counselor.

Memories sparked inside his head, a migraine of memories.

After the first time, Max wouldn't drink the coolers that Anna offered him, so Anna spiked Max's orange juice with vodka and then expounded her philosophy that men are intrinsically violent and women should train boys to be good lovers and to appreciate the mature female form so they won't grow up to be pedophiles who rape little girls.

"That's what causes it, you know," she said, and he tried to focus his eyes on her shifting bulk but the horrid dreaminess meant that she had tricked him again. "Men, raping children. If all men were to suddenly die, the world would be a better place."

At the age of nine, Max's discernment of beauty was undeveloped. It wasn't that Anna was over fifty. That first time, lying on his sheets emblazoned with big trucks, she tried to pound him off, and prepubescent boys' dicks don't work that way. She abraded him until his foreskin ripped. Then she showed him all her sparsely hairy parts and demanded he get stiff.

Afterward, she gave him money and impressed upon him that it was his choice. Her squinty eyes glared at him. "It felt good, didn't it? It felt good because you wanted it. Men have all the choices in this world. For a woman, it's always rape. You raped me."

Max forced himself to inhale. Dust choked him. Once he could breathe again, he staggered to his feet and pounded his clothes to beat out the dust. The grit had ground through his clothes, all the way to his skin.

And why didn't Max tattle? Why did it go on for years?

The usual. The prosaic. Perverts know how to groom children. They find the threats that work. Anna told Max that no one would believe him, that Max would be punished for drinking alcohol, that it was Max's choice, and that he had raped her.

When Anna began to eye Max's younger brothers and sisters, Max saved them. Max never, ever left Aunt Anna alone with them.

When he was seventeen, in a violent parody of everything she had told him about the evils of men, Max stuck a Colt .45 in snobby Anna's mouth and told her to leave him and them alone, and then he beat her. She had made him feel pleasure that shamed him, and she'd flipped on the sex switch in his head, so his libido wanted women. Sex was friction and pain and shame and desperate clinging to control and power and pleasure and orgasm and oblivion.

Afterward, he tried to feel bad about beating up a woman, but she was an abuser. That distinction saved him from most survivors' self-flagellations. Women can be pedophiles, and the psychic damage is just as bad as when a man rapes a little girl. Don't let sexism dissuade you. Max was not a lucky boy initiated into the wiles of women to the envy of his peers. He was forced. He was raped. He knew he was damaged.

Max never repressed these memories. They hover around him constantly like a swarm of killer bees. He compartmentalizes them. He uses them to focus his rage. He hurls them like Thor's thunderbolts.

This time, they ambushed him.

That's the problem with memories. Memories of pain can turn the soul, that little spark of Brahman in all of us, into Shiva the destroyer.

During the whole recitation in the vacant lot, amongst the winter-dead brambles, Diane had stared at P.J. and scrutinized her for any minute sign that the girl might be lying or crazed. Diane was good at detecting lies. As a prosecutor, her own witnesses and sometimes her victims were intrinsic causes of the prosecuted crime. Crimes were tangled wads of provocations and reactions, but eventually Diane found the shred of truth that led to the conviction.

P.J. had evinced no micro-expressions of triumph or insanity. She showed nothing beyond the expected survivor's traumatic shock. She was neither too adamant to suggest lying nor too reticent to suggest other falsehoods.

Damn it, Satanists. The girl teetered on Occam's Razor's thin edge.

Again, Diane reminded herself, she was not battling Satan. She was prosecuting deranged people who committed crimes.

Afterward, Diane sat with her husband Max in her car. He had walked ahead of the rest of them the whole way back from the *locus criminis,* legal Latin for the scene of the crime, and the bayou was a crime scene in Diane's mind. Something had happened there.

When they had reached the vehicles, Vanessa had slithered in her car, slammed the door, and sped away without talking to anybody. She didn't even look at them as she whizzed past. Her angry face accused them of idiocy.

Diane asked Max, "You okay?"

"Yeah. Fine." His face was placid. He didn't even look mad anymore, and he had frowned while he was sleeping that morning.

"Are you still mad about me falling asleep on Daniel's couch?"

"Ancient history."

"You going home?"

"Some paperwork at the office, then I'll be home."

"What time?"

He did not shrug. As a matter of fact, his body had not moved since she got into the car. No hand gestures. No facial expressions. "Five."

"Okay."

He turned to her. His face had such a lack of expression that his facial muscles were slack, and that lack of tone made him look a decade older, around fifty-five, worn out by the law enforcement work, with an empty nest and congestive heart failure. The slackness scared her.

"If you are having an affair," he said, "don't fall in love with him. Don't let him get into your head. Sex is nothing. Sex is bullshit."

The poor guy thought she was screwing around on him. "Oh, Max, I'm not! I wouldn't!"

"It's okay." His hand lifted, and he patted her hand. "Sex is nothing."

She put her arms around him and felt a small, corresponding echo in her heart. Sex was not nothing. Under her arms, he did not move.

"I have to go to the office to write a report. I'll see you at home." Max stepped out of the car, closed the door so gently that it clicked, and drove off in his official car.

Diane watched his car coast away. She shook her head at the change in him, but he was weird like that sometimes. She assumed that it was something to do with Hispanic culture. Sometimes in a cross-cultural marriage, you just have to accept that you will not understand things.

Diane walked over to Pastor Daniel's car. "Can I talk to you for a minute?" she asked.

He got out of the car, leaving P.J. who was bent over with her head resting on her black skirt. They walked into the Lessings' immaculate yard. She said, "Don't forget that I'm picking P.J. up for that doctor's appointment at three o'clock today."

Pastor Daniel ran one finger over his chin, and his chin curled. "I don't like it."

She chose an honorific that suggested equality. "Come on, Brother Daniel. We're not Catholics, as you've noted on many occasions."

"Yet it is an abortion."

"No, it's an emergency contraception pill."

Pastor Daniel dragged his finger over his chin again. "What if it's more than a moral choice, Sister Diane? This child, a virgin, was raped during a Black Mass."

She steeled herself to argue and win. "This minor was raped."

"What if this is how the Anti-Christ chooses to come into the world, Diane? The Temple is going to be rebuilt. The Anti-Christ must occupy it."

"First, Brother Daniel—and I'm sure I don't need to quote scripture to you—the Anti-Christ must occupy the Temple of Jerusalem before Armageddon, so he has to be a Jewish priest, which presupposes that he has to be Jewish, and Judaism is matrilineal. P.J.'s hypothetical child wouldn't qualify. Second, I don't think that the Anti-Christ, the infernal antagonist for the glorious second coming of Our Lord Jesus Christ as foretold in the Book of Revelations by John the Apostle, can be thwarted by the morning-after pill."

Pastor Daniel nodded.

Diane sighed, relieved, because she would not have abandoned P.J. to a pregnancy, whether feared or actual. Diane would have pulled the whole Lessing family out of the Stouts' foster home and bought every air bed in town to camp them in her own living room if necessary, but it was better not to uproot them again.

She asked him, "So what do you think about what P.J. said?"

Pastor Daniel nodded. "I believe her."

"Really? About the altar? A cube of granite, four feet on each side? If it was solid, it would take a crane to lift. Even if they glued granite countertops to a box, it would weigh hundreds of pounds. It would have scraped grooves into the sandstone like wagon wheel tracks." Unless it was on wheels.

Pastor Daniel shook his head, slowly, sadly. "It doesn't matter even if it was just a plywood box sprayed with faux granite-fleck spray paint."

Diane said, "There is no physical evidence. No blood on the ground. No body. No clothes. No enormous cubic block of granite. I only took thirty pictures. If there had been anything, I would have taken hundreds."

"We will never find anything," he said, "not blood, not Ester's body, not marks on the ground, not microscopic fibers. There will be no physical evidence at all."

Diane stopped looking at the cats peering out the front window of the Lessing house and stared at him. There was always evidence. While some guilty people are convicted on means, motive, and opportunity, there was usually at least some circumstantial evidence. Evidence was not required under the law, but it made cases easier to prosecute. "Why will there be no physical evidence?"

Pastor Daniel gazed into the bright sky. "The complete and total lack of evidence *is* the evidence that we are dealing with a Master Satanist."

His words jolted Diane. Prosecuting deranged murderers who believed they were Satanists was within her ken, but he meant they must battle the Satanic supernatural.

Fear rose in her: fear that she was predestined to choose evil because she was too weak, and fear that she could not sacrifice herself properly because she was too afraid.

The sermons that she had heard all through her childhood haunted her. People who sinned went to Hell. She was unworthy and destined for Hell but for the blood sacrifice of Jesus Christ. Some people, those who would not make the blameless choices, were destined for Hell.

She loved the law because she could wrangle with the questions, and laws guided her toward the right. In the whole rest of her life, she felt like the laws amended themselves constantly, with no notice, and her transgressions were inevitable and damning.

She was not an abject rationalist who reduced the world to the merely physical. She longed for the touch of God. God worked in subtle ways on people's hearts, as when he emboldened her to rescue the Lessing children, but He was not limited to mere influence. Miracles happened. People were cured of terminal cancer by prayer. The Vatican catalogued miracles for their saints, and they had a lot of saints.

God performed miracles in the world, *ergo*, it followed that Satan could cause evil supernatural acts. It follows. *Sequitur.*

On the evening news, the ubiquitous picture of smiling, blond Ester James appeared above the left shoulder of the Dallas newscaster. "Today, two people were formally charged in the disappearance and murder of Ester Christina James, the young woman who has been missing for four days." A woman struggled against manacles and hid her face on the perp walk into the women's county jail. "Jennilynn Barkowski, who uses the alias Saffron, and Glen Pappathanasakis, also known as The Tower, were charged with Murder One and First Degree Kidnapping of the missing woman. Earlier today, Assistant Criminal County Attorney Diane Marshall," footage ran of Diane with one ribbon of hair undulating in the wind, "held a press conference that implicated a Satanic cult in the kidnapping and murder. Yesterday, Ms. Vanessa Allen," footage of the hard, busty blond, "a forensic technician from New Orleans, held a news conference to direct public attention to a possible serial killer in the area. No word yet on whether Barkowski and Pappathanasakis allegedly are Satanists or a Bonnie-and-Clyde serial killer team."

The high-haired female newscaster made a rueful moue. "This sounds like a job for the Texas Rangers."

The first anchor looked at his notes page. "Yeah. Sounds bad."

He touched his chest where, directly under his lavalier, tie, shirt, and undershirt, a large gold cross hung from a chain. The cross jostled against his mic, and an electronic squeal ran through the equipment. The sound technician grimaced.

Zeke grieved and stroked Lilypie's heavy head. The sun caught glints of amber in Lilypie's deep red hide and sad eyes. The poor thing.

Deputy Max Konstantin and Vanessa Allen walked across the brown field toward him. "Howdy," Zeke said.

"Hi," Max Konstantin said. "Brought Vanessa Allen to take a look."

"Like I said, I don't see what good it'll do. They were stabbed and their throats were cut. Nothing mysterious." Zeke turned away. Seeing

Vanessa still upset him, even with Max as a buffer. He fidgeted with his hat.

"Always good to have a third set of eyes, though." Max walked around the cow, taking pictures. "I assume you'll prosecute."

"Sure enough." Zeke would hogtie the bastard and drag him from the bumper of his truck if he caught the son of a bitch first. His anger at whoever had taken Ester, long swamped by sorrow, found an outlet.

"Since it's just a cow, we can only charge them with criminal mischief, probably only be a Class A misdemeanor."

"Just a cow, my red-furred butt," Zeke said. "Lilypie was a transgenic organism. In addition to the CMV-Mao A knock-in, she was also transgenic for human erythropoietin with a tet-dependent promoter."

Max blinked twice and pushed his hat back on his head. "What?"

Vanessa frowned at him, stymied.

Zeke explained, "She made an anemia drug for people in her milk if you fed her an antibiotic, and she was insured for one-point-two million dollars, but she would have produced maybe five million dollars worth of erythropoietin in her life. Her calves would have been worth half a million a head. The other two were just Red Angus, though."

Vanessa piped up, "I didn't know you were breeding Frankencows."

Zeke scowled at her flippancy. "I'm not. Lilypie was the next evolutionary step in cattle ranching, a pharmaceutical-grade bioreactor. Look at that coat. Perfectly straight legs. Beautiful animal."

Vanessa pulled on latex gloves, and stuck her fingers in the cow's wounds. "Mao A is your serial killer gene. So she was a serial killer cow?"

"The opposite. She over-expressed Mao A. This cow could love." He stroked her head again. Her blood on the ground was dry. She had died out here, all alone, with just cows for sympathy.

Vanessa Allen had her hand in Lilypie's neck up to her wrist. "He seems to have done a thorough job. The ligaments have been cut all the way back past the trachea. He damn near cut her head off."

Stomach acid burbled in Zeke's belly at the graphic description of what some bastard had done to his sweet little cow. "You do say."

Max said, "So I have to ask you again, Zeke. Who would do this? Rival pharmaceutical company?"

Zeke stopped and sucked on his lips, which tasted like salt sweat. "Might have to do with the Jews."

"You mentioned that. Nazis aren't much of a problem around these parts, and the nearest Jewish temple is in Dallas."

Telling Max made Zeke nervous. The dry facts were all that he had allowed himself to talk about. Names. Prices. Herds. Dates. The reason he was selling these cows to the Jews was far more important than the fact that he was selling cows to the Jews.

Max's unbelieving squint made Zeke's anxious exasperation worse.

"I have to start at the beginning," Zeke said, "in Biblical times. The Israelis' cattle are all descended from the speckled, spotted, and brown cattle that Jacob, son of Isaac, received as wages from his uncle Laban."

The cow's neck sucked shut as Vanessa pulled her hand out and flicked clotted blood from her fingertips onto the grass.

Max clicked his ballpoint pen. "What does this have to do with you?"

"For the Jews to consecrate their temple, they need to sacrifice a red heifer, unblemished, without any spots. You can't breed a purebred red cow from spotted stock. It's like trying to breed an Irish setter from two Dalmatians. Nope, Numbers nineteen is talking about a high-tech, twenty-first century cow, a Red Angus."

Even Max's twitching eyebrows fidgeted, waiting for Zeke to get to the point.

"Jews haven't been able to fully practice their religion since their temple was destroyed. They haven't stood in the presence of God for two thousand years. Doesn't that just break your heart?"

Vanessa, still kneeling on the grass, probed the cow's mouth with her bloody gloves, smearing Lilypie's face. Zeke looked over his field of cattle.

Max stroked his jaw. "How far are you on this transaction?"

Zeke could see that Max didn't understand, from the hesitant chin-stroking to cover a condescending smile to the lack of notes on his notepad. Zeke, Brother Daniel, and the Country Congregational Bible Church were dead serious. "The money is in escrow. The heifers ship in a couple days. Frozen embryos and gametes a few weeks after that, but once the heifers are in Israel, there's no stopping us."

"So why would someone kill your cows?"

"There's a problem with the site the Temple has to be built on. There's a mosque on it. Actually, two mosques."

"Yeah, that's a problem," Max chuckled. Chuckling was odd. The proper reaction was pious grief. He was underestimating the importance of these cows.

Max sighed. "Let's get back to basics: why did someone kill these cows, and why now?"

"Atheists. Jews. Muslims. Now, Satanists. Maybe Satan himself. And animal rights activists, you know, the vegans."

Max stared at his doodle pad and did not meet Zeke's eyes. "Satan."

"The Temple is important in God's plan. Satan wants to stop us."

Deputy Konstantin crooked one side of his mouth in a sardonic grin. "Anybody I should interview, other than Satan?"

"Well, some orthodox Jews believe that it's sacrilege to do these things because only the true Messiah can build the temple, and so on. They think only God can cause a red heifer to be born in Israel. That's Old Testament, the prophet Isaiah."

"They going to wait for those bricks to stack themselves?"

Zeke nodded. God-fearing folks rightly understood that God helps those who help themselves. "If they're right, maybe Jesus is opposed to what we're doing, though I don't think that for a moment."

"Right. I'll interview Jesus Christ right after I interview Satan, the Nazis, and the elders of our local, ultra-orthodox Jewish temple. Do those orthodox folks oppose importing all cattle or just the red ones?"

Zeke could not discern if Max's sarcasm extended to the question. He opted for explaining some more. "Especially these red ones. I knocked out the white-hair genes so all the heifers will have perfect, red coats. Not even two hairs will be white." He nodded. "They're natural redheads, like Ester. Maybe I should cancel their flight to Israel, on Wednesday."

"Redhead?" Max frowned. "Ester is blond in all her pictures."

"They're older photos. She used to bleach her hair. With her blue eyes, she looked good as a blond. Two weeks ago or so, she dyed her hair back to red. Said it was more modest, less worldly, than bleaching it."

Max flipped through his notepad. "She had red hair when she went missing?"

"Oh, yeah. As red as Lilypie, here." He reached down and stroked Lilypie's flank. "Bright, new-copper-penny red."

"No one told me Ester James had red hair." He tried to write but only ripped the paper, and he put the pen away in his breast pocket.

Zeke frowned. "I didn't?"

"No." Max glared at the dead cow on the ground. "You said she 'stopped bleaching it' that first morning in the office, but you didn't say anything about dying it red. Did Daniel Stout know this? Diane Marshall? Did P.J. Lessing know it?"

"Ester dyed it back to red before the last time she went to church." Referring to her outburst again, and in front of Vanessa, would be awful. Zeke stroked his own red beard. "Brother Daniel remarked on it, that Essie and I actually looked like father and daughter, and someone else said that her redheaded temper came back. Sister Diane might've noticed. Ester had been bleaching her hair since high school. Matter of fact," Zeke turned to Vanessa, who was squelching cow blood clots between her gloved fingers, "Vanessa here talked her into bleaching it their freshman year of high school, so they'd be twins."

Vanessa's upper lip contracted, like she smelled peroxide. "I didn't have to talk Ester into anything. She hated being a redhead. People called her Carrot-top and threatened to beat her like a redheaded stepchild. I couldn't believe she dyed it back willingly. Your creepy little church brainwashed her."

"Essie came up with the idea. She didn't like bleaching her roots."

"I wouldn't know." Vanessa smirked at the clouds streaking the sky.

"Of course you do," Zeke said. "I remember you before you two bleached your hair in high school. You're a brunette."

Vanessa gasped. "I am not!"

"Why, certainly you are."

Vanessa smiled slyly at Max and flipped her hair around. "I'm a natural blond, carpet and drapes. You know that."

Zeke caught sexual innuendo. He should have warned Max that Vanessa was a woman of low morals, and Max should have known better. It saddened him to think that Max had betrayed Sister Diane. Vanessa just made him mad. She had come on to Zeke and the deputy. She must be a sad, lonely woman, and he pitied her for confusing sex and intimacy, but he did not like her.

Neither guilt nor outrage showed in Max's blank expression. That nothingness was odd. Vanessa's accusation must have raised some emotion in Max, yet he did not even blink. Max was smooth, as if he had done all this before. Being practiced at adultery was no virtue.

Max asked Vanessa, "So what do you think about the cows?"

She shrugged. "Stab wounds. Deep, lateral cut across the throat. Exsanguination. Disembowelment. There's really not much more to say."

Just as Zeke suspected. They stabbed the cows and cut their throats, and the cows bled to death, then they'd gutted them. The cows moved around less that way. Such brilliant scientific sleuthing Vanessa had done, worthy of one of those forensic television shows. He controlled the urge to snort.

They stabbed the cows. They. Zeke had kind of thought about the other possible killers, atheists and renegade Jews, but Satanists were demonstrably operating in the area. Zeke asked Vanessa, "Can you say anything about when they killed 'em?"

Vanessa shrugged. "I don't have a thermometer. They're still warm inside. I'd say between ten last night and four hours ago."

Zeke said, "That includes midnight."

"Yeah. You're quite a math whiz," Vanessa said.

Zeke did not rise to the bait and lose his temper. Bait is inevitably warm worms, as he reminded himself. "So it might have been the Satanists. In Black Masses, they kill people at midnight. Why not cows, too?"

Vanessa rolled her eyes so hard that her head followed the motion. "This whole town is nuts. People were carrying shotguns in the supermarket. Whatever Pastor Daniel says about his church and crucifixes, the Catholics must be doing brisk business. Seems like everybody has a dead Jesus around their necks."

Vanessa's attitude was repugnant. Zeke did not want to remain in her company, but he didn't want to leave Lilypie yet. He might be a tad harsh in his judgments, but everything she said made him want to shake his head in anger and sorrow. Vanessa must live a sad life, but she was dragging others down with her.

Zeke wondered what his responsibility was to his sister in Christ, Diane. He should confer with Brother Daniel.

Max walked around Lilypie's carcass.

Vanessa stood up and removed her gloves, one, then the other, by yanking on the fingers and then pulling. She ripped one glove in half and had to tear off the rolled latex bracelet. Blood streaked Vanessa's left palm where she had struggled with the destroyed glove.

That's how you take off winter gloves or leather gloves.

No one removes protective gloves like that.

Scientists and doctors and forensic folks, anyone who works with anything more dangerous than bread mold, takes off the worse glove first and peels it off inside out, then holds the contaminated glove in the other hand while they peel that second glove off around it. Then the gloves are inside out and inside each other. Often you knot the wrist of the outside glove, containing both.

Vanessa's de-gloving technique was horrible. Potentially lethal. And disgusting. Zeke did not like it one bit. A forensic tech should know better. Lord Almighty, she had probably already contaminated herself with ethidium bromide and radioisotopes and whatever else she used in that lab.

Max had finished walking a full circle around Lilypie's body. "Zeke, you should take it up with the Sheriff, but I don't think you should cancel that shipment of cattle to Israel on Wednesday night."

"Wednesday?" Vanessa asked. "You're shipping the cows to Israel this Wednesday?"

The prospect of not canceling froze Zeke. "But, if they have Ester, if they do this to her, I'll never forgive myself."

"Look me in the eye, Zeke. You had any threatening phone calls?"

Zeke looked straight into Max's dark brown eyes. The brown was so thick that Zeke could not find a proper pupil. "Nope. My phone is tapped. You'd know."

Max nodded. "Before we tapped it? Any ransom demands?"

Zeke shook his head. His beard swished. "Nope. Nada."

"Most criminals, even the Mafia, coyotes, MS-13, even the Cali cartel, don't make vague threats. Their threats are specific. They tell you exactly what to do, what will happen if you don't, and what leverage they have on you. This isn't like waking up with a cow head in your bed.

This feels random. And if it isn't random, then keeping the timetable may force the Satanists or animal rights activists or whoever to show themselves. If they panic, we'll have them. We can post guards around you and your cattle until Wednesday. If someone does try something nefarious, we'll catch them and charge them with destruction of really expensive property." Max grinned with angry glee. "They didn't know they were killing a million-dollar cow. We'll charge them with a first degree felony and send them to prison for up to ninety-nine years. Those assholes will panic."

Putting his remaining cattle at risk seemed stupid. Five other CMV-MAOA cows were out there, identifiable by their red ear tags among six hundred other cows. Was that how the killers had chosen Lilypie, by her red ear tag, or had she walked right up to them?

Had the men who took Ester chosen her for her bright red hair?

Zeke saw the congruence: he was raising red heifers to build the Anti-Christ's Temple in Jerusalem. His redheaded daughter had been sacrificed to Satan in some other branch of the Divine Plan to end the world.

It was too much, Oh Lord. It was too much to bear. Job had had everything taken from him and he had not cursed God. Zeke did not curse God, but he prayed for God to take him to Heaven now, because his soul was in tatters.

It had to mean something. Signs from God are not meaningless.

He crouched beside Lilypie's dead body. "I will not cancel the flight to Israel. The cattle will go as planned on Wednesday."

Lord, help me.

Zeke read the Good Book for the rest of the afternoon, trying for solace but finding none. Sheriff's cars cruised by his windows every half hour or so, and several horse trailers pulled up as the mounted posse arrived to guard his cattle.

That night, Zeke went to the church for the lock-in, figuring that it was the safest place for him. The fellowship hall was as pious and modest as the rest of the church. A triple line of bent nails held rows of Western hats: straw, felt, fur felt, wool, brown, black, gray, ten-gallon, leather-edged, and junior-sized. One porkpie hat hung on the end that a high school kid had worn in, but at least it was a Stetson.

Pastor Daniel locked the fellowship hall's doors and chained them from the inside. Several people had color-coded keys to the padlocks in case of a fire. Zeke needed to maneuver Pastor Daniel away from the others, to discuss the problem. After all, he had no direct evidence to give Sister Diane, only an insinuation.

The word had gone out about the guarded lock-in, and even families who did not belong to the church had come to sleep. Over a hundred people had come, carrying bedrolls, baggies of dry snacks, and toothbrushes. Smaller children already wore feetie pajamas.

Folks flipped sleeping bags on the floor. Air mattress pumps droned. Beach chairs and camping stools flapped open. Someone reeled out a couple power strips, and folks with laptops pounced on the dozen spots, wrestling to commandeer an outlet, which was terribly rude by Texan standards but as necessary as cannibalism in these circumstances of privation.

Zeke approached the pastor. "Brother Daniel? There's a matter I'd like to discuss with you. A moral issue. Ethical."

"Sure." Daniel's long fingers fluttered in the air, outlining all the things he was thinking that he had to do. "I was going to ask you to bunk down with us to help corral the kids. We're outnumbered. Can we talk after I organize the guards?"

Zeke nodded.

Daniel announced, "I've drawn up a schedule of guards, two-hour shifts, two guards per door. Will Teich Le Guerre, Kendra Moore,

When-Dee Houser, and Nemo Turner kindly bring their weapons and meet me up front for the first shift? Would anyone like their firearms blessed?"

It's midnight again, and most of our people are nestled snug in their sleeping bags, watched over by an amateur, trigger-happy militia, in the fellowship hall of the Country Congregational Bible Church.

Max and Diane are taking their chances at home. They have an excellent security system.

Diane stares at the ceiling, exhausted and flinching at creaks and Max's snorts. It's windy tonight. Their house creaks a lot. Max really should have that airway problem checked. Apnea like that, where the person gurgles and gasps, can cause a heart attack.

Tatiana rolls over in her bed. Her bedsprings creak, almost as if someone has lifted her body out of the bed.

Diane walks down the hall and finds Tatiana asleep.

Diane will leave her bed six more times tonight to make sure the Satanists haven't flown in on the wings of night and stolen one of her children.

Or perhaps Satanists lure children away, like Sirens or Internet predators.

Tuesday

Slam.

Max looked up from his computer at his bullpen desk.

Diane had slammed her palms on his desk and braced her arms wide. Her face was solid red rage. "What in the hell is going on?"

Max tongued his teeth, acting innocent, and asked, "Yes?"

"First thing this morning," she said, "the IT guy calls me about a whole assload of spyware on my computer. What the fuck did you do to it, and why, and when?"

This was going to be bad. He stood. "Conference room?"

She yelled, "You know that since September eleventh we've had massive IT security! We're the damn government. How stupid are you that you emailed those screencaps to your work email account?"

The spyware program had emailed hundreds of screencaps from Diane's account, to the point that Max couldn't look at all of them: she would *love* to have more evidence, she had to prepare for *oral* arguments, data and juries were *anal*yzed. If Max could minimize the damage in front of his co-workers, he might not get fired for it. He nodded. "Pretty stupid."

"I would fucking say so. I should have you fucking arrested, but arresting you would look vindictive while I'm divorcing you."

Max dropped his gaze back to his crumb-littered computer keyboard. He watched her hand, making sure it didn't stray toward her purse, in case she was homicidally mad. Rage like this could torque a person, rev them up, until a bullet's blast seemed cleansing.

She said, "Daniel and Zeke told me this morning about Vanessa Allen's pube comment. Did you screw her?"

Panic boomed in his head, each cannon blast ticking away seconds as the situation worsened. He had to get her out of here. All her opening and closing arguments escalated. This was only going to get even worse. "It was one time. It meant nothing. I'm sorry."

"Oh, my Lord, you did. I didn't really believe it, but you did."

He said, "We should go to the conference room."

She covered her eyes with her hands. "You're a cliché. You're a male chauvinist pig rooting around the nubile women. You're a cop abusing his power." Her hands dropped away. "And I'm a lawyer. I will nail you to the wall. While adultery isn't a crime in Texas, it's sure as hell grounds for divorce. I could have you arrested for wiretapping or criminal trespass or anything I wanted to."

His bones were frozen. "I don't even know why I did it."

"Because you're a man, and you're an idiot, and you were thinking with your dick. You screwed her *ex mero motu,* because you wanted to. Why were you spying on me when you're the one screwing around?"

"I thought you had someone. I thought that if I knew who it was, I could put a stop to it and save the family."

Her hands grabbed at the air beside her ears as if malignant thoughts dive-bombed her like mosquitoes. "And then you fucked Vanessa Allen?"

"Diane, your language."

"Did you fuck her up the ass or just her pussy?"

Too late, and it was too terrible, and he was too far in. Max stood, grabbed Diane's wrist, and led her to the conference room. She yanked her arm a couple times but didn't resist.

When they were in the conference room with the door shut, he mined every sentence that he had seen work when he was called out on domestic problems. "It was one time. I don't love her. I won't do it again. I'm sorry. I didn't mean to hurt you."

"Why?" Her whole being writhed with rage.

Remembering Vanessa reaching her hands toward him iced Max. He was a frozen-over car after an ice storm. He was trying to survive, but he was freezing to death. "I'm sorry. It meant nothing to me. She means nothing to me. I love you."

Diane covered her face. Her fingers purpled, like she was pressing so hard on her eyeballs that she might gouge them out. "And you're still hanging around with her. Yesterday, you two walked all over the site together. Then you two went out to Zeke's together." Diane dropped her hands away from her face and looked horror-struck. "You didn't screw her in my house, did you?"

"Of course not."

"Where? No. Don't tell me. I don't want to know any more details. It wasn't one of the cars, was it?"

"No."

Diane sat with a thump in the chair at the end of the conference table that Vanessa had sat in before she and Max walked the piney woods and he screwed her against the magnolia tree. Diane flipped her purse on the table with a thud. "Already I can't get her out of my head. She's younger. She's taller. She's blond. She has gargantuan tits. Do you want to marry her? Or do you just want out of our marriage?"

"That's not it. I don't want a divorce. It was just a random thing."

Diane squinted with anger. "It wasn't random. You decided."

"I didn't think. I froze up, and I didn't think."

"Of course you thought. No one accidentally has sex."

No, he couldn't have stopped. He had been a speeding bullet on a trajectory that intersected flesh. The implied helplessness shamed him. His body felt like a hoary old lecher's body, corroded and diseased. He didn't want to be divorced, but he did want to be alone somewhere, a hermitage, so no one would be disgusted by him.

Diane drew in a shuddering breath. "The kids and I will sleep at the church tonight. We won't tell them anything yet."

That was weird. "Why would you sleep at the church?"

Another tear slid on her cheek. "Because I can't even look at our bed."

Diane strode out of the conference room.

Max walked back to his desk and stared at his keyboard.

The ice that he had wrapped himself in for so many years engulfed him like the formation of an iceberg, and yet, this time, impure flaws veined its crystalline structure. The ice around him cleaved and chunks fell away.

He would not let this happen. He had let too many things happen to him in his life, and he was not going to let Diane end their marriage like this.

"Diane!" He shouted across the office but she walked out the door at the other end. All the other deputies stared at him. People eyeing him made him irritable.

"Fuck it. Diane!" He sprinted after her, churning his legs hard.

He grabbed her soft arm as she opened the door to the hot little car that he had given her.

"Let go of me." Her voice grated with that dangerous edge with which she cross-examined CEOs of pollution-spewing corporations. She jerked her arm and he let go.

He told her, "That creepy little church of yours is trying to break us up, just like other ministers get between spouses to control them."

Her light brown eyes, fringed with make-up, narrowed with unbelief. "So you didn't bug my computer or screw Vanessa Allen? Is that what you're trying to tell me?" Her tone insinuated he would be lying and she knew it.

"No, but they set this all up."

"Stop it, Max. Don't make this worse than it is." She stepped into her car and he jumped back to avoid her tires as she pulled away.

Rage geysered through the fissures in the ice, and his fists raised first to a pugilist's defensive stance and then to the sides of his pounding head.

Damn it. Damn it. He had screwed around even though he had promised himself that he wouldn't. He knew that people who survived sexual abuse sabotaged relationships, just to prove that the sex didn't matter and because they were inherently unlovable and for a thousand other screwed up reasons, but he had been performing such a perfect role as a normal person that he had forgotten to be constantly on his guard, and he had fucked it all up.

He had destroyed his whole damn life that he had so carefully rebuilt. Damn it. Damn it all to hell.

He marched back into the office and sat at his desk, his head in his hands.

After a startled moment, office chatter resumed around him, even though he could feel all their eyes glancing toward him as he floundered with rage and bewilderment at his own stupidity for screwing around and tapping Diane's computer.

He carefully controlled his face and his breathing.

He was so bereft that he could not even summon the ice to numb him to this rending pain. His chest felt stabbed. Was he having a heart attack? It would serve him right, and the darkness called to him.

The image of sticking his gun in his mouth and blowing his brains out occurred to him, but it was a reaction more than an impulse. He did not even move to take the handgun out of its locked drawer.

Images of suicide and murder of that meddling, creepy little preacher alternated. The minute that Zeke tattled to Stout about Vanessa's stupid-ass blond pubic hair comment, the preacher had used it to drive a wedge between Diane and him.

That creepy preacher wanted Diane. He was just another mind-controlling hypocrite with a God-complex.

Max breathed more evenly as his anguish turned to anger and

focused on Stout.

Within a few hours, he had convinced himself that Stout was trying to screw Diane and shanghai the sheriff's office's investigation because that creepy little church had murdered Ester James for whatever mindfuck reason.

He didn't have to analyse their fucked-up beliefs. It was enough that they believed them.

He would nail that creepy little church and Stout for Ester James's murder. Then Diane would be out from under Stout's influence, and Max could win her back. He had no plans for how he was going to win Diane back, but he could figure that out later.

After an hour, he stood up. There were things to do. He always maintained control, even when everyone in the bullpen eyed him and wondered if he was going to lose it. He walked slowly to the press conference room.

Max officiated at the sheriff's press conference that afternoon at Carlos's insistence, so Carlos might have plausible deniability if the Ester James case went into the crapper. Carlos had to survive elections. Max just had to keep Carlos in office. The petite reporter in the front row harangued Max with rapid, vapid questions in a shrill voice.

He answered calmly into the microphone mushroom farm on the podium for the cannon-barreled cameras. "We recommend that the public take prudent security precautions, including locking their doors at night, but there is no need for alarm. We have no physical or other evidence to cause us to believe a serial killer is operating in the area." Even though local law enforcement always denies the existence of a serial killer until everyone else has figured it out. He felt like a fucking stereotype, the bungling local cop, waiting for the smart guys to show up and solve the case with brilliant deductive reasoning.

Flashbulbs glared in the small room like ground burst pyrotechnics. More frantic gabbling from the goosy blond.

Max said, "We have no physical or other evidence to suggest or cause us to believe a Satanic cult is operating in the area. Arrests are forthcoming in the disappearance of Ester James."

The media buzzards asked their questions.

"How many Satanists are still at large?"

"Is there more than one coven?"

"Do you expect reasonable people to believe a Satanic cult is sacrificing virgins to the full moon?"

"Are their powers like ESP or wizard magic?"

"Can they summon demons?"

"Can they make it rain?" (This, from a drought-paranoid meteorologist pressed into service due to proximity.)

"Are they from California?"

"Have any churches been desecrated?"

"Are they atheists, or just Satanists?"

"How many women have they killed?"

"Will they kill again?"

"*When?*"

Diane clung to the steering wheel and drove back to her office at five miles per hour under the posted speed limit. If she sped, she might be tempted to crash this stupid Christmas present from her unfaithful husband into a wall.

The whole rest of her life, Diane had been searching for the *right* law and the *right* religion and the *right* way to say things and the *right* way to believe, but Max was the only thing in her life that she had been sure was *right*.

Crumbling, everything was crumbling. The road decayed along the curbs into cold pebbles. The winter-leafless trees lining the road were blighted. Heavy clouds tore themselves into rain.

Diane drove and did not disintegrate.

Even a week ago, if Max had screwed some other woman, a younger, blonder, boobier woman, it would have been more than she could bear. But she was stronger now. She had rescued the Lessing kids. She could survive this. No matter what that asshole Max did, she could survive it and she would be fine.

With God's help.

She drove around town, slowly, killing time. She parked at the Lone Star Grocery for half an hour, watching people to see if anyone looked suspicious. She sat in front of her house for fifteen minutes but didn't go in, dreading what she might smash.

P.J.'s gynecologist called Diane's cell phone. The girl had recently had rough sexual intercourse consistent with rape. Her hymen was fully separated and still inflamed. No semen was recovered, not surprising after four days. Something had happened to her.

After an hour, it was time to go back. She prayed to God to help her stay calm if she saw Max and neither fly at him with her fingernails clawing nor scream that he was a cheating bastard. She rehearsed—Not now, Max; Not now, Max—in her head.

Diane met Pastor Daniel and P.J. in the Sheriff's office reception area. Pastor Daniel's eyelids were swollen. P.J. leaned on him, nearly falling. The Sheriff's interrogation room had all the accoutrements: one-way mirror, recording equipment, and a catering-size coffee maker.

"Diane." Pastor Daniel touched her arm. "Are you all right?"

"I'm fine." She bustled the preacher and the teenager toward the interrogation room. The ridiculous and terrible situation rankled her. She stabbed at normalcy. "Hey, P.J., what does it mean when you find a lawyer," or a cheating bastard husband, "up to his neck in cement?"

P.J. shrugged and blinked, slowly.

"Means someone ran out of cement."

They tried to laugh, but the guffaws sounded more like grunts, and she turned to lead them to the conference room.

"Diane," Pastor Daniel said. "We can postpone this. Or you could call someone else from your office to handle it."

"I'm okay," and she kind of thought so, until Max met them at the door of the conference room. Her hands and shoulders rose, more in defense of her battered heart than to strangle him, but if his neck had been between her hands, she might have strangled him. Anger was a shell that buffered all touch and comfort. She said, "Not now, Max."

He said, "I want to sit in on this interview."

"No. This is private."

Max said, "I'll call Carlos. It's his building."

"Sheriff Garcia won't interfere in a County Attorney's investigation."

Max's calm face was an insult. His mild expression was more suitable for considering the quality of the chicken salad sandwich he ate for lunch than for admitting that he had ruined their marriage with one irresponsible screw. That made her even madder. He didn't even care that she was scrambling against an eroding cliff edge.

"Diane."

The anger contracted in her muscles, and her legs trembled, fighting the urge to punch him. "You don't even believe P.J.'s story."

"All the more reason that I should be present. If you can convince me, you can convince a jury."

"Not right now."

"The sheriff's office should have a representative in this questioning," like he didn't give a shit about her, the kids, their home, anything.

She wanted to shake him until his head flew off. "Not you, Max."

"I'm the Chief Deputy, second in charge to Carlos."

Diane's chest hurt from struggling to breathe. "Don't you say anything in there. Not one damned word."

"Unless you're obviously eliciting a false confession."

"She's not confessing to anything. She's a victim." Diane was going to protect P.J. from anyone who thought differently.

"A false accusation, then."

P.J. Lessing watched them argue. Her eyes, mahogany dark irises ringed with kohl, widened. "I don't want him in there."

"Why?" Diane asked.

The girl's exhaustion had been shunted aside by fear. P.J. said, "I don't want anyone else in there."

From her years with the County Attorney's office, Diane was attuned to the moods of witnesses. P.J. was unusually oppositional. "Why not?"

P.J. teared up. "Because."

"He was at the lot yesterday, and you were fine."

P.J. shook her head harder.

That was not normal. Diane said, "We're going back to the County Attorney's office. We'll get it on tape there."

Max cocked his head to the side. "Even if you go back to the County Attorney's office, the sheriff's department needs a representative."

Due to budget constraints, the recording equipment in the County Attorney's conference rooms wasn't nearly as good, and there was no video. She told P.J., "Max will just observe. He won't say anything."

Diane glared at Max to reinforce her point.

He nodded calmly.

She wanted to grab his curly hair and yank it out. The chunky young blonds wouldn't screw him if he was as bald as a brown egg.

"We need another deputy in there for corroboration." He signaled to George, who stood, stretched, and ambled over. "Vanessa Allen, too."

"You have got to be fucking kidding me."

Max said, "She's a forensic scientist."

"Call the Texas Rangers or the state crime lab or the FBI."

"We need someone right now."

"There's very little forensic evidence. There's no need for her."

"You never know, and I've already discussed it with Carlos."

"Fine. You and George and Vanessa Allen sit at the far end of the table and don't any of you say a damn word. Especially to each other."

They filed past the observation booth and into the conference room. Vanessa Allen appeared out of the dark brown paneling like a banshee and came in last. Her blond hair was curled. She was handsome and young. Diane wanted to sue that blond interloper under the torts of criminal conversation and alienation of affection, the bitch, and garnish her measly forensic-scientist wages.

Diane flicked on the recording equipment as she passed.

As dictated, Max, Vanessa, and George the other deputy sat at the far end of the conference room table. P.J., Daniel, and Diane sat near the door.

Diane led P.J. through her answers from the midnight questioning and what she had remembered at the vacant lot. Anger constricted her throat so that she could barely talk. Every time she looked down the table at Vanessa Allen and Max, she wanted to throw something heavy or hot at them.

The presence of her screwing-around husband and his hussy distracted her, and Diane almost forgot to watch P.J. to discern whether she was prosecuting deluded murderers or battling Satan and supernatural evil. She overcame the stupid distraction and focused her attention on P.J.

Diane wanted to be sure that the girl was not lying. Overnight, she had drifted back from her tentative rationalization of the Devil in Texas to suspect that a coven believed they were Satanists, but she could not rule out a Satanic witch explanation.

Diane asked P.J., "And what happened at the clearing by the pond?"

When P.J. blinked, her head swiveled like she was nodding off. "The altar was already set up. They stood in a circle."

She recounted the murder of Ester James while Diane compared her account to her notes. P.J. was spot on in her recollection of the details and the order of events.

At the end of the table, Max cleared his throat.

Diane glared at him and asked, "And the man who sexually assaulted you, P.J., do you remember anything about him? The color of his skin?"

"They shined flashlights on him," P.J. said. "I couldn't tell."

From the far end of the table, Max said, "Let's go back for a minute. P.J., describe Ester James lying on the altar again."

Diane said, "Not now, Max."

P.J. said, "I already told you. The altar was about four feet cubed. Her hands and feet and head dangled off."

Diane said, "She's already been through that several times. Now, P.J., the man who assaulted you, was he black, white, or in-between?"

Max said, "Diane, this is important. P.J., describe how Ester looked when she was lying on that Satanic altar that you think you remember."

Anger lifted Diane. She half-stood. "I told you, not a damned word."

"This is important," Max said, his expression tight and intense. "P.J., describe what Ester looked like for the recording equipment."

P.J. drew her fingers in toward her chest. "I don't know what you mean. She looked like Ester James."

"Did she look like this picture, here?" Max slapped down a picture of Ester James standing beside a red cow on her father's ranch and shoved it down the table. It skidded and stopped between Diane, Daniel, and P.J.

Diane had seen that picture a thousand times. "Max, shut up."

Max yelled down the table, "Did she look just like that, P.J.?"

"Yes," P.J. said. "I mean, it was dark. The Satanists put a robe on me and I couldn't see because the hood kept flapping over my eyes. And I was scared. And I didn't know what was going on. And then he raped me and I don't know what happened."

"So she looked just like this picture," Max said, leaning in. Was he encroaching on P.J. to threaten her?

"That's Ester James," P.J. said. "I saw them kill Ester James."

"What color was her hair, P.J.?" Max asked.

Vanessa Allen said, "Oh," softly, and touched her pink mouth.

"That's enough!" Diane yelled. "That's enough. Max, this is a County Attorney's office investigation. I swear to God, if you say one more word, I'll have you thrown out."

Max said, "Diane, there's a big difference between how you interrogate someone when you want the truth and how you question a witness during a trial to say what you want the jury to hear."

"She said she remembers and I believe her. Now sit down or get out."

"But Ester James didn't look like this picture," Max said. "She dyed her hair. P.J. got it wrong."

Max's inconsequential interruptions were infuriating. "What color was her hair, then?"

Max looked at P.J. "Take her out of the room."

"No. You're trying to confuse the witness. You're trying to contaminate the evidence. All the pictures show her as blond. I've known Ester for months, and she was blond. I don't know where you got this cockamamie idea."

"Her father said she wasn't. You should know. She walked out of that church that Sunday, and her hair wasn't blond. Think!"

When Ester James had flounced out of the church the week before after confronting Pastor Daniel about the mists from the ground, Diane had been sitting halfway back on the left side, taking notes. The golden sun glowed on her blond hair, just like always. Diane remembered it perfectly. "She was blond."

Pastor Daniel frowned.

"You're wrong. You don't remember." Max sat down and chewed whatever else he had been going to say.

This meeting was disastrous. They were getting nowhere, and Max was trying to mislead P.J.

"Okay. Let's do some forensic modeling." Diane tried not to glare at blond, booby Vanessa who, as commanded, had not said a word to anyone. "Max," she did not look at him, "I need flashlights. Four of them. Please get them."

The word please was her concession to professionalism, even though she wanted to order him around or just walk out.

"Yeah," he said. He left the conference room.

While he was gone, Diane did not say a word to any of them, even though she could see Pastor Daniel swaying in his seat, trying to get her attention.

Max returned with flashlights, the high-beam types that the sheriff's department utilized as a psych weapon.

Max dumped the four battery-heavy flashlights on the table. Great. Now, every jerk in the room could have his own flashlight. "These are the high-beam type of flashlight that P.J. said the Satanists used. Who wants to go first?"

The men looked at each other. Pastor Daniel asked, "Pardon me?"

"We're going to have P.J. compare the men's skin tones to see if she can approximate the skin color of the man who assaulted her, because at this point, we have very little to go on, and even ruling out half the possible skin tones would be something. It's convenient that we have here an African-American man," she gestured to Daniel, "a man who's half-Mexican," she gestured toward Max with as little emotion as she could but that dismissive hand flick could have turned obscene, "and a literal paleface."

George, grinning down at the end of the table, had a freckled but porcelain-white hide.

Diane said, "We're going to turn out the lights, and you men are going to stand and take off your shirts, and we're going to aim our flashlights at you. P.J. will observe the result, and determine if her assailant had lighter or darker skin, like an eye test. Who wants to go first?"

Vanessa said, "You have got to be kidding me."

Diane stared into that bitch's too-blue eyes under her curly, gold bangs and stared her down. The skin around Vanessa's angry eyes tightened, but Vanessa finally broke her stare and looked down at the laminate tabletop.

Diane was a lawyer and the voice of authority in Sin Nombre County. Part of law school is learning to write and speak authoritatively. Such a tone goes a long way toward convincing a judge or jury that you know of what you speak. Diane was practiced and damn good at it.

The three men stood: Pastor Daniel, her fuck-around husband Max, and George. Diane rolled two flashlights down the table. Vanessa caught one. Max grabbed the other. Diane and P.J. switched theirs on.

Diane said, "Pastor, the lights, please."

Pastor Daniel reached over with a sinuous wave of his arm and flicked off the lights.

But for the two flashlight beams, the room was tar black. The flashlights were the type with focusable, laser-like beams, so they did not leak light out the sides. Their light bounced off the ceiling and showered down on the six people.

Pastor Daniel unbuttoned his shirt. His fingers were long and spidery against his white shirt. He stripped off his shirt and white undershirt, then maneuvered his gold cross and chain so that it lay down his back. His chest was smooth.

Diane and P.J. shined their lights on him.

At the far end of the table, two more light beams clicked on and caught Pastor Daniel's chest, as if two cars sped out of the night at him.

"No." P.J.'s voice still shook from Max yelling at her, the poor kid. "He was lighter than Pastor Daniel. And more hair. It was kind of a diamond on his chest."

Pastor Daniel said, "Well, that lets out most African Americans."

"All right." Diane pointed her strong flashlight beam at the ceiling and looked down the long table. "Next?"

George the deputy unbuttoned his brown shirt and peeled it off.

They pointed their flashlight beams at him. The strong lights glared off his rolls of white skin, unmarred by body hair, and reflected off his double chin and bulbous nose. A tiny cylinder was tied on a piece of string around his neck.

Max said, "Jeez, George. Don't you wear an undershirt?"

"Nope." He rippled his chub.

Vanessa giggled and Diane wanted to smack her. Vanessa said, "Wow, George, don't swim around sharks."

George jiggled his pale pink man-boobs, and Diane rubbed her eyeballs in embarrassment for him. Diane pointed to the steel cylinder hung around his neck. "What's that?"

George shrugged, which caused another jiggling chain reaction. "Good luck charm."

Pastor Daniel whispered to Diane, "Ten Satanists are still out there."

Diane asked, "Can we see it, George?"

"It's nothing." In the flashlight beams, George pinkened from the waist up. He lifted the string over his head and tossed it down the table. P.J.'s flashlight beam followed the skittering metal tube.

Diane shined her flashlight through the dark as Daniel's long fingers deftly unscrewed the tiny cache and shook out a slim piece of paper. It read: "May the Lord bless you and keep you; may the Lord cause his face to shine upon you and be gracious to you; may the Lord lift up his countenance upon you and grant you peace."

"What is it?" Diane asked him.

"It's from the Book of Numbers. Jews in Israel wore that verse as a talisman against evil, circa Dead Sea Scrolls–era." Daniel carefully rolled the paper, inserted it back into the cylinder, and tossed it back to George. "Where did you get that?"

George shrugged. "Guy at my church was giving them away last night. Said they were extra protection."

"What church?" Diane asked him.

"Lutheran, Missouri Synod."

"And you were there because?"

George shrugged again. "Seemed prudent, what with all those women missing and all, to keep watch during the night."

Diane sat back in her chair. "P.J., how does George's complexion compare to the man's who attacked you?"

P.J. said, "Oh, he's too white. A lot too white. And, um, no offense, sir, but the Master Satanist was, um, like, skinnier."

Diane noted that P.J. used the term "Master Satanist." Diane did not remember saying that around her. She should ask Pastor Daniel about it.

George chuckled and dragged his shirt on. "No offense taken, little lady. You call 'em like you see 'em."

Diane's voice was hard with the force of her control behind it. "Max."

Max's cold glance made her want to tell him to shut up. Max handed the flashlight handle-first to George like you would transfer a gun. Four flashlight beams shone out of the dark room at his brown shirt and flashing copper deputy badge. His eye sockets were dark.

Max flicked open the buttons on his shirt, pulled it off, and jerked his undershirt over his head.

P.J. gasped. Her flashlight spun through the dark across the table. The bright beam splashed the white walls and shocked faces. She knocked her chair over running to the door and yelled, "It's him! It's him!"

Diane yelled, "What?" in the darkness. "Daniel! Get that light on!"

Flashlight beams sliced the dark. One beam lit on Daniel's dark hand slapping the wall, hunting for the light switch.

"It's him! He's the Master Satanist!" She wailed and jerked at the door. The locked door banged its frame.

George's beam shone on Max's calm face. Max lifted his eyebrows.

Vanessa laughed loudly and said, "You have got to be kidding me!"

Diane's straight-up flashlight beam drilled a circle of light on the ceiling. Where had Max been that night? He had gotten the call about four-thirty in the morning, but he had gotten home only a few hours before. "Daniel, the light."

"I'm trying! Where's the darn switch?"

"This is ludicrous," Vanessa said. Her flashlight beam shot the length of the room and poured on P.J., who struggled with the unyielding door. P.J. shielded her eyes from the glare with one hand.

The room filled with light.

P.J. yanked at the door with her whole body, jerking the knob and arching backward.

George switched off his flashlight and slowly laid it on the table. Vanessa looked around the room with a tentative, disbelieving grin.

Max inserted his arms in his undershirt and pulled it over his head, honey-colored skin, and a light patch of chest hair.

P.J. cried, "I didn't recognize him in the daylight. Please, please let me out!"

Diane gestured to the men in the booth behind the mirrored glass that it was okay to release the lock.

A soft buzz sounded, and P.J. fell backward as the door released. She scrambled to her feet and sprinted out. Pastor Daniel followed.

"You're joking." Vanessa chortled. "Come on!"

Diane held the silver barrel of the flashlight between both her hands like a penitent's candle. Shock short-circuited like a sparking, loose wire. Her brain stuttered, trying to reconcile accusation with knowledge.

Max had been her husband for twenty years. He got cavities in his left, lower molars because he brushed them half as much as his other teeth. He pooped at seven o'clock in the morning unless he had recently eaten sweet potatoes.

Max wasn't a Satanist. He couldn't have been at a Black Mass, murdering one girl and raping a child.

Somewhere after his Catholic school education, maybe after she had met him in college, had he so rejected Christianity that he had meandered into the occult? She had seen no signs of it. There were no Tarot cards in his desk or crystals hanging from his car mirror. Yet he had been surprised by her conversion, and she had kept it secret from him for six months.

They talked about superficial things, she realized. They talked about arrests and prosecutions, the kids' schedules and food. They didn't talk about politics or religion or philosophy or culture or opinions, or anything real or personal. She didn't even know why he had insisted that they move to East Texas, away from their families, after college.

The families of serial killers never suspect their loved ones, even after decades. Ted Kaczynski's brother didn't think his brother might be a mail-order terrorist, only that the person who wrote the Unabomber manifesto sounded like his brother. The BTK serial killer's family didn't turn him in. An email trail led to his church computer. Ted Bundy's mother was shocked, *shocked*, at the allegations and laughingly testified at his Florida trial that Ted was a sweet, loving boy.

At the time, Diane thought they were too weak to see the truth. Or thick. Or callused. Maybe the awful truth had rubbed them so long that they had built up resistance in order to bear it.

Maybe Diane was callused to the truth, too. Diane would have bet her life that Max would never fuck around or install spyware on her computer.

Maybe he hadn't suspected her of fooling around, and that whole spiel was a cover for his snooping to find out about the Ester James case.

Would arresting Max be merely quid pro quo for his fucking around?

Max shot P.J.'s adoptive father, The Tower. Maybe The Tower had threatened to turn him in, in exchange for immunity. Saffron hadn't spoken to anyone since Diane had informed her that they knew Saffron was a Satanist and had killed Ester James. Saffron might be afraid for her life while in jail.

Means, motive and opportunity.

Wordless prayer is the opposite of recited mantra. Rather than struggling to fill memorized words with emotion, pure prayer begins with emotion. Diane poured emotion out but even more welled up: devastation for Tatiana and Nicholas if she and Max divorced; guilt at not being able to just forgive Max and have it all be over with; wishing she could forgive him but a knot of anger refusing to untangle; worrying about what divorcing him might do to the kids versus staying married to someone who screwed around and what that might do to the kids; and pity and anger for herself that she might have somehow precipitated this.

At the other end of the room, Vanessa's enormous boobs rested on the table like twin cats, curled up and purring. Should Diane have gotten a boob lift and implants after she nursed the kids? Was that it, the boobs?

Diane was pissed at Max that he had screwed around and bewildered that he had, but she would not allow anger, even life-wrecking rage, to guide this decision. The immorality and terrible ethics of allowing anger to sway her opinion horrified her.

Yet she couldn't err the other way. A woman was dead and a girl raped.

Diane devoutly wished that her boss was here to make this decision.

She could present this evidence to a grand jury, but any decent prosecuting attorney can persuade a grand jury to indict Mother Teresa and Gandhi as a serial murder team. She didn't need a grand jury. When you arrest someone without a grand jury indictment, they just have a right to a speedier arraignment.

Panic had struck P.J. when she saw Max in those harsh flashlight beams. Her fear looked real. P.J. believed what she had said. Identification by an eyewitness fell under the definition of reasonable suspicion, and thus Max could be arrested without a warrant, either grand jury or bench.

Diane's hands around the flashlight cramped. Pain spiraled up her arms. When she had seen Max standing over Saffron's pathetic, begging form and The Tower's dying body, rage transfigured his face until he was alien. Was that the storming demon that had killed Ester and raped P.J.?

Ted Bundy was a perfectly sweet young man until the fiend emerged. In one picture, when Bundy's psychopathic calm composure shattered in court and he roared and bailiffs restrained him, his gaping mouth and black, cadaverous eyes were demonic. That was the face his victims saw.

It could be. Max might be one of those possessed men.

Anger spun. Protecting P.J. and all the other young girls out there was paramount. She had to do the strong thing, even though she hated it. Damn him for making her do it. He got himself into this. He didn't even have an alibi for the middle of the damn night.

"Deputy." She flipped her hand like she was backhanding that stupid idiot at the other end of the table. "Arrest Max Konstantin for the murder of Ester James and the sexual assault of a minor in the case of Peace in Jerusalem 'P.J.' Lessing."

George held out his hand, palm up. "I'm sorry, Max."

"This is fucked up." Max handed over his gun, unclipped his badge, and calmly buttoned his shirt.

Vanessa said, "I don't believe it. You idiots are serious about this bullshit." Her harsh laughter banked on the paneled walls. "Oh my God. I can't believe it. Satanists, and now a Master Satanist. Jesus Christ!"

Diane didn't look up from her white hands strangling that flashlight. The veins in the backs of her hands bulged. "Arrest him right now."

Vanessa watched George handcuff Max and tried to keep her mouth from dropping open, though she was pretty sure her eyes were round Os.

Were they serious? Max, the "Master Satanist?" Someone must be dumping her mother's homemade crystal meth into the water supply.

Vanessa rubbed her eyeballs. A couple of slutty chicks get taken out, and suddenly the town thinks a nest of Satanists is sacrificing virgins. P.J. Lessing had to be stopped. Superstition haunted this town like Civil War cavalry ghosts charging on gaunt horses, lopping off people's brains with curved swords.

The conference room shimmered, taking on the over-lit aura of a television studio with cameras shooting from behind the mirrored glass. Vanessa saw her reflection. She failed at everything she did, but she had to stop this lunacy. She would play the part of a competent human being.

She caught Max's stunned glance and muttered so Diane couldn't hear her, "They've obviously brainwashed the kid. I'll get you out."

P.J. laid her head on Pastor Daniel's legs and sobbed. She had thrown herself on him, and he had lifted her quickly, grabbed someone's leather jacket hanging on the wall, covered his lap, and then let her collapse. She just wanted comfort, someone to tell her that it was okay, that she hadn't been raped, that she hadn't watched a woman murdered.

She sobbed while Pastor Dan stroked her hair. "It's okay," he said. "It's okay."

"It's not okay!"

"Yes, but you did your best, and you told the truth, and God will take care of you."

"I hate this!"

"It'll be okay. God will take care of you."

"You keep saying that." The crying ebbed. She was half cried out.

He leaned his head against the wall and stared across the room into the office area filled with deputies who watched them by not quite looking at them. "It's all I can think of to say."

Black cloth blocked her view of the desks and not-watching men. P.J. looked up at Vanessa Allen, who squatted down and said, "I'm sorry about what happened back there."

P.J. wiped her eyes.

Vanessa said, "That was rough. He didn't seem like the type. I mean, I've been alone with him. That's creepy."

Pastor Daniel's stomach contracted behind P.J., like he had snorted.

Vanessa said, "He might have decided to murder me, too. Creepy."

"I don't know why I didn't recognize him before." P.J. sat up. "He just looked different in the dark, when the lights hit him."

Vanessa said, "I've seen people like that for work. They're like chameleons. They take on the characteristics of the night."

P.J. nodded. "Yeah. Some people are dark like that."

"We should talk more about this," Vanessa said. "You should tell me everything that you can remember about the occult symbols that you saw."

Pastor Daniel laid his hand on P.J.'s shoulder. "I don't think so, Vanessa. P.J. has had a rough week. She needs sleep."

"Okay." Vanessa winked at P.J. as she stood and walked away.

P.J. sat up. Pastor Daniel looked at her seriously. "P.J., that woman is trouble. I don't want to gossip, but don't talk to her."

P.J. wondered what Vanessa had done to earn such condemnation.

Max sat in the jail cell a few yards from his own desk, alert to any flinch from the few other people being held.

His uniform made him an instant target in the cell, but that was the case everywhere. A fellow deputy had died in a hospital a few years back. Substandard care and a stubborn refusal to pass on his increasingly bad symptoms were all it took for him to die of gangrene. Turned out that one of the nurses and an orderly were cousins of people the deputy had arrested. Any vulnerability can be exploited by vicious people.

Five other people populated the two cells. Two women in the other cell pretty much ignored him. Saffron had been transferred out to a long-term facility yesterday after her bail was denied.

Three men sat on benches in the other corners of his cell. Max had arrested the closest one to him, Viking Gutierrez, for drunk and disorderly.

From the back of the cell, joints popped.

Max tensed.

Viking cleared his bearlike throat.

Max glanced at him.

Viking was cleaning his fingernails with the edge of a business card. His expression was macho, but not angry. He nodded at Max, a deferential, conspiratorial bow of his shaggy head, then glared at the thumb-popper in the far corner.

The thumb-popper, a man-mink with a smooth beard, pointed his rodenty eyes toward the clock and thereafter ignored Max.

At least someone had Max's back in here.

Max and Viking had gone to grade school together, years ago, and they had jumped some bullies who had picked on Viking's little sister. It had been a satisfying fight for both of them, enough scrapes and bruises to show it was fair, enough pounding to prove their point.

Besides, Viking knew that breaking a couple chairs and a bottle over a bartender's head will get you thrown in jail. He probably didn't want to go home and hear about it.

Out there, Vanessa had Max's back. At least, she said she did.

All that history between him and Diane—twenty years of marriage, two kids, shared household finances—was corrupted by one extramarital screw that she found out about. Their additional historical weight contributed to the carnage like a bullet train hitting a wall and twisting like a whipping anaconda.

Max spent the night mostly awake, intermittently dozing, because if he and Viking dozed off at the same time, he might wake up with a shiv buried up to its rag-wrapped handle in his throat.

Vanessa watched P.J. through the crowd that was bedding down at the Country Congregational Bible Church.

P.J. had flung her sleeping bag amongst five other high school kids, all of whom twisted into unnatural caricatures of easy poses, elbows and knees wrenched, so that all their ten feet were pointing at the walls, poised for flight. When P.J. looked away, they grimaced behind her back, not in the customary way that in-kids roll their eyes about outsiders, but more subtly, with fear, with guilt. They were predators, those three females and two males. They might be sitting in a church, but they were vampires, predators of men. Not in a literal sense, of course. They were a cool clique, not Gothic darklings. The problem was that they felt guilty about preying on P.J., and Vanessa realized they must have done something. Guilt was unusual in predators. Something had changed for them. P.J. was no longer fair game.

Predators make up rules as part of their rationalizing. Burglars laugh at people who believe glass windowpanes protect diamonds. Drug dealers offer the first one free to the hookable. Child molesters believe that children are sexually precocious and the initiators. Serial killers blame the victim for being so stupid as to get into a car with a stranger.

She needed a cool approach, cooler than the teenagers who P.J. was currently hanging out with. It's easy to out-cool teenagers when you have six years more experience of observing and manipulating people and are in your early twenties, young enough to be cool but old enough to drink, smoke, and stay out all night in bars. Yep, a cool approach, one that confers coolness so P.J. will follow.

Vanessa stood beside P.J. The five high school fledgling raptors pouted with worry and wormed farther into their sleeping bags, picking at threads.

Vanessa pulled a pack of cigarettes out of her purse and tapped it to settle the tobacco, indicating imminent smoking. P.J. frayed the black lace on her vampress-wannabe skirt. Vanessa said, "Come on. Let's go."

Diane's hands shook less. She had been strong, if a little aloof, around her kids, who kept throwing each other coded glances: *something weird is going on*. She did not comment. If she was wrong about Max, then there was nothing to tell them. If he was the Master Satanist, then they should be told gently and privately.

Two hundred-odd people camped on the floor of the Country Congregational Bible Church. The fellowship hall was rated for a hundred and fifty people, but the fire marshal was less of a threat than Satanists.

The fellowship hall was certainly not private, and Diane did not think that she could be gentle right now. She pretended to read a novel.

A woman sitting on the floor behind Diane's back said, "And I just had a feeling that I should go over there, and what do you know? Turkey was on sale. It's like I'm turkey-psychic."

In the cluster beside her, a man said, "A friend of mine saw the UFO over Arizona State University. She said it was right around noon, and it hovered right over the Memorial Union. Then the government men came around and told them it was a weather balloon."

Pastor Daniel leaned over Diane. She jumped.

He asked, "Have you seen P.J. Lessing lately?"

Panic flashed. Another girl missing. She shook her head.

On the other side of Diane's legs, a man said, "Well, I'm a Taurus, so I'm just bull-headed that way."

Diane turned to her teenagers, sitting on sleeping bags and reaching out into the wireless ether via laptop computers. "Tatiana, Nicholas, stay here. You can sit by your friends if you want to, but neither of you is to leave this room unless it is on fire. Actively on fire. The smoke alarms must be screaming. You must document flames with video evidence, cell phone or webcam. Got it?"

The kids nodded, barely glancing up from their laptops.

Daniel and Diane stepped carefully between the rows of sleeping bags. Families were arranged with parents flanking small children. Teenagers clustered heads-in to whisper truths about human nature and philosophy or admonitions about revealing terrible secrets.

Zeke James was bedded down in an orange plaid sleeping bag that nearly matched his hair and beard on the perimeter of the expanded Stout tribe. Pastor Daniel asked him if he had seen P.J., but Zeke frowned and shook his head. "I'll help ask around."

The three of them fanned out among the crowd.

Diane asked people, "Have you seen P.J. Lessing? Have you seen P.J. Lessing?" over and over. Every so often, Zeke or Pastor Daniel stood and caught her eye, then shook his head with increasing worry.

No one asked who she meant. Most people had heard about the young Indian girl who had exposed the Satanist threat in their midst, had seen Ester James murdered, and had been terribly abused in a Satanic ritual. People had surreptitiously pointed her out to each other behind their hands.

One group of teenagers looked extravagantly innocent and exclaimed that they had never met her. Diane questioned them more, but they denied knowing her, at school or here at the church.

The congregants glanced at each other, first worried, then frightened. They gathered their children closer. Rumors ran like fog through the low places in the room, circling ankles, lapping at sleeping bags. People muttered at the horrible silence.

"Did you see anything?"

"No, I didn't see anything."

"How could they have gotten in?"

"The doors are locked."

"The windows?"

"Is anyone else missing?"

"Could they have been already in here, hiding?"

Diane and Zeke checked the bathrooms. Diane asked the ladies in the long line, but no one had seen her.

Zeke, Diane, and Daniel met back at the small stage at one end of the hall. Diane asked, "Anything?"

They shook their heads.

It should have been exciting, being the center of attention, the center of the Satanic coven investigation, suddenly socially acceptable to both her fellow Goths as the virgin sacrifice at a Black Mass and to the cooler Xian kids as a ward of the most Christian church in town.

But P.J. was numb to it all. She couldn't concentrate on anything.

Still images like tableaux in a strobe light beset her: guilty bystanders, chanting, and wildly swinging light.

P.J. climbed over the low wall into her dark yard and counted seven fist-sized rocks from the big white one. Without the yard lights on, the gray rocks smeared together. Straw-sharp grass poked her fingertips.

Vanessa said, "Let's get inside before someone sees us." She shoved her hands in her jacket pockets and glanced at the Gutierrez's house next door, where a single flood lamp threw its light swath toward the vacant lot.

P.J. picked a rock, swiveled the flap on the bottom, and retrieved the key from a hollow. "It's my house. We have the right to be here."

"It's a crime scene, and it's still taped off." Yellow police tape clung to the dark door like thrown paint. Vanessa clawed in her purse and came up with a box cutter. She delicately sliced the tape in the seams of the door.

P.J. unlocked the door, and they slid inside. She said, "Why are we even here? You don't even believe me about the Satanists."

"Nope. Not a word of your bullshit story. You've been brainwashed by that creepy little church, and I'm going to show you why there can't be any Satanists." Gray light pollution filtered through the screened windows and settled on Vanessa's tall outline.

"But I do remember," P.J. said. "Why won't you believe me?"

"That's the difference between science and religion. If something is the truth, it doesn't matter what people believe. If it's all just a story, belief is all you've got."

"I don't like it when people think I'm lying." Soft fur enrobed P.J.'s ankles. "Hi, kitties," she whispered. "You know, Vanessa, before I remembered the Satanists, Ester seemed like Schrödinger's Cat. No one knew if she was alive or dead, so she was both."

"I hate cats." Vanessa's strident voice echoed in the still house.

Hating a whole species seemed malignantly harsh, like the unreasoning stupidity of racism, and designed to present one's sensibilities as superior in order to denigrate other people. P.J. edged away from Vanessa, toward where the computer must be in the dark room. The cats followed her like a cloud of fur.

"Anyway, the whole Schrodinger paradox doesn't describe reality, to whatever extent physicists are, like, concerned with reality. The Copenhagen solution, that the cat is already alive or dead and the observer just looks, seems like a too-easy solution because the equations predict the dual-existence state, but the anti-Copenhagen solution to the paradox, that all quantum alternatives must continue to coexist, is just weird."

Vanessa sniffed loudly. "It stinks in here. What's that smell?"

The ammonia came from the cats' litter boxes, but telling Vanessa might give her a reason to hate cats more. "Glass cleaner."

"God, that really stinks," Vanessa said.

"Saffron must have put in too much ammonia. So, I was over here near the computer."

"Where's the light switch?"

P.J. didn't want Vanessa to see the cats. Though she did not agree with or appreciate Vanessa's unreasoning hatred, she liked Vanessa's good opinion of her. She needed to convince Vanessa that she was telling the truth. Even the Devil's Advocate must believe her about the Devil, or else, something bad might happen. Everyone else might turn on her, too. Her own memories were too precarious to withstand challenge, like a person who suspects their religious belief might be their own fantasy and is thus compelled to proselytize to avoid confrontation. "We probably shouldn't turn on the lights if we're not supposed to be in here. Neighbors might call the cops."

"Good thinking."

P.J. tried to distract her from the literal cats with the fascinating Schrödinger's paradox. It fascinated P.J., anyway. Some people are absurdly fascinated by reality television, which P.J. thought was just amateur actors' bad ad libbing.

"The third solution to Schrödinger's equation is environmental decoherence: that a quantum system cannot be isolated from its surroundings. You sum over each individual measurement of quantum states with a density matrix within the equations, so each possible outcome isn't a quantum state, and they're all entangled. The cat is either alive or dead. It's either in the box or out of it."

One of the cats said, "Mrrrfle."

"What was that?" Vanessa asked.

P.J. was lucky that cat haters are not sensitive to the vast range of feline vocalizations, as Westerners cannot hear Chinese tonal variation. She said loudly, "The ontology of the density matrix is never made clear. Ontology means reality. Physicists who sum over the entangled states aren't concerned with reality."

"Was that a cat?" Vanessa asked.

The cats swirled faster around P.J.'s legs, expecting treats. "I was standing right here when I saw the seven flashlight beams outside."

"You didn't see any flashlights." Vanessa's furious voice scared her.

P.J. remembered seven lines of light undulating in the dark. "I did."

"No, you didn't. You're lying."

"I am not."

"Jesus Christ!" A rumble and a smash as Vanessa's outline flailed. "Something touched my foot."

P.J. started to panic. "Saffron and The Tower are hippies. Some of the furniture is upholstered in purple fur. I saw the Satanists out there."

"I told you, you didn't see anything out there. That creepy little church brainwashed you."

That condescending tone was annoying. "I did see them."

"Holy crap!" The lumbering shadow of Vanessa in the dark room jumped. A cat screamed, and something thudded against a wall.

"What did you do?" P.J. fumbled for the light switch. Glare pounded her eyes. P.J. blinked and saw the brown cat lying limp on the stained carpet. "Oh, Vanessa! What did you do?"

"You do have cats!" Vanessa kicked at an orange tabby, which grabbed the carpeting and jumped away from her. She grabbed it by the tail. "You just can't stop lying, can you?"

"Leave her alone!" P.J. grabbed at the orange cat, but fluffy fur ball Curie rescued herself by twisting like a copperhead and clawing Vanessa's arm. Curie dashed out of the room.

P.J. scooped up all the cats she could and slung them over her arms. She ran two steps for the living room, shooing the rest of the cats with her feet, before Vanessa grabbed her arm.

P.J. said, "Stop it!"

Mendel, a black cat with a bad temper, jumped at Vanessa's arm and clawed her some more, and Vanessa jumped back from P.J.

Vanessa shook off the cat and reached, but Mendel leaped with his hind legs spinning in the air and ran. "Son of a bitch!"

P.J. ran, but Vanessa caught her arm again. The cats spilled from P.J.'s arms and scattered. In the light from the community room, cherry streaks of rage-engorged veins mottled Vanessa's face. Her livid voice grated, and "You didn't see anything! There are no fucking Satanists!"

"I saw them! They walked right through there and The Tower came to the door." She tried to jerk free. The white-painted living room walls were dark, like mud streaked them. "Stop it! You're hurting my arm!"

P.J. smelled burnt coffee and whiskey from Vanessa's screaming mouth. "You're lying! Admit it! Admit that you lied!"

"No!" A terrible realization percolated through P.J. The deputy had been the Master Satanist. At the vacant lot, Vanessa had stuck close to the deputy a lot of the time. More Satanists were still free, and Vanessa was one of them. "You're a Satanist!"

"That's another lie. Another lie!" Bands of light caught Vanessa's pale fiery hair as she tossed her head.

The carpet under her feet was crusty, like the dirt she stood on while she watched the Master Satanist butcher Ester.

Vanessa said, "You lied about everything. I hate liars."

She remembered in the clearing, at that huge cube of an altar, and Vanessa's face jumped out in every scene. Tall Vanessa swished behind P.J. in the line of black robes. She stood to the left of the Master Satanist, almost as tall as he was in the circle of black-draped Satanists. Hanks of blond hair peeked from the sides of her hood.

"You were! You stood beside the Master Satanist. You handed him the knife that he used to cut up Ester."

Vanessa screamed like a jet engine falling toward an inferno.

Burning pain slammed into the side of P.J.'s head.

Again and again and again, pain battered her face and head.

The pain stopped. Blackness squeezed.

She must be floating in space. In free-fall, the gravitational deformation of the fabric of space feels like an embrace.

The empty space that comprised most of P.J.'s atoms engulfed her.

Wednesday

Zeke drove his pickup carefully through town because four men rode in the back. He didn't like folks riding in the bed of his truck, but he had five men wedged in the cab with him, each of them with their arms squeezed tight against their bodies to minimize their contact with other XY flesh, so the other four rode in the back. Only illegal aliens evading *La Migra* and teens heading to a desert party rode crammed into trucks like this.

His hands gripped the plastic-leather steering wheel. They seemed like someone else's hands, someone else who could drive a truck and avoid the few other cars on the road. Surely Zeke could not be driving. Zeke was dead and in his grave somewhere, waiting in the satin-lined box under the cool earth for the Lord-promised resurrection of the dead.

Brother Daniel had sat down with Zeke a few hours ago and explained that P.J. had named Max Konstantin, the deputy who had been helping them, as the Master Satanist who had murdered Ester. Heat waves rose in his brain and smothered all thought. Daniel sat with him until he finally asked, "So that's it? She's been murdered, and she's with God now?"

"Yes, in Jesus' arms. Jesus picked her up and carried her away."

Zeke bent from the waist. "It's worse. I thought that not knowing was worse, but it's not. I miss her so much, and I want her back."

Brother Daniel said, "We Christians believe that we will be reunited in Heaven."

Zeke wiped his eyes. "She's with her mother. Christy will take care of her. She's not alone. She won't be afraid."

Poets and saints have tried to describe it, but the shredding pain when your child is snuffed out is too much to bear. You don't recover. You don't go on. You turn yourself into someone else, a childless parent, a stray dog, an empty-saddled horse, and forage for sustenance until the transformation into a body held together by grief is complete, and then you live out your days because killing yourself might inflict this pain on someone else, a cruel transfer of suffering. Zeke watched the hoary old hands drive his truck and licked his dry lips.

The other three cars that drove away from the church were packed, too. No one was going out alone. Every man had a wing man, and groups of four men were supposed to stay together, in case the Satanists were about tonight. The gibbous moon, just rising, was a quarter gone, and everyone knew that those Satanists had a moon fetish.

Again, Pastor Daniel had printed missing flyers and the terribly efficient maps off his computer, and the men broke up into search parties. This time, Brother Daniel faxed maps and flyers to other churches with a plea for immediate help. It felt like that first night when Ester was missing all over again, like time sadistically replayed itself.

The ladies stayed behind to guard the children, well-armed.

Behind him, in the back seat of the truck's extended cab, Teich Le Guerre and Nemo Turner muttered to each other. Nemo said, "So this means that one of the Satanists was in the church with us."

Teich said, "Or that the Master Satanist escaped from jail."

Zeke swallowed around the angry sick that sprang into this throat. He couldn't even grieve properly for Essie. The wringing anger at the murdering deputy usurped all the well-practiced sadness that swallowed him after Christy had passed away from a silent and probably congenital aneurism, a bulge of weakness in a blood vessel in her brain.

Essie's killer was Max Konstantin, the cold adulterer. In the field with Vanessa Allen, Zeke had felt that Konstantin was capable of worse. In dark moments, Zeke imagined hiring a hit man. In darker ones, he finished the Temple Project and then, with no family nor love left in this world, went out to break a commandment his own self, with his bare hands. His fingers tightened around the steering wheel, practicing.

"He couldn't have gotten out," Nemo said from the dark truck.

Teich said, "Those occultists and Skull-and-Bonesmen have high-placed friends. Someone sneaked him out. Or he turned invisible."

Nemo said, "People can't turn invisible. And Max went to UT, not Yale."

"Maybe he bewitched the girl. Or asked Satan to possess her."

"I don't know, Teich." Nemo ticked his tongue.

"I used to play those role-playing games in high school, before I came to the Lord. There are weird people out there, people who study the occult, the Babylonian and the Mayan demon-gods, who can call down lightning and read Tarot cards. They really believe that stuff."

Zeke parked the truck in the Lone Star's parking lot, two rows away from where he had parked when Ester had gone missing six nights ago.

His cattle must be ready to ship in twenty-two hours. Lord Almighty.

He focused on that: Lord Almighty. Somewhere above the firmament, Almighty God looked down on him. He loved the Lord, surely and deeply. His own dark night of the soul had descended after Christy had died, when he railed against fate and God. Her memory and sweet love of the Lord drew him back, and church was the one place where he felt her, as strong as if her blond head prayed beside him.

The strength that the Lord gave him was the only reason that he could put one foot in front of the other right now, to step out of the truck, to remove his shotgun from the gun rack above the back seat, and to set off through the parking lot, around the back of the grocery store, and into the brush with Pastor Daniel, Teich Le Guerre, and Nemo Turner.

Their flashlight beams roamed the dark wilderness, picking the blind trail out of brush and rocks. Behind Zeke, Teich grunted and rocks clattered.

Zeke pushed on. His exhausted muscles ached. His body was running on adrenaline, caffeine, and God's own strength.

Rage roared like a hurricane blast through a fragile window and flung her arm up into the air and down again and again. Stupid. Little. Cunt.

Exuberance spiraled like a column of fire.

Stupid. *Yes!* Little. *Yes!* Cunt. *Yes!*

Her hard fist crushed eggshell bones and crunched cartilage.

Stupid-little-cunt that got in a car with anyone. Stupid-little-cunt who made up shit about Satanists. It didn't fucking matter if the cat was dead or alive. Nothing the cat did meant shit in this fucked-up world. The fucked-up world was better off without stupid little cunts and their stupid cats.

The light from the back room splashed over the pulped girl and the bloody carpet.

Stupid-little-cunt who made Vanessa so mad with her entangled ontology and fucking cats—Vanessa hated cats—and her fucked-up memory that Vanessa smashed her on the back of the head, first with a wrought iron statue and then with her fists. Two more hard slams had shattered her spinal cord where it fed into her brain and destroyed the lower part of her brain, the, yeah, the cerebellum, the reptilian part of the brain. This kid wouldn't be worrying about Schrödinger's cat anymore.

As always, the exhilaration ebbed.

Three blows had stopped the breathing but, Vanessa noted with irritation, the limbs twitched like a frog trying to crawl on a slick lab benchtop.

Damn. Vanessa just got so angry that she couldn't think and reached out and smashed. She didn't plan it. Manic vigor and ravenous hunger and the noble right to smack someone whipped into a whirlwind rage storm.

They made her so fucking mad. The first time it happened, years ago during the aftermath of Katrina, she surprised the hell out of that slut by punting her until she was practically in pieces. To her surprise, Vanessa thrummed with life, and triumph overwhelmed the straining rage for months.

But the rage returned. People were so stupid that the rage inevitably returned. The irk became wrath became fury became berserker amok.

Ester had tried to cyber-bully Vanessa on the MyOwnRoom site. Ester noticed that several of Vanessa's RoomMates had passed away and wanted to redeem Vanessa from her dangerous lifestyle, so she incited all of her Christ-obsessed RoomMates to message Vanessa, and leave comments on Vanessa's homepage, and IM her, and email, and jump into chat rooms, and reply to her forum posts, imploring her to come to Christ. It was like Christ's Army had taken up cyberstalking. Vanessa couldn't have a coherent conversation with anyone without some little do-gooder popping up and pleading with her to accept Christ as her personal Lord and Savior.

So when Ester invited Vanessa to come home and talk about her church, Vanessa came to shut her up.

Ester had taken eight bashes, but the last five had been unnecessary. Those first three hits had dropped her, but Vanessa kill-kill-killed her until she was dead-dead-dead because she was so fucking stupid to piss off Vanessa.

It raised Vanessa's ire. When Ester got in the car that night, she spouted right off that Vanessa should go to church and get baptized, and the reason for Vanessa's crushing black mood was that she didn't know Jesus.

The watery depression caught fire like a polluted lake, and she swooped down and surprised the hell out of sanctimonious Ester. The checkerboard contrast between her rage and Ester's surprise melded into her triumph and Ester's terror.

Vanessa pulled a long black hair off P.J.'s head and shined her flashlight on it. Goop clung to the end. P.J.'s hair was a black strand like nylon thread. Ester's hairs were pale strands mottled with gross red hair dye. The cheap stuff looks like you scribbled on it with wax crayons.

As always, after the excitement ebbed, depression descended.

The rage was stupid and useless, too. Vanessa didn't even know why she did it. She had to stop. She should never be alone with anyone, because this type of stupid thing happened when stupid people made Vanessa mad.

That's the way this stupid-bastard world works, bee-yatch. They shouldn't piss Vanessa off or else they got what was coming to them.

It was a good thing that Vanessa wasn't a serial killer, one of those cold-blooded, emotionless men who stalked victims, sexually tortured them, and slowly murdered them.

Vanessa turned off the light in the back room, lest the neighbors see her trek across the shorn yard to the vacant lot. The light died.

The depression and rage coalesced into darkness. What's one less person on the face of this evil old Earth, anyway?

Zeke shined the halo of his flashlight on the dark, gumbo mud.

From the dark, a man's voice called, "Ho! Who's that?"

Zeke swung the flashlight beam. Behind him, three more beams searched the dark for the voice.

Four men walked toward them from the dark. They could be Satanists, the ones who were holding P.J. or ones trying to find their way to the Black Mass to kill her.

Brother Daniel yelled back to the men, "Who goes there?"

"Hickock Butler, First Baptist Church of Christ. Who are you?"

Pastor Daniel identified them by his own church, and the two groups of four men each closed warily on each other in the combined light of their flashlights, held before them like torches, shading their eyes from the glaring, oncoming lights. Hickock Butler, a scrawny man armed with a double-barrel shotgun, carried one of Brother Daniel's faxed maps.

Hickock asked, "Have they apprehended any of the other Satanists, Brother Daniel?"

"They got the Master Satanist this afternoon," Pastor Daniel said.

The men rumbled and jostled in the bright flashlight lines.

Hickock said, "So nine more are still out there."

Zeke hated that nine more people who had killed his baby were walking around free. He wanted to shake every person he met until they admitted their Satanism or he was satisfied that they weren't.

One of the other men stepped forward. "Did the Satanists lure her out of the church with their psychic powers? Or did they hypnotize her?"

"We didn't see. We don't know."

Teich asked, "Could they do that, Pastor Daniel?"

"I don't know," Daniel admitted. "The enemies of the Lord will display prodigious powers in the End Times."

"I think she ran away," one of the other Baptists said. "The Satanists have infiltrated the sheriff's office. They knew where she was. She's probably running for her life."

"We were keeping her safe," Pastor Daniel said.

"I'm sure you were doing your best, Brother Daniel," Hickock said, "but once Satan lured her out of your church, she was vulnerable."

The men nodded. The two groups exchanged cellular phone numbers and separated to search.

As they walked apart, Hickock called out of the dark, "The signal will be three owl hoots. If you hear three owl hoots, don't shoot."

Zeke wondered if other Christian groups roaming these woods had been informed of the three-hoot rule.

Zeke, Daniel, Teich, and Nemo hiked gingerly toward the brackish pond that P.J. had identified as the site of the Satanic Black Mass. Zeke feared what he would see when he got there. His eyes caught glimmers of light up ahead and to the sides of him out of the night, but he wasn't sure if that was his own flashlight beam bouncing, or Hickock Butler and his company, or some other search party, or the Satanists.

Out in the dark, a woman's voice yelled, "Hello? Who's there?"

The voice was not P.J.'s, but it was familiar.

Pastor Daniel stepped faster in his flashlight beam. "Who is that?"

"Vanessa Allen!" shouted through the night, and Zeke shuffled his feet on the hard ground.

Thrashing rattled the bushes, and Vanessa blinked in his light. She wore a black blouse and pants, not the right outfit for stumbling around in the dark.

"Whose car were you in?" Zeke asked.

"The last one," Vanessa said. "I jumped in at the last minute. Terrible that another girl is missing."

Zeke didn't remember Pastor Daniel sorting her into a search party, but Zeke's truck had been one of the first vehicles to leave. She must have jumped in a car. He asked, "Where's the rest of your group?"

"I don't know," Vanessa said. "I thought I heard something, and I yelled for them to follow me, and then I couldn't find them. Jeez, I thought I was going to be stuck out here. Can I get a ride back with you?"

"I suppose," Zeke said "One of the other guys will ride in the back so you can sit inside."

"Oh, no need to be chivalrous," she said. "I'm a Texan. I've ridden in the backs of pickups all my life. Have you guys searched over there yet?" She pointed deeper into the lot, away from the houses. "Come on. Let's go."

Max leaned back against the cold wall in his cell and dozed. It was four o'clock Wednesday morning, according to the clock on the wall outside the cell, though the cell was as bright as if it was Tuesday afternoon. He rubbed his palm on his trouser seam. His leg felt unfinished without his heavy holster.

One of the judges should arrive in his court around nine o'clock. Max's arraignment might be soon after that, depending on today's docket. He just needed to wait it out.

At the hearing, Diane might prosecute him.

Surely she would recognize the conflict of interest in prosecuting her own husband—her stupid, delinquent husband—and hand the file off to one of the other ACCAs.

Surely.

Then again, she had probably only had him arrested because a hysterical teen pointing at him had legally cornered her, and she could not, must not, believe those wild accusations. She probably would pull Max's phone LUDs when she got to the office in the morning to see where he was on the night Ester James went missing. Even when a cell phone isn't used, it pings the nearest tower every couple minutes. Cell phones are the best way ever devised to record citizens' movements. Cell phone towers garnish major highways every few miles, and the dozen or so around the town of New Canaan tracked nicely. You need a subpoena to obtain ping records because, when you're driving around without using a cell phone, there is a reasonable and legitimate expectation of privacy under the Fourth Amendment. Max's ping records should show him on the west side of town, in the Sheriff's office, not way over by the Lone Star.

It wasn't an airtight alibi, but it wasn't an old pair of socks, either.

Yet, considering that his arrest was part of the Ester James case, Diane might not see things clearly. His spyware had sent him screencaps of her email, and their tone would startle someone who had not seen how protective she was of Tatiana and Nicholas. She had been territorial to the point of snarling at anything that touched on Ester James.

How had Diane so misunderstood him?

His own stupidity was a good start. He bonked the back of his head gently against the cinderblock wall.

Keys jingled, and the lock on the barred door clicked.

Max opened his eyes. Viking looked over at him, eyebrows raised, tattoos rippling.

Sheriff Carlos Garcia, a part-Navajo, brown walrus of a man, stood outside the cell on his tiny flipper-feet. "Max, you're out of here."

Max glanced at the clock, which read four-twenty. "There can't be a judge on the bench at this hour."

Carlos said, "I'm springing you. Dropping the charges or ROR or just throwing you out of my jail. Let's get your things."

"I'm not afraid to face a judge. I have an alibi. I was logged onto the computer in this very office. You know all this is shit. I didn't rape a teenager, and I'm not a 'Master Satanist.'"

"Doesn't matter what you are," Carlos said. "I'm the sheriff, it's my jail, and I'm springing you. I was over at Our Lady of Perpetual Peace tonight, standing guard, when we got a phone call that we needed to send out search parties. We got maps of areas to search, and this." Carlos held up a computer-printed color picture of P.J. Lessing.

"What about her?"

"She's gone missing."

It took a minute to comprehend, and then he clamped down his agog reaction. "P.J. is missing? Are you sure?"

"Yep. And you're the prime suspect."

Incredulity dawned. "I'm in jail."

Carlos kept his suspicious gaze directed at his own feet. "I don't expect that's going to matter. There are roaming bands of heavily armed men who think you're a 'Master Satanist,' whatever the hell that is, and the girl who was the witness to the ritual murder of a virgin and the victim you supposedly raped at a Black Mass is missing. They're talking crazy, Max. People are calling me, asking whether you could fly out of the jail if you turned into a bat or a raven or smoke. I'm not sure whether they think you're a vampire or a Navajo witch."

Carlos's wary expression was insulting. "Carlos, this is crazy."

"Get in your car—here're your keys—and get out of town. Go to Dallas or Houston. Don't stop at your house. Buy a toothbrush and underwear. Don't tell me where you're going. Just go."

Carlos's insanity didn't impress Max much. Carlos was warm-hearted and shallow, both excellent attributes for an election, but he was none too bright. Carlos had sealed the windows and doors on his rural Texan house with plastic sheeting after September 11th because the terrorists might have improved their weapons access from boxcutters to Sarin or VX.

Max would remove himself from the environs just in case the witch hunters had turned into lynch mobs, sure, but not without his wife and kids. If he left town without Diane, his abandonment would finalize their estrangement.

Luckily, she had told him where she was going.

Diane was tired. She and three other women stood guard at each of the four doors of the fellowship hall. She held the coffee mug in one hand and braced the shotgun on her other hip, planning to drop the coffee on the floor if she needed to shoot anyone who tried to get in. The paranoia was infectious. However far-fetched the notion that the Satanists would try a home invasion, they were standing guard in case of just that scenario.

And P.J. had disappeared. No one knew if she was coerced, grabbed, teleported, or had wandered off, but the witness was gone. The girl's disappearance unnerved everyone.

Knocking pounded the door. Must be one of the last two search parties. Pastor Daniel and Zeke James had been back for an hour.

Around the room, the three bleary-eyed women stood and watched her. When-Dee stepped toward Diane, glanced at her own door, and looked askance as to whether she should provide back-up or guard her own door in case of multi-point ambush. When-Dee had stood duty all night, citing her work-at-home-mom status that would let her sleep during the day.

Diane waved her off. When-Dee gripped her rifle resolutely. Diane turned the key in the deadbolt locks and pressed the crash bar on the door.

Outside, Max pulled the door open.

Diane stumbled back. Oh, Lord, he was supposed to be in jail. "What the hell are you doing here?"

When-Dee, across the sleeping bag-carpeted hall, watched closely.

Max said, "Get the kids. We're getting out of here."

The breast pocket on his brown shirt where his badge usually hung was bare but for a few stretched threads. His holster was empty.

Diane cradled her rifle. "How did you get out of jail?"

Max glanced around, nervous lines working on the corners of his eyes. "Carlos sprang me. Those search parties are turning into crazed mobs. Get the kids. Let's go."

"No." She gripped her weapon tightly. She would use it, if she had to, to protect Tatiana and Nicholas, and herself. She had to protect herself because Tatiana and Nicholas were still just babies. "You need to leave."

Max stood straighter and blinked in the dim light from the hall. "We have to get out of town. New Canaan is too dangerous."

Thousands of reports had crossed her desk in the years that she had been with the County Attorney's office: family annihilators who killed their wives and kids when their secret lives were exposed, spousal murders by paranoid schizophrenics, and every serial killer's family thought he was just a quiet guy, a strong, silent type.

Every flash of rage that had popped out of Max jumped to her mind.

Max had killed fifteen people in the line of duty, including The Tower who had died last night. That was statistically unlikely, even for a deputy with nearly twenty years' experience, especially in the semi-rural, law-abiding Texas piney woods.

He had shot The Tower as soon as Diane left, before backup arrived.

She and Max had been married for twenty years, but they spent most of their lives apart, working, working late, working weekends.

For a few hours a day, anyone can fake it.

She was with her co-workers more than Max. They lunched. They talked about the work they had in common—cases, judges, juries—and they had time around the office and during late-night Chinese take-out to talk about news, politics, and sports. Some of them were having affairs, and she knew which ones and with whom and how.

She could not track Max the same way. It was possible that he had been absent from home at midnight on every full moon, and she hadn't noticed. Max hadn't noticed her going to church on Sunday mornings for six months.

When-Dee stood beside Diane, hitched up her rifle, and said to

Max, "You heard her. You need to leave. Now."

Pastor Daniel stepped beside Diane. He held a pistol, pointing in front of his toes, ready. "This church is private property. Please leave."

"Diane?" Max reached through the open door toward her.

Diane stepped back. His hand grasped air.

"Diane." His voice sounded mournful, and his expression was hurt.

She said, "Sheriff Garcia shouldn't have let you out. He always was an idiot. I'm calling my office to reinstate the charges and get a judge to issue an arrest warrant. You should go back to the jail to turn yourself in."

Max stepped back, turned, and walked toward his car with his hands in his pockets. Diane pressed the door closed and spun the keys, locking it.

Pastor Daniel sighed. "Thank the Lord. That could have turned out badly. Why don't you get some sleep, Diane? I'll take this door for the rest of the night. It's only another couple hours."

Diane shook her head. "I slept earlier. You were out searching. I'll do the rest of my shift."

"Okay." He threaded his way between the sleeping bags to his family's nest, which looked so sparse without P.J.

Diane sank into the chair and wanted to cry. Kidnappings and murders didn't surprise her. She glanced over at her own two kids, asleep next to the Stout clan's enclave. Tatiana and Nicholas were twisted into their sleeping bags.

Next to them, Vanessa Allen slept with an arm flung over her eyes.

When Vanessa had arrived back at the church with Zeke and Daniel's search party, she and Diane had had a long talk. Vanessa had apologized for sleeping with Max, woman to woman. She wept and said that Max had seduced her, somehow, and she was powerless to resist him.

Diane believed in free will, but she also understood how people can fall under the thrall of powerful personalities, become blind, become deaf, become insensible. She had not seen that Max was often out all night and came home with odd scents like smoke or incense clinging to him.

She had been fooled. So had Vanessa.

The embarrassment of being fooled pissed her off. Being angry exhausted her. She just wanted to grieve. Vanessa's confession and apology let her begin grieving. She was grateful.

After they talked, Vanessa kept an eye on Tatiana and Nicholas while Diane stood guard duty. Nicholas was a tender age, only thirteen.

Vanessa took an interest in them. She and Tatiana talked about college for a while. Tatiana needed more friends to talk to about college. In semi-rural New Canaan, college didn't figure in most people's lives, which was all right, nothing wrong with making an honest living. Tatiana, however, was going to a university for a good, long time. If worse came to worst, she could always get an MBA.

Vanessa seemed like a nice girl—a little too easily led, a little too giggly, shallow—but all right.

Outside the church, Max stumbled over to his big, solid SUV. He had convinced himself that Diane would have figured out by now that he wasn't a Master Satanist or even an ordinary, garden-variety Satanist. He had been so insular for so long that even his wife didn't know him well enough to dismiss the bullshit about his participation in Satanism and Satanic ritual murder. What in the hell was wrong with him? How had his life gotten this fucked up?

He beeped the SUV's alarm off then looked at his keychain. He had both alarm beepers on his keychain. Diane's Jaguar was parked on the other side of the SUV.

He strolled around the SUV, retrieved his official duffel bag in which he had stuffed his personal effects, unlocked the Jaguar, and slid the key in the ignition. It caught and roared.

Well, hell. If he was the big, bad Master Satanist, he needed a faster car. Besides, the Jag was low-slung, and its windows were tinted. People couldn't see him in it as well as if he were perched in the high SUV.

He drove slowly out of the parking lot. No sense in drawing attention to himself or pissing people off by shotgunning gravel at their paintjobs.

The first five blocks passed without incident.

As he turned down Armadillo Way, a truck swung around and followed him. He watched, ascertained that it was tailing him, and then flipped a one-eighty and zoomed away.

He was angry at Diane and grimy and tired from the cell, but the faster the trees zoomed backward past the side windows, the better he felt. He bore down on the accelerator pedal and fishtailed around corners.

"Thank you all for coming." Diane adjusted the microphone on the podium outside the Country Congregational Bible Church. Her eyes hurt because all her tears had dried up, and blinking rubbed her dry lids over leathery corneas. "I have two announcements."

One of the photographers, hat pushed to the back of his head, squatted in the gravel of the parking lot to shoot her with the towering, silhouetted cross, a perfectly mortifying shot that would no doubt haunt her the rest of her career. The stiff breeze ruffled the teased up-dos of the reporters, both male and female. The technicians, standing in back of the cameras and eyeing their cables, wore hats: Western, Mexican, fedora, or trucker with a racing car's number stitched on it.

"First," Diane swallowed air down her dusty throat, "we have another girl missing. Peace 'P.J.' Lessing, a girl of fourteen, has been missing since eleven o'clock last night. An Amber Alert has been issued."

The crowd of reporters rumbled, taking notes and composing questions.

"Her picture will be distributed to you momentarily. It is also available for download at the Sheriff's website. She is a witness in the disappearance of Ester James, and it is imperative for her safety to find her immediately."

Diane stared at her large-fonted notes on the rattling paper, not raising her eyes to the crowd. "Second announcement: last night, one man was arrested but erroneously released by Sheriff Carlos Garcia around four o'clock this morning. Maxim Joe Konstantin, a deputy with the sheriff's department, was named as involved in the murder of Ester Christina James. A warrant will be issued for his arrest shortly."

A shrill reporter yelled, "Does that mean he's a Satanist?"

"Satanism is not illegal, *per se*, in the state of Texas. Konstantin is, however, a suspect in the murder of Ester James." Granting him suspect status gave him more rights, one of the few things she could do for her stupid husband. If she had named him only as a person of interest, his rights would have been limited.

A reporter yelled from the dusty, sun-lit crowd, "When Deputy Konstantin gave that press conference yesterday, did he say that 'arrests would be made soon' to throw suspicion off of him?"

"I don't know." She didn't know anything. The cool breeze freshened, pressing her suit sleeves against her arms.

"Are Konstantin and P.J. Lessing together?"

"It appears that P.J. Lessing went missing around eleven o'clock last night. Maxim Konstantin was released near four this morning, five hours later."

"Could she have been kidnapped on his orders?"

"We have no evidence of that." They had no evidence of anything, just suspicions, just elimination of impossibilities. She smoothed her crumpled page of useless notes on the podium.

"How many Satanists are still at large?" asked a hoarse voice from the crowd of ovals topped by blowing cottony hair.

"Nine unknowns plus Konstantin." Her mouth hurt when she said that.

Shouted: "Is Maxim Konstantin your husband?"

Diane swallowed, and her dry throat spasmed. "Yes."

"Did you know that he was a Satanist?"

"No."

"Why not?"

Finally, tears burned in Diane's eyes. She couldn't seem to catch her breath, so she forced air out. "Maybe, like parents of teenagers who don't ask questions about drug use or sex parties or shoplifting or gangs, it never occurred to me that he could ever do anything like this."

"How can people recognize if someone in their family is a Satanist?"

Diane looked over the heads of the reporters at the bruised clouds drifting in the bright morning sky over the dashed lines of suburban roofs. "I don't know."

After scrutinizing the deserted street for law enforcement or vigilantes, Max darted into his house and rifled through Tatiana's closet for her old, half-broken child's microscope. Too bad she didn't have one of those nifty kids' DNA kits from the supergeek store.

In the living room's computer area, Max slammed shut the lid of the laptop with wireless capability, pulled its power supply cord, and sprinted with it into the garage. An armored key box was bolted to the wall near the door. He keyed the access number in, opened the box, and removed a key.

Max dropped to his knees on the garage floor. The door of a safe, two feet square, was sunken vertically into the garage's cement foundation. He turned the lock and opened the door. Below the door, black rubberized rifle butts stuck up.

Carlos didn't need to issue him an official gun. He owned guns. Lots of guns. Max grabbed two rifles and hauled them from where they were sunk vertically into the gun safe. He pulled a rack of pistols out and stuck one in his belt holster. The other handgun in a small holster he strapped around his calf inside his rattlesnake-skin boot. He started to rise but decided to take one more. He pulled a snub-nosed pistol from the rack and stuffed it and its nylon holster down the back of his pants.

You can never have too many guns.

He was out of the house and into the Jaguar in four minutes flat. Diane might have already called a judge and gotten that warrant issued. He needed to highrail it out of his own neighborhood.

He opened the laptop in the Jaguar and connected to a WiFi cheeping out of the house of his neighbor who didn't know crap about security.

The browser opened to its start page, a news site. Among the news items in small red type was the story The End Is Near: Israel Buys Texas Red Heifers. The article stamped a bull's-eye on New Canaan.

Max punched the seat of the Jaguar and clicked back to the website that tracked the GPS unit on the SUV, still bleeping from the church. He revved the Jaguar out of the driveway and down the street. A few blocks away, he parked in an isolated corner of a strip mall's parking lot. The twelve-table Mexican restaurant served the best chicken mole in town.

Max checked his email, more from habit than from hope.

His office email address was listed on the Sheriff's homepage. People had found it. Fifty-seven new emails had subject lines ranging from U R MASTER SATANIST U BURN IN HELL to Are you okay?

Chewy, a childhood friend from Catholic school, wrote, "Why

didn't you come to me, if you were getting into something over your head? Look, I'm a priest now. I've got a friend in the Vatican, a Msgr. Petrocchi-Bianchi, who's an honest-to-God exorcist. He can exorcise whatever demons possess you. Please, Max. It's your soul. And I can testify for leniency. The Church is good at that, trading atonement for leniency. Please, Max."

Max emailed back a few words that this was all a terrible mistake.

Of course, they didn't know him, really. His childhood had revolved around Anna—being injured by Anna, being crippled by Anna, protecting his siblings from Anna, and becoming strong enough to beat Anna to a bleeding pulp. He only wished he shot the babyfucker Anna with a Mozambique drill, twice in the gut and once in the face, bang-bang bang.

Good Lord, did it all stem from that?

His left hand, resting on the keyboard, tremored. Screwing Vanessa a few days ago had frozen an ice coffin around him. Diane's leaving him had shattered it. Now, he looked at the pieces.

It was *not* all traceable to Anna. His whole life—his whole adult life—was *not* an echo of Anna's manicured finger twisting in his ass. He was more than a grown-up raped boy. He was a protective father, and a good husband, and an investigator. He investigated and judged. He wasn't going to be run out of town like a small-time cattle rustler. He was an investigator and he was going to investigate.

On the laptop, Max typed MyOwnRoom.com into the address line of his internet browser and essie tex into the search box amid the gyrating ads and flashing text, expecting to find the same thing he had a few days ago: blond Ester, plain text, a few links, a small group of friends' pictures.

Her homepage had been vandalized.

In her picture—her as a blond standing next to a red heifer—devil's horns sprouted from her head and the cow's head in thick, black scrawls.

Underneath, "I am the Satan Incarnation!" was typed in a slashing font.

He clicked links, but the links were broken. One labeled *Christian Music* redirected his browser to the Church of Satan. This particular Church of Satan was headquartered in Connecticut. They probably wouldn't travel to Texas for a Black Mass. They would be pretty uncomfortable down in the Bible Belt. Might burst into flames or get smote.

Some of the links were not broken. One led into the Country Congregational Bible Church's Revelations webpage, wherein Pastor Daniel extolled the virtues of his own church as the only one that would survive Armageddon.

The link read: Creepy Little Church.

That was what Vanessa called Pastor Daniel's church. That was how she had taught him to think of it.

If he were still wearing a badge, if that idiot Garcia hadn't refused to hand over his shield from his box of personal effects as he had left the jail, investigating the link between Vanessa's idiom "creepy little church" and the vandalism on this webpage would be pretty interesting. Not to mention blood on her car.

Max went back to Ester's MyOwnRoom page and clicked through her links again. On Vanessa Allen's page, the boobie-licious spacer uniform slide show scrolled. In her RoomMates area, a black *in memoriam* ribbon festooned Ester James's picture.

Well, it was pretty likely. Vanessa had said when she was crying in the conference room, "You and I know that three days gone means three days dead. That's the way this bitter old world works. The civilians may not want to believe it, but we know it."

Eight days gone almost certainly meant eight days dead.

And Vanessa had probably known exactly how long Ester had been dead.

Another familiar face caught his eye. If it hadn't been festooned with black crepe, Max might have passed it over. P.J. Lessing's picture, with the appellation PJ_Hawking, was among Vanessa's RoomMates.

P.J. had been missing for only a few hours. Max's jaw clicked, and a sliver of pain scratched up to his temple. That was way too damn quick to declare her dead. That was straight inside information.

He opened another window and logged to the reverse phone book on the sheriff's database. He typed in the address where he had dropped Vanessa off when he gave her a ride home. It was owned by the Saini family. He typed "Inga Allen," which she had said was her mother's name, and an address popped up. He didn't need to map to know it was in the Deuce, a ring of violence around Second Avenue. Man, that was a bad neighborhood, even for Houston or New Orleans, a way station on the meth roads and slavers' highways. Her mother had purchased the house two decades ago, so Vanessa grew up there. Yeesh, the poor girl.

Max clicked over to P.J. Lessing's page, which had not been vandalized, and then clicked to her friends' pages. On one, he found a video clip of P.J. *in flagrante delicto*, or as Max thought of it, *con las manos*. Her drugged, half-open eyes eclipsed her irises to a sliver of a black moon. At first, he thought the video was in black and white because the bedspread under her was gray, but the dull glass lamp caught the emerald highlights in her hair. Her skin was so pale that she looked gray. People stood around the bed. Two unidentified hands passed money between them, a wager paid. The caption: The Rufi Sufi Whirls Another Girl!

Bastards. Max closed his eyes and pressed the backspace key to return to Vanessa's page. He would find the Rufi Sufi later.

On Vanessa's page, he clicked the other twelve black-draped photos and found their names and identifying information.

An African-American woman had died in the aftermath of Hurricane Katrina at the Superdome. Her killer had not been found. A young heroin addict had been beaten to death in the particularly dangerous area of New Orleans, when people still squatted without utilities. Max checked the dates that Vanessa had enlisted the deceased as RoomMates. Most of them were added before their deaths, though a few were posthumous.

Vanessa might be memorializing the victims of the three serial killers that she had discovered in her work in the forensic lab. Police work swallowed some people. That might be why she had so many murder victims among her RoomMates.

Probably not.

He didn't like it at all, but his not liking it didn't mean that there was a connection. He did not cotton to hunches. He worked with discernible facts.

A quick search of the New Orleans police department's website found no references to Vanessa Allen, not in their phone or email directories, not in their previous employees, not in their holiday party pictures. The Louisiana state crime lab also had no listing for her. Neither did the FBI. She wasn't a forensic technician at all.

In the trunk, he shuffled through the detritus in his duffel bag and found the extra blood collection kit.

He set Tatiana's old microscope on the sloping dashboard, angling for the strong sun with the little mirror under the stage. When he looked through the ocular to judge his work, he blinded himself like laser-burning his retina with a magnifying glass. Adjusting the mirror to an angle away from the strong southern sun rectified the problem.

He shook the swab out of the tiny evidence box, wet it with some distilled water from the same kit, smeared the brown crud on a glass slide that was probably clean and laid a cover slip on the fluid.

Those super-scientist forensic television shows had nothing on him.

In the bright circle, squished jelly donut cells floated amidst black dirt boulders, swaying from Brownian motion.

Vanessa Allen had blood on her car.

Max grumbled, "Son of a bitch. How did she manufacture that alibi? Two people swore. Their timelines were right. Usually two consistent people are right."

It wasn't a hundred percent, but it looked like the creepy little church was off the hook. Vanessa Allen had blood on her car. Where there's blood, there's a body.

Because Max is an investigator, and because he has rolled week-old corpses of young women tortured to death in coyotes' dungeons, held captive until their families in Mexico coughed up more money and never released, and because he has seen people brutalized and taken to the hospital with their faces mushy as overripe tomatoes, and the end results of many other crimes, he was not too surprised nor incensed at the revelation that Ester James was probably dead. He had concluded that a few days ago.

Back on the laptop's screen, on Vanessa's MyOwnRoom page, one tiny photo caught his eye. Tatiana's picture was the third from the end on the fifth row. Her NamePlate was "MyDaddysACop." How in the hell had Tatiana opened a MyOwnRoom account without him knowing about it? She was grounded as of right now, for one hell of a long time. On Tatiana's page, she noted that she was looking for "friends" but not "friends with privileges."

She was still grounded.

Max clicked back to Ester's page. It was too bad that he was not technically savvy. He knew how to email a worm to someone and hope they opened it, but he was no hacker. He could not even start to figure out who had vandalized Ester's website.

He exited the MyOwnRoom website and the search engine's front page popped back up, complete with the news story about New Canaan and Zeke's red heifers.

A few neurons clicked in Max's head. Those neurons hadn't been used for thirty-odd years, but they were still up there. Max was vaguely surprised he could remember all the way back to Catholic school.

Zeke was selling Red Angus cattle to Israel so the Jews could rebuild the Temple of Jerusalem.

According to Rapture-obsessed evangelicals, the Jews had to rebuild the Temple of Jerusalem to bring on the end of the world. And God would return to judge the world by fire.

Ah, Jesus. Pastor Daniel's church was a fucking suicide cult. When God didn't oblige, his church would go the way of all doomsday cults and forge their own Armageddon.

There was the off chance that God might exist and stick to the Revelations script, in which case Pastor Daniel's church was trying to destroy the world.

Damn it, Diane was involved, and she had the kids down there. He would deal with Vanessa Allen and the Rufi Sufi later.

Max swung out of the parking lot and down the road, toward the creepy little church. Diane and the kids were leaving that cult. He thought that he could make her listen to reason, this time.

At the end of his street, a pickup passed him. The driver, Gary, a neighborhood acquaintance, stared into his sleek car. In his rearview mirror, Max saw the truck swerve and spin into line behind him.

At the next stoplight, the truck pulled up alongside.

Max pressed the buttons and rolled down his windows.

Gary got out, swinging a baseball bat. "Master Satanist, huh? You don't look so big to me. I'm going to kick your ass."

Max tugged his handgun, a Colt .44 with a seven-inch barrel, out of its holster and laid the handheld cannon across his chest. "You sure?"

Gary got in his pick-up, slammed the door, and squealed his tires.

Max holstered his gun and drove hell-bent to the church.

The dusty parking lot was empty. The doors were locked. No one was there. Damn it, where were Diane and the kids? He powered the laptop and homed in on the SUV's transmitter again.

She was moving out of town, out into the forested roads.

Max left the laptop open on the passenger's seat and followed.

Diane drove the lumbering SUV toward the reconfigured Air Force base that had become Sin Nombre County International Airport, with flights to San Antonio, Phoenix, and the Mexican cities of Monterrey, Saltillo, Torreón, and any other airstrip where a drug lord could charter a cargo flight.

Tatiana and Nicholas were in the wide back seat.

Vanessa Allen rode shotgun.

Diane said, "Pastor Daniel and Zeke are over there. Shall we go help?"

In her rearview mirror, Diane saw Tatiana and Nicholas exchange a wary look. Nicholas jutted his chin at his sister, a gesture that meant, you do it. Tatiana rolled her eyes. "Mom, why do we have to watch cows get on a plane?"

"Because I said so."

"Really. Why?"

Diane sighed. Frightening them was the last thing on her mind, but leaving them alone in the house was foolhardy, especially since Max, her husband, their father, the alleged Master Satanist, was loose. "Because weird stuff is going on."

"You mean the Satanic cult that killed Ester James?" Tatiana asked.

Ah, yes. The high school grapevine had picked up Satanism chatter. "What did you hear?"

Vanessa swiveled in her seat and glared at the kids. Odd.

In the small window of Diane's rearview mirror, Tatiana frowned back at Vanessa. "Everybody knows about the Satanists, plus Ester James's webpage on MyOwnRoom was vandalized. Someone wrote 'I am the Satan Incarnation' all over it."

"Good Lord." Diane turned in her seat to see Tatiana better. "Are you sure?"

Tatiana shrugged with adolescent ennui, as if ritual Satanic murder was part of the teenage wasteland. "It's got pentagrams and stuff scribbled on it."

"When was this?"

"The day after she went missing."

"Oh, my Lord." The sheriff's office could have known about the Satanists days sooner if they had checked out Ester's web pages. Indeed, Zeke had told Diane that no one had checked her computer and that he knew her email passwords. They might have guarded P.J. more seriously if they had known, and now P.J. wouldn't be missing. It was a waste, a horrible waste.

Maybe Max had vandalized Ester's page himself. Loading spyware onto Diane's work computer behind professional firewalls took technical skill. Hacking a social site would not be much harder than that, probably. She didn't know.

Diane grabbed her chest. The pain was inside her heart, not the stab of a heart attack but a longing for happy ignorance. She suspected Max of everything because she had not suspected him of enough or soon enough. She patted her sleek hair back into its tight bun to procrastinate. "Okay," she said. "Okay. Weird stuff is going on. I want you guys with me. Around the other church members is the safest place right now. We'll figure out what to do after the plane takes off."

"Do we have to sleep in the church again? I'm not afraid of Satanists. P.J. Lessing was one of those scary Goth types. She wasn't a Christian. That's why the Satanists got her."

"Just for tonight. After that, we're going to my parents' house." Returning to her parents' house when her marriage had broken down was so medieval, like she was returned goods, still under warranty.

However, her children needed a place to sleep tonight. Her parents' lumbar-mangling hide-a-bed was safer than the back of the SUV in a parking lot, huddled against the winter cold.

"Man," Nicholas grumbled. "Nana and Papa will make us go to church, like, every day."

"Yep." Indeed they would insist on worshipping together at their hellfire-and-damnation Pentecostal Church three times a week. Maybe it was true that one returned to the church of one's childhood.

Pastor Daniel's church wasn't full of hellfire oratory, though. It was literal End of Days. Her childhood church had formed her taste for the law and so she had become a lawyer, and now the law, as a construct of mankind's intellect, instructed her on where to turn for religion. Religion was, of course, another construct of man's intellect.

Nicholas asked, "Is Dad coming with us?"

Diane swallowed and patted her hair again. "Probably not. He has a lot to deal with here. Come on." Diane picked up her heavy purse and opened the heavy door. "Let's help get these cattle loaded. This is a momentous event, kids."

"They're just a bunch of cows," Tatiana said.

Vanessa stood apart from the others, but she always stood apart from the others. The dry wind frizzed her blond hair and whipped it around her face, blocking her view of the red cattle.

The depression had already lifted, and the irritability was back. Her lethal cycle revolved faster every time. Morbid curiosity best described the thrill-hunger, but when you ripped it open, rage filled the empty cavity. Some killers describe the urge as a form of split personality, but that is not how it felt to Vanessa. The urge was not external, any more than hunger or horniness is an alien emotion. The thrill-need was a bored emotion lazily searching for a spark, and then the desultory tension turned inward on itself and burst into a rampaging forest fire. Vanessa didn't know what it was.

Vanessa did not know what she was.

In the car, Tatiana's flippant remarks about Satanists had antagonized Vanessa. Tatiana was one of those stuck-up bitches who drove chinks into the strata of society.

The restless anger latched onto Tatiana's callous comments and drove in lamprey teeth.

Vanessa watched Tatiana's wild black curls wag in the wind. Would those curls cushion a hard blow from a good-sized rock?

Right here, in front of all these people, smashing Tatiana would be insane.

No, it would be random and cruel. That's the way the world works: random and cruel. People should get used to it. Toughen up.

Vanessa was four the first time she saw someone die, when a john convulsed and vomited on the floor and her mother slapped his face and screamed he had to leave. He twitched until he stopped breathing. His face turned blue, then black, and the whites of his eyes turned red. Waiting alone in the house with the puke-covered corpse made Vanessa tough. To pass the time and distract herself from the rotted pork stink of his puke, she played Car Cracker and Ho Hunter video games until her mom returned with some gaunt, stoned friends who rolled the corpse out, chanting over and over, as if it was funnier every time, "Friends help you move. Real friends help you move bodies."

Afterward, her mom's stoner friends clapped her on the back, declared her a moll and a tough kid, and let her have her first drink of vodka and a toddler-sized snort of coke. The giddy euphoria was better than a taffy sugar buzz.

The mental image of smashing Tatiana's black curls became a mantra in Vanessa's head, like an earworm tune that she couldn't stop hearing inside.

Beside Vanessa, Diane pulled out her cell phone and held it in front of her, panning the cattle and plane.

"What're you doing?" Vanessa asked.

Diane shrugged. "Pictures. For posterity."

Posterity. Diane Marshall was a stupid old cow for forgiving and then welcoming Vanessa into her little fold. What a putz. She was too stupid to live, certainly too stupid to be allowed to reproduce. Natural selection should take out Nicholas and Tatiana, any day now.

Several sedans and a truck drove into the gravel lot near Diane's car. The sun glared golden on the swirling dust. Stalwart folks clambered from the vehicles, toting lance-slender rifles or stubby shotguns. Holsters on their belts gave them bulbous, womanly hips.

"Interesting." Vanessa cocked one lightened eyebrow up. "Hey, Tatiana. Do you want to herd the cattle into the stalls inside the airplane?"

Tatiana grinned. The wind tousled her black curls.

Zeke looped the leather straps through the fingers of his left hand and reined the horse to herd the cattle toward the ramp. The cattle would load through two cargo doors, one on each of two decks of stalls, five cattle per stall, fifty stalls per deck in the flying barn. The plane was a cargo version of a DC-10 with special modifications for carrying a herd of cattle. Each deck had seven feet of clearance, floor to ceiling, instead of five on the lower deck and nine on the upper, the usual configuration.

He pulled his hat down to shade his eyes from the sun near the horizon. His dogs scampered back and forth, yelping. Red Angus are mild-mannered cattle, and they obliged by plodding single-file up the ramp and into the belly of the airplane.

Essie should see the cattle and the roaring plane. That first night when Zeke realized that Israel needed a red heifer and that he had hundreds of them milling in the good pasture land of East Texas and that God had a mission for him, he and Ester had been sitting in the parlor. Ester was watching television and he was reading his Bible, and he read the passages about Jacob's spotted cattle and the red heifer sacrifice aloud to her.

She picked up on it fast. "Why not just give them some of ours?"

Lord, give her back. She should see this. The hollows in Zeke's heart ached. He hawed at the cattle, shining in the setting sun.

The cows lowed and trundled up the ramp, but one broke away. Zeke turned his horse sharp on his left lead and cantered fast after the heifer. He spun his stiff rope twice with his right hand and launched it at the cow.

The stiff loop settled over her red neck. He dallied the rope around the saddle horn twice for leverage and tugged the reins. Charlie sat back, tightening the noose.

The cow hit the end of the rope. Charlie stepped backward slowly, playing her like a hooked fish. She twisted, bucked, and fought the rope.

Zeke turned the horse and led the heifer back to the trailers. When she was safely in line, Zeke flipped the rope off her neck and coiled it, flipping it a half-turn with every loop like a snake writhing on the ground. Coiling the rope always reminded him of DNA twisting and coiling around histones into chromosomes.

The two girls, Tatiana and Vanessa, black hair and shining blond, walked up the steep ramp and into the plane. They chatted, flipping their fingers while they talked. He missed Ester anew.

Loading a cow onto the plane took ten seconds per cow, six cows per minute, three hundred and sixty cows an hour, so it would take an hour and a half to load all five hundred head. The sun was settling toward the horizon.

Zeke turned back to Daniel and Diane. "Put those folks to work. Too many people are gawking."

Over by the terminal, several dozen people gathered.

A man laced his fingers in the chain-link fence and rattled it. The thundering wave telegraphed down the fence.

Max sat in the Jaguar in a traffic jam. Traffic jams didn't happen in the smidgeon of New Canaan. Big cities have traffic jams. He opened the car door and stepped out. Cars queued all the way to the airport's entrance. Inside the lot, roving cars vultured for parking spots and stalked nervous employees walking to their pickups.

The rusted-out sedan in front of him bore the bumper stickers *Meat is Murder! Fur is Murder!* and *Visualize World Peace*. Ahead, a minivan with Utah license plates had a sticker in its rear window: *Tabernacle Choir Parking Permit*. Behind him, six college kids bounced in unison in a BMW.

A news van crowned by a satellite dish raced up the wrong side of the road. Law-abiding cars honked long, angry squalls at the interloper. One mighty SUV pulled onto to the other side of the road to block the news truck, which honked furiously. Westerners are fair. You wait your turn, even if you do have a camera.

Max's laptop computer on the passenger seat tracked the SUV's GPS transponder. The SUV was in the airport, chirping its fool head off.

Screw this.

Max couldn't drive up the wrong side of the road because gesturing men had emerged from the blocked news van and huge SUV. Other cars honked support.

Max drove the Jaguar off the road and bounced cross-country. Damn, he should have taken the high-clearance SUV. Or a dune buggy. Or a horse. Weeds scraped paint off the doors right by Max's knees. Damn-damn-damn, that hurt. He steered around boulder chunks and tree stumps.

He didn't see the jagged hulk that tore open the oil pan, but the tearing metal sounded like a rabbit screaming in a trap. He kept driving.

The Jaguar made it another mile before the high-performance, precision engine threw a rod just short of the airport's security fence.

Max retrieved his rifle from the back seat, climbed the chain link fence with two well-placed footholds and a quick hop, and walked cross-country. The sun dipped lower in the sky. His cell phone said the time was four-thirty.

Beyond the dead grass and tarmac, cattle sauntered up ramps onto a looming airplane. People herded the cattle, scurrying like ten minutes after the quitting steam whistle blast. In the shade of the terminal, another crowd coalesced. Some carried picket signs, though they were too far away to read.

When those cattle were boarded, the plane would leave. He had not checked Diane's closet to see if she had packed a suitcase. She might get on that plane and go to Israel, and she might take the kids.

Those cattle were going to cause an international incident, one that might involve suicide bombers or rocket launchers or fuck-all war. If his family was hunkered down over there while he watched shells bursting fiery phosphorus on the television, he would jitter around the television, trying to dive through the screen to land on top of them and shield them. He didn't have a passport. He couldn't follow them if they left.

Max broke into a double-time jog. At a quick-step, he crossed the pebbled field and tarmac, a distance of perhaps a mile and a half, in fifteen minutes. His holstered guns bounced on his hip, back, and ankle.

Vanessa watched Tatiana from two stalls away. The cattle shuffled in the hot plane, sweating though their raw silk fur.

Tatiana was a pretty girl, as pretty as the dry-cleaned bitches in high school, as pretty as Vanessa's own mother in her heyday, but in a different way, of course. Tatiana had vivacious black eyes and boisterous hair.

Vanessa's mother Inga was still a blond beauty, though she complained to anyone who would listen that nursing Vanessa had ruined her breasts. She was as wasp-waisted as Vanessa in a steel-and-leather fetish-wear corset. Methamphetamines kept Inga as lean as a starlet, though some might call her gaunt.

Tatiana was a mercuric amalgam of pretty-boy Max, who had screwed Vanessa against a tree and hadn't had the decency to send flowers, and Diane, that uptight bitch who was too stupid to live.

The ire rose, but Vanessa tamped it down. She held a hand to her temple. This anger was stupid. Vanessa just needed anger management counseling, and other people needed to stop being so stupid.

Vanessa said, "So what do you think about these Satanists?"

"P.J. hung around with the Vampire Goths and other darklings. I guess they really were into Satanism. She narc'd, and they took her out. That's what happens when you hang with the wrong type of people."

Vanessa despised sophomoric elitism that stratified people into wrong and right castes. "So you think there are Satanists."

Tatiana's curly head lifted. "There's this guy at school who had demon horns surgically implanted in his skull. Yeah, he's into Satanism."

"It's just an affect."

"No, they're real. I checked."

"And how did you do that?"

Tatiana's perky expression was annoying. "My friends invited him to a party a couple months ago. We told him not to tell his Goth friends that we invited him because we didn't want a bunch of dorks at the party. He, like, drank too much, you know? He passed out." She giggled. "We wiggled his horns. They're real. Then we tattooed a cross and 'Jesus is Lord' on his ass."

The image of the poor, inebriated Goth, ass-up, getting carved, pissed Vanessa off. Anger condensed and began to vibrate. "That's terrible."

Tatiana reared back like a wavering cobra and her gaze focused down her nose, and Vanessa realized that she was one of those stuck-up, snotty, mean girls. Her sanctimonious tone was harsh. "What about it? Were you one of those cast-offs in high school? What, did no one want to eat lunch with you?"

Vanessa hated snobby bitches.

When Tatiana turned to admire a particularly pretty cow, whatever the hell that was, Vanessa grabbed the orange electrical cord and noosed it over the girl's neck, pulling it tight as a garrote.

Tatiana flailed stupidly. Vanessa choked her harder in retaliation, twisted the cord, and punched her in the face. Finally, she went limp, and Vanessa tied her up and duct-taped her.

Vanessa panted with the effort. That stupid, stuck-up bitch had it coming.

The girl was still alive, though. Vanessa was not a serial killer.

Zeke tied the horse's reins around a bar in the window of the horse trailer. If he was going to be longer than a few minutes, he should take the bridle off Charlie and let him wear the halter for comfort, but checking the cattle on the plane should only take a minute and then he would be back in the saddle again. He waved to the vet that he was going inside and strode up the ramp.

Vanessa Allen, alone on the lower deck, shunted the cattle into waiting pens. Lord in Heaven, that woman turned up everywhere. She was outside by the pens, she was inside the plane, she was in his barn, she was in the dark vacant lot where they had looked for P.J., and she was in the grocery store parking lot when Ester disappeared, a big, blond, busty bad omen.

His chest contracted inward, like cramps. Lord in Heaven, he missed his baby daughter. Ester must be hugging her mother Christy, which she hadn't been able to do for so many years, and then Jesus would embrace both of them. Air leaked into his lungs, and he breathed. That image could brace him for the next couple days, and then despair would settle again.

Around the plane, it looked like the cattle were getting into their pens all right. That's what he was here for, to see to his cattle.

The plane was fuming hot from cattle breath and heat transferred from the sun baking the silver fuselage. He should tell the pilots to start the engines and run the air conditioning. The government has strict regulations about the comfort of livestock on cargo flights.

Zeke called out, "Everything all right up here, Nessie?"

Vanessa continued herding the cattle into pens, but she glanced over her shoulder. "Yep, fine up here. You should look at this, though."

Zeke trudged over to her. Waffle-grid, black rubber mats covered the floor to cushion and provide traction for the heifers' hooves, as well as for drainage. His footsteps made no sound at all on the mats.

The cattle's snuffling and rustling and the occasional bawl echoed on the metal walls curving around and above them like a Quonset hut.

Zeke did not particularly like flying, but flying in a cushy seat with a stewardess and a hot pot of coffee and a movie maintained the safe illusion of civilization better than this minimalist bunker that would soon be suspended in the middle of sky. Brother Daniel would tell Zeke to trust Jesus. Zeke commended his soul to Jesus and trusted the three freelance aeronautical mechanics he had paid overtime to double-check the plane's maintenance yesterday.

The cows, he should think about the cows. "Yes, Nessie?"

"This here." She bent over, which mashed her bosoms together. Zeke did not care to look. She said, "I think this cow has a problem."

He stooped and checked the cow's hind leg. A festering sore oozed pus and smelled like chunky milk. "So much for my overpaid veterinarians."

"Probably an *E. coli* virus," Vanessa said.

Zeke shook his head like a sweat wasp had stung him on the temple. "Virus?"

"Oh, I mean bacteria."

Zeke pursed his lips at her stupid mistake—another stupid mistake about the procedures of science—and went to retrieve his overpaid vet.

When Max approached the plane, he braced himself on his knees to catch his breath and fanned himself with his hat. Weight training in the office gym didn't do squat for his cardiovascular system.

Across the asphalt, he saw Diane and Nicholas standing by the cattle trailers. Tatiana was not in sight.

Max shouldered his rifle like a parading soldier, with the muzzle pointing at the sky, and walked over.

Diane saw him coming about ten yards away and pointed while she backed up.

Securing the rifle with the crook of his elbow, Max spread his hands wide and empty. "Diane!" he yelled across the wind and howling plane engines. "We need to talk!"

"Don't come any closer!" She pulled Nicholas under her arm and behind her, shielding him. Nicholas stared up at her like she was insane. The wind drove tears sideways across her cheeks. "Max, I swear to God, I'll call the sheriff's office and have you arrested."

Loneliness at the prospect of being without her forever gripped him. "Diane, that church of yours, they're a suicide cult like the Branch Davidians!"

"They're not!" The wind whipped meager strands of hair out of her tight bun. Even Nature could not wrest away her tight control. "I mean, we're not! And stay back!"

He walked closer so he wouldn't have to shout. "Come home with me. Bring the kids and come home."

Diane stepped back.

"Diane, stop." He took three quick steps toward her and the wind blew his hat off. It tumbled under a nearby pickup truck.

"Help!" she yelled.

Church people among the trucks swiveled.

"Help!" Diane yelled again.

The church people advanced on him.

"Stay back," Max told them and brought his rifle across his body, not pointing it at anyone, but holding it ready. "I figured out that you guys are sending red heifers to Israel for the Temple of Jerusalem, so that the Rapture and the Tribulation and Armageddon and all that will happen."

Diane smirked, an expression she had never used with him before. He was an adversary to her now. "Figured that all out on your own, did you?"

Church folks wove in a rough circle around them, pacing.

"What is your little church going to do when there is no Rapture?" Max asked. "Is Stout going to brew the cyanide punch?"

The church folk grumbled and paced faster in the red sunlight.

Tendrils of her hair slipped from the tight knot. "No! That's crazy. He wouldn't." She struggled to keep Nicholas behind her back as he danced around, trying to see. "He's said that the Rapture might not be for decades. He told us not to cash out our 401K plans and to make the kids do their homework. Does that sound like a suicide cult?"

Nicholas jumped away from his mother and stared at them with his mouth hanging open.

She said, "Max, let him leave. Don't hurt him."

Max wanted to shake her for insinuating that he might shoot his son. "Get him out of here."

She said, "Nicholas, go help your sister on the plane."

Nicholas stared back and forth at them. "What the hell!"

Max looked at his young son, a pale, weepy version of himself. "Watch your language."

Nicholas moved one of his feet toward the plane then looked at Diane.

"Go!" Silk ribbons of her brown hair flew around her face.

Nicholas said, "Man!" and kicked his feet as he walked through the throng around them. One churchie grabbed Nicholas and hustled him inside the plane.

Max wanted to reach out to Diane, but the multitude might shoot him down for making an aggressive move. He took a little comfort in noting they stood in a circle.

He said, "So what happens when the cows get to Israel and start a war? Do you want Tatiana and Nicholas to live out their lives in some nuked wasteland, reduced to," he thought back to all the dystopian science fiction he read in high school, but he couldn't think of anything terrible enough, "to subsistence cannibalism?"

Her brown eyes flickered upward, dismissing his apocalyptic apoplexy. "Of course not. They'll be raptured."

He wanted to shake these infantile dogmas out of her, but he could not reach her. "Thank God my mother insisted they be baptized Catholic. Even if the Revelations storyline doesn't play out, people believe that those cows are going to cause the Armageddon. There are going to be global waves of terrorism. Do you want to be in Israel when that happens?"

Diane's head twitched, a gesture he recognized as confusion. "We're not going to Israel. Daniel and Zeke are, but I can't take the time off. Nicholas doesn't even have a passport." Her hand flew up to her mouth. Tears welled in her brown eyes. "You're not going to do this! You're not going to just get me talking to you when you screwed around and you're in some kind of a Satanic cult and you killed Ester and now P.J.'s gone and I don't know what to think!"

No matter how insulting or horrifying it was that Diane thought those things about him and said them in front of the people who crowded around them, he had to persevere. "I didn't. I wouldn't."

Diane said, "Not now, Max. We'll talk through lawyers. The whole law system is for talking about things that are too terrible to talk about."

An empty cattle truck moved off. Another pulled up to the cattle gates leading to the airplane's boarding ramp and discharged red cows. A few people helped, but at least forty people ringed them.

"Look," he said.

Her jaw was clenched and bulged at the sides. Diane looked at the pebbled cement, not at him. "I'm calling Carlos to arrest you."

Four guns lay snug on his body: the rifle resting on his shoulder and holsters on his hip, the small of his back, and his ankle. He craved shooting himself in the head or through the mouth. Oblivion was preferable to the only memory that he had left to offer her that explained why.

He couldn't eat a gun. Tatiana and Nicholas would be left with the memory of a father who, when confronted with the image that would become the truth—that he was a "Master Satanist," murderer, and child-rapist—had committed suicide in public, in front of their mother, in front of a crowd of people, rather than accept responsibility.

In the minds of all these people that scowled and paced around him, weaving a tight circle around them with some social black magic that he couldn't escape, blowing his head off would cement their memory of him as a murderer and a coward.

Lies had wrung Diane's image of him and even changed her memories, but they were lies.

His own image of himself in his mind and in other people's minds, all these people's minds around them, was hard-wrought over decades. If his cast-iron image could be so easily hammered with a few lies, truths could forge it back to a true shape.

Not the same shape, but a true shape.

"Look." His voice cracked so hard that his throat hurt.

She grabbed her purse and held it in front of her.

"I screwed Vanessa Allen." His throat hurt like an infection scoured it. "When she grabbed me, it just happened. It's a protective mechanism. It's a stupid protective mechanism, but that's what it is. Sex means nothing."

He stared at his hands clenching around the glassy wood of the rifle stock in front of him. They were an old man's hands, parched and rough. The hands that had beat the snot out of Anna, literally pummeled her until snot clung to her ruined hair, had aged.

Max said, "If sex is meaningless, then I'm all right. Then it didn't kill me. It didn't destroy me. Do you know what I mean?"

He lifted his eyes from the rifle stock, did not look at all the people around them, and risked a glance at her.

Her expression was horrified, an amplification of the workday horror she wore when she artfully euphemized to Max who she had prosecuted that day. "Max? I don't understand what you're talking about."

"Don't make me say it." He drew a breath of scorching air and stared at the rippling wood grain of the rifle again. "I was nine when *it* started."

Vanessa directed cattle into pens by stretching herself into a buxom fence line. The cattle obeyed.

Pastor Daniel, guiding Diane's young son, walked up behind the beasts. "Nicholas is looking for his sister. Isn't she with you?"

"Hmmm?" Vanessa turned and blinked up at the spindly pastor. "Tatiana is on the upper deck. I'll take Nicholas up. All you have to do is stand here. The cows just walk into the pens. No wonder they're so easy to grind up into hamburgers, huh?"

Daniel took Vanessa's place as a human picket fence.

The cattle, indeed, proceeded into the stalls.

Vanessa took Nicholas's arm. He did not protest. She said to Pastor Daniel, "Five per stall. Then switch to the next stall. Just kind of crowd up on them." Daniel moved up, and the cows ahead of him budged up and funneled into the next stall. "Don't forget to close the gate. I've got this one. Nicholas and I will go find Tatiana."

Diane's mouth was open, panting. The air was dusty from the dirt the cattle and crowd kicked up, and grit ground between her teeth. The earth rattled under her feet, unsure if it was going to stay fixed under the firmament. "Max, what are you saying?"

"It started when I was nine," Max said. His head was bowed over the rifle and he clutched the barrel like it was a fencepost and he was fighting a stiff wind. "It was the usual—the grooming, the blackmail, assault."

Lord, oh Lord. Her head spun like the whole planet had whirled out of its orbit and was swinging in ever-widening death spirals. She resorted to interrogating the witness for the jury. "Is that why you became a Satanist?"

"I am not a Satanist. I was never a Satanist. P.J. was a little girl and Ester was just a kid, too. I wouldn't ever hurt a kid."

Assault. Hurt. Euphemisms rose to the top of her mind like swamp scum because the real words evoked horrible images. She fought the perpetrators of child sexual abuse every damn day and had missed the obvious signs of damage in her own macho husband. "Who was it?"

"It was my aunt ... Anna." He coughed the name like he couldn't bear it. His agonized face was heartbreaking.

Anna. She was not invited to their wedding, to Max's father's chagrin, not to Christenings nor holidays. No one in Max's generation mentioned her without a sideways sliding of eyeballs, like she might have appeared in the gloaming at the sigh of her name.

They knew, she realized. The whispers had been disseminated on that warning system that children have, wrapped in mysteries and superstitions: don't go to the haunted shack by the railroad on Friday the thirteenth, don't go over to LeAnn's house when her father is home, don't let Father Sean get you alone in the rectory, don't get in a car with the social studies teacher Mr. Clark, don't eat the Halloween candy from the Steward house.

The crowd of her fellow church-goers swarmed around them. The cattle stomped at their buzzing.

Max had been sexually successful, studly, in college. For a woman, such a dirty laundry list would have branded her as promiscuous or slutty. He was overprotective of their kids to the point of paranoia. He was secretive and didn't trust, even planting spyware on her work computer. His protestations that sex was nothing were a dead giveaway.

At home, he vacillated between ostentatious modesty and exhibitionism. He was ashamed of odd things, like ejaculate and any noise during sex, especially his own.

Tears filming her eyes blurred his outline against the black tarmac.

It was easier to believe that he was a monster who killed people than a molested child whom no one had rescued. Rage is easier to endure than suffering.

All these settled it into the category of probable truth. She had explained away Max's CSA symptoms for years.

Because she worked with victims of CSA, Diane understood how the damage had pulverized Max's psyche, and therefore why he had screwed Vanessa.

As a lawyer, she saw his admission as a guilty plea.

As a Christian, she forgave him and pitied him.

But she was also his wife, and his explanation did not ameliorate the betrayal.

She slapped her hurting chest. "Are you telling me the truth?"

Max nodded. His body crumpled from the knees, and his hands slid down the barrel of the rifle until he was kneeling on the ground, bracing himself around the rifle.

The circling crowd growled and surged toward where he knelt.

Zeke ambled down the stairs from the plane to the ground. A cattle-filled truck backed toward the ramp while people swarmed, waving amateur approximations of semaphore signals. A teenage boy crouched with one leg extended and whipped both hands toward a point beyond his foot, as if the cattle truck was going to morph into a fighter airplane.

Beyond the chain-link fence, the people in the shade of the terminal building had swelled to more than a hundred. The words on the signs and banners resolved as he neared.

Welcome Home, Jesus!

MEAT IS MURDER

White Buffalo Woman Has Returned. Let the Red Heifers Go!

John 3:16

Justice for Palestine

Alongside the cattle trucks and horse trailers, Zeke's fellow parishioners stood around Sister Diane and a man who looked to be her husband, the man P.J. named as the Master Satanist, the man who bled the life out of the chubby legs and slender belly and floral-fresh cheeks of Zeke's baby daughter. Forlorn ache roared and became rage.

Outside, the deputy sank to his knees in the center of the circle.

Zeke broke into a desperate run.

Diane grabbed Max around the shoulders. "Is that what happened?"

He crouched around the rifle like a hysterical cat clinging to a branch in high wind.

Slam. The ground rushed up at Diane and she shoved at the dirt to protect her face. Red hide ran over her and she thought the cattle had stampeded and trampled her but Zeke, red-faced with fury under his orange hair like a bright tiger, had knocked Diane aside and grappled Max.

Max's rifle skittered over the asphalt and rolled underneath Zeke's pickup truck.

"No!" She jumped on Zeke, trying to tear his hands away from Max's throat because Max gurgled and couldn't breathe.

Max clawed at Zeke's hands clamped on his neck.

"Zeke!" Even though Max screwed around, he was still Max and her husband and Zeke couldn't kill him. "No! He didn't do it. I swear to God and I mean it that he didn't hurt Ester! Please let go. Please let go." Her nails scratched the brown-freckled skin and wiry orange hairs on Zeke's hands. "Let go, Zeke. Let go."

Max slammed his fists down on Zeke's forearms, breaking his grip.

Zeke jerked his hands away and staggered back.

The ring of churchgoers grabbed Max. Nemo Turner and Teich Le Guerre, both big men, held Max's arms.

Zeke turned on Diane, furious. "What do you mean he didn't do it?"

Max coughed, spitting. Nemo and Teich edged away from the bloody spittle but held his arms. The rest of the crowd swirled around them, not knowing how to help.

Diane said, "Max didn't do it. I don't think he did."

"You don't think?" Zeke panted. "That's a damn far sight from he didn't. Did he or didn't he kill my daughter?"

"He didn't." Diane looked at Max, who was still coughing. Confusion blocked her. "Right, Max?"

Max held his hand up, a supplication. His voice was strangled. "I didn't hurt Ester or P.J."

"You swear to God!" Zeke yelled at Max. Zeke's fists flinched by his sides. "You swear by the good Lord that you didn't hurt her!"

"I swear," Max said. "I swear in the name of the Father, and the Son and the Holy Spirit."

"None of that Catholic stuff!" shouted Zeke. "Say the name of Jesus!"

Max swallowed hard and rasped out, "I swear by the holy name of Jesus Christ, redeemer of mankind, and of Lord God the Father, that I didn't hurt Ester and that I'm not a Satanist. A possessed person can't say the name of Jesus Christ or God the Father."

"Are you?" Zeke stammered. "Are Satanists possessed?"

Max rubbed his throat. The sadness in his eyes was pitiful. "It didn't come up in confirmation class, but surely that's the point of Satanism."

Evidently the Catholic education he so derided had produced small roots, but it was information, not belief.

"Then where is she?" Zeke cried out.

"I don't know." Max ran his hands around his throat. He muttered, "I think I know who did it, though."

"Damn it, I just want this to be over. I thought she was dead and gone, but now you say you didn't do it. Are there still Satanists? Is she still dead?"

Diane shook her head. P.J.'s witness monopoly had made her seem infallible. Now that the girl was proven wrong, or at least Max was gainsaying her, there might be alternatives. Diane wasn't even sure what color Ester's hair was last Sunday in church. She could picture it as blond and as flaming red as she stood before the congregation, shouting at Pastor Daniel. "I'm not sure, Zeke."

Zeke bent over and braced himself on his knees. He gasped and prayed, "Jesus, sweet Jesus, please tell me if my daughter is dead and in Heaven or if I can find her and bring her home."

The cattle's hooves clomped on the earth, and trucks growled.

Diane crawled a few feet over to Max. "Are you okay?"

"Jesus, his hands are strong." He coughed again. "Can't even swallow."

She looked up. "Zeke, I'm sorry. I don't know what else to do, but we'll look for her. It's like Ester dropped off the face of the Earth."

"Maybe she was raptured," Zeke said. "Maybe once our Red Heifer Project passed the no-return point, the Lord decided to go ahead. The rest of us aren't worthy, but she was." Sad furrows around his eyes guided tears down his cheeks, and Diane wanted to reach out to him but she was on the ground beside Max, who was still rubbing his throat in pain from Zeke trying to throttle him. Lord, so much pain and anger wracked the world.

She said, "Zeke, we'll get back on the case right away, interrogate Saffron again, make her some promises if she'll implicate others. We'll call in the FBI and the psychics and whoever else we can."

Max growled, "No damn feds. No damn psychics. I know who did it, probably."

Zeke said stiffly, "I'm sorry, there, Max. I don't usually lose my temper. It's just all this not-knowing. Damn that Nessie Allen." Diane glanced up at him, startled at his swearing. "If Nessie had been five minutes earlier, this wouldn't have happened."

Max glared at Zeke so sharply that Diane tensed to intervene if Max lunged at him.

Metal rattled and crashed like a chain falling to the ground behind them, near the terminal. The crowd roared.

Diane spun to look.

In the spotlights from the terminal, the chain-link fence lay on the asphalt and an SUV sped over it. Hundreds of people swarmed over the prostrate fence, waving signs and grabbing at each other, fists swinging.

Zeke said, "What in tarnation?"

Max croaked, "Oh, shit."

The scrum neared. The SUV drove in front, weaving.

Diane wavered between running for the trucks or trying for the plane.

Max grabbed her hand and Zeke's shirt and they sprinted.

The crowd broke for the plane as soon as the SUV ran down the fence.

Night was coming on and some of them carried flashlights, but most followed the SUV's headlights through the dusk toward the hot floodlights shining on the last cattle climbing the ramp to the lower deck.

The faithful sprinted to protect the red heifers from the atheists and Satanists. The peaked vegetarians waved carrots and threw tomatoes.

The five Satanists who had flown in from Los Angeles wore red-lined, black satin capes and carried a torn banner that read: WELCOME ANTI-CHRIST! Most of them already sported a black eye or split lip from the righteous devout.

Palestinians threw rocks at the airplane, but they overestimated their pitching capability and the rocks nicked folks herding cows for the Country Congregational Bible Church, who ran back through the crowd and pummeled them.

Forty people linked arms in a phalanx eight across and five rows deep and marched on the plane, singing that Civil War hymn, "Mine eyes have seen the glory of the coming of the Lord! He is trampling out the vintage where the grapes of wrath are stored!" They tried to trample the atheists by stampeding the few remaining cows, but the red heifers wheeled and broke for the open field far away from the screaming plane.

Some signs fell onto the hot blacktop.

Some people toppled into the political and religious mosh pit and skinned themselves on the asphalt, requiring the airport's security to help them limp to ambulances that a prescient security guard had called.

Max pulled his wife and Zeke James by his shirt as if he was the lead sled dog. His boots scrambled on the slick asphalt, and he recovered his balance in panic. "Come on!"

Zeke got the idea and ran.

Diane slipped in her work pumps and they hauled her up by their arms and ran up the ramp to the plane. Her heavy purse flapped around her and thumped Max painfully in the kidneys.

Fear injected fire into Max and he ran like hell, saving Diane and Zeke and himself.

Squeezing by the cattle laboring up the ramp, Max took point, guiding Diane, while Zeke shoved from behind. The three of them whipped around the door of the plane's lower deck and found Pastor Daniel studiously herding the last few heifers into pens. The airplane smelled like sweet shredded grass and cow piss.

Pastor Daniel Stout's grinning face was sweaty. Green alfalfa cud smeared his blue shirt. "Hi! This should be the last of them, right?" He blinked as if clearing his corneas at Max. "Why aren't you in jail?"

Zeke leaned over, breathing hard, and held up one hand to stop Daniel's objections.

Diane stood with one hand braced on the plastic top rail of a pen and the other grabbing her side. Her purse fell to the crook of her elbow and dangled. "Misunderstanding," she said, and Max swelled with hope. "He's not a Satanist. I'd stake my life on it."

"Are you sure?" Daniel Stout the idiot looked at him like he might burst into hellfire flame, revealing himself to be Satan himself. Idiot.

Outside, rioters were halfway across the field. They had to secure the plane or else those boneheads would crawl up inside and they might have a melee amongst the cattle.

Max leaned out of the airplane, pushed the next cow backwards, creating an instant bovine logjam, and yanked the door closed. He dragged the lever in a semi-circle to secure it.

"Hey," Stout said. "What about the other cows?"

Max said, "Those nutcases over by the terminal have broken onto the airstrip. We need to get out of here."

"Get out of the plane? But you closed the door."

"We need to get the plane away from the terminal and the riot."

Stout looked at them all panting. "We've got to get away from those hooligans. If they damage the plane, we're stuck here." His nerves seemed shot, and he vibrated all along his lanky lines.

Zeke nodded. "Let's go."

Finally some sense from the Christians. Max didn't know whether to shout hallelujah or shoot them, for they must be imposters.

Stout said, "We've got to close the top cargo door and tell the pilots."

Diane grabbed Max's arm. "Where are Tatiana and Nicholas?"

Stout said, "Upper deck."

Zeke said, "Nah, Vanessa Allen is the only one up there."

Panic grabbed Max's chest and he sprinted toward the front of the plane, elbowing past Zeke and Stout. He should have suspected what Vanessa Allen was since he first met her, with her narcissism and selfish rants and lying about being a forensic tech, her alibi, and where she lived, and that undercurrent of cavalier ruthlessness.

Vanessa was the last one to see Ester, but Max had cleared her because too many people confirmed her alibi's timeline, and few women were serial killers. As with pedophiles, the gender ratio for serial murderers is skewed due to preconceptions and underreporting.

Vanessa herself was the demon in human clothing that she had been warning everyone about, a serial killer, specifically an anger-retaliatory serial killer. She was the wolf, crying wolf.

He yelled back, "No one saw them get off?"

"No." Diane ran after him.

"Stay here," he told her. "Please stay here."

"Like hell."

Max tore up the tightly spiraled staircase two steps at a time with Diane pounding right behind him.

That crazed bitch was not going to kill his kids. He wouldn't allow it. He would change the course of the universe if necessary to save them. He would hold the sun and the moon in his hands and hurl them into space, to save his Tatiana, Nicholas, and Diane.

He had to get Vanessa alone, without Diane, without the kids. If he got her alone, then he could reason with her, talk to her, and figure out how to end this.

Zeke budged past Pastor Daniel and lumbered to the cockpit. He ducked his head in the door. The pilots fanned themselves with clipboards. Zeke said, "We need to take off, right now."

The co-pilot, incredulous, gestured at the instruments. "The upper deck's cargo door isn't even closed."

"It will be. Let's go."

The co-pilot's voice wound toward hysteria. "We don't have authorization from the tower. We've barely started the pre-flight routine."

Zeke said, "A mob is going to tear this plane apart."

The pilot was a polar bear of a fellow with a wide, white mustache and black eyes. "Sir, you get that upper deck cargo door closed." To the co-pilot, he said, "Junior, you hold on. This is how we did it in 'Nam."

The co-pilot, a technician of little daring and no nerve, looked like a sparrow that had just eaten his first and last poisonous Monarch butterfly and was about to projectile-vomit bright gorge.

Vanessa was disgusted with herself. It was a mess, all a mess, all because she could not control her temper. She kicked a cattle pen, and the animals inside shifted.

The airplane's engines, which had been droning, roared. Clanging like hammers and wrenches rang through the plane's metal skin.

She had to get off this plane and out of town. The sheriff's office or the Texas Rangers might someday find Ester James's body, buried shallow and face-down in Vanessa's stupid mother's weed-lousy yard. They might even figure out that Vanessa had merely announced that she was so late picking Ester up a few times at the bar and then loaned someone her credit card to buy drinks. Alibis are easy. You just tell people what you want them to remember, loudly, and often.

P.J. Lessing's body was still in that house. Her car had been too far away to throw her limp body in the trunk before those stupid search parties arrived, like she had with Ester's corpse.

Both sites had forensic evidence strewn all over the place, like her mother's boyfriends' smoked-down cigarette butts and random chewing gum from under the tables at the Foxhead. Vanessa collected that crap in plastic baggies, just in case, not that she ever thought she would need to use them again but it was best to be prepared. All that DNA should keep them busy for weeks, running down the usual suspects. If she got really lucky, they would conclude that the items were "signature," the unconscious, psychologically motivated scattering of evidence like a maiden's strewments near the body, sweets to the sweet.

Over a chorus of anxious mooing and the metallic barrage, someone shouted "Vanessa!"

Max stood at the far end of the plane, near the spiral staircase by the cockpit. Diane's slicked-back head poked up from the floor behind him.

That looked funny, like Max had cut off her head and dropped it at his feet, except her face kept moving around. Actually, it was funnier with her face moving around.

Diane's head yelled, "Tatiana? Nicholas?"

Vanessa shrugged. "They were bored and got off the plane. Steering cattle into pens is a one-person job."

Behind her, a rhythmic thumping echoed throughout the metal plane: thud-thud-thud; thud, thud, thud; thud-thud-thud.

Max frowned at the odd rhythm.

Diane's eyes widened. She jumped up the last few stairs, knocked Max off balance, and barreled down the center aisle toward Vanessa.

It was blown.

Vanessa braced and absorbed Diane's charge. Vanessa pinned Diane's hands to her sides and picked her up. Diane wrenched her hands free.

Vanessa tried to grab Diane's head to twist and break her neck like they did in the movies, but Diane flowed at her like an attacking jellyfish and scratched the hell out of her face. The scratches on her cheeks and beside her eyes burned and pissed her off more.

Diane looked down into the pen where Tatiana and Nicholas lay bound and gagged.

Vanessa tried to grab the woman's hair but it was so slick and tied down in that bun that Vanessa couldn't get a finger in it, so she grabbed Diane's pearl necklace, spun her around, and pinned her arms behind her back, facing Max, who had taken only a few steps down the aisle.

Diane screamed, "She's got the kids! There!" She jerked her head toward the pen.

Vanessa whipped a knife out of her pocket and held it to Diane's throat. She yelled around Diane to Max, "Stop! All of you just stop!"

"It's okay, Vanessa. Let's all calm down." Max walked forward slowly, but he was encroaching and she wanted to shoot him but she didn't have a fucking gun.

Max said, "You can get away if you go out that cargo door behind you. The crowd broke through. You can get lost in it."

"And then you'll send the cops after me."

"You'll have a head start. That's only fair."

"It's not fair," she protested. "I didn't do anything."

Diane squirmed against her arms, and Vanessa pressed the knife farther into her neck. Killing someone slowly with a knife by pressing the knife in really slowly might allay the anger for months.

"You must be getting antsy." Max gestured toward the pen where the two grubs lay. "Those two kids aren't anything new for you. Ester was a young woman, and P.J. was a teenager."

"What are you talking about? I was going to let them go, although you two are so stupid that I shouldn't."

The top of Diane's head came up to Vanessa's shoulder, and Vanessa wrassled with the screaming, writhing toy-woman. Diane yelled, "Max, shoot her! She's got the kids!"

Max said, "Diane, be quiet." He looked into Vanessa's eyes like they had some sort of psychic connection, coldly ignoring his wife struggling in her grip. Vanessa felt the ping of his retinas reflecting hers. He said, "Most of your dead friends from MyOwnRoom were teenagers and twenty-something females. That must get repetitive after a while."

His still-as-ice face pissed her off even more. "They were all losers. The gene pool is better off without them."

"Is that what you're doing?" His calm voice chanted like monotone plainsong, another religious idiocy. "Chlorinating the gene pool?"

He didn't look away, like their eyes were connected. His black-eyed stare was nerve-wracking, and he should not make her nervous right now. Her knife hand might shake and cut the struggling package of his wife.

"I don't know what you mean," she said. "They provoked me." Diane squirmed in Vanessa's grip, and Vanessa pushed the knife against her windpipe. Vanessa's front teeth grated together. "Don't make me do it."

Max's eyebrows twitched, patronizing, and then his whole face bloomed in revelation. "You don't know what you are, do you?"

The knife was sweating in her hand. She tightened her fist. "I don't know what you're talking about."

He leaned forward, imploring, his face still flushed in aggravating wonder at her, the big, blond specimen. "Do you like killing people?"

"Of course not," Vanessa said. She didn't have to explain herself to this loser. Her arm restraining Diane was tiring.

"You killed Ester." His determined eyes made her squeamish, like trying to stare down a lizard. "And P.J."

Vanessa couldn't think of an answer that would swat him down. "Nuh-uh."

Coiled in Vanessa's arms, Diane yelled, "Max, shoot her!"

Max stared at Vanessa just like his snotty daughter had stared, and she felt like a kid caught torturing snakes. His quiet voice was barely audible above the banshee-wailing jet engines. "You're a classic anger-retaliatory serial killer."

"No I'm not! You're an asshole." She wanted to throw the knife at him but she had never learned how. Slamming a knife through his nose to the back of his skull would be so satisfying. She was pissed at herself for not learning to throw knives.

Diane wiggled against Vanessa's chest and yelled, "Shoot her! She's got the kids tied up right there!"

Max stared, snakelike, retina-to-retina at Vanessa. That wireless communication enervated Vanessa, and her arms restraining Diane felt weak.

Max said, "Serial killers impersonate law enforcement. You're not a forensic technician. You didn't know that Luminol cross-reacts with iron in rust and dirt, and you aren't listed anywhere on the New Orleans police websites. You remove latex gloves like crap. You didn't need an agar gel to analyze those swabs. You just needed a kid's microscope. That blood sample came off your car."

Vanessa back-tracked. "I thought you wanted to know whose blood it was. You got it off my car?"

"Passenger door."

"How in the hell did blood get on my car?" she asked, more to herself than Max. Maybe Essie had a nosebleed.

Diane chose that moment to wriggle again, and Vanessa wrenched her arm, which yielded with a gratifying snap.

Diane screamed a wavering pain-scream, not a strident anger-scream, which bloomed a red tide of triumph in Vanessa. The woman sagged and tried to drag her arm around to hold it, but Vanessa seized her tighter.

Max's wide eyes whirled foolishly. He stutter-stepped, but Vanessa pressed the knife against Diane's throat harder.

"You see that?" Max asked. "You see that? You broke her arm and you don't feel remorse at all, do you?"

"Of course not. The stupid idiot made me do it."

"Classic anger-retaliatory mechanism. You're holding a knife to her throat. She struggled to get away. You're holding her children. She will try to save them. You're provoking her and then blaming her for the attack."

"No, I'm not!" He was being stupid. She should stick his wife just to prove the point.

Max continued, "You provoke them, and they get mad. Usually they say something humiliating, or disrespectful, or scolding, and that sets you off, right?"

"It's more like the fact that they exist, and they're so stupid about it that normal people shouldn't have to suffer their stupidity."

"Because they're stupid?"

"They're just machines for turning food into shit. They deserve it. I'm sifting the global litter box."

The air conditioners blasted sudden icy streams into the wet dog air.

"Have you ever killed a man?" Max asked. "A full-grown man?

Someone over thirty?"

"You're over forty," Vanessa said.

Max smiled a toothy grin, making him less handsome, more manic. He said, "You're just a stupid little girl who couldn't handle killing a man anyway. You're a low-class slut. You've been trailer trash your whole life, and that's never going to change. You're a worthless cunt."

His malicious words wound Vanessa into a furious fit and she could hardly see the tunnel-like plane and cows for thinking about all the ways that she was going to kill him.

Three hundred protesters swarmed across the tarmac and made it to the plane. Parishioners defended the beachheads of the ramps from the invaders.

The men riding in the SUV didn't carry signs. They parked the SUV under the middle of the plane and ran like hell back toward the terminal. When they had safely gained the airport's terminal, they panted for a moment before one of them pulled a cell phone out of his pocket. They walked away from the plate glass windows and around a corner inside the building. There, they crouched, grinning at each other, and the man with the cell phone keyed a phone number into the cell phone with great portent.

When he pushed the last digit, they covered their heads.

After a moment of furtive looks, they peered around the corner at the intact plane and undamaged SUV sitting below it.

They swore in a foreign language and argued to assign blame.

Hot pain sliced Diane's lower arm where the ulna bone broke, though shock and anguish focused her on the duel between her husband and the serial killer behind her. Fear broke over her like arctic waves. Her babies were tied up in that pen. If she died, Max might not be able to save them.

Diane dragged with her unbroken arm at Vanessa's hand that held the knife to her throat, but Vanessa was as big and strong as a man, too strong for Diane to yank her hand and the knife away, and now Diane pulled as hard as she could so Vanessa's arm would not recoil and pierce her throat with the knife.

Diane had to stop her. Her leaden purse, heavy with her gun, swung on her arm. She just needed a chance to save her babies, who had held her hand so softly when they were toddlers, who smiled with happiness at seeing her. She prayed for a chance, any chance.

Behind and above her, Vanessa said to Max, "Toss your gun away."

Diane moved her eyes right and left, trying to shake her head no at Max.

Max's hand strayed toward the gun on his hip.

Diane yelled, "No! Shoot me if you have to and then shoot her!"

Max pinched the butt of the gun between two fingers and tossed it into the nearest cow pen.

"No!" In a fury, Diane lifted her legs to her chest in a classic resistance move and Vanessa almost fell over on her.

Vanessa hissed in her ear, "Stop it or I'll smash your kids."

"Shoot her!" Diane yelled. In vicious case study after monotonous vicious case study, psychopaths simply liked killing people. The more vicious they were, the harder they were to smoke out because, like the exothermic lizards they were, they camouflaged themselves and lied just like they killed: no remorse. Diane screamed, "Shoot her in the head!"

Max frowned at Diane, scaring her more with his grating calm. "It will be okay."

"No!"

Vanessa's voice blasted by her ear and echoed down to the grinding bone-break in her arm. "Turn around and get down on your knees."

Max told Vanessa, "Nothing funny. You let Diane and the kids go, and then you'll have the wildest, most thrilling kill ever. If you don't, if you hurt them, I won't cooperate, and it'll be boring. Got it?"

Diane yelled to Max, "No! You're a good shot. You can hit her at this range. How many people have you killed? Shoot her in the head!"

Max's nonchalant shrug was as frightening as his flat voice. "Eighteen, and I already threw my gun."

Good Lord, he was suicidal. He was trading himself for her life and the kids' lives but he was suicidal. Telling Diane about his abuse had eviscerated him and he was going to let this blond maniac kill him.

Eighteen?

The neurons in Diane's brain stopped transmitting.

Max was suicidal, and that's all. Her children must be saved.

Diane said, "Max, please don't do this. Please save the kids, our babies, please. Shoot her, please?"

Max was already turning away and crouching to his knees.

The scream tore from her throat. "No!"

Vanessa shoved Diane.

Diane stumbled, and Vanessa dragged her one step and then hauled her up by her broken arm. Pain screamed through Diane, blocking her ears and eyes. The cows around them shuffled madly. The knife point pierced her neck, and hot blood trickled to her collarbone.

Vanessa whispered, "Stop it or I'll slice you."

Diane staggered with Vanessa in a sadistic parody of a limping dog toward Max, crouched on the floor. His blue tee shirt hung loose over his blue jeans.

Untucked tee shirts were sloppy, he said. He never wore his tee shirt untucked unless he was wearing a butt holster down the back of his pants.

Diane lurched forward, ready to throw herself out of the way when Max reached for the handgun hiding in the small of his back.

From behind Diane: "Daddy! No!" Tatiana screamed.

Diane turned and half-dragged Vanessa around with her.

In the last pen, Zeke James had the two kids freed and standing. He fumbled his hands toward the kids, trying to herd them toward the cattle ramp. Tatiana pulled at duct tape clinging to her cheek and screamed, "Daddy! Shoot her!"

"Run!" Diane yelled. "Run!" Diane shoved Vanessa hard, away from her kids.

Her purse flew off and skittered.

Vanessa jumped the other way. She grabbed Max and spun him around, trying to get the knife up to his neck.

Zeke James hollered, "Get down that ramp, both of you!"

Tatiana grabbed the door frame, but Zeke pushed her and Nicholas out of the plane. Footsteps pattered down the ramp.

Thank you, Lord. Thank you, Jesus. Now, she had to save herself to finish protecting them.

Diane's purse was far out of reach. She lunged through the hot pain radiating from her arm, grabbed Max around the waist with her good arm, and tried to stick her hand down his pants.

With a roar like a Red Angus bull, Zeke ran over the top of Diane. His foot smashed her good hand. "Damn!"

Zeke stumbled and crashed on the metal floor beyond Diane's head.

Vanessa shoved Diane away and must have noticed Diane going for the back of Max's pants or felt the hard lump over his tailbone because she came up with the handgun and, while grabbing it out of the holster, shot Max in the leg.

His blue jeans and his thigh exploded, splattering the rails, floor, and ceiling with shredded cloth and human meat.

The cattle bawled and threw their heads at the blast.

"Son of a bitch!" Max yelled. "God damn, why the fuck did you shoot me in the fucking leg?"

Vanessa wrestled Max around, sat on his back, and aimed the pistol at Diane and Zeke in turn. "Both of you, leave."

"No." Diane cradled her broken arm that throbbed through the shock filming her vision. "I won't let you kill him."

Max muttered, "Fuck," and laid his head on the rubber mat flooring.

Vanessa's triumphant sneer was shocking. "Get out, or I'll kill both of you, too."

The three men from the SUV, having assigned the blame to the man with a Master's degree in engineering who had wired the cell phone into the explosives, convinced the engineer to go back to the vehicle to rectify his mistake.

He didn't want to. He slouched and shuffled as he sauntered the hundred yards back to the plane, kicking gravel, surly for being designated the martyr.

Rubber mats imprinted waffles into Max's cheekbones.

Vanessa's knee, surprisingly boney, ground into the small of his back.

His right leg screamed agony. His flesh flailed, trying to repair itself and pleading with Max for help because it was dying. A thousand claws flayed him. A million knives flensed him.

Ovals and polygons of light floated on a filmy scrim of pain.

Above him, Vanessa Allen's phony voice said, "Both of you, leave."

Yes. When they left, he could goad her, stick in that verbal cattle prod and buzz it hard until she attacked him. An anger-retaliatory killer blitz-attacks the head and face, using hands or a hand-held implement. She probably wouldn't shoot him. When she lost control and hit berserker, her attention would be diverted inward to her own frenzy, and he could pull the gun from his ankle-holster and blast her with a Mozambique drill.

He was fairly certain he could remain conscious long enough.

"No," Diane said from somewhere beyond the pain veil. "I won't let you kill him."

Max muttered, "Fuck," and rolled his face on the matting, trying to shield himself from the pain in his leg by gouging his face. They had to leave. If they didn't leave, he couldn't be an ass and drive Vanessa amok because she might kill them instead.

Vanessa wasn't a rattlesnake that struck with hypodermic punctures. She was a grenade.

And was he a rattlesnake? Was he a sidewinder, an unblinking desert hunter? The woven pain drifted lower, settling light folds over that thought, yet his body was sinuous, ready to bend and release the gun concealed in his boot.

Flying above him, Van-anna-nessa's voice said, "Get out, or I'll kill both of you, too."

Max coiled and waited, ready to strike, resisting the darkness.

Zeke's temper swelled like one of his red bulls huffing and pawing the dirt. That blond murderer had to be stopped before she killed someone else.

Zeke crushed his temper. It solidified into an angry ball.

Beside him, Diane supported her broken arm with the hand he had stepped on and panted with pain.

Gunshot-rattled cows snorted and kicked their pens, thundering the solid rails, threatening the fragile humans if only they could escape.

Max lay on the rubber mats, bleeding. "Both of you, get out."

Zeke asked calmly, "Why are you doing this, Nessie?"

"That's a stupid question," said Vanessa, "and don't call me Nessie."

Zeke leaned toward Vanessa. "Really, I want to know why. Was it a broken home? The wrong crowd? Or does it feel innate?"

"I don't know what the hell you're talking about." She pointed the pistol straight at him.

Under Vanessa's legs, Deputy Max Konstantin groaned, "Get out."

She shoved the barrel of the gun against the back of Max's head.

"Now, now, Vanessa," Zeke called to her, desperate to slow her anger. "Stop there. That's a girl."

Her blue eyes flickered at him, wary. Mascara clumped her eyelashes.

"That's a girl," he said, gentling her like he would a colt slashing at him with metal-shod hooves. "Move the gun away."

She pointed the hollow muzzle at Zeke. "I'm not a serial killer."

"Of course you're not," Zeke said quickly. The appellation meant nothing. She could call herself Saint Nessie the Chaste if Max and Diane got off the plane alive. "But your temper might be genetic."

"She had a choice." Diane gestured with her unbroken arm to Vanessa, who watched them sharply. "She still has a choice. She could put that gun down and walk off the plane," another pain-pressed breath, "and I could help her."

Vanessa nodded. The hollow barrel of the handgun wove between the two of them like Orpheus's tunnel that might suck them in.

Diane turned to Vanessa. "You can tell us how it happened," she nose-inhaled again, "and we can explain things to a judge, and I'll bet you'll be out in three years, maximum." Her black, patent leather purse was near her feet, and she stooped to retrieve it. "I can make sure it's at a minimum-security, Club Fed kind of place."

Vanessa rolled her eyes. "I don't think so."

Zeke wanted to shake his head. Diane was going about this wrong. A person like Vanessa wouldn't turn herself over to the law, even though Diane was surely lying about how little time she would serve. The low levels of Mao A protein in Vanessa's brain convinced her that she was entitled to kill other people because they had no importance. Vanessa was less empathetic than Lilypie. He felt sorry for her.

"You see, Zeke?" Diane turned back to him and grabbed her broken arm with a teeth-clenched grimace. "She has a choice, and this is the choice she's made. If we don't have a choice, the legal system should be turned into a big mental health care system because there is no crime, only crazy."

Zeke looked over at Max, who stared hard at him from prone on the floor. His gaze flicked toward the cargo door, commanding Zeke to take Diane and leave. Zeke could not leave Max here. Two children needed him alive.

Vanessa ran her fingers through Max's thick black hair and pulled his head up by his curly-headed scalp. "Max here has made his choice. You two, get out."

Zeke said, "Vanessa, don't kill him."

"Did you hear what he said to me? He called me a cunt and a serial killer. The world will be better off without him." She squirmed with anger and pistol-whipped Max on the back of the head.

Max grunted and closed his eyes.

"Stop!" Diane shrilled, and her voice cracked. "Please stop!"

Vanessa yelled, "Why are you two still here? If I'm an 'anger-retaliatory serial killer,' why the hell aren't you two running for your lives?"

"You're not crazy," Zeke said to Vanessa. "I'll bet you're the rarest genotype of all: a female with two low-activity promoters. You had a rough time growing up, too, didn't you?"

"I'm tough. You've got to be tough to survive in this world." Vanessa's prideful voice saddened Zeke.

Under her knee, Max said, "Your mother isn't tough, is she?"

"Shut up," Vanessa said. "My dad ruined her. She got sucked down in meth and turned tricks for drug money. She should have been tough. She's pure-blooded German, and both her parents are from Argentina."

Zeke did the math by skipping two decades at a time. Maybe there was a eugenics link, though Zeke hated to think that. "So your grandparents were Nazis?"

"Of course they were," Vanessa said. "My idiot mother wouldn't tell me who they were, but I think my grandfather was Mengele. Why else would she change her name to 'Inga Allen?' It's almost an anagram."

"You're making it sound like Vanessa didn't have a choice." Diane inhaled through pain again and grabbed her purse with one hand, trying to manipulate it. It swung heavily. "There's always a choice. If there is no free will and some souls are damned," and she pain-inhaled through her nose, blinking with effort, "then Jesus can't save everybody. Then, there are Chosen People, an Israel of the flesh, or of the genes. There must be free will. Without a choice, it's," a pain-wracked breath, "Calvinism. Genetic Calvinism."

Her fumbling in her purse became purposeful.

Diane mustn't try anything stupid. Vanessa would shoot them all.

Zeke reached over to Diane's hand and carefully pulled it out of her purse. Panic lit her eyes as he raised her hand.

Zeke held her good hand and glanced into her purse. A bar of metal glinted. If she had pulled a gun, Vanessa would have shot her.

The tube lights firefly-flickered, and darkness plastered them.

The open cargo door funneled a wan cone of sunlight into the plane. Cows wove their heads above the pens like a shadowy shipment of cobras.

In the dim light, Diane's brow crease looked more horrified than pained.

Clanging echoed from the lower deck of the plane, and Vanessa whipped around, thought she saw a head prairie-dogging through the deck, and shot at it.

Recoil shunted the gun upward.

The shot ricocheted off the metal floor with a bang-zing. Sulfur-steel smoke pierced the cows' green smells.

The crowd of cattle stomped and screamed.

Zeke yelled, "Stop!" Diane shouted, "Don't!"

From below, a man's voice yelled, "There's a truckbomb! Get out!"

God fucking damn it, the shot missed. Her thighs hurt from straddling Max. She should end this all now.

These idiots, they were all idiots.

A cow nudged her shoulder warmly and smeared crap on her.

And the shit about her being a serial killer, what shit was that? She was surrounded by bullshit and cowshit. She was not a fucking serial killer. She should shoot Max now, even though she had a black widow fantasy about blowing his head off while she fucked him.

Serial killers were men like Ted Bundy who lured girls with long hair into his car and then killed them because they looked like the ex-girlfriend who had rejected him, or like Gary Ridgeway, who picked up and killed sluts because he had some misogynist thing, or like the BTK killer, Dennis Rader, the bald guy with the pointy Devil-beard who sneaked into his neighbor's houses and then bound, tortured, and killed them.

They sought murder. They planned and executed. Those men had techniques and *modi operandi* and signatures.

Vanessa didn't do any of that. She was not a serial killer.

She *wasn't.*

From between her legs, Max said, "Go ahead and shoot me, Vanessa. Get it out of your system. You'll feel better for a couple weeks. It releases the tension."

"I don't know what you're talking about."

But she did. The release was not orgasmic but deflating the balloon of rage. For a couple weeks, she felt relaxed, bold and dangerous. People backed off because they sensed that assertiveness. Then her dangerousness ebbed, and the idiots got more confrontational, and frustration bloated until she blew someone away.

But she wasn't a serial killer. That's not what a serial killer was. Vanessa was a cauldron of anger. Lily-livered ladylike emotions dunked in and came up Lady Macbeth boiling bloody. She wasn't strident or shrill. The rage that simmers in every woman overflowed in her, hissing on the burner and exploding like a grease fire.

From below her, Max inhaled, and his ribs pushed against her thighs. He sighed hard. "I should have known what you were when you said you wished I had killed your father."

"Anyone would want my father dead." Her image of her father was of a Cthulhu-like monster with fists waving from a hundred tentacles.

"Did he sexually abuse you?"

"No. And it's none of your business. And no." Of course he hadn't touched her. He left when she was six. Of course not. That was stupid.

"So who abused you?"

"No one. I would have shot anyone who touched me." She was convinced this was true. If any one of the men who lined up outside the trailer had touched her, she knew where the guns were kept: under the couch, in the gumbo cooking pot, and under her mother's ragged lingerie. She had held them as a first-grader, fingered them, made sure they were there in case she needed them.

Max grunted, "Can you remember the abuse, or did you repress it?"

"That's stupid. Either you remember it or it didn't happen."

Max's head rolled on the floor, and he looked up at her with one black-irised eye. "It's easy to lie to yourself. Even easier than lying to other people. And you lie exceptionally well. You are a serial killer and a world-class whore and a failure at everything you try."

Vanessa's temper flared like an untempered gas flame.

She aimed the gun at the black hole of his eye.

The engineer in the SUV twisted wires.

He had wired it correctly the first time, damn it.

That idiot in the terminal who was so impressed with his own knowledge of the Holy Text must have dialed the wrong phone number. Leave it to that idiot to not be able to remember ten digits.

The engineer rested his head on the back seat of the SUV, trying to figure out if anything else could go wrong.

The crowd of American hippies rocked the SUV.

He sat up and yelled and shook his fist at them. They didn't know what they were dealing with, damn it. He was flaming Death incarnate. He was from and destined for another world. His privileged upbringing—travel, private schooling, and adherence to religion—had taught him of his superiority, right, and duty to accomplish this sacrifice. Six years of American university education couldn't overwrite it.

When Vanessa's head bent down and her long, blond tresses trickled past her shoulders and blocked her face, Diane yanked her hand away from Zeke, dipped into her purse, and brought up her pistol.

As soon as the sights on Diane's gun cleared Max's head and leveled on Vanessa, Diane started shooting. She didn't bother to line up the sights at the range of ten feet.

The first shot went wild and hit a cattle pen. The cattle screamed and bucked.

Vanessa threw herself sideways and scrambled away, running toward the open cargo door.

Diane followed her with the sights, loathe to shoot even a psychopathic murderer in the back, even though Texas law permits deadly force against a perpetrator fleeing the scene of a crime.

Max writhed on the floor, reaching for his ankle holster and gritting his teeth against the pain. The leg that took the bullet pulsed like someone was clubbing it in time with his drumroll heartbeat.

Diane's shot zinged above his head, and Max covered his head with his left arm while he aimed at Vanessa's retreating back. He squeezed the trigger but missed.

Vanessa whipped around and brought her pistol to bear on Max.

Zeke yelled, "No!" and lumbered, diving at Vanessa. He caught her legs and took her down.

Max yelled, "Clear! Clear! Get out of the way!"

Zeke wrestled Vanessa Allen on the cow urine-soaked rubber mats of the plane. "Run!" he roared, and the steed of anger in his heart strengthened him. "Diane, take your husband and run!"

The silky material on Vanessa's legs slipped in Zeke's hands, but he grabbed one of her arms like a bulldogger and held fast. She swung the pistol around on him.

Red sun glared behind her. If Vanessa shot him and he passed from this world to the next, the Temple Project would endure. Pastor Daniel would see to it that the Jews consecrated their temple. Zeke wasn't altogether sure if the Temple would hasten the end of creation, but the Jews should stand in the sight of God.

Zeke slammed her pistol away from his head and swiveled for a moment to see Diane hauling Max from the floor.

He yelled again, "Run! Both of you! Run!"

Zeke was not as tall but heavier and stronger than Vanessa. She might be practiced at killing, but he was practiced in wrestling steers and heifers that outweighed him and slashed wicked horns and sharp hooves. He was a powerful man, and he batted her gun-wielding arm away from him.

He glanced back, and three shadows stood in the scarlet light.

"There's a bomb!" Pastor Daniel yelled, his hand out.

Diane, on the far side of Max, looked at him. Her terrified eyes were haunting.

Zeke slammed Vanessa's flailing arm against a pen and yelled, "Run! Your children are down there!"

Footsteps clattered out of the plane.

Vanessa's body writhed in anger, then whipped in rage, and then she lost control and shouted obscenities, shooting the gun beside his head and blasting pain into his ears until it ran out of ammunition and clicked.

She was possessed by demons, and he yelled into her face, "I cast thee out, Satan! I cast thee out in the name of the Lord and his only begotten Son and my Savior, Jesus Christ!"

She looked shocked for a moment, and a sly craftiness sneaked around her eyes. "Yes," she said. "I'm possessed. Yes!" She screamed a demonic wail, baring her ground teeth all the way back to her molars.

More lies from the Prince of Lies, Zeke knew. She wasn't a Satanist. Some people are just plain evil inside, deep down in their genes, lacking love more thoroughly than even God can mend.

Diane grappled Max and supported him, lifting him onto her side because his gunshot leg wouldn't support his weight.

Pastor Daniel, who had climbed the staircase from the dark belly of the plane, yelling about a bomb, hoisted Max's other arm onto his shoulder.

Diane yanked Max and started down the plane ramp, into the crowd, pulling her husband and Daniel, trying to get clear. Pain pierced her broken arm, and she held Max's shoulder with her good arm.

Outside, the sun burned like a Soviet retaliatory nuclear blast on the horizon, streaming red light over the crowd that chased the remaining cattle in a muddled fray.

Outside the gate, ambulances screamed to enter and flashed red halos.

Diane and Daniel hobbled with Max through the crowd. He crumpled with each step, nearly unconscious, slinging his legs forward. His head rocked on Diane's shoulder. Her hose soaked up the blood and wicked it into her slippery shoes.

They reached the terminal and fell inside an unlocked door.

An airline worker hurried over to them, spouting as he ran, "That door is to remain locked during operating hours."

Tatiana and Nicholas were there, and they all charged inside the terminal, passing three men huddled on the floor.

Diane turned and, even so broken by pain and horror, caught one of the men's eyes and was repelled by the ophidian glint of madness.

"No! No!" the engineer screamed as the SUV rocked wildly. If he left the SUV now, these unbelievers would rip the wires out and destroy everything. Faces, mostly white faces, leered in the windows. "We're not finished yet!"

The protesters watched the engineer throw a temper tantrum in the back seat.

Inside the terminal, one of his compatriots said, "Oh, that's a five, not a three," and dialed the phone again.

The world turned to fire.

The plane burned with exceeding softness, with soft and delicious fire.

Diane loaded Max into one of the first ambulances to depart for the hospital, pulling rank because he was law enforcement wounded in the line of duty. The medic bundled him in because he was ready to go, and the screaming-siren parade past the news vans must begin.

As his stretcher was loaded and the wheeled legs collapsed against the ambulance, Max's strong hand turned over, and he reached for her.

The symbol was there for the taking.

Their children, Tatiana and Nicholas, watched.

Somehow, they had all survived the truck bomb, the airplane inferno, and Diane's attempt to end the world.

Yes, Diane's attempt. She accepted the blame. When Zeke and Daniel had broached the subject of selling red heifers to Israel, she knew why, and she did the paperwork. Without her, the project would have wandered in the desert forever. They were nice guys, but they did not understand the law.

She understood that their liability for the inferno that now cast her flickering shadow into the ambulance was several and plural, meaning that she and Zeke and Daniel and all the others were each entirely responsible for every death they had caused. Diane estimated that a hundred murders rested on her soul.

She was ready for the Rapture. She was Christian. Being raptured was a fringe benefit. Her two children were sweet, not headstrong, not defiant. When she told them the Good News, and then the very bad news, they would have come to Christ.

She was prepared for the Rapture and for Armageddon. Everything else—serial killers and Satanists and terrorists—she was not prepared for. Car accidents, drug pushers, rape parties—she was not prepared for. If she had ended the world, in her way, by her own hand, she would not have been afraid anymore.

Fear drove Diane to religion. Fear drove Diane at work. Fear dominated her home. She warned her children, but she did not ask questions about things that frightened her, like Max. Every time that she said, "You're so weird sometimes," she should have asked, "Why?"

But she was afraid of what he might tell her, so she let the fear dictate her life. She thought that, if she was just afraid enough, she could handle anything.

Max's palm was up and his fingers, outstretched. Soot streaked his palm over the film of blood. His fingers twitched, supplicating.

Her fear had almost killed her and her children and Max and the whole world.

Behind her, the plane vented flaming kerosene and charred beef into the sky. The last she had seen, Zeke had pinned Vanessa to the rubber-matted floor inside the plane. She hoped that Jesus had swept Zeke into His arms and carried him straight up to Heaven.

The molten tarmac was too hot to retrieve the dead from the crowd that had stormed the plane, grasping at its landing gear. Glass, blown through and out the other side of the terminal, crunched under their feet.

Pastor Daniel, his hands protecting his face from the broiling heat, dragged injured protesters away. Gray ash powdered him. While others gibbered with terror, Pastor Daniel shouted and directed and helped. He had, she remembered, seen horror before.

Her fear had killed all those smoldering husks huddled under the plane. It had opened her to the idea that Satanists were performing human sacrifices. It had ripped apart P.J.'s family and killed her and The Tower.

Max had killed eighteen people, he had said.

Fear was too dangerous to indulge in. She had not been prepared for the consequences of fear.

Max lifted his head and looked at her, imploring.

Could she take him back? Could they go on with their lives? The evidence was in shambles. The opposing counsels, having no points of law or case to stand on, merely argued.

She couldn't judge her own case. *In propria causa nemo iudex.*

Their children stared.

She was afraid to take him back. He killed people. Her fear had shut off that thought, but she examined it now. He killed people because he was afraid too.

Her fear insisted that she step back and avert her eyes.

If there is an Israel of the genes, as it were, Diane's DNA relented. No pragmatic reason forced her: not financial security, not repressive laws. She longed for the false and fearful serenity of a few days ago, but love, produced in excess, can change behavior.

Diane reached. Her fingers slid down Max's warm hand as the stretcher bumped into the ambulance.

About the author

TK Kenyon is an Iowa Writers' MFA Workshop graduate, Truman Capote Fellow, novelist, CEO of TK Consulting (pharmaceutical industry consultants, www.consultingtk.com,) herpesvirologist, Ph.D., postdoctoral neuroscientist, toddler mother, happy wife, cat slave, jogger, surfer, high-handicap golfer, scuba diver, quilter, vegetarian gourmet chef, chocolatier, capsaicin addict, caffeine junkie, Apache and Scot descendant, native Arizonan, New York resident, Hawaiian kama'aina wannabe, radical feminist, subversive Republican, philosophical agnostic, Hindu, Buddhist, Tamil Ayer Brahmin by marriage, ex-actress, grown-up child beauty queen, ASU Sun Devil, Iowa Hawkeye, UPenn Quaker, and always looking for something interesting to do.

Her fiction has been recently published in *Big Muddy*, *New York Stories*, and *American Short Fiction* (Summer, 2006).

Her first novel, *Rabid* (April, 2007), received a starred review in Booklist, which called it "...a genre-bending story—part thriller, part literary slapdown with dialogue as the weapon of choice (think *Who's Afraid of Virginia Woolf*). Kenyon is definitely a keeper."

Her website includes essays on fiction writing, religion, science, philosophy, and politics (www.tkkenyon.com.)

KÜNATI

Kunati Book Titles

Provocative. Bold. Controversial.

MADicine

■ **Derek Armstrong**

What happens when an engineered virus, meant to virally lobotomize psychopathic patients, is let loose on the world? Only Bane and his new partner, Doctor Ada Kenner, can stop this virus of rage.

■ "In his follow-up to the excellent *The Game*.... Armstrong blends comedy, parody, and adventure in genuinely innovative ways." *The Last Troubadour —Booklist*

■ "Tongue-in-cheek thriller." *The Game —Library Journal*

US$ 24.95 | Pages 352, cloth hardcover
ISBN 978-1-60164-017-8 | EAN: 9781601640178

Bathtub Admirals

■ **Jeff Huber**

Are the armed forces of the world's only superpower really run by self-serving "Bathtub Admirals"? Based on a true story of military incompetence.

■ *"Witty, wacky, wildly outrageous...A remarkably accomplished book, striking just the right balance between ridicule and insight." —Booklist*

US$ 24.95
Pages 320, cloth hardcover
ISBN 978-1-60164-019-2
EAN 9781601640192

Belly of the Whale

■ **Linda Merlino**

Terrorized by a gunman, a woman with cancer vows to survive and regains her hope and the will to live.

■ *"A riveting story, both powerful and poignant in its telling. Merlino's immense talent shines on every page." —Howard Roughan, Bestselling Author*

US$ 19.95
Pages 208, cloth hardcover
ISBN 978-1-60164-018-5
EAN 9781601640185

Hunting the KIng

■ **Peter Clenott**

An intellectual thriller about the most coveted archeological find of all time: the tomb of Jesus.

■ *"Fans of intellectual thrillers and historical fiction will find a worthy new voice in Clenott... Given such an auspicious start, the sequel can't come too soon." —ForeWord*

US$ 24.95
Pages 384, cloth hardcover
ISBN 978-1-60164-148-9
EAN 9781601641489

KÜNATI

Kunati Book Titles

www.kunati.com

Callous

■ **T K Kenyon**

A routine missing person call turns the town of New Canaan, Texas, inside out as claims of Satanism, child abuse and serial killers clash, and a radical church prepares for Armageddon and the Rapture. Part thriller, part crime novel, *Callous* is a dark and funny page-turner.

■ "Kenyon is definitely a keeper." *Rabid*, STARRED REVIEW. *—Booklist*

■ "Impressive." *Rabid*, *—Publishers Weekly*

US$ 24.95 | Pages 384, cloth hardcover
ISBN 978-1-60164-022-2 | EAN: 9781601640222

Janeology

■ **Karen Harrington**

Tom is certain he is living the American dream. Until one day in June, the police tell him the unthinkable—his wife has drowned their toddler son.

■ *"Harrington begins with a fascinating premise and develops it fully. Tom and his wife emerge as compelling, complexly developed individuals." —Booklist*

US$ 24.95
Pages 256, cloth hardcover
ISBN 978-1-60164-020-8
EAN 9781601640208

Miracle MYX

■ **Dave Diotalevi**

For an unblinking forty-two hours, Myx's synesthetic brain probes a lot of dirty secrets in Miracle before arriving at the truth.

■ *"Exceptional." STARRED REVIEW. —Booklist*

■ *"What a treat to be in the mind of Myx Amens, the clever, capable, twice-dead protagonist who is full of surprises."—Robert Fate, Academy Award winner*

US$ 24.95
Pages 288, cloth hardcover
ISBN 978-1-60164-155-7
EAN 9781601641557

Unholy Domain

■ **Dan Ronco**

A fast-paced techno-thriller depicts a world of violent extremes, where religious terrorists and visionaries of technology fight for supreme power.

■ *"A solid futuristic thriller." —Booklist*

■ *"Unholy Domain...top rate adventure, sparkling with ideas." —Piers Anthony*

US$ 24.95
Pages 352, cloth hardcover
ISBN 978-1-60164-021-5
EAN 9781601640215

Provocative. Bold. Controversial.

Kunati Book Titles

Available at your favorite bookseller

www.kunati.com

The Last Troubadour

Historical fiction by Derek Armstrong

Against the flames of a rising medieval Inquisition, a heretic, an atheist and a pagan are the last hope to save the holiest Christian relic from a sainted king and crusading pope. Based on true events.

■ "... brilliance in which Armstrong blends comedy, parody, and adventure in genuinely innovative ways." —*Booklist*

US$ 24.95 | Pages 384, cloth hardcover
ISBN-13: 978-1-60164-010-9
ISBN-10: 1-60164-010-2
EAN: 9781601640109

Recycling Jimmy

A cheeky, outrageous novel by Andy Tilley

Two Manchester lads mine a local hospital ward for "clients" as they launch Quitters, their suicide-for-profit venture in this off-the-wall look at death and modern life.

■ "Energetic, imaginative, relentlessly and unabashedly vulgar." —*Booklist*

■ "Darkly comic story unwinds with plenty of surprises." —*ForeWord*

US$ 24.95 | Pages 256, cloth hardcover
ISBN-13: 978-1-60164-013-0
ISBN-10: 1-60164-013-7
EAN 9781601640130

Women Of Magdalene

A hauntingly tragic tale of the old South by Rosemary Poole-Carter

An idealistic young doctor in the post-Civil War South exposes the greed and cruelty at the heart of the Magdalene Ladies' Asylum in this elegant, richly detailed and moving story of love and sacrifice.

■ "A fine mix of thriller, historical fiction, and Southern Gothic." —*Booklist*

■ "A brilliant example of the best historical fiction can do." —*ForeWord*

US$ 24.95 | Pages 288, cloth hardcover

ISBN-13: 978-1-60164-014-7
ISBN-10: 1-60164-014-5 | EAN: 9781601640147

On Ice

A road story like no other, by Red Evans

The sudden death of a sad old fiddle player brings new happiness and hope to those who loved him in this charming, earthy, hilarious coming-of-age tale.

■ "Evans' humor is broad but infectious ... Evans uses offbeat humor to both entertain and move his readers." —*Booklist*

US$ 19.95 | Pages 208, cloth hardcover

ISBN-13: 978-1-60164-015-4
ISBN-10: 1-60164-015-3
EAN: 9781601640154

Truth Or Bare

Offbeat, stylish crime novel by Richard Cahill

The characters throb with vitality, the prose sizzles in this darkly comic page-turner set in the sleazy world of murderous sex workers, the justice system, and the rich who will stop at nothing to get what they want.

■ "Cahill has introduced an enticing character ... Let's hope this debut novel isn't the last we hear from him." —*Booklist*

US$ 24.95 | Pages 304, cloth hardcover

ISBN-13: 978-1-60164-016-1
ISBN-10: 1-60164-016-1
EAN: 9781601640161

The Secret Ever Keeps

A novel by Art Tirrell

An aging Godfather-like billionaire tycoon regrets a decades-long life of "shady dealings" and seeks reconciliation with a granddaughter who doesn't even know he exists. A sweeping adventure across decades—from Prohibition to today—exploring themes of guilt, greed and forgiveness.

■ "Riveting ... Rhapsodic ... Accomplished." *ForeWord*

US$ 24.95
Pages 352, cloth hardcover
ISBN 978-1-60164-004-8
EAN 9781601640048
LCCN 2006930185

Toonamint of Champions

A wickedly allegorical comedy by Todd Sentell

Todd Sentell pulls out all the stops in his hilarious spoof of the manners and mores of America's most prestigious golf club. A cast of unforgettable characters, speaking a language only a true son of the South could pull off, reveal that behind the gates of fancy private golf clubs lurk some mighty influential freaks.

■ "Bubbly imagination and wacky humor." *ForeWord*

US$ 19.95
Pages 192, cloth hardcover
ISBN 978-1-60164-005-5
EAN 9781601640055
LCCN 2006930186

Mothering Mother

A daughter's humorous and heartbreaking memoir.
Carol D. O'Dell

Mothering Mother is an authentic, "in-the-room" view of a daughter's struggle to care for a dying parent. It will touch you and never leave you.

■ "Beautiful, told with humor... and much love." *Booklist*

■ "I not only loved it, I lived it. I laughed, I smiled and shuddered reading this book." Judith H. Wright, author of over 20 books.

US$ 19.95
Pages 208, cloth hardcover
ISBN 978-1-60164-003-1
EAN 9781601640031
LCCN 2006930184

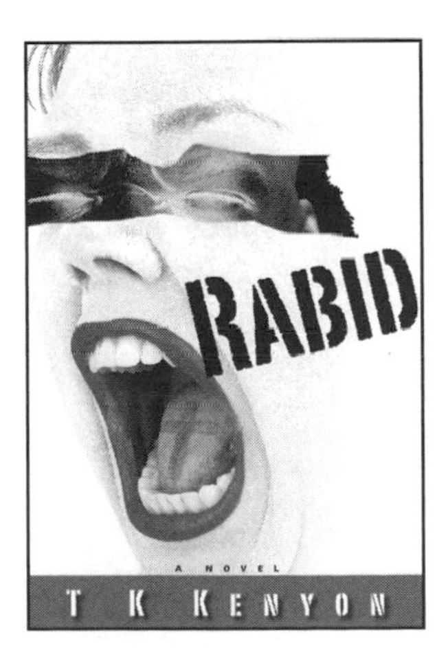

Rabid

A novel by T K Kenyon

A sexy, savvy, darkly funny tale of ambition, scandal, forbidden love and murder. Nothing is sacred. The graduate student, her professor, his wife, her priest: four brilliantly realized characters spin out of control in a world where science and religion are in constant conflict.

■ "Kenyon is definitely a keeper." STARRED REVIEW, *Booklist*

US$ 26.95 | Pages 480, cloth hardcover
ISBN 978-1-60164-002-4 | EAN: 9781601640024
LCCN 2006930189